Number One *New York Times* bestselling author **Nora Roberts** is "a storyteller of immeasurable diversity and talent" according to *Publishers Weekly*. She has published over one hundred and sixty novels, her work has been optioned and made into films, and her books have been translated into over twenty-five different languages and published all over the world.

Nora Roberts

Engaging the Enemy

MILLS & BOON

Mills & Boon, an imprint of Harlequin (UK) Limited,
Eton House, 18-24 Paradise Road, Richmond, Surrey TW9 1SR

ENGAGING THE ENEMY © Harlequin Books S.A. 2003

The publisher acknowledges the copyright holder of the individual works as follows:

A Will and A Way © Nora Roberts 1986
Boundary Lines © Nora Roberts 1985

ISBN: 978 0 263 89007 5

026-0511

Harlequin (UK) policy is to use papers that are natural, renewable and recyclable products and made from wood grown in sustainable forests. The logging and manufacturing processes conform to the legal environmental regulations of the country of origin.

Printed and bound in Spain
by Blackprint CPI, Barcelona

CONTENTS

A Will and a Way

For my family members, who, fortunately,
aren't as odd as the relatives in this book

Chapter 1

One hundred fifty million dollars was nothing to sneeze at. No one in the vast, echoing library of Jolley's Folley would have dared. Except Pandora. She did so with more enthusiasm than delicacy into a tattered tissue. After blowing her nose, she sat back, wishing the antihistamine she had taken would live up to its promise of fast relief. She wished she'd never caught the wretched cold in the first place. More, she wished she were anywhere else in the world.

Surrounding her were dozens of books she'd read and hundreds more she'd never given a thought to, though she'd spent hours and hours in the library. The scent of the leather-bound volumes mixed with the lighter, homier scent of dust. Pandora preferred either to the strangling fragrance of lilies that filled three stocky vases.

In one corner of the room was a marble-and-ivory

chess set, where she'd lost a great many highly dis-
puted matches. Uncle Jolley, bless his round, innocent
face and pudgy fingers, had been a compulsive and
skilled cheat. Pandora had never taken a loss in stride.
Maybe that's why he'd so loved to beat her, by fair
means or foul.

Through the three arching windows the light shone
dull and a little gloomy. It suited her mood and, she
thought, the proceedings. Uncle Jolley had loved to set
scenes.

When she loved—and she felt this emotion for a
select few who'd touched her life—she put everything
she had into it. She'd been born with boundless energy. She'd developed iron-jawed stubbornness. She'd
loved Uncle Jolley in her uninhibited, expansive fashion, acknowledging then accepting all of his oddites.
He might have been ninety-three, but he'd never been
dull or fussy.

A month before his death, they'd gone fishing—
poaching actually—in the lake that was owned and
stocked by his neighbor. When they'd caught more
than they could eat, they'd sent a half-dozen trout back
to the owner, cleaned and chilled.

She was going to miss Uncle Jolley with his round
cherub's face, high, melodious voice and wicked hu-
mors. From his ten-foot, extravagantly framed portrait,
he looked down at her with the same little smirk he'd
worn whether he'd been making a million-dollar
merger or handing an unsuspecting vice-president a
drink in a dribble glass. She missed him already. No
one else in her far-flung, contrasting family understood
and accepted her with the same ease. It had been one
more reason she'd adored him.

Miserable with grief, aggravated by a head cold, Pandora listened to Edmund Fitzhugh drone on, and on, with the preliminary technicalities of Uncle Jolley's will. Maximillian Jolley McVie had never been one for brevity. He'd always said if you were going to do something, do it until the steam ran out. His last will and testament bore his style.

Not bothering to hide her disinterest in the proceedings, Pandora took a comprehensive survey of the other occupants of the library.

To have called them mourners would have been just the sort of bad joke Jolley would have appreciated.

There was Jolley's only surviving son, Uncle Carlson, and his wife. What was her name? Lona—Mona? Did it matter? Pandora saw them sitting stiff backed and alert in matching shades of black. They made her think of crows on a telephone wire just waiting for something to fall at their feet.

Cousin Ginger—sweet and pretty and harmless, if rather vacuous. Her hair was Jean Harlow blond this month. Good old Cousin Biff was there in his black Brooks Brothers suit. He sat back, one leg crossed over the other as if he were watching a polo match. Pandora was certain he wasn't missing a word. His wife—was it Laurie?—had a prim, respectful look on her face. From experience, Pandora knew she wouldn't utter a word unless it were to echo Biff. Uncle Jolley had called her a silly, boring fool. Hating to be cynical, Pandora had to agree.

There was Uncle Monroe looking plump and successful and smoking a big cigar despite the fact that his sister, Patience, waved a little white handkerchief in front of her nose. Probably because of it, Pandora corrected. Uncle Monroe liked nothing better than to make his ineffectual sister uncomfortable.

Cousin Hank looked macho and muscular, but hardly more than his tough athletic wife, Meg. They'd hiked the Appalachian Trail on their honeymoon. Uncle Jolley had wondered if they stretched and limbered up before lovemaking.

The thought caused Pandora to giggle. She stifled it halfheartedly with the tissue just before her gaze wandered over to cousin Michael. Or was it second cousin Michael? She'd never been able to get the technical business straight. It seemed a bit foolish when you weren't talking blood relation anyway. His mother had been Uncle Jolley's niece by Jolley's son's second marriage. It was a complicated state of affairs, Pandora thought. But then Michael Donahue was a complicated man.

They'd never gotten along, though she knew Uncle Jolley had favored him. As far as Pandora was concerned, anyone who made his living writing a silly television series that kept people glued to a box rather than doing something worthwhile was a materialistic parasite. She had a momentary flash of pleasure as she remembered telling him just that.

Then, of course, there were the women. When a man dated centerfolds and showgirls it was obvious he wasn't interested in intellectual stimulation. Pandora smiled as she recalled stating her view quite clearly the last time Michael had visited Jolley's Folley. Uncle Jolley had nearly fallen off his chair laughing.

Then her smile faded. Uncle Jolley was gone. And if she was honest, which she was often, she'd admit that of all the people in the room at that moment, Mi-

chael Donahue had cared for and enjoyed the old man more than anyone but herself.

You'd hardly know that to look at him now, she mused. He looked disinterested and slightly arrogant. She noticed the set, grim line around his lips. Pandora had always considered Donahue's mouth his best feature, though he rarely smiled at her unless it was to bare his teeth and snarl.

Uncle Jolley had liked his looks, and had told Pandora so in his early stages of matchmaking. A hobby she'd made sure he'd given up quickly. Well, he hadn't given it up precisely, but she'd ignored it all the same.

Being rather short and round himself, perhaps Jolley had appreciated Donahue's long lean frame, and the narrow intense face. Pandora might have liked it herself, except that Michael's eyes were often distant and detached.

At the moment he looked like one of the heroes in the action series he wrote—leaning negligently against the wall and looking just a bit out of place in the tidy suit and tie. His dark hair was casual and not altogether neat, as though he hadn't thought to comb it into place after riding with the top down. He looked bored and ready for action. Any action.

It was too bad, Pandora thought, that they didn't get along better. She'd have liked to have reminisced with someone about Uncle Jolley, someone who appreciated his whimsies as she had.

There was no use thinking along those lines. If they'd elected to sit together, they'd have been picking little pieces out of each other by now. Uncle Jolley, smirking down from his portrait, knew it very well.

With a half sigh she blew her nose again and tried to listen to Fitzhugh. There was something about a bequest to whales. Or maybe it was whalers.

Another hour of this, Michael thought, and he'd be ready to chew raw meat. If he heard one more *whereas…* On a long breath, Michael drew himself in. He was here for the duration because he'd loved the crazy old man. If the last thing he could do for Jolley was to stand in a room with a group of human vultures and listen to long rambling legalese, then he'd do it. Once it was over, he'd pour himself a long shot of brandy and toast the old man in private. Jolley had had a fondness for brandy.

When Michael had been young and full of imagination and his parents hadn't understood, Uncle Jolley had listened to him ramble, encouraged him to dream. Invariably on a visit to the Folley, his uncle had demanded a story then had settled himself back, bright-eyed and eager, while Michael wove on. Michael hadn't forgotten.

When he'd received his first Emmy for *Logan's Run*, Michael had flown from L.A. to the Catskills and had given the statuette to his uncle. The Emmy was still in the old man's bedroom, even if the old man wasn't.

Michael listened to the dry impersonal attorney's voice and wished for a cigarette. He'd only given them up two days before. Two days, four hours and thirty-five minutes. He'd have welcomed the raw meat.

He felt stifled in the room with all these people. Every one of them had thought old Jolley was half-mad and a bit of a nuisance. The one hundred fifty-million-dollar estate was different. Stocks and bonds

were extremely sane. Michael had seen several assessing glances roaming over the library furniture. Big, ornate Georgian might not suit some of the streamlined life-styles, but it would liquidate into very tidy cash. The old man, Michael knew, had loved every clunky chair and oversize table in the house.

He doubted if any of them had been to the big echoing house in the past ten years. Except for Pandora, he admitted grudgingly. She might be an annoyance, but she'd adored Jolley.

At the moment she looked miserable. Michael didn't believe he'd ever seen her look unhappy before—furious, disdainful, infuriating, but never unhappy. If he hadn't known better, he'd have gone to sit beside her, offer some comfort, hold her hand. She'd probably chomp it off at the wrist.

Still, her shockingly blue eyes were red and puffy. Almost as red as her hair, he mused, as his gaze skimmed over the wild curly mane that tumbled, with little attention to discipline or style, around her shoulders. She was so pale that the sprinkling of freckles over her nose stood out. Normally her ivory-toned skin had a hint of rose in it—health or temperament, he'd never been sure.

Sitting among her solemn, black-clad family, she stood out like a parrot among crows. She'd worn a vivid blue dress. Michael approved of it, though he'd never say so to Pandora. She didn't need black and crepe and lilies to mourn. That he understood, if he didn't understand her.

She annoyed him, periodically, with her views on his life-style and career. When they clashed, it didn't take long for him to hurl criticism back at her. After

all, she was a bright, talented woman who was content
to play around making outrageous jewelry for bou-
tiques rather than taking advantage of her Master's degree in education.

She called him materialistic, he called her idealistic.
She labeled him a chauvinist, he labeled her a pseudo-
intellectual. Jolley had sat with his hands folded and
chuckled every time they argued. Now that he was
gone, Michael mused, there wouldn't be an opportunity for any more battles. Oddly enough, he found it
another reason to miss his uncle.

The truth was, he'd never felt any strong family ties
to anyone but Jolley. Michael didn't think of his parents very often. His father was somewhere in Europe
with his fourth wife, and his mother had settled placidly into Palm Springs society with husband number
three. They'd never understood their son who'd opted
to work for a living in something as bourgeois as television.

But Jolley had understood and appreciated. More,
much more important to Michael, he'd enjoyed Michael's work.

A grin spread over his face when he heard Fitzhugh
drone out the bequest for whales. It was so typically
Jolley. Several impatient relations hissed through their
teeth. A hundred fifty thousand dollars had just spun
out of their reach. Michael glanced up at the larger-
than-life-size portrait of his uncle. You always said
you'd have the last word, you old fool. The only trouble is you're not here to laugh about it.

"To my son, Carlson..." All the quiet muttering
and whispers died as Fitzhugh cleared his throat. Without much interest Pandora watched her relatives come

to attention. The charities and servants had their bequests. Now it was time for the big guns. Fitzhugh glanced up briefly before he continued. "Whose— aaah—mediocrity was always a mystery to me, I leave my entire collection of magic tricks in hopes he can develop a sense of the ridiculous."

Pandora choked into her tissue and watched her uncle turn beet red. First point Uncle Jolley, she thought and prepared to enjoy herself. Maybe he'd left the whole business to the A.S.P.C.A.

"To my grandson, Bradley, and my granddaughter by marriage, Lorraine, I leave my very best wishes. They need nothing more."

Pandora swallowed and blinked back tears at the reference to her parents. She'd call them in Zanzibar that evening. They would appreciate the sentiment even as she did.

"To my nephew Monroe who has the first dollar he ever made, I leave the last dollar I made, frame included. To my niece, Patience, I leave my cottage in Key West without much hope she'll have the gumption to use it."

Monroe chomped on his cigar while Patience looked horrified.

"To my grand-nephew, Biff, I leave my collection of matches, with the hopes that he will, at last, set the world on fire. To my pretty grand-niece, Ginger, who likes equally pretty things, I leave the sterling silver mirror purported to have been owned by Marie Antoinette. To my grand-nephew, Hank, I leave the sum of $3528. Enough, I believe, for a lifetime supply of wheat germ."

The grumbles that had begun with the first bequest

continued and grew. Anger hovered on the edge of outrage. Jolley would have liked nothing better. Pandora made the mistake of glancing over at Michael. He didn't seem so distant and detached now, but full of admiration. When their gazes met, the giggle she'd been holding back spilled out. It earned her several glares.

Carlson rose, giving new meaning to the phrase controlled outrage. "Mr. Fitzhugh, my father's will is nothing more than a mockery. It's quite obvious that he wasn't in his right mind when he made it, nor do I have any doubt that a court will overturn it."

"Mr. McVie." Again Fitzhugh cleared his throat. The sun began to push its way through the clouds but no one seemed to notice. "I understand perfectly your sentiments in this matter. However, my client was perfectly well and lucid when this will was drawn. He may have worded it against my advice, but it is legal and binding. You are, of course, free to consult with your own counsel. Meanwhile, there's more to be read."

"Hogwash." Monroe puffed on his cigar and glared at everyone. "Hogwash," he repeated while Patience patted his arm and chirped ineffectually.

"Uncle Jolley liked hogwash," Pandora said as she balled her tissue. She was ready to face them down, almost hoped she'd have to. It would take her mind off her grief. "If he wanted to leave his money to the Society for the Prevention of Stupidity, it was his right."

"Easily said, my dear." Biff polished his nails on his lapel. The gold band of his watch caught a bit of

the sun and gleamed. "Perhaps the old lunatic left you a ball of twine so you can string more beads."

"You haven't got the matches yet, old boy." Michael spoke lazily from his corner, but every eye turned his way. "Careful what you light."

"Let him read, why don't you?" Ginger piped up, quite pleased with her bequest. Marie Antoinette, she mused. Just imagine.

"The last two bequests are joint," Fitzhugh began before there could be another interruption. "And, a bit unorthodox."

"The entire document's unorthodox," Carlson tossed out, then harrumphed. Several heads nodded in agreement.

Pandora remembered why she always avoided family gatherings. They bored her to death. Quite deliberately, she waved a hand in front of her mouth and yawned. "Could we have the rest, Mr. Fitzhugh, before my family embarrasses themselves any further?"

She thought, but couldn't be sure, that she saw a quick light of approval in the fusty attorney's eyes. "Mr. McVie wrote this portion in his own words." He paused a moment, either for effect or courage. "To Pandora McVie and Michael Donahue," Fitzhugh read. "The two members of my family who have given me the most pleasure with their outlook on life, their enjoyment of an old man and old jokes, I leave the rest of my estate, in entirety, all accounts, all business interests, all stocks, bonds and trusts, all real and personal property, with all affection. Share and share alike."

Pandora didn't hear the half-dozen objections that sprang out. She rose, stunned and infuriated. "I can't

take his money." Towering over the family who sat around her, she strode straight up to Fitzhugh. The lawyer, who'd anticipated attacks from other areas, braced for the unexpected. "I wouldn't know what to do with it. It'd just clutter up my life." She waved a hand at the papers on the desk as if they were a minor annoyance. "He should've asked me first."

"Miss McVie..."

Before the lawyer could speak again, she whirled on Michael. "You can have it all. You'd know what to do with it, after all. Buy a hotel in New York, a condo in L.A., a club in Chicago and a plane to fly you back and forth, I don't care."

Deadly calm, Michael slipped his hands in his pockets. "I appreciate the offer, cousin. Before you pull the trigger, why don't we wait until Mr. Fitzhugh finishes before you embarrass yourself any further?"

She stared at him a moment, nearly nose to nose with him in heels. Then, because she'd been taught to do so at an early age, she took a deep breath and waited for her temper to ebb. "I don't want his money."

"You've made your point." He lifted a brow in the cynical, half-amused way that always infuriated her. "You're fascinating the relatives by the little show you're putting on."

Nothing could have made her find control quicker. She angled her chin at him, hissed once, then subsided. "All right then." She turned and stood her ground. "I apologize for the interruption. Please finish reading, Mr. Fitzhugh."

The lawyer gave himself a moment by taking off his glasses and polishing them on a big white handker-

chief. He'd known when Jolley had made the will the day would come when he'd be forced to face an enraged family. He'd argued with his client about it, cajoled, reasoned, pointed out the absurdities. Then he'd drawn up the will and closed the loopholes.

"I leave all of this," he continued, "the money, which is a small thing, the stocks and bonds, which are necessary but boring, the business interests, which are interesting weights around the neck. And my home and all in it, which is everything important to me, the memories made there, to Pandora and Michael because they understood and cared. I leave this to them, though it may annoy them, because there is no one else in my family I can leave what is important to me. What was mine is Pandora and Michael's now, because I know they'll keep me alive. I ask only one thing of each of them in return."

Michael's grip relaxed, and he nearly smiled again. "Here comes the kicker," he murmured.

"Beginning no more than a week after the reading of this document, Pandora and Michael will move into my home in the Catskills, known as Jolley's Folley. They will live there together for a period of six months, neither one spending more than two nights in succession under another roof. After this six-month period, the estate reverts to them, entirely and without encumbrance, share and share alike.

"If one does not agree with this provision, or breaks the terms of this provision within the six-month period, the estate, in its entirety will be given over to all my surviving heirs and the Institute for the Study of Carnivorous Plants in joint shares.

"You have my blessing, children. Don't let an old, dead man down."

For a full thirty seconds there was silence. Taking advantage of it, Fitzhugh began straightening his papers.

"The old bastard," Michael murmured. Pandora would've taken offense if she hadn't agreed so completely. Because he judged the temperature in the room to be on the rise, Michael pulled Pandora out, down the hall and into one of the funny little parlors that could be found throughout the house. Just before he closed the door, the first explosion in the library erupted.

Pandora drew out a fresh tissue, sneezed into it, then plopped down on the arm of a chair. She was too flabbergasted and worn-out to be amused. "Well, what now?"

Michael reached for a cigarette before he remembered he'd quit. "Now we have to make a couple of decisions."

Pandora gave him one of the long lingering stares she'd learned made most men stutter. Michael merely sat across from her and stared back. "I meant what I said. I don't want his money. By the time it's divided up and the taxes dealt with, it's close to fifty million apiece. Fifty million," she repeated, rolling her eyes. "It's ridiculous."

"Jolley always thought so," Michael said, and watched the grief come and go in her eyes.

"He only had it to play with. The trouble was, every time he played, he made more." Unable to sit, Pandora paced to the window. "Michael, I'd suffocate with that much money."

"Cash isn't as heavy as you think."

With something close to a sneer, she turned and sat on the window ledge. "You don't object to fifty million or so after taxes I take it."

He'd have loved to have wiped that look off her face. "I haven't your fine disregard for money, Pandora, probably because I was raised with the illusion of it rather than the reality."

She shrugged, knowing his parents existed, and always had, mainly on credit and connections. "So, take it all then."

Michael picked up a little blue glass egg and tossed it from palm to palm. It was cool and smooth and worth several thousand. "That's not what Jolley wanted."

With a sniff, she snatched the egg from his hand. "He wanted us to get married and live happily ever after. I'd like to humor him...." She tossed the egg back again. "But I'm not that much of a martyr. Besides, aren't you engaged to some little blond dancer?"

He set the egg down before he could heave it at her. "For someone who turns their pampered nose up at television, you don't have the same intellectual snobbery about gossip rags."

"I *adore* gossip," Pandora said with such magnificent exaggeration Michael laughed.

"All right, Pandora, let's put down the swords a minute." He tucked his thumbs in his pockets and rocked back on his heels. Maybe they could, if they concentrated, talk civilly with each other for a few minutes. "I'm not engaged to anyone, but marriage wasn't a term of the will in any case. All we have to

do is live together for six months under the same roof.''

As she studied him a sense of disappointment ran through her. Perhaps they'd never gotten along, but she'd respected him if for nothing more than what she'd seen as his pure affection for Uncle Jolley. ''So, you really want the money?''

He took two furious steps forward before he caught himself. Pandora never flinched. ''Think whatever you like.'' He said it softly, as though it didn't matter. Oddly enough, it made her shudder. ''You don't want the money, fine. Put that aside a moment. Are you going to stand by and watch this house go to the clan out there or a bunch of scientists studying Venus's-flytraps? Jolley loved this place and everything in it. I always thought you did, too.''

''I do.'' The others would sell it, she admitted. There wasn't one person in the library who wouldn't put the house on the market and run with the cash. It would be lost to her. All the foolish, ostentatious rooms, the ridiculous archways. Jolley might be gone, but he'd left the house like a dangling carrot. And he still held the stick.

''He's trying to run our lives still.''

Michael lifted a brow. ''Surprised?''

With a half laugh, Pandora glanced over. ''No.''

Slowly she walked around the room while the sun shot through the diamond panes of glass and lit her hair. Michael watched her with a sense of detached admiration. She'd look magnificent on the screen. He'd always thought so. Her coloring, her posture. Her arrogance. The five or ten pounds the camera would

add couldn't hurt that too angular, bean-pole body, either. And the fire-engine-red hair would make a statement on the screen while it was simply outrageous in reality. He'd often wondered why she didn't do something to tone it down.

At the moment he wasn't interested in any of that— just in what was in her brain. He didn't give a damn about the money, but he wasn't going to sit idly by and watch everything Jolley had had and built go to the vultures. If he had to play rough with Pandora, he would. He might even enjoy it.

Millions. Pandora cringed at the outrageousness of it. That much money could be nothing but a headache, she was certain. Stocks, bonds, accountants, trusts, tax shelters. She preferred a simpler kind of living. Though no one would call her apartment in Manhattan primitive.

She'd never had to worry about money and that was just the way she liked it. Above or below a certain income level, there were nothing but worries. But if you found a nice, comfortable plateau, you could just cruise. She'd nearly found it.

It was true enough that a share of this would help her tremendously professionally. With a buffer sturdy enough, she could have the artistic freedom she wanted and continue the life-style that now caused a bit of a strain on her bank account. Her work was artistic and critically acclaimed but reviews didn't pay the rent. Outside of Manhattan, her work was usually considered too unconventional. The fact that she often had to create more mainstream designs to keep her head above water grated constantly. With fifty or sixty thousand to back her, she could…

Furious with herself, she blocked it off. She was thinking like Michael, she decided. She'd rather die. He'd sold out, turned whatever talent he had to the main chance, just as he was ready to turn these circumstances to his own financial advantage. She would think of other areas. She would think first of Jolley.

As she saw it, the entire scheme was a maze of problems. How like her uncle. Now, like a chess match, she'd have to consider her moves.

She'd never lived with a man. Purposely. Pandora liked running by her own clock. It wasn't so much that she minded sharing *things*, she minded sharing space. If she agreed, that would be the first concession.

Then there was the fact that Michael was attractive, attractive enough to be unsettling if he hadn't been so annoying. Annoying and easily annoyed, she recalled with a flash of amusement. She knew what buttons to push. Hadn't she always prided herself on the fact that she could handle him? It wasn't always easy; he was too sharp. But that made their altercations interesting. Still, they'd never been together for more than a week at a time.

But there was one clear, inarguable fact. She'd loved her uncle. How could she live with herself if she denied him a last wish? Or a last joke.

Six months. Stopping, she studied Michael as he studied her. Six months could be a very long time, especially when you weren't pleased with what you were doing. There was only one way to speed things up. She'd enjoy herself.

"Tell me, cousin, how can we live under the same roof for six months without coming to blows?"

"We can't."

He'd answered without a second's hesitation, so she laughed again. "I suppose I'd be bored if we did. I can tidy up loose ends and move in in three days. Four at the most."

"That's fine." When his shoulders relaxed, he realized he'd been tensed for her refusal. At the moment he didn't want to question why it mattered so much. Instead he held out a hand. "Deal."

Pandora inclined her head just before her palm met his. "Deal," she agreed, surprised that his hand was hard and a bit callused. She'd expected it to be rather soft and limp. After all, all he did was type. Perhaps the next six months would have some surprises.

"Shall we go tell the others?"

"They'll want to murder us."

Her smile came slowly, subtly shifting the angles of her face. It was, Michael thought, at once wicked and alluring. "I know. Try not to gloat."

When they stepped out, several griping relatives had spilled out into the hallway. They did what they did best together. They argued.

"You'd blow your share on barbells and carrot juice," Biff said spitefully to Hank. "At least I know what to do with money."

"Lose it on horses," Monroe said, and blew out a stream of choking cigar smoke. "Invest. Tax deferred."

"You could use yours to take a course in how to speak in complete sentences." Carlson stepped out of the smoke and straightened his tie. "I'm the old man's only living son. It's up to me to prove he was incompetent."

"Uncle Jolley had more competence than the lot of you put together." Feeling equal parts frustration and disgust, Pandora stepped forward. "He gave you each exactly what he wanted you to have."

Biff drew out a flat gold cigarette case as he glanced over at his cousin. "It appears our Pandora's changed her mind about the money. Well, you worked for it, didn't you, darling?"

Michael put his hand on Pandora's shoulder and squeezed lightly before she could spring. "You'd like to keep your profile, wouldn't you, cousin?"

"It appears writing for television's given you a taste for violence." Biff lit his cigarette and smiled. If he'd thought he could get in a blow below the belt... "I think I'll decline a brawl," he decided.

"Well, I think it's fair." Hank's wife came forward, stretching out her hand. She gave both Pandora and Michael a hearty shake. "You should put a gym in this place. Build yourself up a little. Come on, Hank."

Silent, and his shoulders straining the material of his suit, Hank followed her out.

"Nothing but muscles between the head," Carlson mumbled. "Come, Mona." He strode ahead of his wife, pausing long enough to level a glare at Pandora and Michael. The inevitable line ran though Michael's mind before Carlson opened his mouth and echoed it. "You haven't heard the last of this."

Pandora gave him her sweetest smile. "Have a nice trip home, Uncle Carlson."

"Probate," Monroe said with a grunt, and waddled his way out behind them.

Patience fluttered her hands. "Key West, for

heaven's sake. I've never been south of Palm Beach. My, oh my.''

"Oh, Michael." Fluttering her lashes, Ginger placed a hand on his arm. "When do you think I might have my mirror?"

He glanced down into her perfectly lovely, heart-shaped face. Her eyes were as pure a blue as tropical waters. He thanked God Jolley hadn't asked that he spend six months with Cousin Ginger. "I'm sure Mr. Fitzhugh will have it shipped to you as soon as possible."

"Come along, Ginger, we'll give you a ride to the airport." Biff pulled Ginger's hand through his arm, patted it and smiled down at Pandora. "I'd be worried if I didn't know you better. You won't last six days with Michael much less six months. Beastly temper," he said confidentially to Michael. "The two of you'll murder each other before a week's out."

"Don't spend the old man's money yet," Michael warned. "We'll make the six months if for no other reason than to spite you." He smiled when he said it, a chummy, well-meaning smile that took the arrogance from Biff's face.

"We'll see who wins the game." Straight backed, Biff turned toward the door. His wife walked out behind him without having said a word since she'd walked in.

"Biff," Ginger began as they walked out. "What are you going to do with all those matches?"

"Burn his bridges, I hope," Pandora muttered. "Well, Michael, though I can't say there was a lot of love before, there's nearly none lost now."

"Are you worried about alienating them?"

With a shrug of her shoulders, she walked toward a bowl of roses, then gave him a considering look. "Well, I've never had any trouble alienating you. Why is that, do you suppose?"

"Jolley always said we were too much alike."

"Really?" Haughty, she lifted a brow. "I find myself disagreeing with him again. You and I, Michael Donahue, have almost nothing in common."

"If that's so we have six months to prove it." On impulse he moved closer and put a finger under her chin. "You know, darling, you might've been stuck with Biff."

"I'd've given the place to the plants first."

He grinned. "I'm flattered."

"Don't be." But she didn't move away from him. Not yet. It was an interesting feeling to be this close without snarling. "The only difference is you don't bore me."

"That's enough," he said with a hint of a smile. "I'm easily flattered." Intrigued, he flicked a finger down her cheek. It was still pale, but her eyes were direct and steady. "No, we won't bore each other Pandora. In six months we might experience a lot of things, but boredom won't be one of them."

It might be an interesting feeling, she discovered, but it wasn't quite a safe one. It was best to remember that he didn't find her appealing as a woman but would, for the sake of his own ego, string her along if she permitted it. "I don't flatter easily. I haven't decided exactly what your reasons are for going through with this farce, but I'm doing it only for Uncle Jolley. I can set up my equipment here quite easily."

"And I can write here quite easily."

Pandora plucked a rose from the bowl. "If you can call those implausible scripts writing."

"The same way you call the bangles you string together art."

Color came back to her cheeks and that pleased him. "You wouldn't know art if it reached up and bit you on the nose. My jewelry expresses emotion."

His smile showed pleasant interest. "How much is lust going for these days?"

"I would have guessed you'd be very familiar with the cost." Pandora fumbled for a tissue, sneezed into it, then shut her bag with a click. "Most of the women you date have price tags."

It amused him, and it showed. "I thought we were talking about work."

"My profession is a time-honored one, while yours—yours stops for commercial breaks. And furthermore—"

"I beg your pardon."

Fitzhugh paused at the doorway of the library. He wanted nothing more than to be shed of the McVie clan and have a quiet, soothing drink. "Am I to assume that you've both decided to accept the terms of the will?"

Six months, she thought. It was going to be a long, long winter.

Six months, he thought. He was going to have the first daffodil he found in April bronzed.

"You can start counting the days at the end of the week," he told Fitzhugh. "Agreed, cousin?"

Pandora set her chin. "Agreed."

Chapter 2

It was a pleasant trip from Manhattan along the Hudson River toward the Catskills. Pandora had always enjoyed it. The drive gave her time to clear her mind and relax. But then, she'd always taken it at her own whim, her own pace, her own convenience. Pandora made it a habit to do everything just that way. This time, however, there was more involved than her own wants and wishes. Uncle Jolley had boxed her in.

He'd known she'd have to go along with the terms of the will. Not for the money. He'd been too smart to think she could be lured into such a ridiculous scheme with money. But the house, her ties to it, her need for the continuity of family. That's what he'd hooked her with.

Now she had to leave Manhattan behind for six months. Oh, she'd run into the city for a few hours here and there, but it was hardly the same as living in

the center of things. She'd always liked that—being in the center, surrounded by movement, being able to watch and become involved whenever she liked. Just as she'd always liked long weekends in the solitude of Jolley's Folley.

She'd been raised that way, to enjoy and make the most of whatever environment she was in. Her parents were gypsies. Wealth had meant they'd traveled first class instead of in covered wagons. If there'd been campfires, there had also been a servant to gather kindling, but the spirit was the same.

Before she'd been fifteen, Pandora had been to more than thirty countries. She'd eaten sushi in Tokyo, roamed the moors in Cornwall, bargained in Turkish markets. A succession of tutors had traveled with them so that by her calculations, she'd spent just under two years in a classroom environment before college.

The exotic, vagabond childhood had given her a taste for variety—in people, in foods, in styles. And oddly enough the exposure to widely diverse cultures and mores had formed in her an unshakable desire for a home and a sense of belonging.

Though her parents liked to meander through countries, recording everything with pen and film, Pandora had missed a central point. Where was home? This year in Mexico, next year in Athens. Her parents made a name for themselves with their books and articles on the unusual, but Pandora wanted roots. She'd discovered she'd have to find them for herself.

She'd chosen New York, and in her way, Uncle Jolley.

Now, because her uncle and his home had become her central point, she was agreeing to spend six months

living with a man she could hardly tolerate so that she could inherit a fortune she didn't want or need. Life, she'd discovered long ago, never moved in straight lines.

Jolley McVie's ultimate joke, she thought as she turned up the long drive toward his Folley. Well, he could throw them together, but he couldn't make them stick.

Still, she'd have felt better if she'd been sure of Michael. Was it the lure of the millions of dollars, or an affection for an old man that would bring him to the Catskills? She knew his *Logan's Run* was in its very successful fourth year, and that he'd had other lucrative ventures in television. But money was a seduction itself. After all, her Uncle Carlson had more than he could ever spend, yet he was already taking the steps for a probate of the will.

That didn't worry her. Uncle Jolley had believed in hiring the best. If Fitzhugh had drawn up the will, it was air-tight. What worried her was Michael Donahue.

Because of the trap she'd fallen into, she'd found herself thinking of him a great deal too much over the past couple of days. Ally or enemy, she wasn't sure. Either way, she was going to have to live with him. Or around him. She hoped the house was big enough.

By the time she arrived, she was worn-out from the drive and the lingering head cold. Though her equipment and supplies had been shipped the day before, she still had three cases in the car. Deciding to take one at a time, Pandora popped the trunk, then simply looked at Jolley's Folley.

He'd built it when he'd been forty, so the house was already over a half century old. It went in all directions

at once, as if he'd never been able to decide where he wanted to start and where he wanted to finish. The truth about Jolley, she admitted, was that he'd never wanted to finish. The project, the game, the puzzle, was always more interesting to him before the last pieces were in place.

Without the wings, it might have been a rather somber and sedate late-nineteenth-century mansion. With them, it was a mass of walls and corners, heights and widths. There was no symmetry, yet to Pandora it had always seemed as sturdy as the rock it had been built on.

Some of the windows were long, some were wide, some of them were leaded and some sheer. Jolley had made up his mind then changed it again as he'd gone along.

The stone had come from one of his quarries, the wood from one of his lumberyards. When he'd decided to build a house, he'd started his own construction firm. McVie Construction, Incorporated was one of the five biggest companies in the country.

It struck her suddenly that she owned half of Jolley's share in the company and her mind spun at how many others. She had interests in baby oil, steel mills, rocket engines and cake mix. Pandora lifted the case and set her teeth. What on earth had she let herself in for?

From the upstairs window, Michael watched her. The jacket she wore was big and baggy with three vivid colors, blue, yellow and pink patched in. The wind caught at her slacks and rippled them from thigh to ankle. She wasn't looking teary-eyed and pale this time, but grim and resigned. So much the better. He'd

been tempted to comfort her during their uncle's funeral. Only the knowledge that too much sympathy for a woman like Pandora was fatal had prevented him.

He'd known her since childhood and had considered her a spoiled brat from the word go. Though she'd often been off for months at a time on one of her parents' journalistic safaris, they'd seen enough of each other to feed a mutual dislike. Only the fact that she had cared for Jolley had given Michael some tolerance for her. And the fact, he was forced to admit, that she had more honesty and humanity in her than any of their other relations.

There had been a time, he recalled, a brief time, during late adolescence that he'd felt a certain…stirring for her. A purely shallow and physical teenage hunger, Michael assured himself. She'd always had an intriguing face; it could be unrelentingly plain one moment and striking the next, and when she'd hit her teens…well, that had been a natural enough reaction. And it had passed without incident. He now preferred a woman with more subtlety, more gloss and femininity—and shorter fangs.

Whatever he preferred, Michael left the arranging of his own office to wander downstairs.

"Charles, did my shipment come?" Pandora pulled off her leather driving gloves and dropped them on a little round table in the hall. Since Charles was there, the ancient butler who had served her uncle since before she was born, she felt a certain pleasure in coming.

"Everything arrived this morning, miss." The old man would have taken her suitcase if she hadn't waved him away.

"No, don't fuss with that. Where did you have them put everything?"

"In the garden shed in the east yard, as you instructed."

She gave him a smile and a peck on the cheek, both of which pleased him. His square bulldog's face grew slightly pink. "I knew I could count on you. I didn't tell you before how happy I was that you and Sweeney are staying. The place wouldn't be the same without you serving tea and Sweeney baking cakes."

Charles managed to pull his back a bit straighter. "We wouldn't think about going anywhere else, miss. The master would have wanted us to stay."

But made it possible for them to go, Pandora mused. Leaving each of them three thousand dollars for every year of service. Charles had been with Jolley since the house was built, and Sweeney had come some ten years later. The bequest would have been more than enough for each to retire on. Pandora smiled. Some weren't made for retirement.

"Charles, I'd love some tea," she began, knowing if she didn't distract him, he'd insist on carrying her bags up the long staircase.

"In the drawing room, miss?"

"Perfect. And if Sweeney has any of those little cakes…"

"She's been baking all morning." With only the slightest of creaks, he made his way toward the kitchen.

Pandora thought of rich icing loaded with sugar. "I wonder how much weight a person can gain in six months."

"A steady diet of Sweeney's cakes wouldn't hurt

you,'' Michael said from above her head. ''Men are generally more attracted to flesh than bone.''

Pandora spun around, then found herself in the awkward position of having to arch her neck back to see Michael at the top of the stairs. ''I don't center my life around attracting men.''

''I'd be the last one to argue with that.''

He looked quite comfortable, she thought, feeling the first stirrings of resentment. And negligently, arrogantly attractive. From several feet above her head, he leaned against a post and looked down on her as though he was the master. She'd soon put an end to that. Uncle Jolley's will had been very clear. Share and share alike.

''Since you're already here and settled in, you can come help me with the rest of my bags.''

He didn't budge. ''I always thought the one point we were in perfect agreement on was feminism.''

Pandora paused at the door to toss a look over her shoulder. ''Social and political views aside, if you don't help me up with them before Charles comes back, he'll insist on doing it himself. He's too old to do it and too proud to be told he can't.'' She walked back out and wasn't surprised when she heard his footsteps on the gravel behind her.

She took a deep breath of crisp autumn air. All in all, it was a lovely day. ''Drive up early?''

''Actually, I drove up late last night.''

Pandora turned at the open trunk of her car. ''So eager to start the game, Michael?''

If he hadn't been determined to start off peacefully, he'd have found fault with the tone of her voice, with the look in her eyes. Instead he let it pass. ''I wanted

to get my office set up today. I was just finishing it when you drove in.''

''Work, work, work,'' she said with a long sigh. ''You must put in slavish hours to come up with an hour of chase scenes and steam a week.''

Peace wasn't all that important. As she reached for a suitcase, he closed a hand over her wrist. Later he'd think about how slim it was, how soft. Now he could only think how much he wished she were a man. Then he could've belted her. ''The amount of work I do and what I produce is of absolutely no concern to you.''

It occurred to Pandora, oddly, she thought, just how much she enjoyed seeing him on the edge of temper. All of her other relatives were so bland, so outwardly civilized. Michael had always been a contrast, and therefore of more interest. Smiling, she allowed her wrist to stay limp.

''Did I indicate that it was? Nothing, I promise you, could be further from the truth. Shall we get these in and have that tea? It's a bit chilly.''

He'd always admired, grudgingly, how smoothly she could slip into the lady-of-the-manor routine. As a writer who wrote for actors and for viewers, he appreciated natural talent. He also knew how to set a scene to his best advantage. ''Tea's a perfect idea.'' He hauled one case out and left the second for her. ''We'll establish some guidelines.''

''Will we?'' Pandora pulled out the case, then let the trunk shut quietly. Without another word, she started back toward the house, holding the front door open for him, then breezing by the suitcase she'd left in the main hall. Because she knew Michael was fond

of Charles, she hadn't a doubt he'd pick it up and follow.

The room she always took was on the second floor in the east wing. Jolley had let her decorate it herself, and she'd chosen white on white with a few startling splashes of color. Chartreuse and blazing blue in throw pillows, a long horizontal oil painting, jarring in its colors of sunset, a crimson waist-high urn stuffed with ostrich plumes.

Pandora set her case by the bed, noted with satisfaction that a fire had been laid in the small marble fireplace, then tossed her jacket over a chair.

"I always feel like I'm walking into *Better Homes*," he commented as he let her cases drop.

Pandora glanced down at them briefly, then at him. "I'm sure you're more at home in your own room. It's more—*Field and Stream*. I expect tea's ready."

He gave her a long, steady survey. Her jacket had concealed the trim cashmere sweater tucked into the narrow waist of her slacks. It reminded Michael quite forcibly just what had begun to attract him all those teenage years ago. For the second time he found himself wishing she were a man.

Though they walked abreast down the stairs, they didn't speak. In the drawing room, amid the Mideast opulence Jolley had chosen there, Charles was setting up the tea service.

"Oh, you lit the fire. How lovely." Pandora walked over and began warming her hands. She wanted a moment, just a moment, because for an instant in her room she thought she'd seen something in Michael's eyes. And she thought she'd felt the same something

in response. "I'll pour, Charles. I'm sure Michael and I won't need another thing until dinner."

Casually she glanced around the room, at the flowing drapes, the curvy brocade sofas, the plump pillows and brass urns. "You know, this has always been one of my favorite rooms." Going to the tea set, she began to fill cups. "I was only twelve when we visited Turkey, but this room always makes me remember it vividly. Right down to the smells in the markets. Sugar?"

"No." He took the cup from her, plopped a generous slice of cake on a dish, then chose a seat. He preferred the little parlor next door with its tidy English country air. This was the beginning, he thought, with the old butler and plump cook as witnesses. Six months from today, they'd all sign a document swearing that the terms of the will had been adhered to and that would be that. It was the time in between that concerned him.

"Rule number one," Michael began without preamble. "We're both in the east wing because it makes it easier for Charles and Sweeney. But—" he paused, hoping to emphasize his point "—both of us will, at all times, respect the other's area."

"By all means." Pandora crossed her legs and sipped her tea.

"Again, because of the staff, it seems fair that we eat at the same time. Therefore, in the interest of survival, we'll keep the conversations away from professional matters."

Pandora smiled at him and nibbled on cake. "Oh yes, let's do keep things personal."

"You're a nasty little package—"

"See, we're off to a perfect start. Rule number two.

Neither of us, no matter how bored or restless, will disturb the other during his or her set working hours. I generally work between ten and one, then again between three and six.''

"Rule number three. If one of us is entertaining, the other will make him or herself scarce.''

Pandora's eyes narrowed, only for a moment. "Oh, and I so wanted to meet your dancer. Rule number four. The first floor is neutral ground and to be shared equally unless specific prior arrangements are made and agreed upon.'' She tapped her finger against the arm of the chair. "If we both play fair, we should manage.''

"I don't have any trouble playing fair. As I recall, you're the one who cheats.''

Her voice became very cool, her tone very rounded. "I don't know what you're talking about.''

"Canasta, poker, gin.''

"That's absurd and you have absolutely no proof.'' Rising, she helped herself to another cup of tea. "Besides, cards are entirely different.'' Warmed by the fire, soothed by the tea, she smiled at him. As Michael recalled, that particular smile was lethal. And stunning. "Are you still holding a grudge over that five hundred I won from you?''

"I wouldn't if you'd won it fairly.''

"I won it,'' she countered. "That's what counts. If I cheated and you didn't catch me, then it follows that I cheated well enough for it to be legal.''

"You always had a crooked sense of logic.'' He rose as well and came close. She had to admire the way he moved. It wasn't quite a swagger because he didn't put the effort into it. But it was very close.

"If we play again, whatever we play, you won't cheat me."

Confident, she smiled at him. "Michael, we've known each other too long for you to intimidate me." She reached a hand up to pat his cheek and found her wrist captured a second time. And a second time she saw and felt that same dangerous something she'd experienced upstairs.

There was no Uncle Jolley as a buffer between them now. Perhaps they'd both just begun to realize it. Whatever was between them that made them snarl and snap would have a long, cold winter to surface.

Perhaps neither one of them wanted to face it, but both were too stubborn to back down.

"Perhaps we're just beginning to know each other," Michael murmured.

She believed it. And didn't like it. He wasn't a posturing fool like Biff nor a harmless hulk like Hank. He might be a cousin by marriage only, but the blood between them had always run hot. There was violence in him. It showed sometimes in a look in his eyes, in the way he held himself. As though he wouldn't ward off a blow but counter it. Pandora recognized it because there was violence in her, as well. Perhaps that was why she always felt compelled to shoot darts at him, just to see how many he could boomerang back at her.

They stood as they were a moment, gauging each other, reassessing. The wise thing to do was for each to acknowledge a hit and step aside. Pandora threw up her chin. Michael set for the volley. "We'll go to the mat another time, Michael. At the moment, I'm a bit tired from the drive. If you'll excuse me?"

"Rule number five," he said without releasing her. "If one of us takes potshots at the other, they'll damn well pay the consequences." When he freed her arm, he went back for his cup. "See you at dinner, cousin."

Pandora awoke just past dawn fully awake, rested and bursting with energy. Whether it had been the air in the mountains or the six hours of deep sleep, she was ready and eager to work. Breakfast could wait, she decided as she showered and dressed. She was going out to the garden shed, organizing her equipment and diving in.

The house was perfectly quiet and still dim as she made her way downstairs. The servants would sleep another hour or two, she thought as she stuck her head in the pantry and chose a muffin. As she recalled, Michael might sleep until noon.

They had made it through dinner without incident. Perhaps they'd been polite to each other because of Charles and Sweeney or perhaps because both of them had been too tired to snipe. Pandora wasn't sure herself.

They'd dined under the cheerful lights of the big chandelier and had talked, when they'd talked, about the weather and the food.

By nine they'd gone their separate ways. Pandora to read until her eyes closed and Michael to work. Or so he'd said.

Outside the air was chill enough to cause Pandora's skin to prickle. She hunched up the collar of her jacket and started across the lawn. It crunched underfoot with the early thin frost. She liked it—the absolute solitude,

the lightness of the air, the incredible smell of mountain and river.

In Tibet she'd once come close to frostbite because she hadn't been able to resist the snow and the swoop of rock. She didn't find this slice of the Catskills any less fascinating. The winter was best, she'd always thought, when the snow skimmed the top of your boots and your voice came out in puffs of smoke.

Winter in the mountains was a time for the basics. Heat, food, work. There were times Pandora wanted only the basics. There were times in New York she'd argue for hours over unions, politics, civil rights because the fact was, she loved an argument. She wanted the stimulation of an opposing view over broad issues or niggling ones. She wanted the challenge, the heat and the exercise for her brain. But...

There were times she wanted nothing more than a quiet sunrise over frost-crisped ground and the promise of a warm drink by a hot fire. And there were times, though she'd rarely admit it even to herself, that she wanted a shoulder to lay her head against and a hand to hold. She'd been raised to see independence as a duty, not a choice. Her parents had the most balanced of relationships, equal to equal. Pandora saw them as something rare in a world where the scales tipped this way or that too often. At age eighteen, Pandora had decided she'd never settle for less than a full partnership. At age twenty, she decided marriage wasn't for her. Instead she put all her passion, her energy and imagination into her work.

Straight-line dedication had paid off. She was successful, even prominent, and creatively she was fulfilled. It was more than many people ever achieved.

Now she pulled open the door of the utility shed. It was a big square building, as wide as the average barn, with hardwood floors and paneled walls. Uncle Jolley hadn't believed in the primitive. Hitting the switch, she flooded the building with light.

As per her instructions, the crates and boxes she'd shipped had been stacked along one wall. The shelves where Uncle Jolley had kept his gardening tools during his brief, torrid gardening stage had been packed away. The plumbing was good, with a full-size stainless-steel sink and a small but more than adequate bath with shower enclosed in the rear. She counted five workbenches. The light and ventilation were excellent.

It wouldn't take her long, Pandora figured, to turn the shed into an organized, productive workroom.

It took three hours.

Along one shelf were boxes of beads in various sizes—jet, amethyst, gold, polished wood, coral, ivory. She had trays of stones, precious and semiprecious, square cut, brilliants, teardrops and chips. In New York, they were kept in a safe. Here, she never considered it. She had gold, silver, bronze, copper. There were solid and hollow drills, hammers, tongs, pliers, nippers, files and clamps. One might have thought she did carpentry. Then there were scribes and drawplates, bottles of chemicals, and miles of string and fiber cord.

The money she'd invested in these materials had cost her every penny of an inheritance from her grandmother, and a good chunk of savings she'd earned as an apprentice. It had been worth it. Pandora picked up a file and tapped it against her palm. Well worth it.

She could forge gold and silver, cast alloys and string impossibly complex designs with the use of a

few beads or shells. Metals could be worked into thin, threadlike strands or built into big bold chunks. Pandora could do as she chose, with tools that had hardly changed from those used by artists two centuries earlier.

It was and always had been, both the sense of continuity and the endless variety that appealed to her. She never made two identical pieces. That, to her, would have been manufacturing rather than creating. At times, her pieces were elegantly simple, classic in design. Those pieces sold well and allowed her a bit of artistic freedom. At other times, they were bold and brash and exaggerated. Mood guided Pandora, not trends. Rarely, very rarely, she would agree to create a piece along specified lines. If the lines, or the client, interested her.

She turned down a president because she'd found his ideas too pedestrian but had made a ring at a new father's request because his idea had been unique. Pandora had been told that the new mother had never taken the braided gold links off. Three links, one for each of the triplets she'd given birth to.

At the moment, Pandora had just completed drafting the design for a three-tiered necklace commissioned to her by the husband of a popular singer. Emerald. That was her name and the only requirement given to Pandora. The man wanted lots of them. And he'd pay, Pandora mused, for the dozen she'd chosen just before leaving New York. They were square, three karats apiece and of the sharp, sharp green that emeralds are valued for.

This was, she knew, her big chance, professionally and, most importantly, artistically. If the necklace was

a success, there'd not only be reviews for her scrap-
book, but acceptance. She'd be freer to do more of
what she wanted without compromise.

The trick would be to fashion the chain so that it
held like steel and looked like a cobweb. The stones
would hang from each tier as if they'd dripped there.

For the next two hours, she worked in gold.

Between the two heaters at each end of the shed and
the flame from her tools, the air became sultry. Sweat
rolled down under her sweater, but she didn't mind.
In fact, she barely noticed as the gold became pliable.
Again and again, she drew the wire through the draw-
plate, smoothing out the kinks and subtly, slowly,
changing the shape and size. When the wire looked
like angel hair she began working it with her fingers,
twisting and braiding until she matched the design in
her head and on her drawing paper.

It would be simple—elegantly, richly simple. The
emeralds would bring their own flash when she attached them.

Time passed. After careful, meticulous use of draw-
plate, flame and her own hands, the first thin, gold tier
formed.

She'd just begun to stretch out the muscles in her
back when the door of the shed opened and cool air
poured in. Her face glowing with sweat and concentration, she glared at Michael.

"Just what the hell do you think you're doing?"

"Following orders." He had his hands stuffed in his
jacket pockets for warmth, but hadn't buttoned the
front. Nor, she noticed, had he bothered to shave.
"This place smells like an oven."

"I'm working." She lifted the hem of the big apron

she wore and wiped at her brow. It was being interrupted that annoyed her, Pandora told herself. Not the
fact that he'd walked in on her when she looked like
a steelworker. "Remember rule number three?"

"Tell that to Sweeney." Leaving the door ajar, he
wandered in. "She said it was bad enough that you
skipped breakfast, but you're not getting away with
missing lunch." Curious, he poked his finger into a
tray that held brilliant colored stones. "I have orders
to bring you back."

"I'm not ready."

He picked up a tiny sapphire and held it to the light.
"I had to stop her from tramping out here herself. If
I go back alone, she's going to come for you. Her
arthritis is acting up again."

Pandora swore under her breath. "Put that down,"
she ordered, then yanked the apron off.

"Some of this stuff looks real," he commented.
Though he put the sapphire back, he picked up a
round, winking diamond.

"Some of this stuff is real." Pandora crouched to
turn the first heater down.

The diamond was in his hand as he scowled down
at her head. "Why in hell do you have it sitting out
like candy? It should be locked up."

Pandora adjusted the second heater. "Why?"

"Don't be any more foolish than necessary. Someone could steal it."

"Someone?" Straightening, Pandora smiled at him.
"There aren't many someones around. I don't think
Charles and Sweeney are a problem, but maybe I
should worry about you."

He cursed her and dropped the diamond back.

"They're your little bag of tricks, cousin, but if I had several thousand dollars sitting around that could slip into a pocket, I'd be more careful."

Though under most circumstances she fully agreed, Pandora merely picked up her jacket. After all, they weren't in Manhattan but miles away from anyone or anything. If she locked everything up, she'd just have to unlock it again every time she wanted to work. "Just one of the differences between you and me, Michael. I suppose it's because you write about so many dirty deeds."

"I also write about human nature." He picked up the sketch of the emerald necklace she had drawn. It had the sense of scale that would have pleased an architect and the flare and flow that would appeal to an artist. "If you're so into making bangles and baubles, why aren't you wearing any?"

"They get in the way when I'm working. If you write about human nature, how come the bad guy gets caught every week?"

"Because I'm writing for people, and people need heroes."

Pandora opened her mouth to argue, then found she agreed with the essence of the statement. "Hmm," was all she said as she turned out the lights and went out ahead of him.

"At least lock the door," Michael told her.

"I haven't a key."

"Then we'll get one."

"*We* don't need one."

He shut the door with a snap. "*You* do."

Pandora only shrugged as she started across the

lawn. "Michael, have I mentioned that you've been more crabby than usual?"

He pulled a piece of hard candy out of his pocket and popped it into his mouth. "Quit smoking."

The candy was lemon. She caught just a whiff. "So I noticed. How long?"

He scowled at some leaves that skimmed across the lawn. They were brown and dry and seemed to have a life of their own. "Couple weeks. I'm going crazy."

She laughed sympathetically before she tucked her arm into his. "You'll live, darling. The first month's the toughest."

Now he scowled at her. "How would you know? You never smoked."

"The first month of anything's the toughest. You just have to keep your mind occupied. Exercise. We'll jog after lunch."

"We?"

"And we can play canasta after dinner."

He gave a quick snort but brushed the hair back from her cheek. "You'll cheat."

"See, your mind's already occupied." With a laugh, she turned her face up to his. He looked a bit surly, but on him, oddly, it was attractive. Placid, good-natured good looks had always bored her. "It won't hurt you to give up one of your vices, Michael. You have so many."

"I like my vices," he grumbled, then turned his head to look down at her. She was giving him her easy, friendly smile, one she sent his way rarely. It always made him forget just how much trouble she caused him. It made him forget he wasn't attracted to dramatically bohemian women with wild red hair and

sharp bones. "A woman who looks like you should have several of her own."

Her mouth was solemn, her eyes wicked. "I'm much too busy. Vices take up a great deal of time."

"When Pandora opened the box, vices popped out."

She stopped at the back stoop. "Among other miseries. I suppose that's why I'm careful about opening boxes."

Michael ran a finger down her cheek. It was the sort of gesture he realized could easily become a habit. She was right, his mind was occupied. "You have to lift off the lid sooner or later."

She didn't move back, though she'd felt the little tingle of tension, of attraction, of need. Pandora didn't believe in moving back, but in plowing through. "Some things are better off locked up."

He nodded. He didn't want to release what was in their private box any more than she did. "Some locks aren't as strong as they need to be."

They were standing close, the wind whistling lightly between them. Pandora felt the sun on her back and the chill on her face. If she took a step nearer, there'd be heat. That she'd never doubted and had always avoided. He'd use whatever was available to him, she reminded herself. At the moment, it just happened to be her. She let her breath come calmly and easily before she reached for the doorknob.

"We'd better not keep Sweeney waiting."

Chapter 3

The streets are almost deserted. A car turns a corner and disappears. It's drizzling. Neon flashes off puddles. It's garish rather than festive. There's a gray, miserable feel to this part of the city. Alleyways, cheap clubs, dented cars. The small, neatly dressed blonde walks quickly. She's nervous, out of her element, but not lost. Close-up on the envelope in her hands. It's damp from the rain. Her fingers open and close on it. Tires squeal off screen and she jolts. The blue lights of the club blink off and on in her face as she stands outside. Hesitates. Shifts the envelope from hand to hand. She goes in. Slow pan of the street. Three shots and freeze.

Three knocks sounded at the door of Michael's office. Before he could answer, Pandora swirled in. "Happy anniversary, darling."

Michael looked up from his typewriter. He'd been

up most of the night working the story line out in his mind. It was nine in the morning, and he'd only had one cup of coffee to prime him for the day. Coffee and cigarettes together were too precious a memory. The scene that had just jelled in his mind dissolved.

"What the hell are you talking about?" He reached his hand into a bowl of peanuts and discovered he'd already eaten all but two.

"Two full weeks without any broken bones." Pandora swooped over to him, clucked her tongue at the disorder, then chose the arm of a chair. It was virtually the only free space. She brushed at the dust on the edge of the table beside her and left a smear. "And they said it wouldn't last."

She looked fresh with her wild mane of red pulled back from her face, comfortable in sweater and slacks that were too big for her. Michael felt like he'd just crawled out of a cave. His sweatshirt had ripped at the shoulder seam two years before, but he still favored it. A few weeks before, he'd helped paint a friend's apartment. The paint smears on his jeans showed her preference for baby pink. His eyes felt as though he'd slept facedown in the sand.

Pandora smiled at him like some bright, enthusiastic kindergarten teacher. She had a fresh, clean, almost woodsy scent. "We have a rule about respecting the other's work space," he reminded her.

"Oh, don't be cranky." It was said with the same positive smile. "Besides, you never gave me any schedule. From what I've noticed in the past couple of weeks, this is early for you."

"I'm just starting the treatment for a new episode."

"Really?" Pandora walked over and leaned over his

shoulder. "Hmm," she said, though she wondered who had shot whom. "Well, I don't suppose that'll take long."

"Why don't you go play with your beads?"

"Now you're being rude when I came up here to invite you to go with me into town." After brushing off the sleeve of her sweater, she sat on the edge of the desk. She didn't know exactly why she was so determined to be friendly. Maybe it was because the emerald necklace was nearly finished and was exceeding even her standards. Maybe it was because in the past two weeks she'd found a certain enjoyment in Michael's company. Mild enjoyment, Pandora reminded herself. Nothing to shout about.

Suspicious, Michael narrowed his eyes. "What for?"

"I'm going in for some supplies Sweeney needs." She found the turtle shell that was his lampshade intriguing, and ran her fingers over it. "I thought you might like to get out for a while."

He would. It had been two weeks since he'd seen anything but the house and grounds. He glanced back at the page in his typewriter. "How long will you be?"

"Oh, two, three hours I suppose." She moved her shoulders. "It's an hour's round trip to begin with."

He was tempted. Free time and a change of scene. But the half-blank sheet remained in his typewriter. "Can't. I have to get this fleshed out."

"All right." Pandora rose from the desk a bit surprised by the degree of disappointment she felt. Silly, she thought. She loved to drive alone with the radio blaring. "Don't strain your fingers."

He started to growl something at her back, then be-

cause his bowl of nuts was empty, thought better of it. "Pandora, how about picking me up a couple pounds of pistachios?"

As she stopped at the door, she lifted a brow. "Pistachios?"

"Real ones. No red dye." He ran a hand over the bristle on his chin and wished for a pack of cigarettes. One cigarette. One long deep drag.

She glanced at the empty bowl and nearly smiled. The way he was nibbling, he'd lose that lean, rangy look quickly. "I suppose I could."

"And a copy of the *New York Times*."

Her brow rose. "Would you like to make me a list?"

"Be a sport, will you? Next time Sweeney needs supplies, I'll go in."

She thought about it a moment. "Very well then, nuts and news."

"And some pencils," he called out.

She slammed the door smartly.

Nearly two hours passed before Michael decided he deserved another cup of coffee. The story line was bumping along just as he'd planned, full of twists and turns. The fans of *Logan's Run* expected the gritty with occasional bursts of color and magic. That's just the way it was panning out.

Critics of the medium aside, Michael enjoyed writing for the small screen. He liked knowing his stories would reach literally millions of people every week and that for an hour, they could involve themselves with the character he had created.

The truth was, Michael liked Logan—the reluctant but steady heroism, the humor and the flaws. He'd

made Logan human and fallible and reluctant because Michael had always imagined the best heroes were just that.

The ratings and the mail proved he was on target. His writing for Logan had won him critical acclaim and awards, just as the one-act play he'd written had won him critical acclaim and awards. But the play had reached a few thousand at best, the bulk of whom had been New Yorkers. *Logan's Run* reached the family of four in Des Moines, the steelworkers in Chicago and the college crowd in Boston. Every week.

He didn't see television as the vast wasteland but as the magic box. Michael figured everyone was entitled to a bit of magic.

Michael switched off the typewriter so that the humming died. For a moment he sat in silence. He'd known he could work at the Folley. He'd done so before, but never long-term. What he hadn't known was that he'd work so well, so quickly or be so content. The truth was, he'd never expected to get along half so well with Pandora. Not that it was any picnic, Michael mused, absently running the stub of a pencil between his fingers.

They fought, certainly, but at least they weren't taking chunks out of each other. Or not very big ones. All in all he enjoyed the evenings when they played cards if for no other reason than the challenge of trying to catch her cheating. So far he hadn't.

Also true was the odd attraction he felt for her. That hadn't been in the script. So far he'd been able to ignore, control or smother it. But there were times... There were times, Michael thought as he rose and stretched, when he'd like to close her smart-tongued

mouth in a more satisfactory way. Just to see what it'd be like, he told himself. Curiosity about people was part of his makeup. He'd be interested to see how Pandora would react if he hauled her against him and kissed her until she went limp.

He let out a quick laugh as he wandered to the window. Limp? Pandora? Women like her never went soft. He might satisfy his curiosity, but he'd get a fist in the gut for his trouble. Even that might be worth it....

She wasn't unmoved. He'd been sure of that since the first day they'd walked back together from her workshop. He'd seen it in her face, heard it, however briefly in her voice. They'd both been circling around it for two weeks. Or twenty years, Michael speculated.

He'd never felt about another woman exactly the way he felt about Pandora McVie. Uncomfortable, challenged, infuriated. The truth was that he was almost always at ease around women. He liked them—their femininity, their peculiar strengths and weaknesses, their style. Perhaps that was the reason for his success in relationships, though he'd carefully kept them short-term.

If he romanced a woman, it was because he was interested in her, not simply in the end result. True enough he was interested in Pandora, but he'd never considered romancing her. It surprised him that he'd caught himself once or twice considering seducing her.

Seducing, of course, was an entirely different matter than romancing. But all in all, he didn't know if attempting a casual seduction of Pandora would be worth the risk.

If he offered her a candlelight dinner or a walk in the moonlight—or a mad night of passion—she'd

come back with a sarcastic remark. Which would, inevitably, trigger some caustic rebuttal from him. The merry-go-round would begin again.

In any case, it wasn't romance he wanted with Pandora. It was simply curiosity. In certain instances, it was best to remember what had happened to the intrepid cat. But as he thought of her, his gaze was drawn toward her workshop.

They weren't so very different really, Michael mused. Pandora could insist from dawn to dusk that they had nothing in common, but Jolley had been closer to the mark. They were both quick-tempered, opinionated and passionately protective of their professions. He closed himself up for hours at a time with a typewriter. She closed herself up with tools and torches. The end result of both of their work was entertainment. And after all, that was...

His thoughts broke off as he saw the shed door open. Odd, he hadn't thought she was back yet. His rooms were on the opposite end of the house from the garage, so he wouldn't have heard her car, but he thought she'd drop off what she'd picked up for him.

He started to shrug and turn away when he saw the figure emerge from the shed. It was bundled deep in a coat and hat, but he knew immediately it wasn't Pandora. She moved fluidly, unselfconsciously. This person walked with speed and wariness. Wariness, he thought again, that was evident in the way the head swiveled back and forth before the door was closed again. Without stopping to think, Michael dashed out of the room and down the stairs.

He nearly rammed into Charles at the bottom. "Pandora back?" he demanded.

"No, sir." Relieved that he hadn't been plowed down, Charles rested a hand on the rail. "She said she might stay in town and do some shopping. We shouldn't worry if—"

But Michael was already halfway down the hall.

With a sigh for the agility he hadn't had in thirty years, Charles creaked his way into the drawing room to lay a fire.

The wind hit Michael the moment he stepped outside, reminding him he hadn't stopped for a coat. As he began to race toward the shed, his face chilled and his muscles warmed. There was no one in sight on the grounds. Not surprising, he mused as he slowed his pace just a bit. The woods were close at the edge, and there were a half a dozen easy paths through them.

Some kid poking around? he wondered. Pandora would be lucky if he hadn't pocketed half her pretty stones. It would serve her right.

But he changed his mind the minute he stood in the doorway of her workshop.

Boxes were turned over so that gems and stones and beads were scattered everywhere. Balls of string and twine had been unraveled and twisted and knotted from wall to wall. He had to push some out of his way to step inside. What was usually almost pristine in its order was utter chaos. Gold and silver wire had been bent and snapped, tools lay where they'd been carelessly tossed to the floor.

Michael bent down and picked up an emerald. It glinted sharp and green in his palm. If it had been a thief, he decided, it had been a clumsy and short-sighted one.

"Oh, God!" Pandora dropped her purse with a thud and stared.

When Michael turned, he saw her standing in the doorway, ice pale and rigid. He swore, wishing he'd had a moment to prepare her. "Take it easy," he began as he reached for her arm.

She shoved him aside forcibly and fought her way into the shed. Beads rolled and bounced at her feet. For a moment there was pure shock, disbelief. Then came a white wall of fury. "How could you?" When she turned back to him she was no longer pale. Her color was vivid, her eyes as sharp as the emerald he still held.

Because he was off guard, she nearly landed the first blow. The air whistled by his face as her fist passed. He caught her arms before she tried again. "Just a minute," he began, but she threw herself bodily into him and knocked them both against the wall. Whatever had been left on the shelves shuddered or fell off. It took several moments, and a few bruises on both ends, before he managed to pin her arms back and hold her still.

"Stop it." He pressed her back until she glared up at him, dry-eyed and furious. "You've a right to be upset, but putting a hole in me won't accomplish anything."

"I knew you could be low," she said between her teeth. "But I'd never have believed you could do something so filthy."

"Believe whatever the hell you want," he began, but he felt her body shudder as she fought for control. "Pandora," and his voice softened. "I didn't do this.

Look at me,'' he demanded with a little shake. ''Why would I?''

Because she wanted to cry, her voice, her eyes were hard. ''You tell me.''

Patience wasn't one of his strong points, but he tried again. ''Pandora, listen to me. Try for common sense a minute and just listen. I got here a few minutes before you. I saw someone coming out of the shed from my window and came down. When I got here, this is what I found.''

She was going to disgrace herself. She felt the tears backing up and hated them. It was better to hate him. ''Let go of me.''

Perhaps he could handle her anger better than her despair. Cautiously Michael released her arms and stepped back. ''It hasn't been more than ten minutes since I saw someone coming out of here. I figured they cut through the woods.''

She tried to think, tried to clear the fury out of her head. ''You can go,'' she said with deadly calm. ''I have to clean up and take inventory.''

Something hot backed up in his throat at the casual dismissal. Remembering his own reaction when he'd opened the shed door, he swallowed it. ''I'll call the police if you like, but I don't know if anything was stolen.'' He opened his palm and showed her the emerald. ''I can't imagine any thief leaving stones like this behind.''

Pandora snatched it out of his hand. When her fingers closed over it, she felt the slight prick of the hoop she'd fastened onto it only the day before. The emerald seemed to grow out of the braided wire.

Her heart was thudding against her ribs as she

walked to her worktable. There was what was left of the necklace she'd been fashioning for two weeks. The deceptively delicate tiers were in pieces, the emeralds that had hung gracefully from them, scattered. Her own nippers had been used to destroy it. She gathered up the pieces in her hands and fought back the urge to scream.

"It was this, wasn't it?" Michael picked up the sketch from the floor. It was stunning on paper—at once fanciful and bold. He supposed what she had drawn had some claim to art. He imagined how he'd feel if someone took scissors to one of his scripts. "You'd nearly finished."

Pandora dropped the pieces back on the table. "Leave me alone." She crouched and began to gather up stones and beads.

"Pandora." When she ignored him, Michael grabbed her by the shoulders and shook. "Dammit, Pandora, I want to help."

She sent him a long, cold look. "You've done enough, Michael. Now leave me alone."

"All right, fine." He released her and stormed out. Anger and frustration carried him halfway across the lawn. Michael stopped, swore and wished bitterly for a cigarette. She had no right to accuse him. Worse, she had no right to make him feel responsible. The guilt he was experiencing was nearly as strong as it would have been if he'd actually vandalized her shop. Hands in his pockets, he stood staring back at the shed and cursing her.

She really thought he'd done that to her. That he was capable of such meaningless, bitter destruction. He'd tried to talk to her, soothe her. Every offer of

help had been thrown back at him. Just like her, he thought with his teeth gritted. She deserved to be left alone.

He nearly started back to the house again when he remembered just how shocked and ill she'd looked in the doorway of the shed. Calling himself a fool, he went back.

When he opened the door of the shed again, the chaos was just as it had been. Sitting in the middle of it on the floor by her workbench was Pandora. She was weeping quietly.

He felt the initial male panic at being confronted with feminine tears and surprise that they came from Pandora who never shed them. Yet he felt sympathy for someone who'd been dealt a bull's-eye blow. Without saying a word, he went to her and slipped his arms around her.

She stiffened, but he'd expected it. "I told you to go away."

"Yeah. Why should I listen to you?" He stroked her hair.

She wanted to crawl into his lap and weep for hours. "I don't want you here."

"I know. Just pretend I'm someone else." He drew her against his chest.

"I'm only crying because I'm angry." With a sniff, she turned her face into his shirt.

"Sure." He kissed the top of her head. "Go ahead and be angry for a while. I'm used to it."

She told herself it was because she was weakened by shock and grief, but she relaxed against him. The tears came in floods. When she cried, she cried wholeheartedly. When she was finished, she was done.

Tears dry, she sat cushioned against him. Secure. She wouldn't question it now. Along with the anger came a sense of shame she was unaccustomed to. She'd been filthy to him. But he'd come back and held her. Who'd have expected him to be patient, or caring? Or strong enough to make her accept both. Pandora let out a long breath and kept her eyes shut for just a moment. He smelled of soap and nothing else.

"I'm sorry, Michael."

She was soft. Hadn't he just told himself she wouldn't be? He let his cheek brush against her hair. "Okay."

"No, I mean it." When she turned her head her lips skimmed across his cheek. It surprised them both. That kind of contact was for friends—or lovers. "I couldn't think after I walked in here. I—" She broke off a moment, fascinated by his eyes. Wasn't it strange how small the world could become if you looked into someone's eyes? Why hadn't she ever noticed that before? "I need to sort all this out."

"Yeah." He ran a fingertip down her cheek. She was soft. Softer than he'd let himself believe. "We both do."

It was so easy to settle herself in the crook of his arm. "I can't think."

"No?" Her lips were only an inch from his—too close to ignore, too far to taste. "Let's both not think for a minute."

When he touched his mouth to hers, she didn't draw away but accepted, experimented with the same sense of curiosity that moved through him. It wasn't an explosion or a shock, but a test for both of them. One they'd both known would come sooner or later.

She tasted warm, and her sweetness had a bite. He'd known her so long, shouldn't he have known that? Her body felt primed to move, to act, to race. Soft, yes, she was soft, but not pliant. Perhaps he'd have found pliancy too easy. When he slipped his tongue into her mouth hers met it teasingly, playfully. His stomach knotted. She made him want more, much more of that unapologetically earthy scent, the taut body. His fingers tangled in her hair and tightened.

He was as mysterious and bold as she'd always thought he would be. His hands were firm, his mouth giving. Sometimes she'd wondered what it would be like to meet him on these terms. But she'd always closed her mind before any of the answers could slip through. Michael Donahue was dangerous simply because he was Michael Donahue. By turns he'd attracted and alienated her since they'd been children. It was more than any other man had been able to do for more than a week.

Now, as her mouth explored his, she began to understand why. He was different, for her. She didn't feel altogether safe in his arms, and not completely in control. Pandora had always made certain she was both those things when it came to a man. The scrape of his unshaved cheek didn't annoy her as she'd thought it would. It aroused. The discomfort of the hard floor seemed suitable, as was the quick rush of cold air through the still-open door.

She felt quietly and completely at home. Then the quick nip of his teeth against her lip made her feel as though she'd just stepped on uncharted land. New territory was what she'd been raised on, and yet, in all

her experience, she'd never explored anything so unique, so exotic or so comfortable.

She wanted to go on and knew she had to stop.

Together they drew away.

"Well." She scrambled for composure as she folded her hands in her lap. Be casual, she ordered herself while her pulse thudded at her wrists. Be careless. She couldn't afford to say anything that might make him laugh at her. "That's been coming for a while, I suppose."

He felt as though he'd just slid down a roller coaster without a cart. "I suppose." He studied her a moment, curious and a bit unnerved. When he saw her fingers twist together he felt a small sense of satisfaction. "It wasn't altogether what I'd expected."

"Things rarely are." Too many surprises for one day, Pandora decided, and rose unsteadily to her feet. She made the mistake of looking around and nearly sunk to the floor again.

"Pandora—"

"No, don't worry." She shook her head as he rose. "I'm not going to fall apart again." Concentrating on breathing evenly, she took one long look at her workshop. "It looks like you were right about the locks. I suppose I should be grateful you haven't said I told you so."

"Maybe I would if it applied." Michael picked up the emeralds scattered on her table. "I'm no expert, cousin, but I'd say these are worth a few thousand."

"So?" She frowned as her train of thought began to march with his. "No thief would've left them behind." Reaching down, she picked up a handful of

stones. Among them were two top-grade diamonds. "Or these."

As was his habit, he began to put the steps together in a sort of mental scenario. Action and reaction, motive and result. "I'd wager once you've inventoried, you won't be missing anything. Whoever did this didn't want to risk more than breaking and entering and vandalism."

With a huff, she sat down on her table. "You think it was one of the family."

"'They said it wouldn't last,'" he quoted, and stuck his hands in his pockets. "You may've had something there, Pandora. Something neither of us considered when we were setting out the guidelines. None of them believed we'd be able to get through six months together. The fact is, we've gotten through the first two weeks without a hitch. It could make one of them nervous enough to want to throw in a complication. What was your first reaction when you saw all this?"

She dragged her hand through her hair. "That you'd done it for spite. Exactly what our kith and kin would expect me to think. Dammit, I hate to be predictable."

"You outsmarted them once your mind cleared."

She sent him a quick look, not certain if she should thank him or apologize again. It was best to do neither. "Biff," Pandora decided with relish. "This sort of low-minded trick would be just up his alley."

"I'd only vote for Biff if you find a few rocks missing." Michael rocked back on his heels. "He'd never be able to resist picking up a few glitters that could be liquidated into nice clean cash."

"True enough." Uncle Carlson—no, it seemed a bit crude for his style. Ginger would've been too fasci-

nated with the sparkles to have done any more than fondle. Pulling a hand through her hair, she tried to picture one of her bland, civilized relations wielding a pair of nippers. "Well, I don't suppose it matters a great deal which one of them did it. They've put me two weeks behind on my commission." Again she picked up pieces of thin gold. "It'll never be quite the same," she murmured. "Nothing is when it's done over."

"Sometimes it's better."

With a shake of her head, she walked over to a heater. If he gave her any more sympathy now, she wouldn't be able to trust herself. "One way or the other I've got to get started. Tell Sweeney I won't make it in for lunch."

"I'll help you clean this up."

"No." She turned back when he started to frown. "No, really, Michael, I appreciate it. I need to be busy. And alone."

He didn't like it, but understood. "All right. I'll see you at dinner."

"Michael…" He paused at the doorway and looked back. Amid the confusion she looked strong and vivid. He nearly closed the door and went back to her. "Maybe Uncle Jolley was right."

"About what?"

"You may have one or two redeeming qualities."

He smiled at her then, quick and dashing. "Uncle Jolley was always right, cousin. That's why he's still pulling the strings."

Pandora waited until the door shut again. Pulling the strings he was, she mused. "But you're not playing matchmaker with my life," she mumbled. "I'm stay-

ing free, single and unattached. Just get that through your head.''

She wasn't superstitious, but Pandora almost thought she heard her uncle's high, cackling laugh. She rolled up her sleeves and got to work.

Chapter 4

Because after a long, tedious inventory Pandora discovered nothing missing, she vetoed Michael's notion of calling in the police. If something had been stolen, she'd have seen the call as a logical step. As it was, she decided the police would poke and prod around and lecture on the lack of locks. If the vandal had been one of the family—and she had to agree with Michael's conclusion there—a noisy, official investigation would give the break-in too much importance and undoubtedly too much publicity.

Yes, the press would have a field day. Pandora had already imagined the headlines. "Family vs. family in the battle of eccentric's will." There was, under her independent and straightforward nature, a prim part of her that felt family business was private business.

If one or more of the members of the family were keeping an eye on Jolley's Folley and the goings-on

there, Pandora wanted them to think that she'd brushed off the vandalism as petty and foolish. As a matter of pride, she didn't want anyone to believe she'd been dealt a stunning blow. As a matter of practicality, she didn't want anyone to know that she had her eyes open. She was determined to find out who had broken into her shop and how they'd managed to pick such a perfect time for it.

Michael hadn't insisted on calling the police because his thoughts had run along the same lines as Pandora's. He'd managed, through a lot of maneuvering and silence, to keep his career totally separate from his family. In his business, he was known as Michael Donahue, award-winning writer, not Michael Donahue, relative of Jolley McVie, multimillionaire. He wanted to keep it that way.

Stubbornly, each had refused to tell the other of their reasons or their plans for some personal detective work. It wasn't so much a matter of trust, but more the fact that neither of them felt the other could do the job competently. So instead, they kept the conversation light through one of Sweeney's four-star meals and let the vandalism rest. More important, they carefully avoided any reference that might trigger some remark about what had happened on a more personal level in Pandora's workshop.

After two glasses of wine and a generous portion of chicken fricassee, Pandora felt more optimistic. It would have been much worse if any of her stock or tools had been taken. That would have meant a trip into Manhattan and days, perhaps weeks of delay. As it was, the worst crime that she could see was the fact that she'd been spied on. Surely that was the only ex-

planation for the break-in coinciding so perfectly with her trip to town. And that would be her first order of business.

"I wonder," Pandora began, probing lightly, "if the Saundersons are in residence for the winter."

"The neighbors with the pond." Michael had thought of the Saunderson place himself. There were certain points on that property where, with a good set of binoculars, someone could watch the Folley easily. "They spend a lot of time in Europe, don't they?"

"Hmm." Pandora toyed with her chicken. "He's in hotels, you know. They tend to pop off here or there for weeks at a time."

"Do they ever rent the place out?"

"Oh, not that I know of. I'm under the impression that they leave a skeleton staff there even when they fly off. Now that I think of it, they were home a few months ago." The memory made her smile. "Uncle Jolley and I went fishing and Saunderson nearly caught us. If we hadn't scrambled back to the cabin—" She broke off as the thought formed.

"Cabin." Michael picked up where she'd left off. "That old two-room wreck Jolley was going to use as a hunting lodge during his eat-off-the-land stage? I'd forgotten all about it."

Pandora shrugged as though it meant nothing while her mind raced ahead. "He ended up eating more beans than game. In any case, we caught a bundle of trout, ate like pigs and sent the rest along to Saunderson. He never sent a thank-you note."

"Poor manners."

"Well, I've heard his grandmother was a barmaid in Chelsea. More wine?"

"No, thanks." He thought it best to keep a clear head if he was going to carry out the plans that were just beginning to form. "Help yourself."

Pandora set the bottle down and sent him a sweet smile. "No, I'm fine. Just a bit tired really."

"You're entitled." It would clear his path beautifully if he could ship her off to bed early. "What you need is a good night's sleep."

"I'm sure you're right." Both of them were too involved with their own moves to notice how excruciatingly polite the conversation had become. "I'll just skip coffee tonight and go have a bath." She feigned a little yawn. "What about you? Planning to work late?"

"No—no, I think I'll get a fresh start in the morning."

"Well then." Pandora rose, still smiling. She'd give it an hour, she calculated, then she'd be out and gone. "I'm going up. Good night, Michael."

"Good night." Once the light in her room was off, he decided, he'd be on his way.

Pandora sat in her darkened room for exactly fifteen minutes and just listened. All she had to do was get outside without being spotted. The rest would be easy. Opening her door a crack, she held her breath, waited and listened a little longer. Not a sound. It was now or never, she decided and bundled into her coat. Into the deep pockets, she shoved a flashlight, two books of matches and a small can of hair spray. As good as mace, Pandora figured, if you ran into something unfriendly. She crept out into the hall and started slowly down the stairs, her back to the wall.

An adventure, she thought, feeling the familiar pulse of excitement and anxiety. She hadn't had one since Uncle Jolley died. As she let herself out one of the side doors, she thought how much he'd have enjoyed this one. The moon was only a sliver, but the sky was full of stars. The few clouds that spread over them were hardly more than transparent wisps. And the air—she took a deep breath—was cool and crisp as an apple. With a quick glance over her shoulder at Michael's window, she started toward the woods.

The starlight couldn't help her there. Though the trees were bare, the branches were thick enough to block out big chunks of sky. She dug out her flashlight and, turning it side to side, found the edges of the path. She didn't hurry. If she rushed, the adventure would be over too soon. She walked slowly, listened and imagined.

There were sounds—the breeze blew through pine needles and scattered the dry leaves. Now and again there was a skuddle in the woods to the right or left. A fox, a raccoon, a bear not quite settled down to hibernate? Pandora liked not being quite certain. If you walked through the woods alone, in the dark, and didn't have some sense of wonder, it was hardly worth the trip.

She liked the smells—pine, earth, the hint of frost that would settle on the ground before morning. She liked the sense of being alone, and more, of having something up ahead that warranted her attention.

The path forked, and she swung to the left. The cabin wasn't much farther. She stopped once, certain she'd heard something move up ahead that was too big to be considered a fox. For a moment she had a few

uncomfortable thoughts about bears and bobcats. It was one thing to speculate and another to have to deal with them. Then there was nothing. Shaking her head, Pandora went on.

What would she do if she got to the cabin, and it wasn't dusty and deserted? What would she do if she actually found one of her dear, devoted relatives had set up housekeeping? Uncle Carlson reading the *Wall Street Journal* by the fire? Aunt Patience fussing around the rocky wooden table with a dust cloth? The thought was almost laughable. Almost, until Pandora remembered her workshop.

Drawing her brows together, she walked forward. If someone was there, they were going to answer to her. In moments, the shadow of the cabin loomed up before her. It looked as it was supposed to look, desolate, deserted, eerie. She kept her flashlight low as she crept toward the porch, then nearly let out a scream when her own weight caused the narrow wooden stair to creak. She held a hand to her heart until it no longer felt as though it would break her ribs. Then slowly, quietly, stealthily, she reached for the doorknob and twisted it.

The door moaned itself open. Wincing at the sound, Pandora counted off ten seconds before she took the next step. With a quick sweep of her light, she stepped in.

When the arm came around her neck, she dropped the flashlight with a clatter. It rolled over the floor, sending an erratic beam over the log walls and brick fireplace. Even as she drew the breath to scream, she reached in her pocket for the hair spray. After she was whirled around, she found herself face-to-face with

Michael. His fist was poised inches from her face, her can inches from his. Both of them stood just as they were.

"Dammit!" Michael dropped his arm. "What are you doing here?"

"What are you doing here?" she tossed back. "And what do you mean by grabbing me that way? You may've broken my flashlight."

"I almost broke your nose."

Pandora shook back her hair and walked over to retrieve her light. She didn't want him to see her hands tremble. "Well, I certainly think you should find out who someone is before you throw a headlock on them."

"You followed me."

She sent him a cool, amused look. It helped to be able to do so when her stomach was still quaking. "Don't flatter yourself. I simply wanted to see if something was going on out here, and I didn't want you to interfere."

"Interfere." He shone his own light directly in her face so that she had to throw up a hand in defense. "And what the hell were you going to do if something was going on? Overpower them?"

She thought of how easily he'd taken her by surprise. It only made her lift her chin higher. "I can take care of myself."

"Sure." He glanced down at the can she still held. "What have you got there?"

Having forgotten it, Pandora looked down herself, then had to stifle a chuckle. Oh, how Uncle Jolley would've appreciated the absurdity. "Hair spray," she said very precisely. "Right between the eyes."

He swore, then laughed. He couldn't have written a scene so implausible. "I guess I should be glad you didn't get a shot off at me."

"I look before I pounce." Pandora dropped the can back into her pocket. "Well, since we're here, we might as well look around."

"I was doing just that when I heard your catlike approach." She wrinkled her nose at him, but he ignored her. "It looks like someone's been making themselves at home." To prove his point, Michael shone his light at the fireplace. Half-burnt logs still smoldered.

"Well, well." With her own light, Pandora began to walk around the cabin. The last time she'd been there, the chair with the broken rung had been by the window. Jolley had sat there himself, keeping a lookout for Saunderson while she'd opened a tin of sardines to ward off starvation. Now the chair was pulled up near the fire. "A vagrant, perhaps."

Watching her, Michael nodded. "Perhaps."

"But not likely. Suppose they'll be back?"

"Hard to say." The casual glance showed nothing out of place. The cabin was neat and tidy. Too tidy. The floor and table surfaces should have had a film of dust. Everything had been wiped clean. "It could be they've done all the damage they intend to do."

Disgruntled, Pandora plopped down on the bunk and dropped her chin in her hands. "I'd hoped to catch them."

"And what? Zap them with environmentally safe hair spray?"

She glared up at him. "I suppose you had a better plan."

"I think I might've made them a bit more uncomfortable."

"Black eyes and broken noses." She made an impatient sound. "Really, Michael, you should try to get your mind out of your fists."

"I suppose you just wanted to talk reasonably with whichever member of our cozy family played search and destroy with your workshop."

She started to snap, caught herself, then smiled. It was the slow, wicked smile Michael could never help admiring. "No," she admitted. "Reason wasn't high on my list. Still, it appears we've both missed our chance for brute force. Well, you write the detective stories—so to speak—shouldn't we look for clues?"

His lips curved in something close to a sneer. "I didn't think to bring my magnifying glass."

"You can almost be amusing when you put your mind to it." Rising, Pandora began to shine her light here and there. "They might've dropped something."

"A name tag?"

"Something," she muttered, and dropped to her knees to look under the bunk. "Aha!" Hunkering down, she grabbed at something.

"What is it?" Michael was beside her before she'd straightened up.

"A shoe." Feeling foolish and sentimental, she held it in both hands. "It's nothing. It was Uncle Jolley's."

Because she looked lost, and more vulnerable than he'd expected, Michael offered the only comfort he knew. "I miss him, too."

She sat a moment, the worn sneaker in her lap. "You know, sometimes it's as though I can almost feel him. As though he's around the next corner, in

the next room, waiting to pop up and laugh at the incredible joke he's played.''

With a quick laugh, Michael rubbed a hand over her back. ''I know what you mean.''

Pandora looked at him, steady, measuring. ''Maybe you do,'' she murmured. Briskly she set the sneaker on the bunk and rose. ''I'll have a look in the cupboards.''

''Let me know if you find any cookies.'' He met the look she tossed over her shoulder with a shrug. ''In the early stages of nonsmoking, you need a lot of oral satisfaction.''

''You ought to try chewing gum.'' Pandora opened a cupboard and shone her light over jars and cans. There was peanut butter, chunky, and caviar, Russian. Two of Jolley's favorite snacks. She passed over taco sauce and jumbo fruit cocktail, remembering that her ninety-three-year-old uncle had had the appetite of a teenager. Then reaching in, she plucked out a can and held it up.

''Aha!''

''Again?''

''Tuna fish,'' Pandora announced waving the can at Michael. ''It's a can of tuna.''

''Right you are. Any mayo to go with it?''

''Don't be dense, Michael. Uncle Jolley hated tuna.''

Michael started to say something sarcastic, then stopped. ''He did, didn't he?'' he said slowly. ''And he never kept anything around he didn't like.''

''Exactly.''

''Congratulations, Sherlock. Now which of the suspects has an affection for canned fish?''

"You're just jealous because I found a clue and you didn't."

"It's only a clue," Michael pointed out, a little annoyed at being outdone by an amateur, "if you can do something with it."

He'd never give her credit, she thought, for anything, not her craft, her intelligence and never her womanhood. There was an edge to her voice when she spoke again. "If you're so pessimistic, why did you come out here?"

"I was hoping to find someone." Restless, Michael moved his light from wall to wall. "As it is all we've done is prove someone was here and gone."

Pandora dropped the can of tuna in disgust. "A waste of time."

"You shouldn't've followed me out."

"I didn't follow you out." She shone her light back at him. He looked too male, too dangerous in the shadows. She wished, only briefly, that she had the spectacular build and stunning style that would bring him whimpering to his knees. Their breath came in clouds and merged together. "For all I know, you followed me."

"Oh, I see. That's why I was here first."

"Beside the point. If you'd planned to come out here tonight, why didn't you tell me?"

He came closer. But if he came too close to her, he discovered, he began to feel something, something like an itch along the skin. Try to scratch it, he reminded himself, and she'd rub you raw in seconds. "For the same reason you didn't tell me. I don't trust you, cousin. You don't trust me."

"At least we can agree on something." She started

to brush by him and found her arm captured. In one icy movement, she tilted her head down to look at his hand, then up to look at his face. "That's a habit you should try to break, Michael."

"They say when you break one habit, you pick up another."

The ice in Pandora's voice never changed, but her blood was warming. "Do they?"

"You're easier to touch than I'd once thought, Pandora."

"Don't be too sure, Michael." She took a step back, not in retreat, she told herself. It was a purely offensive move. Still, he moved with her.

"Some women have trouble dealing with physical attraction."

The temper that flared in her eyes appealed to him as much as the passion he'd seen there briefly that afternoon. "Your ego's showing again. This dominant routine might work very well with your centerfolds, but—"

"You've always had an odd fascination with my sex life." Michael grinned at her, pleased to see frustration flit over her face.

"The same kind of educated fascination one has with the sex lives of lower mammals." It infuriated her that her heart was racing. And not from anger. She was too honest to pretend it was anger. She'd come looking for an adventure, and she'd found one. "It's getting late," she said, using the tone of a parochial schoolteacher to a disruptive student. "You'll have to excuse me."

"I've never asked about your sex life." When she took another step away, he boxed her neatly into a

corner. Pandora's hand slipped into her pocket and rested on the can of hair spray. "Let me guess. You prefer a man with a string of initials after his name who philosophizes about sex more than he acts on it."

"Why you pompous, arrogant—"

Michael shut her mouth the way he'd once fantasized. With his own.

The kiss was no test this time, but torrid, hot, edging toward desperate. Whatever she might feel, she'd dissect later. Now she'd accept the experience. His mouth was warm, firm, and he used it with the same cocky male confidence that would have infuriated her at any other time. Now she met it with her own.

He was strong, insistent. For the first time Pandora felt herself body to body with a man who wouldn't treat her delicately. He demanded, expected and gave a completely uninhibited physicality. Pandora didn't have to think her way through the kiss. She didn't have to think at all.

He'd expected her to rear back and take a swing at him. Her instant and full response left him reeling. Later Michael would recall that nothing as basic and simple as a kiss had made his head spin for years.

She packed a punch, but she did it with soft lips. If she knew just how quickly she'd knocked him out, would she gloat? He wouldn't think of it now. He wouldn't think of anything now. Without a moment's hesitation, he buried his consciousness in her and let the senses rule.

The cabin was cold and dark without even a single stream of moonlight for romance. It smelled of dying smoke and settling dust. The wind had kicked up enough to moan grumpily at the windows. Neither of

them noticed. Even when they broke apart, neither of them noticed.

He wasn't steady. That was something else he'd think about later. At least he had the satisfaction of seeing she wasn't steady, either. She looked as he felt, stunned, off balance and unable to set for the next blow. Needing some equilibrium, he grinned at her.

"You were saying?"

She wanted to slug him. She wanted to kiss him again until he didn't have the strength to grin. He'd expect her to fall at his feet as other women probably did. He'd expect her to sigh and smile and surrender so he'd have one more victory. Instead she snapped, "Idiot."

"I love it when you're succinct."

"Rule number six," Pandora stated, aiming a killing look. "No physical contact."

"No physical contact," Michael agreed as she stomped toward the doorway, "unless both parties enjoy it."

She slammed the door and left him grinning.

When two people are totally involved in their own projects, they can live under the same roof for days at a time and rarely see each other. Especially if the roof is enormous and the people very stubborn. Pandora and Michael brushed together at meals and otherwise left each other alone. This wasn't out of any sense of politeness or consideration. It was simply because each of them was too busy to heckle the other.

Separately, however, each felt a smug satisfaction when the first month passed. One down, five to go.

When they were into their second month, Michael

drove into New York for a day to handle a problem with a script that had to be dealt with personally. He left, cross as a bear and muttering about imbeciles. Pandora prepared to enjoy herself tremendously in his absence. She wouldn't have to keep up her guard or share the Folley for hours. She could do anything she wanted without worrying about anyone coming to look over her shoulder or make a caustic remark. It would be wonderful.

She ended up picking at her dinner, then watching for his car through the heavy brocade drapes. Not because she missed *him*, she assured herself. It was just that she'd become used to having someone in the house.

Wasn't that one of the reasons she'd never lived with anyone before? She wanted to avoid any sense of dependence. And dependence, she decided, was natural when you shared the same space—even when it was with a two-legged snake.

So she waited, and she watched. Long after Charles and Sweeney had gone to bed, she continued to wait and watch. She wasn't concerned, and certainly not lonely. Only restless. She told herself she didn't go to bed herself because she wasn't tired. Wandering the first floor, she walked into Jolley's den. Game room would have been a more appropriate name. The decor was a cross between video arcade and disco lounge with its state-of-the-art components and low, curved-back sofas.

She turned on the huge, fifty-four-inch television, then left it on the first show that appeared. She wasn't going to *watch* it. She just wanted the company.

There were two pinball tables where she passed

nearly an hour trying to beat the high scores Jolley had left behind. Another legacy. Then there was an arcade-size video game that simulated an attack on the planet Zarbo. Under her haphazard defense system, the planet blew up three times before she moved on. There was computerized chess, but she thought her mind too sluggish to take it on. In the end she stretched out on the six-foot sofa in front of the television. Just to rest, not to watch.

Within moments, she was hooked on the late-night syndication of a cop show. Squealing tires and blasting bullets. Head pillowed on her arms, one leg thrown over the top of the sofa, she relaxed and let herself be entertained.

When Michael came to the doorway, she didn't notice him. He'd had a grueling day and had hit some nasty traffic on the drive back. The fact was he'd considered staying in the city overnight—the sensible thing to do. He'd found himself making a dozen weak excuses why he had to go back instead of accepting the invitation of the assistant producer—a tidily built brunette with big brown eyes.

He'd intended to crawl upstairs, fall into his bed and sleep until noon, but he'd seen the lights and heard the racket. Now, here was Pandora, self-proclaimed critic of the small screen, sprawled on a sofa watching reruns at one in the morning. She looked suspiciously as though she were enjoying herself.

Not a bad show, Michael mused, recognizing the series. In fact, he'd written a couple of scripts for it in his early days. The central character had a sly sort of wit and a fumbling manner that caused the perpetrator

to spill out enough information for an arrest by the end of the show.

Michael watched Pandora as she shifted comfortably on the couch. He waited until the commercial break. ''Well, how the mighty have fallen.''

She nearly did, rolling quickly to look back toward the doorway. She sat up, scowled and searched her mind for a plausible excuse. ''I couldn't sleep,'' she told him, which was true enough. She wouldn't add it was because he hadn't been home. ''I suppose television is made for the insomniac. Valium for the mind.''

He was tired, bone tired, but he realized how glad he was she'd had a comeback. He came over, plopped down beside her and propped his feet on a coffee table made out of a fat log. ''Who done it?'' he asked, and sighed. It was good to be home.

''The greedy business partner.'' She was too pleased to have him back to be embarrassed. ''There's really very little challenge in figuring out the answers.''

''This show wasn't based on the premise of figuring out who did the crime, but in how the hero maneuvers them into betraying themselves.''

She pretended she wasn't interested, but shifted so that she could still see the screen. ''So, how did things go in New York?''

''They went.'' Michael pried off one shoe with the toe of the other. ''After several hours of hair tearing and blame casting, the script's intact.''

He looked tired. Really tired, she realized, and unbent enough to take off his other shoe. He merely let out a quick grunt of appreciation. ''I don't understand why people would get all worked up about one silly hour a week.''

He opened one eye to stare at her. "It's the American way."

"What's there to get so excited about? You have a crime, the good guys chase the bad guys and catch them before the final credits. Seems simple enough."

"I can't thank you enough for clearing that up. I'll point it out at the next production meeting."

"Really, Michael, it seems to me things should run fairly smoothly, especially since you've been on the air with this thing for years."

"Know anything about ego and paranoia?"

She smiled a little. "I've heard of them."

"Well, multiply that with artistic temperament, the ratings race and an escalating budget. Don't forget to drop in a good dose of network executives. Things haven't run smoothly for four years. If *Logan* goes another four, it still won't run smoothly. That's show biz."

Pandora moved her shoulders. "It seems a foolish way to make a living."

"Ain't it just," Michael agreed, and fell sound asleep.

She let him doze for the next twenty minutes while she watched the sly, fumbling cop tighten the ropes on the greedy business partner. Satisfied that justice had been done, Pandora rose to switch off the set and dim the lights.

She could leave him here, she considered as she watched Michael sleep. He looked comfortable enough at the moment. She thought about it as she walked over to brush his hair from his forehead. But he'd probably wake up with a stiff neck and a nasty disposition. Bet-

ter get him upstairs into bed, she decided, and shook
his shoulder.

"Michael."

"Mmm?"

"Let's go to bed."

"Thought you'd never ask," he mumbled, and
reached halfheartedly for her.

Amused, she shook him harder. "Never let your
reach exceed your grasp. Come on, cousin, I'll help
you upstairs."

"The director's a posturing idiot," he grumbled as
she dragged him to his feet.

"I'm sure he is. Now, see if you can put one foot
in front of the other. That's the way. Here we go."
With an arm around his waist, she began to lead him
from the room.

"He kept screwing around with my script."

"Of all the nerve. Here come the steps."

"Said he wanted more emotional impact in the second act. Bleaches his hair," Michael muttered as she
half pulled him up the steps. "Lot he knows about
emotional impact."

"Obviously a mental midget." Breathlessly she
steered him toward his room. He was heavier than he
looked. "Here we are now, home again." With a little
strategy and a final burst of will, she shoved him onto
the bed. "There now, isn't that cozy?" Leaving him
fully dressed, she spread an afghan over him.

"Aren't you going to take my pants off?"

She patted his head. "Not a chance."

"Spoilsport."

"If I helped you undress this late at night, I'd probably have nightmares."

"You know you're crazy about me." The bed felt like heaven. He could've burrowed in it for a week.

"You're getting delirious, Michael. I'll have Charles bring you some warm tea and honey in the morning."

"Not if you want to live." He roused himself to open his eyes and smile at her. "Why don't you crawl in beside me? With a little encouragement, I could show you the time of your life."

Pandora leaned closer, closer, until her mouth was inches from his. Their breath mixed quickly, intimately. She hovered there a moment while her hair fell forward and brushed his cheek. "In a pig's eye," she whispered.

Michael shrugged, yawned and rolled over. "'Kay."

In the dark, Pandora stood for a moment with her hands on her hips. At least he could've acted insulted. Chin up, she walked out—making sure she slammed the door at her back.

Chapter 5

Tier by painstaking tier, Pandora had completed the emerald necklace. When it was finished, she was pleased to judge it perfect. This judgment pleased her particularly because she was her own toughest critic. Pandora didn't feel emotionally attached or creatively satisfied by every piece she made. With the necklace, she felt both. She examined it under a magnifying glass, held it up in harsh light, went over the filigree inch by inch and found no flaws. Out of her own imagination she'd conceived it, then with her own skill created it. With a kind of regret, she boxed the necklace in a bed of cotton. It wasn't hers any longer.

With the necklace done, she looked around her workshop without inspiration. She'd put so much into that one piece, all her concentration, her emotion, her skill. She hadn't made a single plan for the next project. Restless, wanting to work, she picked up her pad and began to sketch.

Earrings perhaps, she mused. Something bold and chunky and ornate. She wanted a change after the fine, elegant work she'd devoted so much time to. Circles and triangles, she thought. Something geometric and blatantly modern. Nothing romantic like the necklace.

Romantic, she mused, and sketched strong, definite lines. She'd been working with a romantic piece; perhaps that's why she'd nearly made a fool of herself with Michael. Her emotions were involved with her work, and her work had been light and feminine and romantic. It made sense, she decided, satisfied. Now, she'd work with something strong and brash and arrogant. That should solve the problem.

There shouldn't be a problem in the first place. Teeth gritted, she flipped a page and started over. Her feelings for Michael had always been very definite. Intolerance. If you were intolerant of someone, it went against the grain to be attracted to him.

It wasn't real attraction in any case. It was more some sort of twisted…curiosity. Yes, curiosity. The word satisfied her completely. She'd been curious, naturally enough, to touch on the sexuality of a man she'd known since childhood. Curious, again naturally, to find out what it was about Michael Donahue that attracted all those poster girls. She'd found out.

So he had a way of making a woman feel utterly a woman, utterly involved, utterly willing. It wasn't something that had happened to her before nor something she'd looked for. As Pandora saw it, it was a kind of skill. She decided he'd certainly honed it as meticulously as any craftsman. Though she found it difficult to fault him for that, *she* wasn't about to fall in with the horde. If he knew, if he even suspected,

that she'd had the same reaction to him that she imagined dozens of other women had, he'd gloat for a month. If he guessed that from time to time she'd wished—just for a moment—that he'd think of her the way he thought of those dozens of other women, he'd gloat for twice as long. She wouldn't give him the pleasure.

Individuality was part of her makeup. She didn't want to be one of his women, even if she could. Now that her curiosity had been satisfied, they'd get through the next five months without any more…complications.

Just because she'd found him marginally acceptable as a human being, almost tolerable as a companion wouldn't get in the way. It would, if anything, make the winter pass a bit easier.

And when she caught herself putting the finishing touches on a sketch of Michael's face, she was appalled. The lines were true enough, though rough. She'd had no trouble capturing the arrogance around the eyes or the sensitivity around the mouth. Odd, she realized; she'd sketched him to look intelligent. She ripped the sheet from her pad, crumpled it up in a ball and tossed it into the trash. Her mind had wandered, that was all. Pandora picked up her pencil again, put it down, then dug the sketch out again. Art was art, after all, she told herself as she smoothed out Michael's face.

He wasn't having a great deal of success with his own work. Michael sat at his desk and typed like a maniac for five minutes. Then he stared into space for fifteen. It wasn't like him. When he worked, he

worked steadily, competently, smoothly until the scene
was set.

Leaning back in his chair, he picked up a pencil and
ran his fingers from end to end. Whatever the statistics
said, he should never have given up smoking. That's
what had him so edgy. Restless, he pushed away from
the desk and wandered over to the window. He stared
down at Pandora's workshop. It looked cheerful under
a light layer of snow that was hardly more than a dusting. The windows were blank.

That's what had him so edgy.

She wasn't what he'd expected. She was softer,
sweeter. Warmer. She was fun to talk to, whether she
was arguing and snipping and keeping you on the edge
of temper, or whether she was being easy and companionable. There wasn't an overflow of small talk
with Pandora. There weren't any trite conversations.
She kept your mind working, even if it was in defense
of her next barb.

It wasn't easy to admit that he actually enjoyed her
company. But the weeks they'd been together at the
Folley had gone quickly. No, it wasn't easy to admit
he liked being with her, but he'd turned down an interesting invitation from his assistant producer because... Because, Michael admitted on a long breath,
he hadn't wanted to spend the night with one woman
when he'd known his thoughts would have been on
another.

Just how was he going to handle this unwanted and
unexpected attraction to a woman who'd rather put on
the gloves and go a few rounds than walk in the moonlight?

Romantic women had always appealed to him be-

cause he was, unashamedly, a romantic himself. He enjoyed candlelight, quiet music, long, lonely walks. Michael courted women in old-fashioned ways because he felt comfortable with old-fashioned ways. It didn't interfere with the fact that he was, and had been since college, a staunch feminist. Romance and socio-political views were worlds apart. He had no trouble balancing equal pay for equal work against offering a woman a carriage ride through the park.

And he knew if he sent Pandora a dozen white roses, she'd complain about the thorns.

He wanted her. Michael was too much a creature of the senses to pretend otherwise. When he wanted something, he worked toward it in one of two ways. First, he planned out the best approach, then took the steps one at a time, maneuvering subtly. If that didn't work, he tossed out subtlety and went after it with both hands. He'd had just as much success the first way as the second.

As he saw it, Pandora wouldn't respond to patience and posies. She wouldn't go for being swept off her feet, either. With Pandora, he might just have to toss his two usual approaches and come up with a whole new third.

An interesting challenge, Michael decided with a slow smile. He liked nothing better than arranging and rearranging plot lines and shifting angles. And hadn't he always thought Pandora would make a fascinating character? So, he'd work it like a screenplay.

Hero and heroine living as housemates, he began. Attracted to each other but reluctant. Hero is intelligent, charming. Has tremendous willpower. Hadn't he given up smoking—five weeks, three days and four-

teen hours ago? Heroine is stubborn and opinionated, often mistakes arrogance for independence. Hero gradually cracks through her brittle shield to their mutual satisfaction.

Michael leaned back in his chair and grinned. He might just make it a play. A great deal of the action would be ad-lib, of course, but he had the general theme. Satisfied, and looking forward to the opening scene, Michael went back to work with a vengeance.

Two hours breezed by with Michael working steadily. He answered the knock at his door with a grunt.

"I beg your pardon, Mr. Donahue." Charles, slightly out of breath from the climb up the stairs, stood in the doorway.

Michael gave another grunt and finished typing the paragraph. "Yes, Charles?"

"Telegram for you, sir."

"Telegram?" Scowling, he swiveled around in the chair. If there was a problem in New York—as there was at least once a week—the phone was the quickest way to solve it. "Thanks." He took the telegram, but only flapped it against his palm. "Pandora still out in her shop?"

"Yes, sir." Grateful for the chance to rest, Charles expanded a bit. "Sweeney is a bit upset that Miss McVie missed lunch. She intends to serve dinner in an hour. I hope that suits your schedule."

Michael knew better than to make waves where Sweeney was concerned. "I'll be down."

"Thank you, sir, and if I may say, I enjoy your television show tremendously. This week's episode was particularly exciting."

"I appreciate that, Charles."

"It was Mr. McVie's habit to watch it every week in my company. He never missed an episode."

"There probably wouldn't have been a *Logan's Run* without Jolley," Michael mused. "I miss him."

"We all do. The house seems so quiet. But I—" Charles reddened a bit at the thought of overstepping his bounds.

"Go ahead, Charles."

"I'd like you to know that both Sweeney and I are pleased to remain in your service, yours and Miss McVie's. We were glad when Mr. McVie left you the house. The others..." He straightened his back and plunged on. "They wouldn't have been suitable, sir. Sweeney and I had both discussed resigning if Mr. McVie had chosen to leave the Folley to one of his other heirs." Charles folded his bony hands. "Will there be anything else before dinner, sir?"

"No, Charles. Thank you."

Telegram in hand, Michael leaned back as Charles went out. The old butler had known him since childhood. Michael could remember distinctly when Charles had stopped calling him Master Donahue. He'd been sixteen and visiting the Folley during the summer months. Charles had called him Mr. Donahue and Michael had felt as though he'd just stepped from childhood, over adolescence and into adulthood.

Strange how much of his life had been involved with the Folley and the people who were a part of it. Charles had served him his first whisky—with dignity if not approval on his eighteenth birthday. Years before that, Sweeney had given him his first ear boxing. His parents had never bothered to swat him and his tutors wouldn't have dared. Michael still remembered

that after the sting had eased, he'd felt like part of a family.

Pandora had been both bane and fantasy during his adolescence. Apparently that hadn't changed as much as Michael had thought. And Jolley. Jolley had been father, grandfather, friend, son and brother.

Jolley had been Jolley, and Michael had spoken no less than the truth when he'd told Charles he missed the old man. In some part of himself, he always would. Thinking of other things, Michael tore open the telegram.

Your mother gravely ill. Doctors not hopeful. Make arrangements to fly to Palm Springs immediately. L. J. KEYSER.

Michael stared at the telegram for nearly a minute. It wasn't possible; his mother was never ill. She considered it something of a social flaw. He felt a moment's disbelief, a moment's shock. He was reaching for the phone before either had worn off.

When Pandora walked by his room fifteen minutes later, she saw him tossing clothes into a bag. She lifted a brow, leaned against the jamb and cleared her throat. "Going somewhere?"

"Palm Springs." He tossed in his shaving kit.

"Really?" Now she folded her arms. "Looking for a sunnier climate?"

"It's my mother. Her husband sent me a telegram."

Instantly she dropped her cool, sarcastic pose and came into the room. "Is she ill?"

"The telegram didn't say much, but it doesn't sound good."

"Oh, Michael, I'm sorry. Can I do anything? Call the airport?"

"I've already done it. I've got a flight in a couple of hours. They're routing me through half a dozen cities, but it was the best I could do."

Feeling helpless, she watched him zip up his bag. "I'll drive you to the airport if you like."

"No, thanks anyway." He dragged a hand through his hair as he turned to face her. The concern was there, though he realized she'd only met his mother once, ten, perhaps fifteen years before. The concern was for him and unexpectedly solid. "Pandora, it's going to take me half the night to get to the coast. And then I don't know—" He broke off, not able to imagine his mother seriously ill. "I might not be able to make it back in time—not in forty-eight hours."

She shook her head. "I don't want you to think about it. I'll call Fitzhugh and explain. Maybe he'll be able to do something. After all, it's an emergency. If he can't, he can't."

He was taking a step that could pull millions of dollars out from under her. Millions of dollars and the home she loved. Torn, Michael went to her and rested his hands on her shoulders. She was so slender. He'd forgotten just how fragile a strong woman could be. "I'm sorry, Pandora. If there was any other way…"

"Michael, I told you I didn't want the money. I meant it."

He studied her a moment. Yes, the strength was there, the stubbornness and the basic goodness he often overlooked. "I believe you did," he murmured.

"As for the rest, well, we'll see. Now go ahead before you miss your plane." She waited until he'd

grabbed his bag then walked with him to the hall. "Call me if you get the chance and let me know how your mother is."

He nodded, started for the stairs, then stopped. Setting his bag down, he came back and pulled her against him. The kiss was hard and long, with hints of a fire barely banked. He drew her away just as abruptly. "See you."

"Yeah." Pandora swallowed. "See you."

She stood where she was until she heard the front door slam.

She had a long time to think about the kiss, through a solitary dinner, during the hours when she tried to read by the cheery fire in the parlor. It seemed to Pandora that there'd been more passion concentrated in that brief contact than she'd experienced in any of her carefully structured relationships. Was it because she'd always been able to restrict passion to her temper, or her work?

It might have been because she'd been sympathetic, and Michael had been distraught. Emotions had a way of feeding emotions. But for the second time she found herself alone in the house, and to her astonishment, lonely. It was foolish because the fire was bright, the book entertaining and the brandy she sipped warming.

But lonely she was. After little more than a month, she'd come to depend on Michael's company. Even to look forward to it, as strange as that may have been. She liked sitting across from him at meals, arguing with him. She especially liked watching the way he fought, exploding when she poked pins in his work. Perverse? she wondered with a sigh. Perhaps she was,

but life was so boring without a bit of friction. No one seemed to provide it more satisfactorily than Michael Donahue.

She wondered when she'd see him again. And she wondered if now they'd have to forgo spending the winter together. If the terms of the will were broken, there would be no reason for them to stay on together. In fact, they'd have no right to stay at the Folley at all. They'd both go back to New York where, due to separate life-styles, they never saw one another. Not until now, when it was a possibility, did Pandora fully realize how much she didn't want it to happen.

She didn't want to lose the Folley. There were so many memories, so many important ones. Wouldn't they begin to fade if she couldn't walk into a room and bring them back? She didn't want to lose Michael. His companionship, she amended quickly. It was more satisfying than she'd imagined to have someone near who could meet you head to head. If she lost that daily challenge, life would be terribly flat. Since it was Michael who was adding that certain spark to the days, it was only natural to want him around. Wasn't it?

With a sigh, Pandora shut the book and decided an early night would be more productive than idle speculation. Just as she reached over to shut out the lamp, it went out on its own. She was left with the glow of the fire.

Odd, she thought and reached for the switch. After turning it back and forth, she rose, blaming a defective bulb. But when she walked into the hall she found it in darkness. The light she'd left burning was out, along with the one always left on at the top of the stairs.

Again Pandora reached for a switch and again she found it useless.

Power failure, she decided but found herself hesitating in the dark. There was no storm. Electricity at the Folley went out regularly during snow and thunderstorms, but the back-up generator took over within minutes. Pandora waited, but the house remained dark. It occurred to her as she stood there hoping for the best, that she'd never really considered how dark dark could be. She was already making her way back into the parlor for a candle when the rest occurred to her. The house was heated with electricity, as well. If she didn't see about the power soon, the house was going to be very cold as well as very dark before too long. With two people in their seventies in the house, she couldn't let it go.

Annoyed, she found three candles in a silver holder and lit them. It wasn't any use disturbing Charles's sleep and dragging him down to the basement. It was probably only a faulty fuse or two. Holding the candles ahead of her, Pandora wound her way through the curving halls to the cellar door.

She wasn't bothered about going down into the cellar in the dark. So she told herself as she stood with her hand on the knob. It was, after all, just another room. And one, if memory served, which was full of the remains of several of Uncle Jolley's rejected hobbies. The fuse box was down there. She'd seen it when she'd helped her uncle cart down several boxes of photographic equipment after he'd decided to give up the idea of becoming a portrait photographer. She'd go down, check for faulty fuses and replace them. After

the lights and heat were taken care of, she'd have a hot bath and go to bed.

But she drew in a deep breath before she opened the door.

The stairs creaked. It was to be expected. And they were steep and narrow as stairs were in any self-respecting cellar. The light from her candles set the shadows dancing over the crates and boxes her uncle had stored there. She'd have to see if she could talk Michael into helping her sort through them. On some bright afternoon. She was humming nervously to herself before she reached the bottom stair.

Pandora held the candles high and scanned the floor as far as the light circled. She knew mice had an affection for dark, dank cellars and she had no affection for them. When nothing rushed across the floor, she skirted around two six-foot crates and headed for the fuse box. There was the motorized exercise bike that Uncle Jolley had decided took the fun out of staying fit. There was a floor-to-ceiling shelf of old bottles. He'd once been fascinated by a ten-dollar bottle cutter. And there, she saw with a sigh of relief, was the fuse box. Setting the candles on a stack of boxes, she opened the big metal door and stared inside. There wasn't a single fuse in place.

"What the hell's this?" she muttered. Then as she shifted to look closer, her foot sent something rattling over the concrete floor. Jolting, she stifled a scream and the urge to run. Holding her breath, she waited in the silence. When she thought she could manage it, she picked up the candles again and crouched. Scattered at her feet were a dozen fuses. She picked one up and let it lay in her palm. The cellar might have its

quota of mice, but they weren't handy enough to empty a fuse box.

She felt a little shudder, which she ignored as she began to gather up the fuses. Tricks, she told herself. Just silly tricks. Annoying, but not as destructive as the one played in her workshop. It wasn't even a very clever trick, she decided, as it was as simple to put fuses back as it had been to take them out.

Working quickly, and trying not to look over her shoulder, Pandora put the fuses back in place. Whoever had managed to get into the basement and play games had wasted her time, nothing more.

Finished, she went over to the stairs, and though she hated herself, ran up them. But her sigh of relief was premature. The door she'd carefully left open was closed tightly. For a few moments she simply refused to believe it. She twisted the knob, pushed, shoved and twisted again. Then she forgot everything but the fear of being closed in a dark place. Pandora beat on the door, shouted, pleaded, then collapsed half sobbing on the top step. No one would hear her. Charles and Sweeney were on the other side of the house.

For five minutes she gave in to fear and self-pity. She was alone, all alone, locked in a dark cellar where no one would hear her until morning. It was already cold and getting colder. By morning…her candles would go out by then, and she'd have no light at all. That was the worst, the very worst, to have no light.

Light, she thought, and called herself an idiot as she wiped away tears. Hadn't she just fixed the lights? Scrambling up, Pandora hit the switch at the top of the stairs. Nothing happened. Holding back a scream, she

held the candles up. The socket over the stairs was empty.

So, they'd thought to take out the bulbs. It had been a clever trick after all. She swallowed fresh panic and tried to think. They wanted her to be incoherent, and she refused to give them the satisfaction. When she found out which one of her loving family was playing nasty games...

That was for later, Pandora told herself. Now she was going to find a way out. She was shivering, but she told herself it was anger. There were times it paid to lie to yourself. Holding the candles aloft, she forced herself to go down the steps again when cowering at the top seemed so much easier.

The cellar was twice the size of her apartment in New York, open and barnlike without any of the ornate decorating Uncle Jolley had been prone to. It was just dark and slightly damp with concrete floors and stone walls that echoed. She wouldn't think about spiders or things that scurried into corners right now. Slowly, trying to keep calm, she searched for an exit.

There were no doors, but then she was standing several feet underground. Like a tomb. That particular thought didn't soothe her nerves so she concentrated on other things. She'd only been down in the cellar a handful of times and hadn't given a great deal of thought to the setup. Now she had to think about it—and pretend her palms weren't clammy.

She eased by a pile of boxes as high as her shoulders, then let out a scream when she ran into a maze of cobwebs. More disgusted than frightened, she brushed and dragged at them. It didn't sit well with her to make a fool out of herself, even if no one was

around to see it. Someone was going to pay, she told herself as she fought her way clear.

Then she saw the window, four feet above her head and tiny. Though it was hardly the size of a transom, Pandora nearly collapsed in relief. After setting the candles on a shelf, she began dragging boxes over. Her muscles strained and her back protested, but she hauled and stacked against the wall. The first splinter had her swearing. After the third, she stopped counting. Out of breath, streaming with sweat, she leaned against her makeshift ladder. Now all she had to do was climb it. With the candles in one hand, she used the other to haul herself up. The light shivered and swayed. The boxes groaned and teetered a bit. The thought passed through her mind that if she fell, she could lie there on the frigid concrete with broken bones until morning. She pulled herself high and refused to think at all.

When she reached the window, she found the little latch rusted and stubborn. Swearing, praying, she balanced the candles on the box under her and used both hands. She felt the latch give, then stick again. If she'd only thought to find a tool before she'd climbed up. She considered climbing back down and finding one, then made the mistake of looking behind her. The stack of boxes looked even more rickety from up there.

Turning back to the window, she tugged with all the strength she had. The latch gave with a grind of metal against metal, the boxes swayed from the movement. She saw her candles start to tip and grabbed for them. Out of reach, they slid from the box and clattered to the concrete, their tiny flames extinguished as they hit the ground. She almost followed them, but managed

to fight for balance. Pandora found herself perched nine feet off the floor in pitch-darkness.

She wouldn't fall, she promised herself as she gripped the little window ledge with both hands. Using her touch to guide her, she pulled the window out and open, then began to ease herself through. The first blast of cold air made her almost giddy. After she'd pushed her shoulders through she gave herself a moment to breathe and adjust to the lesser dark of starlight. From somewhere to the west, she heard a hardy night bird call twice and fall silent. She'd never heard anything more beautiful.

Grabbing the base of a rhododendron, she pulled herself through to the waist. When she heard the crash of boxes behind her, she laid her cheek against the cold grass. Inch by inch, she wiggled her way out, ignoring the occasional rip and scratch. At last, she was flat on her back, looking up at the stars. Cold, bruised and exhausted, she lay there, just breathing. When she was able, Pandora dragged herself up and walked around to the east terrace doors.

She wanted revenge, but first, she wanted a bath.

After three layovers and two plane changes, Michael arrived in Palm Springs. Nothing, as far as he could see, had changed. He never came to the exclusive little community but that he came reluctantly. Now, thinking of his mother lying ill, he was swamped with guilt.

He rarely saw her. True, she was no more interested in seeing him than he was her. Yet, she was still his mother. They had been on a different wavelength since the day he'd been born, but she'd taken care of him. At least, she'd hired people to take care of him. Af-

fection, Michael realized, didn't have to enter into a child's feelings for his parent. The bond was there whether or not understanding followed it.

With no more than a flight bag, he bypassed the crowd at baggage claim and hailed a cab. After giving his mother's address, he sat back and checked his watch, subtracting time zones. Even with the hours he'd gained, it was probably past visiting hours. He'd get around that, but first he had to know what hospital his mother was in. If he'd been thinking straight, he would have called ahead and checked.

If his mother's husband wasn't in, one of the servants could tell him. It might not be as bad as the telegram made it sound. After all his mother was still young. Then it struck Michael that he didn't have the vaguest idea how old his mother was. He doubted his father knew, and certainly not her current husband. At another time, it might have struck him as funny.

Impatient, he watched as the cab glided by the gates and pillars of the elite. His career had caused him to stay in California for extended lengths of time, but he preferred L.A. to Palm Springs. There, at least, was some action, some movement, some edge. But he liked New York best of all; the pace matched his own and the streets were tougher.

He thought of Pandora. Both of them lived in New York, but they never saw each other unless it was miles north of the city at the Folley. The city could swallow you. Or hide you. It was another aspect Michael appreciated.

Didn't he often use it to hide—from his stifling upbringing, from his recurring lack of faith in the human race? It was at the Folley that he felt the easiest, but

it was in New York that he felt the safest. He could be anonymous there if he chose to be. There were times he wanted nothing more. He wrote about heroes and justice, sometimes rough but always human. He wrote, in his own fashion, about basic values and simple rights.

He'd been raised with the illusions and hypocrisy of wealth and with values that were just as unstable. He'd broken away from that, started on his own. New York had helped make it possible because in the city backgrounds were easily erased. So easily erased, Michael mused, that he rarely thought of his.

The cab cruised up the long semicircle of macadam, under the swaying palms, toward the towering white house where his mother had chosen to live. Michael remembered there was a lily pond in the back with goldfish the size of groupers. His mother refused to call them carp.

"Wait," he told the driver, then dashed up two levels of stairs to the door. The butler who answered was new. It was his mother's habit to change the staff regularly, before, as she put it, they got too familiar. "I'm Michael Donahue, Mrs. Keyser's son."

The butler glanced over his shoulder at the waiting cab, then back at Michael's disheveled sweater and unshaven face. "Good evening, sir. Are you expected?"

"Where's my mother? I want to go to the hospital directly."

"Your mother isn't in this evening, Mr. Donahue. If you'll wait, I'll see if Mr. Keyser's available."

Intolerant, as always, of cardboard manners, he

stepped inside. "I know she's not in. I want to go see her tonight. What's the name of the hospital?"

The butler gave a polite nod. "What hospital, Mr. Donahue?"

"Jackson, where did that cab come from?" Wrapped in a deep-rose smoking jacket, Lawrence Keyser strolled downstairs. He had a thick cigar between the fingers of one hand and a snifter of brandy in the other.

"Well, Lawrence," Michael began over a wave of fury. "You look comfortable. Where's my mother?"

"Well, well, it's—ah, it's Matthew."

"It's Michael."

"Michael, of course. Jackson, pay off Mr. ah, Mr. Donavan's cab."

"No, thanks, Jackson." Michael held up a hand. Another time, he'd have been amused at his stepfather's groping for his name. "I'll use it to get to the hospital. Wouldn't want to put you out."

"No trouble at all, not at all." Big, round and only partially balding, Keyser gave Michael a friendly grin. "Veronica will be pleased to see you, though we didn't know you were coming. How long are you in town?"

"As long as I'm needed. I left the minute I got the telegram. You didn't mention the name of the hospital. Since you're home and relaxing," he said with only the slightest trace of venom, "should I assume that my mother's condition's improved?"

"Condition?" Keyser gave a jovial laugh. "Well now, I don't know how she'd take to that term, but you can ask her yourself."

"I intend to. Where is she?"

"Playing bridge at the Bradleys'. She'll be coming along in about an hour. How about a brandy?"

"Playing bridge!" Michael stepped forward and grabbed his surprised stepfather by the lapels. "What the hell do you mean she's playing bridge?"

"Can't stomach the game myself," Keyser began warily. "But Veronica's fond of it."

It came to Michael, clear as a bell. "You didn't send me a telegram about Mother?"

"A telegram?" Keyser patted Michael's arm, and hoped Jackson stayed close. "No need to send you a telegram about a bridge game, boy."

"Mother's not ill?"

"Strong as a horse, though I wouldn't let her hear me say so just that way."

Michael swore and whirled around. "Someone's going to pay," he muttered.

"Where are you going?"

"Back to New York," Michael tossed over his shoulder as he ran down the steps.

Relieved, Keyser opted against the usual protests about his departure. "Is there a message for your mother?"

"Yeah." Michael stopped with a hand on the door of the cab. "Yeah, tell her I'm glad she's well. And I hope she wins—in spades." Michael slammed the door shut behind him.

Keyser waited until the cab shot out of sight. "Odd boy," Keyser grumbled to his butler. "Writes for television."

Chapter 6

Pandora, sleeping soundly, was awakened at seven in the morning when Michael dropped on her bed. The mattress bounced. He snuggled his head into the pillow beside her and shut his eyes.

"Sonofabitch," he grumbled.

Pandora sat up, remembered she was naked and grabbed for the sheets. "Michael! You're supposed to be in California. What are you doing in my bed?"

"Getting horizontal for the first time in twenty-four hours."

"Well, do that in your own bed," she ordered, then saw the lines of strain and fatigue. "Your mother." Pandora grabbed for his hand. "Oh, Michael, is your mother—"

"Playing bridge." He rubbed his free hand over his face. Even to him it felt rough and seedy. "I bounced across country, once in a tuna can with propellers, to

find out she was sipping sherry and trumping her partner's ace.''

"She's better then?"

"She was always better. The telegram was a hoax." He yawned, stretched and settled. "God, what a night."

"You mean..." Pandora tugged on the sheets and glowered. "Well, the rats."

"Yeah. I plotted out several forms of revenge when I was laid over in Cleveland. Maybe our friend who stomped through your workshop figured it was my turn. Now we each owe them one."

"I owe 'em two." Pandora leaned back against the headboard with the sheets tucked under her arms. Her hair fell luxuriously over her naked shoulders. "Last night while you were off on your wild-goose chase, I was locked in the cellar."

Michael's attention shot away from the thin sheet that barely covered her. "Locked in? How?"

Crossing one ankle over the other, Pandora told him what happened from the time the lights went out.

"Climbed up on boxes? To that little window? It's nearly ten feet."

"Yes, I believe I noticed that at the time."

Michael scowled at her. The anger he'd felt at being treated to a sleepless night doubled. He could picture her groping her way around in the dank cellar all too well. Worse, he could see her very clearly climbing on shaky boxes and crates. "You could've broken your neck."

"I didn't. What I did do was rip my favorite pair of slacks, scratch both knees and bruise my shoulder."

Michael managed to hold back his fury. He'd let it

go, he promised himself, when the time was right. "It could've been worse," he said lightly, and thought of what he'd do to whoever had locked her in.

"It was worse," Pandora tossed back, insulted. "While you were sipping Scotch at thirty thousand feet, I was locked in a cold, damp cellar with mice and spiders."

"We might reconsider calling the police."

"And do what with them? We can't prove anything. We don't even know whom we can't prove anything against."

"New rule," Michael decided. "We stick together. Neither of us leaves the house overnight without the other. At least until we find out which of our devoted relations is playing games."

Pandora started to protest, then remembered how frightened she'd been, and before the cellar, before the fear, how lonely. "Agreed. Now…" With one hand hanging onto the sheet, she shifted toward him. "I vote for Uncle Carlson on this one. After all, he knows the house better than any of the others. He lived here."

"It's as good a guess as any. But it's only a guess." Michael stared up at the ceiling. "I want to know. Biff stayed here for six weeks one summer when we were kids."

"That's right." Pandora frowned at the ceiling herself. The mirror across the room reflected them lying companionably, hip to hip. "I'd forgotten about that. He hated it."

"He's never had a sense of humor."

"True enough. As I recall he certainly didn't like you."

"Probably because I gave him a black eye."

Pandora's brow lifted. "You would." Then, because the image of Biff with a shiner wasn't so unappealing, she added: "Why did you? You never said."

"Remember the frogs in your dresser?"

Pandora sniffed and smoothed at the sheets. "I certainly do. It was quite immature of you."

"Not me. Biff."

"Biff?" Astonished, she turned toward him again. "You mean that little creep put the frogs in my underwear?" The next thought came, surprisingly pleasing. "And you punched him for it?"

"It wasn't hard."

"Why didn't you deny it when I accused you?"

"It was more satisfying to punch Biff. In any case, he knows the house well enough. And I imagine if we checked up, we'd find most of our happy clan has stayed here, at least for a few days at a time. Finding a fuse box in the cellar doesn't take a lot of cunning. Think it through, Pandora. There are six of them, seven with the charity added on. Split a hundred fifty million seven ways and you end up with plenty of motive. Every one of them has a reason for wanting us to break the terms of the will. None of them, as far as I'm concerned, is above adding a little pressure to help us along."

"Another reason the money never appealed to me," she mused. "They haven't done anything but vandalize and annoy, but, dammit, Michael, I want to pay them back."

"The ultimate payback comes in just under five months." Without thinking about it, Michael put his arm around her shoulders. Without thinking about it, Pandora settled against him. A light fragrance clung to

her skin. "Can't you see Carlson's face when the will holds up and he gets nothing but a magic wand and a trick hat?"

His shoulder felt more solid than she'd imagined. "And Biff with three cartons of matchbooks." Comfortable, she chuckled. "Uncle Jolley's still having the last laugh."

"We'll have it with him in a few months."

"It's a date. And you've got your shoes on my sheets."

"Sorry." With two economical movements, he pried them off.

"That's not exactly what I meant. Don't you want to wander off to your own room now?"

"Not particularly. Your bed's nicer than mine. Do you always sleep naked?"

"No."

"My luck must be turning then." He shifted to press his lips to a bruise on her shoulder. "Hurt?"

She shrugged and prayed it came off as negligent. "A little."

"Poor little Pandora. And to think I always thought you were tough-skinned."

"I am—"

"Soft," he interrupted, and skimmed his fingers down her arm. "Very soft. Any more bruises?" He brushed his lips over the curve of her neck. They both felt her quick, involuntary shudder.

"Not so you'd notice."

"I'm very observant." He rolled, smoothly, so that his body pressed more intimately into hers as he looked down on her. He was tired. Yes, he was tired and more than a little punchy with jet lag, but he

hadn't forgotten he wanted her. Even if he had, the way her body yielded, the way her face looked rosy and soft with sleep, would've jogged his memory. "Why don't I look for myself?" He ran his fingers down to where the sheet lay, neat, prim and arousing, at her breast.

She sucked in her breath, incredibly moved by his lightest touch. She couldn't let it show...could she? She couldn't reach out for something that was only an illusion. He wasn't stable. He wasn't real. He was with her now because she was here and no one else was. Why was it becoming so hard to remember that?

His face was close, filling her vision. She saw the little things she'd tried not to notice over the years. The way a thin ring of gray outlined his irises, the straight, almost aristocratic line of his nose that had remained miraculously unbroken through countless fistfights. The soft, sculpted, somehow poetic shape of his mouth. A mouth, she remembered, that was hot and strong and inventive when pressed against hers.

"Michael..." The fact that she hesitated, then fumbled before she reached down to take his hand both pleased and unnerved him. She wasn't as cool and self-contained as she'd always appeared. And because she wasn't, he could slip his way under her skin. But he might not slip out again so easily.

Be practical, she told herself. Be realistic. "Michael, we have almost five months more to get through."

"Good point." He needed the warmth. He needed the woman. Maybe it was time to risk the consequences. He lowered his head and nibbled at her mouth. "Why waste it?"

She let herself enjoy him. For just a moment, she

promised herself. For only a moment. He was warm
and his hands were easy. The night had been long and
cold and frightening. No matter how much she hated
to admit it, she'd needed him. Now, with the sun pouring through the tiny square panes in the windows, falling bright and hard on the bed, she had him. Close,
secure, comforting.

Her lips opened against his.

He'd had no plan when he'd come into her room.
He'd simply been drawn to her; he'd wanted to lie
beside her and talk to her. Passion hadn't guided him.
Desire hadn't pushed him. There'd only been the basic
need to be home, to be home with her. When she'd
snuggled against him, hair tousled, eyes heavy, it had
been so natural that the longing had snuck up on him.
He wanted nothing more than to stay where he was,
wrapped around her, slowly heating.

And for her, passion didn't bubble wildly, but easily, like a brew that had been left to simmer through
the day while spices were added. One sample, then
another, and the taste changed, enriched, deepened.
With Michael, there the flavors were only hinted at, an
aroma to draw in and savor. She could have gone on,
and on, hour after hour, until what they made between
them was perfected. She wanted to give in to the need,
the beginnings of greed. If she did, everything would
change. It was a change she couldn't predict, couldn't
see clearly, could only anticipate. So she resisted him
and herself and what could happen between them.

"Michael…" But she let her fingers linger in his
hair for just a minute more. "This isn't smart."

He kissed her eyes closed. It was something no one

had done before. "It's the smartest thing either of us has done in years."

She wanted to agree, felt herself on the edge of agreeing. "Michael, things are complicated enough. If we were lovers and things went wrong, how could we manage to go on here together? We've made a commitment to Uncle Jolley."

"The will doesn't have a damn thing to do with you and me in this bed."

How could she have forgotten just how intense he could look when he was bent on something? How was it she'd never noticed how attractive it made him? She'd have to make a stand now or go under. "The will has everything to do with you and me in this house. If we go to bed together and our relationship changes, then we'll have to deal with all the problems and complications that go with it."

"Name some."

"Don't be amusing, Michael."

"Giving you a laugh wasn't my intention." He liked the way she looked against the pillow—hair spread out like wildfire, cheeks a bit flushed, her mouth on the edge of forming a pout. Strange he'd never pictured her this way before. It didn't take any thought to know he'd picture her like this again and again. "I want you, Pandora. There's nothing amusing about it."

No, that wasn't something she could laugh or shrug off, not when the words brushed over her skin and made her muscles limp. He didn't mean it. He couldn't mean it. But she wanted to believe it. If she couldn't laugh it off, she had to throw up a guard and block it.

"Becoming lovers is something that takes a lot of thought. If we're going to discuss it—"

"I don't want to discuss it." He pressed his lips against hers until he felt her body soften. "We're not making a corporate merger, Pandora, we're making love."

"That's just it." She fought back an avalanche of longing. Be practical. It was her cardinal rule. "We're business partners. Worse, we're family business partners, at least for the next few months. If we change that now it could—"

"If," he interrupted. "It could. Do you always need guarantees?"

Her brows drew together as annoyance competed with desire. "It's a matter of common sense to look at all the angles."

"I suppose you have any prospective lover fill out an application form."

Her voice chilled. It was, in a distorted way, close to the truth. "Don't be crude, Michael."

Pushed to the limit, he glared down at her. "I'd rather be crude than have your brand of common sense."

"You've never had any brand of common sense," she tossed back. "Why else would every busty little blonde you've winked at be public knowledge? You don't even have the decency to be discreet."

"So that's it." Shifting, Michael drew her into a sitting position. There was no soft yielding now. She faced him with fire in her eyes. "Don't forget the brunettes and the redheads."

She hadn't. She promised herself she wouldn't. "I don't want to discuss it."

"You brought it up, and we'll finish it. I've gone to bed with women. So put me in irons. I've even enjoyed it."

She tossed her hair behind her shoulder. "I'm sure you have."

"And I haven't had a debate with every one of them beforehand. Some women prefer romance and mutual enjoyment."

"Romance?" Her brows shot up under her tousled hair. "I've always had another word for it."

"You wouldn't recognize romance if it dropped on your head. Do you consider it discreet to take lovers and pretend you don't? To pledge undying fidelity to one person while you're looking for another? What you want to call discretion, I call hypocrisy. I'm not ashamed of any of the women I've known, in bed or out."

"I'm not interested in what you are or aren't ashamed of. I'm not going to be your next mutual enjoyment. Keep your passion for your dancers and starlets and chorus girls."

"You're as big a snob as the rest of them."

That hit home and had her shoulders stiffening. "That's not true. I've simply no intention of joining a crowd."

"You flatter me, cousin."

"There's another word for that, too."

"Think about this." He gave her a shake, harder than he'd intended. "I've never made love with a woman I didn't care for and respect." Before he cut loose and did more than shake her, he got up and walked to the door while she sat in the middle of the bed clutching sheets and looking furious.

"It appears you give respect easily."

He turned back to study her. "No," he said slowly. "But I don't make people jump through hoops for it."

A cold war might not be as stimulating as an active battle, but with the right participants, it could be equally destructive. For days Pandora and Michael circled around each other. If one made a sarcastic comment, the other reached into the stockpile and used equal sarcasm. Neither drew out the red flag for full-scale attack, instead they picked and prodded at each other while the servants rolled their eyes and waited for bloodshed.

"Foolishness," Sweeney declared as she rolled out the crust for two apple pies. "Plain foolishness." She was a sturdy, red-faced woman, as round as Charles was thin. In her pragmatic, no-nonsense way, she'd married and buried two husbands, then made her way in the world by cooking for others. Her kitchen was always neat and tidy, all the while smelling of the sinfully rich food she prepared. "Spoiled children," she told Charles. "That's what they are. Spoiled children need the back of the hand."

"They've over four months to go." Charles sat gloomily at the kitchen table, hunched over a cup of tea. "They'll never make it."

"Hah!" Sweeney slammed the rolling pin onto a fresh ball of dough. "They'll make it. Too stubborn not to. But it's not enough."

"The master wanted them to have the house. As long as they do, we won't lose it."

"What'll we be doing in this big empty house when both of them go back to the city? How often will either

of them be visiting with the master gone?'' Sweeney turned the crust into a pan and trimmed it expertly. ''The master wanted them to have the house, true enough. And he wanted them to have each other. The house needs a family. It's up to us to see it gets one.''

''You didn't hear them over breakfast.'' Charles sipped his tea and watched Sweeney pour a moist apple mixture into the crust.

''That has nothing to do with it. *I've* seen the way they look at each other when they think the other one's not noticing. All they need's a push.''

With quick, economic movements, she filled the second crust. ''We're going to give 'em one.''

Charles stretched out his legs. ''We're too old to push young people.''

Sweeney gave a quick grunt as she turned. Her hands were thick, and she set them on her hips. ''Being old's the whole trick. You've been feeling poorly lately.''

''No, to tell you the truth, I've been feeling much better this week.''

''You've been feeling poorly,'' Sweeney repeated, scowling at him. ''Now here's our Pandora coming in for lunch. Just follow my lead. Look a little peaked.''

Snow had come during the night, big fat flakes that piled on the ground and hung in the pines. As she walked, Pandora kicked it up, pleased with herself. Her work couldn't have been going better. The earrings she'd finally fashioned had been unique, so unique, she'd designed a necklace to complement them. It was chunky and oversize with geometric shapes of copper and gold. Not every woman could wear it, but the one who could wouldn't go unnoticed.

It was, to Pandora, a statement of the strong, disci-
plined woman. She was just as pleased with the shoul-
der-brushing earrings she was making with jet and silver beads. They had been painstakingly strung together
and when finished would be elegantly flirtatious. Another aspect of woman. If her pace kept steady, she'd
have a solid inventory to ship off to the boutique she
supplied. In time for the Christmas rush, she reminded
herself smugly.

When she opened the kitchen door, she was raven-
ously hungry and in the best of moods.

"...if you're feeling better in a day or two,"
Sweeney said briskly, then turned as if surprised to see
Pandora inside. "Oh, time must've got away from me.
Lunch already and I'm just finishing up the pies."

"Apple pies?" Grinning, Pandora moved closer.
But Sweeney saw with satisfaction that Pandora was
already studying Charles. "Any filling left?" she began, and started to dip her fingers into the bowl. Sweeney smacked them smartly.

"You've been working with those hands. Wash
them up in the sink, and you'll have your lunch as
soon as I can manage it."

Obediently, Pandora turned on a rush of water. Under the noise, she murmured to Sweeney. "Is Charles
not feeling well?"

"Bursitis is acting up. Cold weather's a problem.
Just being old's a problem in itself." She pushed a
hand at the small of her back as though she had a pain.
"Guess we're both slowing down a bit. Aches and
pains," Sweeney sighed and cast a sidelong look at
Pandora. "Just part of being old."

"Nonsense." Concerned, Pandora scrubbed her

hands harder. She told herself she should have been keeping a closer eye on Charles. "You just try to do too much."

"With the holidays coming..." Sweeney trailed off and made a business out of arranging a top crust. "Well, decorating the house is a lot of work, but it's its own reward. Charles and I'll deal with the boxes in the attic this afternoon."

"Don't be silly." Pandora shut off the water and reached for a towel. "I'll bring the decorations down."

"No, now, missy, there're too many boxes and most of them are too heavy for a little girl like you. That's for us to see to. Isn't that right, Charles?"

Thinking of climbing the attic stairs a half-dozen times, Charles started to sigh. A look from Sweeney stopped him. "Don't worry, Miss McVie, Sweeney and I will see to it."

"You certainly will not." Pandora hung the towel back on the hook. "Michael and I will bring everything down this afternoon, and that's that. Now I'll go tell him to come to lunch."

Sweeney waited until the door swung shut behind Pandora before she grinned.

Upstairs, Pandora knocked twice on Michael's office door, then walked in. He kept on typing. Putting her pride on hold, Pandora walked over to his desk and folded her arms. "I need to talk to you."

"Come back later. I'm busy."

Abuse rose up in her throat. Remembering Sweeney's tired voice, she swallowed it. "It's important." She ground her teeth on the word, but said it. "Please."

Surprised, Michael stopped typing in midword.

''What? Has one of the family been playing games again?''

''No, it's not that. Michael, we have to decorate the house for Christmas.''

He stared at her a moment, swore and turned back to his machine. ''I've got a twelve-year-old boy kidnapped and being held for a million-dollar ransom. That's important.''

''Michael, will you put away fantasyland for a moment? This is real.''

''So's this. Just ask my producer.''

''Michael!'' Before he could stop her, Pandora pulled the sheet from the typewriter. He was halfway out of his chair to retaliate. ''It's Sweeney and Charles.''

It stopped him, though he snatched the paper back from her. ''What about them?''

''Charles's bursitis is acting up again, and I'm sure Sweeney's not feeling well. She sounded, well, old.''

''She is old.'' But Michael tossed the paper on the desk. ''Think we should call in a doctor?''

''No, they'd be furious.'' She swung around his desk, trying to pretend she wasn't reading part of his script. ''I'd rather just keep an eye on them for a few days and make sure they don't overdo. That's where the Christmas decorations come in.''

''I figured you'd get to them. Look, if you want to deck the halls, go ahead. I haven't got time to fool with it today.''

''Neither do I.'' She folded her arms in a manner that amused him. ''Sweeney and Charles have it in their heads that it has to be done. Unless we want them

dragging up and down the attic stairs, we have to take care of it.''

"Christmas is three weeks away.''

"I know the date." Frustrated, she strode to the window then back. "They're old and they're set on it. You know Uncle Jolley would've had them up the day after Thanksgiving. It's traditional.''

"All right, all right." Trapped, Michael rose. "Let's get started.''

"Right after lunch." Satisfied she'd gotten her way, Pandora swept out.

Forty-five minutes later, she and Michael were pushing open the attic door. The attic was, in Jolley's tradition, big enough to house a family of five. "Oh, I'd forgotten what a marvelous place this is." Forgetting herself, Pandora grabbed Michael's hand and pulled him in. "Look at this table, isn't it horrible?''

It was. Old and ornate with curlicues and cupids, it had been shoved into a corner to hold other paraphernalia Jolley had discarded. "And the bird cage out of Popsicle sticks. Uncle Jolley said it took him six months to finish it, then he didn't have the heart to put a bird inside.''

"Lucky for the bird," Michael muttered, but found himself, as always, drawn to the dusty charm of the place. "Spats," he said, and lifted a pair from a box. "Can't you see him in them?''

"And this hat." Pandora found a huge circular straw with a garden of flowers along the brim. "Aunt Katie's. I've always wished I'd met her. My father said she was just as much fun as Uncle Jolley.''

Michael watched Pandora tip the brim over her eyes.

"If that was her hat, I believe it. How about this?" He found a black derby and tilted it rakishly.

"It's you," Pandora told him with her first easy laugh in days. "All you need's a high white collar and a walking stick. Look." She pulled him in front of a tall cheval mirror that needed resilvering. Together, they studied themselves.

"An elegant pair," Michael decided, though his sweater bagged over his hips, and she already had dust on her nose. "All you need is one of those slim little skirts that sweep the floor and a lace blouse with padded shoulders."

"And a cameo on a ribbon," she added as she tried to visualize herself. "No, I probably would've worn bloomers and picketed for women's rights."

"The hat still suits you." He turned to adjust it just a bit. "Especially with your hair long and loose. I've always liked it long, though you looked appealingly lost and big-eyed when you had it all chopped short."

"I was fifteen."

"And you'd just come back from the Canary Islands with the longest, brownest legs I'd ever seen in my life. I nearly ate my saucer when you walked into the parlor."

"You were in college and had some cheerleader hanging on your arm."

Michael grinned. "You had better legs."

Pandora pretended little interest. She remembered the visit perfectly, but was surprised, and pleased, that he did. "I'm surprised you noticed or remembered."

"I told you I was observant."

She acknowledged the thrust with a slight nod. There were times when it was best to pad quietly over

dangerous ground. "We'd better start digging out the decorations. Sweeney said the boxes were back along the left and clearly marked." Without waiting for agreement, she turned and began to look. "Oh good grief." She stopped again when she saw the stacks of boxes, twenty, perhaps twenty-five of them. Michael stood at her shoulder and stuck his hands in his pockets.

"Think we can hire some teamsters?"

Pandora blew out a breath. "Roll up your sleeves."

On some trips, they could pile two or three boxes apiece and maneuver downstairs. On others, it took both of them to haul one. Somewhere along the way they'd stopped arguing. It was just too much effort.

Grimy and sweaty, they dropped the last boxes in the parlor. Ignoring the dust on her slacks, Pandora collapsed in the nearest chair. "Won't it be great fun hauling them all up again after New Year's?"

"Couldn't we've settled on a plastic Santa?"

"It'll be worth it." Drumming up the energy, she knelt on the floor and opened the first box. "Let's get started."

Once they did, they went at it with a vengeance. Boxes were opened, garland strewed and bulbs tested. They squabbled good-naturedly about what looked best where and the proper way to drape lights at the windows. When the parlor, the main hall and the staircase were finished, Pandora stood at the front door and took a long look.

The garland was white and silver, twisting and twining down the banister. There were bright red bells, lush green ribbon and tiny lights just waiting for evening.

"It looks good," she decided. "Really good. Of

course, Sweeney and Charles will want to decorate the servants' quarters and that entire box goes into the dining room, but it's a wonderful start.''

"Start?" Michael sat on the stairs. "We're not entering a contest, cousin."

"These things have to be done right. I wonder if my parents will make it home for Christmas. Well..." She brushed that off. They always considered wherever they were home. "I'd say we're ready for the tree. Let's go find one."

"You want to drive into town now?"

"Of course not." Pandora was already pulling coats out of the hall closet. "We'll go right out in the woods and dig one up."

"We?"

"Certainly. I hate it when people cut trees down and then toss them aside after the new year. The woods are loaded with nice little pines. We'll dig one up, then replant it after the holidays."

"How handy are you with a shovel?"

"Don't be a spoilsport." Pandora tossed his coat to him, then pulled on her own. "Besides, it'll be nice to spend some time outside after being in that stuffy attic. We can have some hot buttered rum when we're finished."

"Heavy on the rum."

They stopped at the toolshed for a shovel. Michael picked two and handed one to Pandora. She took it without a blink, then together they walked through the ankle-high snow to the woods. The air had a bite and the scent of pine was somehow stronger in the snow.

"I love it when it's like this." Pandora balanced the shovel on her shoulder and plowed through the woods.

"It's so quiet, so—separated. You know, sometimes I think I'd rather live here and visit the city than the other way around."

He'd had the same thought, but was surprised to hear it from her. "I always thought you liked the bright lights and confusion."

"I do. But I like this, too. How about this one?" She paused in front of a spruce. "No, the trunk's too crooked." She walked on. "Besides, I wonder if it wouldn't be more exciting to go into the city for a week now and again and know you had someplace like this to come back to. I seem to work better here. Here's one."

"Too tall. We're better off digging up a young one. Wouldn't it put a crimp in your social life?"

"What?" She studied the tree in question and was forced to agree with him. "Oh. My social life isn't a priority, my work is. In any case, I could entertain here."

He had a picture of her spending long, cozy weekends with flamboyant, artsy types who read Keats aloud. "You don't have to come all the way to the Catskills to play house."

Pandora merely lifted a brow. "No, I don't. This one looks good." She stopped again and took a long study of a four-and-a-half-foot spruce. Behind her, Michael worked hard to keep his mouth shut. "It's just the right size for the parlor."

"Fine." Michael stuck his shovel into the ground. "Put your back into it."

As he bent over to dig, Pandora scooped up a shovelful of snow and tossed it into his face. "Oh, sorry."

She smiled and batted her eyes. "Looks like my aim's off." Digging with more effort, she began to hum.

He let it go, probably because he appreciated the move and wished he'd thought of it himself. Within fifteen minutes, they had the hole dug.

"There now." Only a little out of breath, Pandora leaned on her shovel. "The satisfaction of a job well done."

"We only have to carry it back to the house, set it up and…damn, we need something to wrap the roots and dirt in. There was burlap in the shed."

They eyed each other blandly.

"All right," he said after a moment. "I'll go get it, then you have to sweep up the needles and dirt we trail on the floor."

"Deal."

Content, Pandora turned away to watch a cardinal when a snowball slapped into the back of her head. "Sorry." Michael gave her a companionable smile. "Aim must be off." He whistled as he walked back to the shed.

Pandora waited until he was out of sight, then smiling smugly, knelt down to ball snow. By the time he got back, she calculated, she could have an arsenal at hand. He wouldn't have a chance. She took her time, forming and smoothing each ball into a sophisticated weapon. Secure in her advantage, she nearly fell on her face when she heard a sound behind her. She had the ball in her hand and was already set to throw as she whirled. No one was there. Narrowing her eyes, she waited. Hadn't she seen a movement back in the trees? It would be just like him to skirt around and try to sneak up on her. She saw the cardinal fly up again

as if startled and heard the quiet plop of snow hitting snow as it was shaken from branches.

"All right, Michael, don't be a coward." She picked up a ball in her left hand, prepared to bombard.

"Guarding your flank?" Michael asked so that this time when she whirled back around, she slid onto her bottom. He grinned at her and dropped the burlap sack in her lap.

"But weren't you..." She trailed off and looked behind her again. How could he be here if he was there? "Did you circle around?"

"No, but from the looks of that mound of balls, I should've. Want to play war?"

"It's just a defense system," she began, then looked over her shoulder again. "I thought I heard you. I would've sworn there was someone just beyond the trees there."

"I went straight to the shed and back." He looked beyond her. "You saw something out there?"

"Michael, if you're playing tricks—"

"No." He cut her off and reached down to pull her to her feet. "No tricks. Let's have a look."

She moved her shoulders but didn't remove her hand from his as they walked deeper into the trees. "Maybe I was a bit jumpy."

"Or expecting me to be sneaky?"

"That, too. It was probably just a rabbit."

"A rabbit with big feet," he murmured as he looked down at the tracks. They were clear enough in the snow, tracks leading to and away from the spot ten yards behind where they'd dug up the tree. "Rabbits don't wear boots."

"So, we still have company. I was beginning to

think they'd given the whole business up.'' She kept her voice light, but felt the uneasiness of anyone who'd been watched. ''Maybe it's time we talked to Fitzhugh, Michael.''

''Maybe, in the meantime—'' The sound of an engine cut him off. He was off in a sprint with Pandora at his heels. After a five-minute dash, they came, clammy and out of breath, to what was hardly more than a logging trail. Tire tracks had churned up the snow and blackened it. ''A Jeep, I'd guess.'' Swearing, Michael stuck his hands in his pockets. If he'd started out right away, he might have caught someone or at least have caught a glimpse of someone.

Pandora let out an annoyed breath. Racing after someone was one thing, being outmaneuvered another. ''Whoever it is is only wasting his time.''

''I don't like being spied on.'' He wanted physical contact. Longed for it. Frustrated, he stared at the tracks that led back to the main road. ''I'm not playing cat and mouse for the next four months.''

''What are we going to do?''

His smile spread as he looked at the tracks. ''We'll spread the word through Fitzhugh that we've been bothered by trespassers. Being as there's any number of valuables on the premises, we've decided to haul out one of Jolley's old .30-.30's.''

''Michael! They may be a nuisance, but they're still family.'' Unsure, she studied him. ''You wouldn't really shoot at anyone.''

''I'd rather shoot at family than strangers,'' he countered, then shrugged. ''They're also fond of their own skin. I can't think of one of them who wouldn't hes-

itate to play around if they thought they might be picking buckshot out of embarrassing places.''

"I don't like it. Guns, even the threat of guns, are trouble.''

"Got a better idea?''

"Let's buy a dog. A really big, mean dog.''

"Great, then we can let him loose and have him sink his teeth into one of our favorite relatives. They'd like that a lot better than buckshot.''

"He doesn't have to be that mean.''

"We'll compromise and do both.''

"Michael—''

"Let's call Fitzhugh.''

"And take his advice?'' Pandora demanded.

"Sure…if I like it.''

Pandora started to object, then laughed. It was all as silly as a plot of one of his shows. "Sounds reasonable,'' she decided, then tucked her arm through his. "Let's get the tree inside first.''

Chapter 7

"I know it's Christmas Eve, Darla." Michael picked up his coffee cup, found it empty and lifted the pot from his hot plate. Dregs. He bit off a sigh. The trouble with the Folley was that you had to hike a half a mile to the kitchen whenever the pot ran dry. "I know it'll be a great party, but I can't get away."

That wasn't precisely true, Michael mused as he listened to Darla's rambles about a celebration in Manhattan. *Everyone*, according to her estimate, was going to be there. That meant a loud, elbow-to-elbow party with plenty of booze. He could have taken a day and driven into the city to raise a glass or two with friends. He was well ahead of schedule. So far ahead, he could have taken off a week and not felt the strain. The precise truth was, he didn't want to get away.

"I appreciate that…you'll just have to tell everyone Merry Christmas for me. No, I like living in the coun-

try, Darla. Weird? Yeah, maybe." He had to laugh.
Darla was a top-notch dancer and a barrel of laughs,
but she didn't believe life went on outside of the island
of Manhattan. "New Year's if I can manage it. Okay,
babe. Yeah, yeah, *ciao*."

More than a little relieved, Michael hung up. Darla
was a lot of fun, but he wasn't used to being clung to
by a woman, especially one he'd only dated casually.
The truth was, she was just as attracted to the influence
he had with certain casting agents as she was interested
in him. He didn't hold it against her. She had ambition
and talent, a combination that could work in the tough-
edged business of entertaining if a dash of luck was
added. After the holidays he'd make a few calls and
see what he could do.

From the doorway, Pandora watched as Michael ran
a hand along the back of his neck. Darla, she repeated
silently. She imagined the women his taste leaned toward had names like Darla, or Robin and Candy.
Sleek, smooth, sophisticated and preferably empty-
headed.

"Popularity's such a strain, isn't it, darling?"

Michael turned in his chair to give her a long, narrowed look. "Eavesdropping's so rude, isn't it, darling?"

She shrugged but didn't come in. "If you'd wanted
privacy, you should've closed your door."

"Around here you have to nail it shut for privacy."

One brow raised, head slightly inclined, Pandora
looked as aloof as royalty. "Your phone conversations
have absolutely no interest for me. I only came up as
a favor to Charles. You've a package downstairs."

"Thanks." He didn't bother to hide amusement at

her tone. If he knew Pandora, and he did, she'd listened to every word. "I thought these were your sacred working hours."

"Some of us schedule our work well enough that we can take some time off during the holidays. No, no, let's not bicker," she decided abruptly before he could retaliate. "It is nearly Christmas after all, and we've had three weeks of peace from our familial practical jokers. Truce," Pandora offered with a smile Michael wasn't sure he should trust. "Or a moratorium if you prefer."

"Why?"

"Let's just say I'm a sucker for holly and ivy. Besides, I'm relieved we didn't have to buy a big drooling dog or a supply of buckshot."

"For now." Not completely satisfied, Michael tipped back in his chair. "Fitzhugh's notion of notifying the local police of trespassers and spreading the rumor of an official investigation might be working temporarily. Or maybe our friends and family are just taking a holiday break themselves. Either way I'm not ready to relax."

"You'd rather break someone's nose than solve things peaceably," Pandora began, then waved a hand. "Never mind. I, for one, am going to enjoy the holidays and not give any of our dear family a thought." She paused a moment, toying with her braided chain of gold and amethyst. "I suppose Darla was disappointed."

Michael watched the way the stones caught the thin winter light and made sparks from it. "She'll pull through."

Pandora twisted the chain one way, twisted it back,

then let it go. It was the sort of nervous gesture Michael hadn't expected from her. "Michael, you know you don't have to stay. I really will be fine if you want to run into New York for the holiday."

"Rule number six," he reminded her. "We stick together, and you've turned down a half-dozen invitations for the holidays yourself."

"My choice." She reached for the chain again, then dropped her hands. "I don't want you to feel obligated—"

"My choice," he interrupted. "Or have you suddenly decided I'm chivalrous and unselfish?"

"Certainly not," she tossed back, but smiled. "I prefer thinking you're just too lazy to make the trip."

He shook his head, but his lips curved in response. "I'm sure you would."

She hesitated in the doorway until he lifted a brow in question. "Michael, would you become totally obnoxious if I told you I'm glad you're staying?"

He studied her as she stood, looking slim and neat in the doorway, her hair a riotous contrast to the trim sweater and stovepipe pants. "I might."

"Then I won't tell you." Without another word, she slipped out of the doorway and disappeared.

Contrary woman, Michael thought. He was close to being crazy about her. And crazy was the perfect word. She baited him or, he admitted, he baited her at every possible opportunity. He could imagine no two people less inclined to peaceful coexistence, much less harmony. And yet…and yet he was close to being crazy about her. Knowing better than to try to go back to work, he rose and followed her downstairs.

He found her in the parlor, rearranging packages under the tree. "How many have you shaken?"

"All of them," she said easily. But she didn't turn because he might have seen how pleased she was he'd come downstairs with her. "I don't want to show any preference. Thing is," she added, poking at an elegantly wrapped box, "I seem to have missed my present from you."

Michael gave her a bland smile. "Who says I got you anything?"

"You would have been terribly rude and insensitive otherwise."

"Yep. In any case, you seem to've done well enough." He crouched down to study the stacks of boxes under the tree. "Who's Boris?" Idly he picked up a small silver box with flowing white ribbon.

"A Russian cellist who defected. He admires my…gold links."

"I bet. And Roger?"

"Roger Madison."

His mouth dropped open, but only for a moment. "The Yankee shortstop who batted .304 last year?"

"That's right. You may've noticed the silver band he wears on his right wrist. I made that for him last March. He seems to think it straightened out his bat or something." She lifted the blue-and-gold box and shook it gently. "He tends to be very generous."

"I see." Michael took a comprehensive study of the boxes. "There don't seem to be a great many packages here for you from women."

"Really?" Pandora took a scan herself. "It appears you make up for that with your pile. Chi-Chi?" she asked as she picked up a box with a big pink bow.

"She's a marine biologist," Michael said with his tongue in his cheek.

"Fascinating. And I imagine Magda's a librarian."

"Corporate attorney," he said blandly.

"Hmm. Well, whoever sent this one's obviously shy." She picked up a magnum of champagne with a glittering red ribbon. The tag read "Happy Holidays, Michael," and nothing more.

Michael scanned the label with approval. "Some people don't want to advertise their generosity."

"How about you?" She tilted her head. "After all, it is a magnum. Are you going to share?"

"With whom?"

"I should've known you'd be greedy." She picked up a box with her name on it. "Just for that I'm eating this entire box of imported chocolates myself."

Michael eyed the box. "How do you know they're chocolates?"

She only smiled. "Henri always gives me chocolate."

"Imported?"

"Swiss."

Michael put out a hand. "Share and share alike."

Pandora accepted it. "I'll chill the wine."

Hours later when there was starlight on the snow and a fire in the hearth, Pandora lit the tree. Like Michael, she didn't miss any of the crowded, frenzied parties in the city. She was where she wanted to be. It had taken Pandora only a matter of weeks to discover she wasn't as attached to the rush of the city as she'd once thought. The Folley was home. Hadn't it always been? No, she no longer thought of going back to

Manhattan in the spring. But what would it be like to live in the Folley alone?

Michael wouldn't stay. True, he'd own half of the Folley in a few months, but his life—including his active social life—was in the city. He wouldn't stay, she thought again, and found herself annoyed with her own sense of regret. Why should he stay? she asked herself as she wandered over to poke at the already crackling fire. How could he stay? They couldn't go on living together indefinitely. Sooner or later she'd have to approach him about her decision to remain there. To do so, she'd have to explain herself. It wouldn't be easy.

Still, she was grateful to Jolley for doing something she'd once resented. Boxing her in. She may have been forced into dealing with Michael on a day-to-day level, but in the few months she'd done so, her life had had more energy and interest than in the many months before. It was that, Pandora told herself, that she hated to give up.

She'd dealt with her attraction to him semisuccessfully. The fact was, he was no more her type than she was his. She jammed hard at a log. From all the many reports, Michael preferred a more flamboyant, exotic sort of woman. Actresses, dancers, models. And he preferred them in droves. She, on the other hand, looked for more intellectual men. The men she spent time with could discuss obscure French novelists and appreciate small, esoteric plays. Most of them wouldn't have known if *Logan's Run* was a television show or a restaurant in SoHo.

The fact that she had a sort of primitive desire for Michael was only a tempest in a teapot. Pandora

smiled as she replaced the poker. She couldn't deny she enjoyed a tempest now and again.

When a small one erupted behind her, Pandora turned in disbelief. A little white dog with oversize feet scrambled into the room, slid on the Aubusson carpet and rammed smartly into a table. Barking madly, it rolled over twice, righted itself, then dashed at Pandora to leap halfheartedly and loll its tongue. Entertained, Pandora crouched down and was rewarded when the puppy sprang onto her lap and licked her face.

"Where'd you come from?" Laughing, and defending herself as best she could, Pandora found the card attached to the red bow around the puppy's neck. It read:

My name is Bruno. I'm a mean, ugly dog looking for a lady to defend.

"Bruno, huh?" Laughing again, Pandora stroked his unfortunately long ears. "How mean are you?" she asked as he contented himself with licking her chin.

"He especially likes to attack discontented relatives," Michael announced as he wheeled in a tray carrying an ice bucket and champagne. "He's been trained to go after anyone wearing a Brooks Brothers suit."

"We might add Italian loafers."

"That's next."

Moved, incredibly moved, she concentrated on the puppy. She hadn't the least idea how to thank Michael without making a fool of herself. "He isn't really ugly," she murmured.

"They promised me he would be."

"They?" She buried her face in the puppy's fur a moment. "Where did you get him?"

"Pound." Watching her, Michael ripped the foil from the champagne. "When we went into town for supplies last week and I deserted you in the supermarket."

"And I thought you'd gone off somewhere to buy pornographic magazines."

"My reputation precedes me," he said half to himself. "In any case, I went to the pound and walked through the kennels. Bruno bit another dog on the— on a sensitive area in order to get to the bars first. Then he grinned at me with absolutely no dignity. I knew he was the one."

The cork came out with a bang and champagne sprayed up and dripped onto the floor. Bruno scrambled out of Pandora's lap and greedily licked it up. "Perhaps his manners are lacking a bit," Pandora observed. "But his taste is first class." She rose, but waited until Michael had poured two glasses. "It was a lovely thing to do, dammit."

He grinned and handed her a glass. "You're welcome."

"It's easier for me when you're rude and intolerable."

"I do the best I can." He touched his glass to hers.

"When you're sweet, it's harder for me to stop myself from doing something foolish."

He started to lift his glass, then stopped. "Such as?"

"Such as." Pandora set down her champagne, then took Michael's and set it on the table as well. Watching him, only him, she put her arms around his neck.

Very slowly—unwise acts done slowly often take on a wisdom of their own—she touched her mouth to his.

It was, as she'd known it would be, warm and waiting. His hands came to her shoulders, holding her without pressure. Perhaps they'd both come to understand that pressure would never hold her. When she softened, when she gave, she gave through her own volition, not through seduction, not through demand. So it was Pandora who moved closer, Pandora who pressed body to body, offering hints of intimacy with no submission.

It wasn't submission he wanted. It wasn't submission he looked for, though it was often given to him. He didn't look for matching strength, but strength that meshed. In Pandora, where he'd never thought to search for it, he found it. Her scent twisted around him, heightening emotions her taste had just begun to stir. Under his hands, her body was firm with the underlying softness women could exploit or be exploited by. He thought she'd do neither, but would simply be. By being alone, she drew him in.

She didn't resist his touch, not when his hands slipped down to her hips or skimmed up again. It seemed he'd done so before, though only in dreams she'd refused to acknowledge. If this was the time for acceptance, she'd accept. If this was the time for pleasure, she'd take it. If she found both with him, she wouldn't refuse. Even questions could come later. Maybe tonight was a night without questions.

She drew back, but only to smile at him. "You know, I don't think of you as a cousin when I'm kissing you."

"Really?" He nipped at her lips. She had an in-

credibly alluring mouth—full and pouty. ''What do you think of me as?''

She cocked a brow. His arms surrounded her, but didn't imprison. Pandora knew she'd have to analyze the difference later. ''I haven't figured that out yet.''

''Then maybe we should keep working it out.'' He started to pull her back, but she resisted.

''Since you've broken tradition to give me my Christmas present a few hours early, I'll do the same.'' Going to the tree, Pandora reached down and found the square, flat box. ''Happy Christmas, Michael.''

He sat down on the arm of a chair to open it while Pandora picked up her glass of champagne. She sipped, watching a bit nervously for his reaction. It was only a token after all, she told herself, as she played with the stem of her glass. When he ripped off the paper then said nothing, she shrugged. ''It's not as inventive as a guard dog.''

Michael stared down at the pencil sketch of their uncle without any idea what to say. The frame she'd made herself, he knew. It was silver and busily ornate in a style Jolley would have appreciated. But it was the sketch that held him silent. She'd drawn Jolley as Michael remembered him best, standing, a bit bent forward from the waist as though he were ready to pop off on a new tangent. What thin hair he'd had left was mussed. His cheeks were stretched out in a big, wide-open grin. It had been drawn with love, talent and humor, three qualities Jolley had possessed and admired. When Michael looked up, Pandora was still twisting the stem of the glass in her hands.

Why she's nervous, he realized. He'd never expected her to be anything but arrogantly confident

about her work. About herself. The secrets he was un-
covering were just as unnerving to him as they were
to her. A man tended to get pulled into a woman who
had soft spots in unexpected places. If he was pulled
in, how would he work his way out again? But she
was waiting, twisting the stem of her glass in her hand.

"Pandora. No one's ever given me anything that's
meant more."

The line between her brows smoothed out as her
smile bloomed. The ridiculous sense of pleasure was
difficult to mask. "Really?"

He held a hand out to her. "Really." He glanced
down at the sketch again and smiled. "It looks just
like him."

"It looks like I remember him." She let her fingers
link with Michael's. Pandora could tell herself it was
Jolley who drew them together, and nothing else. She
could nearly believe it. "I thought you might remember him that way, too. The frame's a bit gaudy."

"And suitable." He studied it with more care. The
silver shone dully, set off with the deep curls and lines
she'd etched. It could, he realized, be put in an antique
shop and pass for an heirloom. "I didn't know you
did this sort of thing."

"Now and again. The boutique carries a few of
them."

"Doesn't fit in the same category as bangles and
beads," he mused.

"Doesn't it?" Her chin tilted. "I thought about
making you a big gold collar with rhinestones just to
annoy you."

"It would have."

"Maybe next year then. Or perhaps I'll make one for Bruno." She glanced around. "Where'd he go?"

"He's probably behind the tree gnawing on presents. During his brief stay in the garage, he ate a pair of golf shoes."

"We'll put a stop to that," Pandora declared, and went to find him.

"You know, Pandora, I'd no idea you could draw like this." Michael settled against the back of the chair to study the sketch again. "Why aren't you painting?"

"Why aren't you writing the Great American Novel?"

"Because I enjoy what I'm doing."

"Exactly." Finding no sign of the puppy around the tree, Pandora began to search under the furniture. "Though certainly a number of painters have toyed with jewelry design successfully enough—Dali for one—I feel...Michael!"

He set his untouched champagne back down and hurried over to where she knelt by a divan. "What is it?" he demanded, then saw for himself. Eyes closed, breathing fast and heavy, the puppy lay half under the divan. Even as Pandora reached for him, Bruno whimpered and struggled to stand.

"Oh, Michael, he's sick. We should get him to a vet."

"It'll be midnight before we get to town. We won't find a vet at midnight on Christmas Eve." Gently Michael laid a hand on Bruno's belly and heard him moan. "Maybe I can get someone on the phone."

"Do you think it's something he ate?"

"Sweeney's been supervising his feeding like a new mother." On cue Bruno struggled and shuddered and

relieved himself of what offended his stomach. Exhausted from the effort, he lay back and dozed fitfully.

"Something he drank," Michael murmured.

Pampering and soothing, Pandora stroked the dog. "That little bit of champagne shouldn't have made him ill." Because the dog was already resting easier, she relaxed a bit. "Charles isn't going to be pleased Bruno cast up his accounts on the carpet. Maybe I should—" She broke off as Michael grabbed her arm.

"How much champagne did you drink?"

"Only a sip. Why—" She broke off again to stare. "The champagne. You think something's wrong with it?"

"I think I'm an idiot for not suspecting an anonymous present." He grabbed her by the chin. "Only a sip. You're sure? How do you feel?"

Her skin had gone cold, but she answered calmly enough. "I'm fine. Look at my glass, it's still full." She turned her head to look at it herself. "You—you think it was poisoned?"

"We'll find out."

Logic seeped through, making her shake her head. "But, Michael, the wine was corked. How could it have been tampered with?"

"The first season on *Logan* I used a device like this." He thought back, remembering how he'd tested the theory by adding food coloring to a bottle of Dom Perignon. "The killer poisoned champagne by shooting cyanide through the cork with a hypodermic."

"Fiction," Pandora claimed, and fought a shiver. "That's just fiction."

"Until we find out differently, we're going to treat

it as fact. The rest of the bottle's going into New York to Sanfield Labs for testing.''

Shaky, Pandora swallowed. ''For testing,'' she said on an unsteady breath. ''All right, I suppose we'll both be easier when we're sure. Do you know someone who works there?''

''We own Sanfield.'' He looked down at the sleeping puppy. ''Or we will own it in a matter of months. That's just one of the reasons someone might've sent us some doctored champagne.''

''Michael, if it was poisoned…'' She tried to imagine it and found it nearly impossible. ''If it was poisoned,'' she repeated, ''this wouldn't just be a game anymore.''

He thought of what might have happened if they hadn't been distracted from the wine. ''No, it wouldn't be a game.''

''It doesn't make any sense.'' Uneasy and fighting to calm herself, Pandora rose. ''Vandalism I can see, petty annoyances I can understand, but I just can't attribute something like this to one of the family. We're probably overreacting. Bruno's had too much excitement. He could very well have picked up something in the pound.''

''I had him sent to the vet for his shots before he was delivered here yesterday.'' Michael's voice was calm, but his eyes were hot. ''He was healthy, Pandora, until he lapped up some spilled champagne.''

One look at him told her rationalizing was useless. ''All right. The wine should be tested in any case so we can stop speculating. We can't do anything about it until day after tomorrow. In the meantime, I don't want to dwell on it.''

"Pulling the blinds down, Pandora?"

"No." She picked up Bruno, who whimpered and burrowed into her breast. "But until it's proven, I don't want to consider that a member of my family tried to kill me. I'll fix him something warm to drink, then I'm going to take him upstairs. I'll keep an eye on him tonight."

"All right." Fighting a combination of frustration and fury, Michael stood by the fire.

Long after midnight when he couldn't sleep, couldn't work, Michael looked in on her. She'd left a light burning low across the room so that the white spreads and covers took on a rosy hue. Outside snow was falling again in big, festive flakes. Michael could see her, curled in the wide bed, the blankets up to her chin. The fire was nearly out. On the rug in front of it, the puppy snored. She'd put a mohair throw over him and had set a shallow bowl filled with what looked like tea nearby. Michael crouched beside the dog.

"Poor fella," he murmured. As he stroked, Bruno stirred, whimpered, then settled again.

"I think he's better."

Glancing over, Michael saw the light reflected in Pandora's eyes. Her hair was tousled, her skin pale and soft. Her shoulders, gently sloped, rose just above the covers pooled around her. She looked beautiful, desirable, arousing. He told himself he was mad. Pandora didn't fit into his carefully detailed notion of beauty. Michael looked back at the dog.

"Just needs to sleep it off. You could use another log on this fire." Needing to keep busy, Michael dug in the woodbox, then added a log to the coals.

"Thanks. Can't sleep?"

"No."

"Me, either." They sat in silence a moment, Pandora in the big bed, Michael on the hearth rug. The fire crackled greedily at the fresh log and flickered light and shadow. At length, she drew her knees up to her chest. "Michael, I'm frightened."

It wasn't an easy admission. He knew it cost her to tell him. He stirred at the fire a moment, then spoke lightly as he replaced the screen. "We can leave. We can drive into New York tomorrow and stay there. Forget this whole business and enjoy the holidays."

She didn't speak for a minute, but she watched him carefully. His face was turned away toward the fire so that she had to judge his feelings by the way he held himself. "Is that what you want to do?"

He thought of Jolley, then he thought of Pandora. Every muscle in his body tightened. "Sure." He tossed it off like a shrug. "I've got to think about myself." He said it as if to remind himself it had once been true.

"For someone who earns his living by making up stories, you're a lousy liar." She waited until he turned to face her. "You don't want to go back. What you want is to gather all our relatives together and beat them up."

"Can you see me pounding Aunt Patience?"

"With a few exceptions," Pandora temporized. "But the last thing you want is to give up."

"All right, that's me." He rose and, hands in pockets, paced back and forth in front of the fire. He could smell the woodsmoke mixed with some light scent from one of the bottles on Pandora's dresser. "What

about you? You didn't want to hassle with this whole business from the beginning. I talked you into it. I feel responsible.''

For the first time in hours she felt her humor return. ''I hate to dent your ego, Michael, but you didn't talk me into anything. No one does. And I'm completely responsible for myself. I don't want to quit,'' she added before he could speak. ''I said I didn't want the money, and that was true. I also said I didn't need it, and that's not precisely true. Over and above that, there's pride. I'm frightened, yes, but I don't want to quit. Oh, stop pacing around and come sit down.'' The order was cross and impatient, nearly making him smile. He came over and sat on the bed.

''Better?''

She gave him a long, steady look that had the hint of a smile fading. ''Yes. Michael, I've been lying here for hours thinking this thing through. I've realized a few things. You called me a snob once, and perhaps you were right in a way. I've never thought much about money. Never allowed myself to. When Uncle Jolley cut everyone out, I thought of it as a cross between a joke and a slap on the wrist. I figured they'd grumble and complain certainly, but that was all.'' She lifted her hand palm up. ''It was only money, and every one of them has their own.''

''Ever heard of greed or the lust for power?''

''That's just it, I didn't think. How much do I know about any of those people? They bore or annoy me from time to time, but I've never thought about them as individuals.'' Now she ran the hand through her hair so that the blankets fell to her waist. ''Ginger must be about the same age as I am, and I can't think of two

things we have in common. I'd probably pass Biff's wife on the street without recognizing her.''

"I have a hard time remembering her name,'' Michael put in, and earned a sigh from Pandora.

"That's my point. We don't really know them. The family, in a group, is a kind of parlor joke. Separately, who are they and what are they capable of? I've just begun to consider it. It's not a joke, Michael.''

"No, it's not.''

"I want to fight back, but I don't know how.''

"The surest way is by staying. And maybe,'' he added, and took her hand. It was cool and soft. "Add a little psychological warfare.''

"Such as?''

"What if we sent each one of our relatives a nice bottle of champagne?''

Her smile came slowly. "A magnum.''

"Naturally. It'd be interesting to see what sort of reaction we get.''

"It would be a nasty gesture, wouldn't it?''

"Uh-hmm.''

"Maybe I haven't given your creative brain enough credit.'' She fell silent as he wound her hair around his finger. "I suppose we should get some sleep.''

"I suppose.'' But his fingers skimmed down her shoulders.

"I'm not very tired.''

"We could play canasta.''

"We could.'' But she made no move to stop him when he nudged the thin straps of her chemise from her shoulders. "There's always cribbage.''

"That, too.''

"Or...'' It was her decision, they both understood

that. "We might finish playing out the hand we started downstairs earlier."

He lifted her hand and pressed his lips to the palm. "Always best to finish what you start before going on. As I recall, we were...here." He lowered his mouth to hers. Slowly, on a sigh, she wound her arms around his neck.

"That seems about right."

Holding fast, they sunk into the bed together.

Perhaps it was because they knew each other well. Perhaps it was because they'd already waited a lifetime, but each moved slowly. Desire, for the moment, was comfortable, easy to satisfy with a touch, a taste. Passion curled inside him then unwound with a sigh. There was inch after inch of her to explore with his fingertips, with his lips. He'd waited too long, wanted too long, to miss any part of what they could give to each other.

She was more generous than he'd imagined, less inhibited, more open. She didn't ask to be coaxed, she didn't pretend to need persuasion. She ran her hands over him with equal curiosity. Her mouth took from him and gave again. When his lips parted from hers, her eyes were on him, clouded with desire, dark with amusement of a shared joke. They were together, Michael thought as he buried his face in her hair. About to become lovers. The joke was on both of them.

Her hands were steady when she pulled his sweatshirt over his head, steady still as she ran them over his chest. Her pulse wasn't. She'd avoided this, refused this. Now she was accepting it though she knew there would be consequences she couldn't anticipate.

The fire crackled steadily. The soft light glowed. Consequences were for more practical times.

Her skin slid over his with each movement. Each movement enticed. With his heartbeat beginning to hammer in his head, he journeyed lower. With open-mouthed kisses he learned her body in a way he'd only been able to imagine. Her scent was everywhere, subtle at the curve of her waist, stronger at the gentle underside of her breasts. He drew it in and let it swim in his head.

He felt the instant her lazy enjoyment darkened with power. When her breath caught on a moan, he took her deeper. They reached a point where he no longer knew what they did to each other, only that strength met need and need became desperation.

His skin was damp. She tasted the moistness of it and craved more. So this was passion. This was the trembling, churning hunger men and women longed for. She'd never wanted it. That's what she told herself as her body shuddered. Pleasure and pain mixed, needs and fears tangled. Her mind was as swamped with sensations as her flesh—heat and light, ecstasy and terror. The vulnerability overwhelmed her though her body arched taut and her hands clung. No one had ever brushed back her defenses so effortlessly and taken. Taken and taken.

Breathless and desperate, she dragged his mouth back to hers. They rolled over the bed, rough, racing. Neither had had enough. While she tugged and pulled at his jeans, Michael drove her higher. He'd wanted the madness, for himself and for her. Now he felt the wild strength pouring out of her. No thought here, no

logic. He rolled on top of her again, reveling in her frantic breathing.

She curled around him, legs and arms. When he plunged into her, they watched the astonishment on each other's faces. Not like this—it had never been like this. They'd come home. But home, each discovered, wasn't always a peaceful place.

There was silence, stunned, awkward silence. They lay tangled in the covers as the log Michael had set to fire broke apart and showered sparks against the screen. They knew each other well, too well to speak of what had happened just yet. So they lay in silence as their skin cooled and their pulses leveled. Michael shifted to pull the spread up over them both.

"Merry Christmas," he murmured.

With a sound that was both sigh and laugh, Pandora settled beside him.

Chapter 8

They left the Folley in the hard morning light the day after Christmas. Sun glared off snow, melting it at the edges and forming icicles down branches and eaves. It was a postcard with biting wind.

After a short tussle they'd agreed that Pandora would drive into the city and Michael would drive back. He pushed his seat back to the limit and managed to stretch out his legs. She maneuvered carefully down the slushy mountain road that led from the Folley. They didn't speak until she'd reached clear highway.

''What if they don't let us in?''

''Why shouldn't they?'' Preferring driving to sitting, Michael shifted in his seat. For the first time he was impatient with the miles of road between the Folley and New York.

''Isn't that like counting your chickens?'' Pandora

turned the heat down a notch and loosened the buttons of her coat. "We don't own the place yet."

"Just a technicality."

"Always cocky."

"You always look at the negative angles."

"Someone has to."

"Look..." He started to toss back something critical, then noticed how tightly she gripped the wheel. All nerves, he mused. Though the scenery was a print by Currier and Ives, it wasn't entirely possible to pretend they were off on a holiday jaunt. He was running on nerves himself, and they didn't all have to do with doctored champagne. How would he have guessed he'd wake up beside her in the cool light of dawn and feel so involved? So responsible. So hungry.

He took a deep breath and watched the scenery for another moment. "Look," he began again in a lighter tone. "We may not own the lab or anything else at the moment, but we're still Jolley's family. Why should a lab technician refuse to do a little analysis?"

"I suppose we'll find out when we get there." She drove another ten miles in silence. "Michael, what difference is an analysis going to make?"

"I have this odd sort of curiosity. I like to know if someone's tried to poison me."

"So we'll know if, and we'll know why. We still won't know who."

"That's the next step." He glanced over. "We can invite them all to Folley for New Year's and take turns grilling them."

"Now you're making fun of me."

"No, actually, I'd thought of it. I just figure the time's not quite right." He waited a few minutes. In

thin leather gloves, her fingers curled and uncurled on the wheel. "Pandora, why don't you tell me what's really bothering you?"

"Nothing is." Everything was. She hadn't been able to think straight for twenty-four hours.

"Nothing?"

"Nothing other than wondering if someone wants to kill me." She tossed it off arrogantly. "Isn't that enough?"

He heard the edge under the sarcasm. "Is that why you hid in your room all day yesterday."

"I wasn't hiding." She had enough pride to sound brittle. "I was tending to Bruno. And I was tired."

"You hardly ate any of that enormous goose Sweeney slaved over."

"I'm not terribly fond of goose."

"I've had Christmas dinner with you before," he corrected. "You eat like a horse."

"How gallant of you to point it out." For no particular reason, she switched lanes, pumped the gas and passed another car. "Let's just say I wasn't in the mood."

"How did you manage to talk yourself into disliking what happened between us so quickly?" It hurt. He felt the hurt, but it didn't mean he had to let it show. His voice, as hers had been, was cool and hard.

"I haven't. That's absurd." Dislike? She hadn't been able to think of anything else, feel anything else. It scared her to death. "We slept together." She managed to toss it off with a shrug. "I suppose we both knew we would sooner or later."

He'd told himself precisely the same thing. He'd lost count of the number of times. He'd yet to figure

out when he'd stopped believing. For himself. "And that's it?"

The question was deadly calm, but she was too preoccupied with her own nerves to notice. "What else?" She had to stop dwelling on a moment of impulse. Didn't she? She couldn't go on letting her common sense be overrun by an attraction that would lead nowhere. Could she? "Michael, there's no use blowing what happened out of proportion."

"Just what is that proportion?"

The car felt stuffy and close. Pandora switched off the heat and concentrated on the road. "We're two adults," she began, but had to swallow twice.

"And?"

"Dammit, Michael, I don't have to spell it out."

"Yes, you do."

"We're two adults," she said again, but with temper replacing nerves. "We have normal adult needs. We slept together and satisfied them."

"How practical."

"I am practical." Abruptly, and very badly, she wanted to weep. "Much too practical to weave fantasies about a man who likes his women in six packs. Too practical," she went on, voice rising, "to picture myself emotionally involved with a man I spent one night with. And too practical to romanticize what was no more than an exchange of normal and basic lust."

"Pull over."

"I will not."

"Pull over to the shoulder, Pandora, or I'll do it for you."

She gritted her teeth and debated calling his bluff. There was just enough traffic on the road to force her

hand. With only a slight squeal of tires, Pandora pulled off to the side of the road. Michael turned off the key then grabbed her by the lapels and pulled her half into his seat. Before she could struggle away, he closed his mouth over hers.

Heat, anger, passion. They seemed to twist together into one emotion. He held her there as cars whizzed by, shaking the windows. She infuriated him, she aroused him, she hurt him. In Michael's opinion, it was too much for one man to take from one woman. As abruptly as he'd grabbed her, he released her.

"Make something practical out of that," he challenged.

Breathless, Pandora struggled back into her own seat. In a furious gesture, she turned the key, gunning the motor. "Idiot."

"Yeah." He sat back as she pulled back onto the highway. "We finally agree on something."

It was a long ride into the city. Longer still when you sat in a car in tense silence. Once they entered Manhattan, Pandora was forced to follow Michael's directions to the lab.

"How do you know where it is?" she demanded after they left the car in a parking garage. The sidewalk was mobbed with people hurrying to exchange what had been brightly boxed and wrapped the day before. As they walked, Pandora held her coat closed against the wind.

"I looked the address up in Jolley's files yesterday." Michael walked the half block hatless, his coat flapping open, clutching the box with the champagne under one arm. He wasn't immune to the cold but

found it a relief after the hot tension of the drive. With a brisk gesture to Pandora, he pushed through revolving doors and entered the lobby of a steel-and-glass building. "He owned the whole place."

Pandora looked across the marble floor. It sloped upward and widened into a crowded, bustling area with men and women carrying briefcases. "This whole place?"

"All seventy-two floors."

It hit her again just how complicated the estate was. How many companies operated in the building? How many people worked there? How could she possibly crowd her life with this kind of responsibility? If she could get her hands on Uncle Jolley—Pandora broke off, almost amused. How he must be enjoying this, she thought.

"What am I supposed to do with seventy-two floors in midtown?"

"There are plenty of people to do it for you." Michael gave their names to the guard at the elevators. With no delay, they were riding to the fortieth floor.

"So there are people to do it for us. Who keeps track of them?"

"Accountants, lawyers, managers. It's a matter of hiring people to look after people you hire."

"That certainly clears that up."

"If you're worried, think about Jolley. Having a fortune didn't seem to keep him from enjoying himself. For the most part, he looked at the whole business as a kind of hobby."

Pandora watched the numbers above the door. "A hobby."

"Everyone should have a hobby."

"Tennis is a hobby," she muttered.

"The trick is to keep the ball moving. Jolley tossed it in our court, Pandora."

She folded her arms. "I'm not ready to be grateful for that."

"Look at it this way then." He put a hand on her shoulder and squeezed lightly. "You don't have to know how to build a car to own one. You just have to drive steady and follow the signs. If Jolley didn't think we could follow the signs, he wouldn't have given us the keys."

It helped to look at it that way. Still it was odd to consider she was riding on an elevator she would own when the six months were up. "Do we know whom to go to?" Pandora glanced at the box Michael held, which contained the bottle of champagne.

"A man named Silas Lockworth seems to be in charge."

"You did your homework."

"Let's hope it pays off."

When the elevator stopped, they walked into the reception area for Sanfield Laboratories. The carpet was pale rose, the walls lacquered in cream. Two huge split-leaf philodendrons flanked the wide glass doors that slid open at their approach. A woman behind a gleaming desk folded her hands and smiled.

"Good morning. May I help you?"

Michael glanced at the computer terminal resting on an extension of her desk. Top of the line. "We'd like to see Mr. Lockworth."

"Mr. Lockworth's in a meeting. If I could have your names, perhaps his assistant can help you."

"I'm Michael Donahue. This is Pandora McVie."

"McVie?"

Pandora saw the receptionist's eyebrows raise. "Yes, Maximillian McVie was our uncle."

Already polite and efficient, the receptionist became gracious. "I'm sure Mr. Lockworth would have greeted you himself if we'd known you were coming. Please have a seat. I'll ring through."

It took under five minutes.

The man who strode out into reception didn't look like Pandora's conception of a technician or scientist. He was six-three, lean as a gymnast with blond hair brushed back from a tanned, lantern-jawed face. He looked, Pandora thought, more like a man who'd be at home on the range than in a lab with test tubes.

"Ms. McVie." He walked with an easy rolling gait, hand outstretched. "Mr. Donahue. I'm Silas Lockworth. Your uncle was a good friend."

"Thank you." Michael accepted the handshake. "I apologize for dropping in unannounced."

"No need for that." Lockworth's smile seemed to mean it. "We never knew when Jolley was going to drop in on us. Let's go back to my office."

He led them down the corridor. Lockworth's office was the next surprise. It was plush enough, with curvy chairs and clever lithographs, to make you think of a corporate executive. The desk was piled high with enough files and papers to make you think of a harried clerk. It carried the scent from the dozens of leather-bound books on a floor-to-ceiling shelf. Built into one wall was a round aquarium teeming with exotic fish.

"Would you like coffee? I can guarantee it's hot and strong."

"No." Pandora was already twisting her gloves in

her hands. "Thank you. We don't want to take too much of your time."

"It's my pleasure," Lockworth assured her. "Jolley certainly spoke often of both of you," Lockworth went on as he gestured to chairs. "There was never a doubt you were his favorites."

"And he was ours," Pandora returned.

"Still you didn't come to pass the time." Lockworth leaned back on his desk. "What can I do for you?"

"We have something we'd like analyzed," Michael began. "Quickly and quietly."

"I see." Silas stopped there, brow raised. Lockworth was a man who picked up impressions of people right away. In Pandora he saw nerves under a sheen of politeness. In Michael he saw violence, not so much buried as thinly coated. He thought he detected a bond between them though they hadn't so much as looked at each other since entering the room.

Lockworth could have refused. His staff was slimmed down during the holidays, and work was backlogged. He was under no obligation to either of them yet. But he never forgot his obligation to Jolley McVie. "We'll try to accommodate you."

In silence, Michael opened the box and drew out the bottle of champagne. "We need a report on the contents of this bottle. A confidential report. Today."

Lockworth took it and examined the label. His lips curved slightly. "Seventy-two. A good year. Were you thinking of starting a vineyard?"

"We need to know what's in there other than champagne."

Rather than showing surprise, Lockworth leaned

back on the desk again. "You've reason to think there is?"

Michael met the look. "We wouldn't be here otherwise."

Lockworth only inclined his head. "All right. I'll run it through the lab myself."

With a quick scowl for Michael's manners, Pandora rose and offered her hand. "We appreciate the trouble, Mr. Lockworth. I'm sure you have a great many other things to do, but the results are important to Michael and me."

"No problem." He decided he'd find out why it was important after he'd analyzed the wine. "There's a coffee shop for the staff. I'll show you where it is. You can wait for me there."

"There was absolutely no reason to be rude." Pandora settled herself at a table and looked at a surprisingly varied menu.

"I wasn't rude."

"Of course you were. Mr. Lockworth was going out of his way to be friendly, and you had a chip on your shoulder. I think I'm going to have the shrimp salad."

"I don't have a chip on my shoulder. I was being cautious. Or maybe you think we should spill everything to a total stranger."

Pandora folded her hands and smiled at the waitress. "I'd like the shrimp salad and coffee."

"Two coffees," Michael muttered. "And the turkey platter."

"I've no intention of spilling, as you put it, everything to a total stranger." Pandora picked up her nap-

kin. "However, if we weren't going to trust Lock-worth, we'd have been better off to buy a chemistry set and try to handle it ourselves."

"Drink your coffee," Michael muttered, and picked up his own the moment the waitress served it.

Pandora frowned as she added cream. "How long do you think it'll take?"

"I don't know. I'm not a scientist."

"He didn't look like one, either, did he?"

"Bronc rider." Michael sipped his black coffee and found it as strong as Lockworth had promised.

"What?"

"Looks like a bronc rider. I wonder if Carlson or any of the others have any interest in this building."

Pandora set her coffee down before she tasted it. "I hadn't thought of that."

"As I remember, Jolley turned over Tristar Corporation to Monroe about twenty-five years ago. I remember my parents talking about it."

"Tristar. Which one is that?"

"Plastics. I know he gave little pieces of the pie out here and there. He told me once he wanted to give all his relatives a chance before he crossed them off the list."

After a moment's thought, she shrugged and picked up her coffee again. "Well, if he did give a few shares of Sanfield to one of them, what difference does it make?"

"I don't know how much we should trust Lock-worth."

"You'd have felt better if he'd been bald and short with Coke-bottle glasses and a faint German accent."

"Maybe."

"See?" Pandora smiled. "You're just jealous because he has great shoulders." She fluttered her lashes. "Here's your turkey."

They ate slowly, drank more coffee, then passed more time with pie. After an hour and a half, both of them were restless and edgy. When Lockworth came in, Pandora forgot to be nervous about the results.

"Thank God, here he comes."

After maneuvering around chairs and employees on lunch break, Lockworth set a computer printout on the table and handed the box back to Michael. "I thought you'd want a copy." He took a seat and signaled for coffee. "Though it's technical."

Pandora frowned down at the long, chemical terms printed out on the paper. It meant little more than nothing to her, but she doubted trichloroethanol or any of the other multisyllabic words belonged in French champagne. "What does it mean?"

"I wondered that myself." Lockworth reached in his pocket and drew out a pack of cigarettes. Michael looked at it for a moment with longing. "I wondered why anyone would put rose dust in vintage champagne."

"Rose dust?" Michael repeated. "Pesticide. So it was poisoned."

"Technically, yes. Though there wasn't enough in the wine to do any more than make you miserably ill for a day or two. I take it neither one of you had any?"

"No." Pandora looked up from the report. "My puppy did," she explained. "When we opened the bottle, some spilled and he lapped it up. Before we'd gotten around to drinking it, he was ill."

"Luckily for you, though I find it curious that you'd

jumped to the conclusion that the champagne had been poisoned because a puppy was sick.''

"Luckily for us, we did.'' Michael folded the report and slipped it into his pocket.

"You'll have to pardon my cousin," Pandora said. "He has no manners. We appreciate you taking time out to do this for us, Mr. Lockworth. I'm afraid it isn't possible to fully explain ourselves at this point, but I can tell you that we had good reason to suspect the wine."

Lockworth nodded. As a scientist he knew how to theorize. "If you find you need a more comprehensive report, let me know. Jolley was an important person in my life. We'll call it a favor to him."

As he rose, Michael stood with him. "I'll apologize for myself this time." He held out a hand.

"I'd be a bit edgy myself if someone gave me pesticide disguised as Moët et Chandon. Let me know if I can do anything else."

"Well," Pandora began when they were alone. "What next?"

"A little trip to the liquor store. We've some presents to buy."

They sent, first-class, a bottle of the same to each of Jolley's erstwhile heirs. Michael signed the cards simply, "One good turn deserves another." After it was done and they walked outside in the frigid wind, Pandora huffed and pulled on her gloves.

"An expensive gesture."

"Look at it as an investment," Michael suggested.

It wasn't the money, she thought, but the sudden futility she felt. "What good will it do really?"

"Several bottles'll be wondered over, then appre-

ciated. But one,'' Michael said with relish. ''One makes a statement, even a threat.''

''An empty threat,'' Pandora returned. ''It's not as if we'll be there when everyone gets one to gauge reactions.''

''You're thinking like an amateur.''

Michael was halfway across the street when Pandora grabbed his arm. ''Just what does that mean?''

''When an amateur plays a practical joke, he thinks he has to be in on the kill.''

Ignoring the people who brushed by them, Pandora held her ground. ''Since when is pesticide poisoning a practical joke?''

''Revenge follows the same principle.''

''Oh, I see. And you're an expert.''

The light changed. Cars started for them, horns blaring. Gritting his teeth, Michael grabbed her arm and pulled her to the curb. ''Maybe I am. It's enough for me to know someone's going to look at the bottle and be very nervous. Someone's going to look at it and know we intend to give as good as we get. Your trouble is you don't like to let your emotions loose long enough to appreciate revenge.''

''Leave my emotions alone.''

''That's the plan,'' he said evenly, and started walking again.

In three strides she'd caught up with him. Her face was pink from the wind, the anger in her voice came out in thin wisps. ''You're not annoyed with Lockworth or about the champagne or over differing views on revenge. You're mad because I defined our relationship in practical terms.''

He stared at her as her phrasing worked on both his

temper and his humor. "Okay," he declared, turning to walk on. Patience straining, he turned back when Pandora grabbed his arm. "You want to hash this out right here?"

"I won't let you make me feel inadequate just because I broke things off before you had a chance to."

"Before I had a chance to?" He took her by the coat. With the added height from the heels on her boots, she looked straight into his eyes. Another time, another place, he might have considered her magnificent. "I barely had the chance to recover from what happened before you were shoving me out. I wanted you. Dammit, I still want you. God knows why."

"Well, I want you, too, and I don't like it, either."

"Looks like that puts us in the same fix, doesn't it?"

"So what're we going to do about it?"

He looked at her and saw the anger. But he looked closely enough to see confusion, as well. One of them had to make the first move. He decided it was going to be him. Taking her hand, he dragged her across the street.

"Where are we going?"

"The Plaza."

"The Plaza Hotel? Why?"

"We're going to get a room, put the chain on the door and make love for the next twenty-four hours. After that, we'll decide how we want to handle it."

There were times, Pandora decided, when it was best to go along for the ride. "We don't have any luggage."

"Yeah. My reputation's about to be shattered."

She made a sound that might have been a laugh.

When they walked into the elegant lobby, the heat warmed her skin and stirred up her nerves. It was all impulse, she told herself. She knew better than to make any important decision on impulse. He could change everything. That was something she hadn't wanted to admit but had known for years. When she started to draw away, his hand locked on her arm.

"Coward," he murmured. He couldn't have said anything more perfectly designed to make her march forward.

"Good afternoon." Michael smiled at the desk clerk. Pandora wondered briefly if the smile would have been so charming if the clerk had been a man. "Checking in."

"You have a reservation?"

"Donahue. Michael Donahue."

The clerk punched some buttons and stared at her computer screen. "I'm afraid I don't show anything under Donahue for the twenty-sixth."

"Katie," Michael said on a breath of impatience. He sent Pandora a long suffering look. "I should never have trusted her to handle this."

Catching the drift, Pandora patted his hand. "You're going to have to let her go, Michael. I know she's worked for your family for forty years, but when a person gets into their seventies..." She trailed off and let Michael take the ball.

"We'll decide when we get home." He turned back to the desk clerk. "Apparently there's been a mix-up between my secretary and the hotel. We'll only be in town overnight. Is anything available?"

The clerk went back to her buttons. Most people in her experience raised the roof when there was a mix-

up in reservations. Michael's quiet request touched her sympathies. "You understand there's a problem because of the holiday." She punched more buttons, wanting to help. "We do have a suite available."

"Fine." Michael took the registration form and filled it out. With the key in his hand, he sent the clerk another smile. "I appreciate the trouble." Noting the bellhop hovering at his elbow, he handed him a bill. "We'll handle it, thanks."

The clerk looked at the twenty in his palm and the lack of luggage. "Yes, sir!"

"He thinks we're having an illicit affair," Pandora murmured as they stepped onto the elevator.

"We are." Before the doors had closed again, Michael grabbed her to him and locked her in a kiss that lasted twelve floors. "We don't know each other," he told her as they stepped into the hallway. "We've just met. We don't have mutual childhood memories or share the same family." He put the key in the lock. "We don't give a damn what the other does for a living nor do we have any long-standing opinions about each other."

"Is that supposed to simplify things?"

Michael drew her inside. "Let's find out."

He didn't give her a chance to wonder, a chance to debate. The moment the door was shut behind them, he had her in his arms. He took questions away. He took choice away. For once, she wanted him to. In a fury of passions, of hungers, of cravings, they came together. Each fought to draw more, still more out of the other, to touch faster, to possess more quickly. They forgot what they knew, what they thought and reveled in what they felt.

Coats, still chill from the wind, were pushed to the floor. Sweaters and shirts followed. Hardly more than a foot inside the door, they slid to the carpet.

"Damn winter," Michael muttered as he fought with her boots.

Laughing, Pandora struggled with his, then moaned when he pressed his lips to her breast.

It was a race, part warring, part loving. Neither gave the other respite. When their clothes were shed, they sprinted ahead, hands reaching, lips arousing. There was none of the dreamy déjà vu they'd experienced the first time. This was new. The fingers tracing her skin had never been felt before. The lips, hot and searing, had never been tasted. Fresh, erotically fresh, their mouths met and clung.

Her heart had never beat so fast. She was sure of it. Her body had never ached and pulsed so desperately. She'd never wanted it to. Now she wanted more, everything. Him. She rolled so that she could press quick, hungry kisses over his face, his neck, his chest. Everywhere.

His mind was teeming with her, with every part of her that he could touch or taste or smell. She was wild in a way he'd never imagined. She was demanding in a way any man would desire. His body seemed to fascinate her, every curve, every angle. She exploited it until he was half mad, then he groped for her.

She'd never known a man could give so much. Racked with sensations, she arched under him. Hot and ready, she offered. But he was far from through. The taste of her thighs was subtle, luring him toward the heat. He found her, drove her and kept her helplessly trapped in passion. Helplessly. The sensation shivered

over her. She'd never known what it had meant to be truly vulnerable to another. He could have taken anything from her then, asked anything and she couldn't have refused. But he didn't ask, he gave.

She crested wave after wave. Between heights and depths she pinwheeled, delighting in the spin. On the rug with the afternoon light streaming through the windows, she was locked in blinding darkness without any wish to see. *Make me feel,* her mind seemed to shout. More. Again. Still.

And he was inside her, joined, melded. She found there was more. Impossibly more.

They stayed where they were, sprawled on scattered clothes. Gradually Pandora found her mind swimming back to reality. She could see the pastel walls, the sunlight. She could smell the body heat that was a mix of hers and his. She could feel Michael's hair brushing over her cheek, the beat of his heart, still fast, against her breast.

It happened so fast, she thought. Or had it taken hours? All she was certain of was that she'd never experienced anything like it. Never permitted herself to, she amended. Strange things could happen to a woman who lifted the lid from her passion. Other things could sneak in before the top closed again. Things like affection, understanding. Even love.

She caught herself stroking Michael's hair and let her hand fall to the carpet. She couldn't let love in, not even briefly. Love took as well as gave. That she'd always known. And it didn't always give and take in equal shares. Michael wasn't a man a woman could

love practically, and certainly not wisely. That she understood. He wouldn't follow the rules.

She'd be his lover, but she wouldn't love him. Though there would be no pretending they could live with each other for the next three months platonically, she wouldn't risk her heart. For an instant Pandora thought she felt it break, just a little. Foolishness, she told herself. Her heart was strong and unimpaired. What she and Michael had together was a very basic, very uncomplicated arrangement. Arrangement, she thought, sounded so much more practical than romance.

But her sigh was quiet, and a little wistful.

"Figure it all out?" He shifted a little as he spoke, just enough so that he could brush his lips down her throat.

"What do you mean?"

"Have you figured out the guidelines for our relationship?" Lifting his head, he looked down at her. He wasn't smiling, but Pandora thought he was amused.

"I don't know what you're talking about."

"I can almost hear the wheels turning. Pandora, I can see just what's going on in your head."

Annoyed that he probably could, she lifted a brow. "I thought we'd just met."

"I'm psychic. You're thinking...." He trailed off to nibble at her lips. "That there should be a way to keep our...relationship on a practical level. You're wondering how you'll keep an emotional distance when we're sleeping together. You've decided that there'll be absolutely no romantic overtones to any arrangement between us."

"All right." He made her feel foolish. Then he ran

a hand over her hip and made her tremble. "Since you're so smart, you'll see that I've only been using common sense."

"I like it better when your skin gets hot, and you haven't any sense at all. But—" he kissed her before she could answer "—we can't stay in bed all the time. I don't believe in practical affairs, Pandora. I don't believe in emotional distance between lovers."

"You've had a great deal of experience there."

"That's right." He sat up, drawing her with him. "And I'll tell you this. You can wall up your emotions all you want. You can call whatever we have here by any practical term you can dream up. You can turn up your nose at candlelight dinners and quiet music. It's not going to make any difference." He gathered her hair in his hand and pulled her head back. "I'm going to get to you, cousin. I'm going to get to you until you can't think of anything, anyone but me. If you wake up in the middle of the night and I'm not there, you'll wish I were. And when I touch you, any time I touch you, you're going to want me."

She had to fight the shudder. She knew, as well as she'd ever known anything, that he was right. And she knew, perhaps they both did, that she'd fight it right down to the end. "You're arrogant, egocentric and simpleminded."

"True enough. And you're stubborn, willful and perverse. The only thing we can be sure of at this point is that one of us is going to win."

Sitting on the pile of discarded clothes, they studied each other. "Another game?" Pandora murmured.

"Maybe. Maybe it's the only game." With that, he stood and lifted her into his arms.

''Michael, I don't need to be carried.''

''Yes, you do.''

He walked across the suite toward the bedroom. Pandora started to struggle, then subsided. Maybe just this once, she decided, and relaxed in his arms.

Chapter 9

January was a month of freezing wind, pelting snow and gray skies. Each day was as bitterly cold as the last, with tomorrow waiting frigidly in the wings. It was a month of frozen pipes, burst pipes, overworked furnaces and stalled engines. Pandora loved it. The frost built up on the windows of her shop, and the inside temperature always remained cool even with the heaters turned up. She worked until her fingers were numb and enjoyed every moment.

Throughout the month, the road to the Folley was often inaccessible. Pandora didn't mind not being able to get out. It meant no one could get in. The pantry and freezer were stocked, and there was over a cord of wood stacked beside the kitchen door. The way she looked at it, they had everything they needed. The days were short and productive, the nights long and relaxing. Since the incident of the champagne, it had been a quiet, uneventful winter.

Uneventful, Pandora mused, wasn't precisely the right term. With quick, careful strokes, she filed the edges of a thick copper bracelet. It certainly wasn't as though nothing had happened. There'd been no trouble from outside sources, but... Trouble, as she'd always known, was definitely one of Michael Donahue's greatest talents.

Just what was he trying to pull by leaving a bunch of violets on her pillow? She was certain a magic wand would have been needed to produce the little purple flowers in January. When she'd questioned him about them, he'd simply smiled and told her violets didn't have thorns. What kind of an answer was that? Pandora wondered, and examined the clasp of the bracelet through a magnifying glass. She was satisfied with the way she'd designed it to blend with the design.

Then, there'd been the time she'd come out of the bath to find the bedroom lit with a dozen candles. When she'd asked if there'd been a power failure, Michael had just laughed and pulled her into bed.

He did things like reaching for her hand at dinner and whispering in her ear just before dawn. Once he'd joined her in the shower uninvited and silenced her protests by washing every inch of her body himself. She'd been right. Michael Donahue didn't follow the rules. He'd been right. He was getting to her.

Pandora removed the bracelet from the vise, then absently began to polish it. She'd made a half a dozen others in the last two weeks. Big chunky bracelets, some had gaudy stones, some had ornate engraving. They suited her mood—daring, opinionated and a bit silly. She'd learned to trust her instincts, and her in-

stincts told her they'd sell faster than she could possibly make them—and be copied just as quickly.

She didn't mind the imitations. After all, there was only one of each type that was truly a Pandora McVie. Copies would be recognized as copies because they lacked that something special, that individuality of the genuine.

Pleased, she turned the bracelet over in her hand. No one would mistake any of her work for an imitation. She might often use glass instead of precious or semiprecious stones because glass expressed her mood at the time. But each piece she created carried her mark, her opinion and her honesty. She never gave a thought to the price of a piece when she crafted it or its market value. She created what she needed to create first, then after it was done, her practical side calculated the profit margin. Her art varied from piece to piece, but it never lied.

Looking down at the bracelet, Pandora sighed. No, her art never lied, but did she? Could she be certain her emotions were as genuine as the jewelry she made? A feeling could be imitated. An emotion could be fraudulent. How many times in the past few weeks had she pretended? Not pretended to feel, Pandora thought, but pretended not to feel. She was a woman who'd always prided herself on her honesty. Truth and independence went hand in hand with Pandora's set of values. But she'd lied—over and over again—to herself, the worst form of deception.

It was time to stop, Pandora told herself. Time to face the truth of her feelings if only in the privacy of her own heart and mind.

How long had she been in love with Michael? She

had to stand and move around the shop as the question formed in her mind. Weeks? Months? Years? It wasn't something she could answer because she would never be sure. But she was certain of the emotion. She loved. Pandora understood it because she loved only a few people, and when she did, she loved boundlessly. Perhaps that was the biggest problem. Wasn't it a sort of suicide to love Michael boundlessly?

Better to face it, she told herself. No problem resolved itself without being faced first and examined second. However much a fool it made her, she loved Michael. Pandora rubbed at the steam on the windows and looked out at the snow. Strange, she'd really believed once she accepted it she'd feel better. She didn't.

What options did she have? She could tell him. And have him gloat, Pandora thought with a scowl. He would, too, before he trotted off to his next conquest. *She* certainly wasn't fool enough to think he'd be interested in a long-term relationship. Of course, she wasn't interested in one either, Pandora told herself as she began to noisily pack her tools.

Another option was to cut and run. What the relatives hadn't been able to accomplish with their malice and mischief, her own heart would succeed in doing. She could get in the car, drive to the airport and fly to anywhere. Escape was the honest word. Then, she'd not only be a coward, she'd be a traitor. No, she wouldn't let Uncle Jolley down; she wouldn't run. That left her, as Pandora saw it, with one option.

She'd go on as she was. She'd stay with Michael, sleep with Michael, share with Michael—share with him everything but what was in her heart. She'd take

the two months they had left together and prepare herself to walk away with no regrets.

He'd gotten to her, Pandora admitted. Gotten to her in places no other man had touched. She loved him for it. She hated him for it. With her mood as turbulent as her thoughts, she locked the shop and stomped across the lawn.

"Here she comes now." With a new plan ready to spring, Sweeney turned away from the kitchen window and signaled to Charles.

"It's never going to work."

"Of course it is. We're going to push those children together for their own good. Any two people who spat as much as they do should be married."

"We're interfering where it's not our place."

"What malarkey!" Sweeney took her seat at the kitchen table. "Whose place is it to interfere if not ours, I'd like to know? Who'll be knocking around this big empty house if they go back to the city if not us? Now pick up that cloth and fan me. Stoop over a bit and look feeble."

"I am feeble," Charles muttered, but picked up the cloth.

When Pandora walked into the kitchen she saw Sweeney sprawled back in a chair, eyes closed, with Charles standing over her waving a dishcloth at her face.

"God, what's wrong? Charles, did she faint?" Before he could answer, Pandora had dashed across the room. "Call Michael," she ordered. "Call Michael quickly." She brushed Charles away and crouched. "Sweeney, it's Pandora. Are you in pain?"

Barely suppressing a sigh of satisfaction, Sweeney

let her eyes flutter open and hoped she looked pale. "Oh, missy, don't you worry now. Just one of my spells is all. Now and then my heart starts to flutter so that I feel it's coming right out of my head."

"I'm going to call the doctor." Pandora had taken only one step when her hand was caught in a surprisingly strong grip.

"No need for that." Sweeney made her voice thin and weary. "Saw him just a few months past and he told me I'd have to expect one of these now and again."

"I don't believe that," Pandora said fiercely. "You're just plain working too hard, and it's going to stop."

A little trickle of guilt worked its way in as Sweeney saw the concern. "Now, now, don't fret."

"What is it?" Michael swung through the kitchen door. "Sweeney?" He knelt down beside her and took her other hand.

"Now look at all this commotion." Mentally she leaped up and kicked her heels. "It's nothing but one of my little spells. The doctor said I'd have to watch for them. Just a nuisance, that's all." She looked hard at Charles when he came in. Eventually she looked hard enough so that he remembered his cue.

"And you know what he said."

"Now, Charles—"

"You're to have two or three days of bed rest."

Pleased that he'd remembered his lines, Sweeney pretended to huff. "Pack of nonsense. I'll be right as rain in a few minutes. I've dinner to cook."

"You won't be cooking anything." In a way

Sweeney considered properly masterful, Michael picked her up. "Into bed with you."

"Just who'll take care of things?" Sweeney demanded. "I'll not have Charles spreading his germs around my kitchen."

Michael was nearly out of the room with Sweeney before Charles remembered the next step. He coughed into his hand, looked apologetic and coughed again.

"Listen to that!" Pleased, Sweeney let her head rest against Michael's shoulder. "I won't go to bed and let him infect my kitchen."

"How long have you had that cough?" Pandora demanded. When Charles began to mutter, she stood up. "That's enough. Both of you into bed. Michael and I will take care of everything." Taking Charles's arm, she began to lead him into the servant's wing. "Into bed and no nonsense. I'll make both of you some tea. Michael, see that Charles gets settled, I'll look after Sweeney."

Within a half hour, Sweeney had them both where she wanted them. Together.

"Well, they're all settled in and there's no fever." Satisfied, Pandora poured herself a cup of tea. "I suppose all they need is a few days' rest and some pampering. Tea?"

He made a face at the idea and switched on the coffee. "Since the days of house calls are over, I'd think they'd be better off here in bed than being dragged into town. We can take turns keeping an eye on them."

"Mmm-hmm." Pandora opened the refrigerator and studied. "What about meals? Can you cook?"

"Sure." Michael rattled cups in the cupboard.

"Badly, but I can cook. Meat loaf's my specialty." When this was met with no enthusiasm, he turned his head. "Do you?"

"Cook?" Pandora lifted a plastic lid hopefully. "I can broil a steak and scramble eggs. Anything else is chancy."

"Life's nothing without a risk." Michael joined her in her rummage through the refrigerator. "Here's almost half an apple cobbler."

"That's hardly a meal."

"It'll do for me." He took it out and went for a spoon. Pandora watched as he sat down at the table and dug in. "Want some?"

She started to refuse on principle, then decided not to cut off her nose. Going to the cupboard, she found a bowl. "What about the bedridden?" she asked as she scooped out cobbler.

"Soup," Michael said between bites. "Nothing better than hot soup. Though I'd let them rest awhile first."

With a nod of agreement, she sat across from him. "Michael…" She trailed off as she played with her cobbler. The steam from her tea rose up between them. She'd been thinking about how to broach the subject for days. It seemed the time had come. "I've been thinking. In two months, the will should be final. When Fitzhugh wrote us last week, he said Uncle Carlson's lawyers were advising him to drop the probate."

"So?"

"The house, along with everything else, will be half yours, half mine."

"That's right."

She took a bite of cobbler, then set down her spoon. "What're you smiling at?"

"You're nice to look at. I find it relaxing to sit here alone in the kitchen, in the quiet, and look at you."

It was that sort of thing, just that sort of thing, that left her light-headed and foolish. She stared at him a moment, then dropped her gaze to her bowl. "I wish you wouldn't say things like that."

"No, you don't. So you've been thinking," he prompted.

"Yes." She gave herself a moment, carefully spooning out another bite of cobbler. "We'll have the house between us, but we won't be living here together any longer. Sweeney and Charles will be here alone. I've worried about that for a while. Now, after this, I'm more concerned than ever. They can't stay here alone."

"No, I think you're right. Ideas?"

"I mentioned before that I was considering moving here on a semipermanent basis." She found she had no appetite after all and switched back to her tea. "I think I'm going to make it permanent all around."

He heard a trace of nervousness in her voice. "Because of Charles and Sweeney?"

"Only partly." She drank more tea, set the cup down and toyed with her cobbler again. She wasn't accustomed to discussing her decisions with anyone. Though she found it difficult, Pandora had already resolved that she had an obligation to do so. More, she'd realized she needed to talk to him, to be, as she couldn't be on other levels, honest. "I always felt the Folley was home, but I didn't realize just how much

of a home. I need it, for myself. You see, I never had one.'' She lifted her gaze and met his. ''Only here.''

To say her words surprised him was to say too little. All his life he'd seen her as the pampered pet, the golden girl with every advantage. ''But your parents—''

''Are wonderful,'' Pandora said quickly. ''I adore them. There's nothing about them I'd change. But...'' How could she explain? How could she not? ''We never had a kitchen like this—a place you could come back to day after day and know it'd be the same. Even if you changed the wallpaper and the paint, it would be the same. It sounds silly.'' She shifted restlessly. ''You wouldn't understand.''

''Maybe I would.'' He caught her hand before she could rise. ''Maybe I'd like to.''

''I want a home,'' she said simply. ''The Folley's been that to me. I want to stay here after the term's up.''

He kept her hand in his, palm to palm. ''Why are you telling me this, Pandora?''

Reasons. Too many reasons. She chose the only one she could give him safely. ''In two months, the house belongs to you as much as to me. According to the terms of the will—''

He swore and released her hand. Rising, he stuck his hands in his back pockets and strode to the window. He'd thought for a moment, just for a moment, she'd been ready to give him more. By God, he'd waited long enough for only a few drops more. There'd been something in her voice, something soft and giving. Perhaps he'd just imagined it because he'd

wanted to hear it. Terms of the will, he thought. It was
so like her to see nothing else.

"What do you want, my permission?"

Disturbed, Pandora stayed at the table. "I suppose
I wanted you to understand and agree."

"Fine."

"You needn't be so curt about it. After all, you
haven't any plans to use the house on a regular basis."

"I haven't made any plans," he murmured. "Perhaps it's time I did."

"I didn't mean to annoy you."

He turned slowly, then just as slowly smiled. "No,
I'm sure you didn't. There's never any doubt when
you annoy me intentionally."

There was something wrong here, something she
couldn't quite pinpoint. So she groped. "Would you
mind so much if I were to live here?"

It surprised him when she rose to come to him, offering a hand. She didn't make such gestures often or
casually. "No, why should it?"

"It would be half yours."

"We could draw a line down the middle."

"That might be awkward. I could buy you out."

"No."

He said it so fiercely, her brows shot up. "It was
only an offer."

"Forget it." He turned to look for soup.

Pandora stood back a moment, watching his back,
the tension in the muscles. "Michael..." With a sigh,
she wrapped her arms around his waist. She felt him
stiffen, but didn't realize it was from surprise. "I seem
to be saying all the wrong things. Maybe I have an

easier time when we snap at each other than when I try to be considerate.''

"Maybe we both do.'' He turned to frame her face with his hands. For a moment they looked like friends, like lovers. "Pandora....'' Could he tell her he found it impossible to think about leaving her or her leaving him? Would she understand if he told her he wanted to go on living with her, being with her? How could she possibly take in the fact that he'd been in love with her for years when he was just becoming able to accept it himself? Instead he kissed her forehead. "Let's make soup.''

They couldn't work together without friction, but they discovered over the next few days that they could work together. They cooked meals, washed up, dusted furniture while the servants stayed in bed or sat, bundled up, on sofas drinking tea. True, there were times when Sweeney itched to get up and be about her business, or when Charles suffered pangs of conscience, but they were convinced they were doing their duty. Both servants felt justified when they heard laughter drift through the house.

Michael wasn't sure there had been another time in his life when he'd been so content. He was, in essence, playing house, something he'd never had the time or inclination for. He would write for hours, closed off in his office, wrapped up in plots and characters and what-ifs. Then he could break away and reality was the scent of cooking or furniture polish. He had a home, a woman, and was determined to keep them.

Late in the afternoon, he always laid a fire in the parlor. After dinner they had coffee there, sometimes

quietly, sometimes during a hard-fought game of rummy. It seemed ordinary, Michael admitted. It was ordinary, unless you added Pandora. He was just setting fire to the kindling when Bruno raced into the room and upset a table. Knickknacks went flying.

"We're going to have to send you to charm school," Michael declared as he rose to deal with the rubble. Though it had been just over a month, Bruno had nearly doubled in size already. He was, without a doubt, going to grow into his paws. After righting the table, he saw the dog wiggling its way under a sofa. "What've you got there?"

Besides being large, Bruno had already earned a reputation as a clever thief. Just the day before, they'd lost a slab of pork chops. "All right, you devil, if that's tonight's chicken, you're going into solitary confinement in the garage." Getting down on all fours, Michael looked under the couch. It wasn't chicken the dog was gnawing noisily on, but Michael's shoe.

"Damn!" Michael made a grab but the dog backed out of reach and kept on chewing. "That shoe's worth five times what you are, you overgrown mutt. Give it here." Flattening, Michael scooted halfway under the sofa. Bruno merely dragged the shoe away again, enjoying the game.

"Oh, how sweet." Pandora walked into the parlor and eyed Michael from the waist down. He did, she decided, indeed have some redeeming qualities. "Are you playing with the dog, Michael, or dusting under the sofa?"

"I'm going to make a rug out of him."

"Dear, dear, we sound a little cross this evening. Bruno, here baby." Carrying the shoe like a trophy,

Bruno squirmed out from under the couch and pranced over to her. "Is this what you were after?" Pandora held up the shoe while petting Bruno with her other hand. "How clever of you to teach Bruno to fetch."

Michael pulled himself up, then yanked the shoe out of her hand. It was unfortunately wet and covered with teeth marks. "That's the second shoe he's ruined. And he didn't even have the courtesy to take both from one pair."

She looked down at what had been creamy Italian leather. "You never wear anything but tennis shoes or boots anyway."

Michael slapped the shoe against his palm. Bruno, tongue lolling, grinned up at him. "Obedience school."

"Oh, Michael, we can't send our child away." She patted his cheek. "It's just a phase."

"This phase has cost me two pairs of shoes, my dinner and we never did find that sweater he dragged off."

"You shouldn't drop your clothes on the floor," Pandora said easily. "And that sweater was already ratty. I'm sure Bruno thought it was a rag."

"He never chews up anything of yours."

Pandora smiled. "No, he doesn't, does he?"

Michael gave her a long look. "Just what're you so happy about?"

"I had a phone call this afternoon."

Michael saw the excitement in her eyes and decided the issue of the shoe could wait. "And?"

"From Jacob Morison."

"The producer?"

"*The* producer," Pandora repeated. She'd promised

herself she wouldn't overreact, but the excitement threatened to burst inside her. "He's going to be filming a new movie. Jessica Wainwright's starring."

Jessica Wainwright, Michael mused. Grande dame of the theater and the screen. Eccentric and brilliant, her career had spanned two generations. "She's retired. Wainwright hasn't made a film in five years."

"She's making this one. Billy Mitchell's directing."

Michael tilted his head in consideration as he studied Pandora's face. It made him think of the cat and the canary. "Sounds like they're pulling out all the stops."

"She plays a half-mad reclusive countess who's dragged back to reality by a visit from her granddaughter. Cass Barkley's on the point of signing for the part of the granddaughter."

"Oscar material. Now, are you going to tell me why Morison called you?"

"Wainwright's an admirer of my work. She wants me to design all her jewelry for the movie. All!" After an attempt to sound businesslike, Pandora laughed and did a quick spin. "Morison said the only way he could talk her out of retirement was to promise her the best. She wants me."

Michael grabbed her close and spun her around. Bruno raced around the room barking and shaking tables. "We'll celebrate," he decided. "Champagne with our fried chicken."

Pandora held on tight. "I feel like an idiot."

"Why?"

"I've always thought I was, well, beyond star adoration. I'm a professional." Bubbling with excitement, she clung to Michael. "While I was talking to Morison

I told myself it was a great career opportunity, a wonderful chance to express myself in a large way. Then I hung up and all I could think was Jessica Wainwright! A Morison production! I felt as silly as any bubble-headed fan.''

''Proves you're not half the snob you think you are.'' Michael cut off her retort with a kiss. ''I'm proud of you,'' he murmured.

That threw her off. All of her pleasure in the assignment was dwarfed by that one sentence. No one but Jolley had ever been proud of her. Her parents loved her, patted her head and told her to do what she wanted. Pride was a valued addition to affection. ''Really?''

Surprised, Michael drew her back and kissed her again. ''Of course I am.''

''But you've never thought much of my work.''

''No, that's not true. I've never understood why people feel the need to deck themselves out in bangles, or why you seemed content to design on such a small scale. But as far as your work goes I'm not blind, Pandora. Some of it's beautiful, some of it's extraordinary and some of it's incomprehensible. But it's all imaginative and expertly crafted.''

''Well.'' She let out a long breath. ''This is a redletter day. I always thought you felt I was playing with beads because I didn't want to face a real job. You even said so once.''

He grinned. ''Only because it made you furious. You're spectacular to look at when you're furious.''

She thought about it a moment, then let out a sigh. ''I suppose this is the best time to tell you.''

He tensed, but forced his voice to come calmly. "To tell me what?"

"I watch the Emmy Awards every time you're nominated."

Tension flowed out in a laugh. There'd been guilt in every syllable. "What?"

"Every time," Pandora repeated, amazed that her cheeks were warm. "It made me feel good to watch you win. And…" She paused to clear her throat. "I've watched a few episodes of *Logan's Run*."

Michael wondered if she realized she sounded as though she was confessing a major social flaw. "Why?"

"Uncle Jolley was always going on about it; I'd even hear it discussed at parties. So I thought I'd see for myself. Naturally, it was just a matter of intellectual curiosity."

"Naturally. And?"

She moved her shoulders. "Of its kind—"

He stopped that line of response by twisting her ear. "Some people only tell the truth under duress."

"All right." Half laughing, she reached to free herself. "It's good!" she shouted when he held on. "I liked it."

"Why?"

"Michael, that hurts!"

"We have ways of making you talk."

"I liked it because the characters are genuine, the plots are intelligent. And—" she had to swallow hard on this one "—it has style."

When he let go of her ear to kiss her soundly, she gave him a halfhearted shove. "If you repeat that to anyone, I'll deny it."

"It'll be our little secret." He kissed her again, not so playfully.

Pandora was almost becoming used to the sensation of having her muscles loosen and feeling as if her bones were dissolving. She moved closer, delighting in the feeling of having her body mold against his. When his heart thudded, she felt the pulse inside herself. When his tiny moan escaped, she tasted it on her tongue. When the need leaped forward, she saw it in his eyes.

She pressed her mouth to his again and let her own hunger rule. There would be consequences. Hadn't she already accepted it? There would be pain. She was already braced for it. She couldn't stop what would happen in the weeks ahead, but she could direct what would happen tonight and perhaps tomorrow. It had to be enough. Everything she felt, wanted, feared, went into the kiss.

It left him reeling. She was often passionate, wildly so. She was often demanding, erotically so. But he'd never felt such pure emotion from her. There was a softness under the strength, a request under the urgency. He drew her closer, more gently than was his habit, and let her take what she wanted.

Her head tilted back, inviting, luring. His grip tightened. His fingers wound into her hair and were lost in the richness of it. He felt the need catapult through his body so that he was tense against her sudden, unexpected yielding. She never submitted, and until that moment he hadn't known how stirring it could be to have her do so. Without a thought to time and place, they lowered to the sofa.

Because she was pliant, he was tender. Because he

was gentle, she was patient. In a way they'd never experienced, they made love without rush, without fire, without the whirlwind. Thoroughly, they gave to each other. A touch, a taste, a murmured request, a whispered answer. The fire sizzled gently behind them as night fell outside the windows. Fingers brushed, lips skimmed so that they learned the power of quiet arousal. Though they'd been lovers for weeks, they brought love to passion for the first time.

The room was quiet, the light dim. If she'd never looked for romance, it found her there, wrapped easily in Michael's arms. Closer they came, but comfortably. Deeper they dived, but lazily. As they came together, Pandora felt her firm line of independence crack to let him in. But the weakness she'd expected didn't follow. Only contentment.

It was contentment that followed her into that quick and final burst of pleasure.

They were still wrapped together, half dozing, when the phone rang. With a murmur of complaint, Michael reached over his head to the table and lifted the receiver.

"Hello."

"Michael Donahue, please."

"Yeah, this is Michael."

"Michael, it's Penny."

He rubbed a hand over his eyes as he tried to put a face with the name. Penny—the little blonde in the apartment next to his. Wanted to be a model. He remembered vaguely leaving her the number of the Folley in case something important was delivered to his apartment. "Hi." He watched Pandora's eyes flutter open.

"Michael, I hate to do this, but I had to call. I've already phoned the police. They're on their way."

"Police?" He struggled into a half-sitting position. "What's going on?"

"You've been robbed."

"What?" He sat bolt upright, nearly dumping Pandora on the floor. "When?"

"I'm not sure. I got home a few minutes ago and noticed your door wasn't closed all the way. I thought maybe you'd come back so I knocked. Anyway, I pushed the door open a bit. The place was turned upside down. I came right over here and called the cops. They asked me to contact you and told me not to go back over."

"Thanks." Dozens of questions ran through his mind but there was no one to answer them. "Look, I'll try to come in tonight."

"Okay. Hey, Michael, I'm really sorry."

"Yeah. I'll see you."

"Michael?" Pandora grabbed his hand as soon as he hung up the receiver.

"Somebody broke into my apartment."

"Oh no." She'd known the peace couldn't last. "Do you think it was—"

"I don't know." He dragged a hand through his hair. "Maybe. Or maybe it was someone who noticed no one had been home for a while."

She felt the anger in him but knew she couldn't soothe it. "You've got to go."

Nodding, he took her hand. "Come with me."

"Michael, one of us has to be here with Sweeney and Charles."

"I'm not leaving you alone."

"You have to go," she repeated. "If it was one of the family, maybe you can find something to prove it. In any case, you have to see to this. I'll be fine."

"Just like the last time I was away."

Pandora lifted a brow. "I'm not incompetent, Michael."

"But you'll be alone."

"I have Bruno. Don't give me that look," she ordered. "He may not be ferocious, but he certainly knows how to bark. I'll lock every door and window."

He shook his head. "Not good enough."

"All right, we'll call the local police. They have Fitzhugh's report about trespassers. We'll explain that I'm going to be alone for the night and ask them to keep an eye on the place."

"Better." But he rose to pace. "If this is a setup..."

"Then we're prepared for it this time."

Michael hesitated, thought it through, then nodded. "I'll call the police."

Chapter 10

The moment Michael left, Pandora turned the heavy bolt on the main door. Though it had taken them the better part of an hour, she was grateful he'd insisted on checking all the doors and windows with her. The house, with Pandora safely in it, was locked up tight.

It was entirely too quiet.

In defense, Pandora went to the kitchen and began rattling pots and pans. She had to be alone, but she didn't have to be idle. She wanted to be with Michael, to stand by him when he faced the break-in of his apartment. Was it as frustrating for him to go on alone, she wondered, as it was for her to stay behind? It couldn't be helped. There were two old people in the house who couldn't be left. And they needed to eat.

The chicken was to have been a joint effort and a respite from the haphazard meals they'd managed to date. Michael had claimed to know at least the basics

of deep frying. While he'd volunteered to deal with the chicken, she'd been assigned to try her hand at mashing potatoes. She'd thought competition if nothing else would have improved the end result.

Pandora resigned herself to a solo and decided the effort of cooking would keep her mind off fresh trouble. Needing company, she switched on the tuner on the kitchen wall unit and fiddled with the dial until she found a country-music station. Dolly Parton bubbled out brightly. Satisfied, she pulled one of Sweeney's cookbooks from the shelf and began to search the index. Fried chicken went on picnics, she mused. How much trouble could it be?

She had two counters crowded and splattered, and flour up to her wrists when the phone rang. Using a dishcloth, Pandora plucked the receiver from the kitchen extension. Her foot was tapping to a catchy rendition of "On the Road Again."

"Hello."

"Pandora McVie?"

Her mind on more immediate matters, Pandora stretched the cord to the counter and picked up a drumstick. "Yes."

"Listen carefully."

"Can you speak up?" Tongue caught between her teeth, Pandora dipped the drumstick in her flour mixture. "I can't hear you very well."

"I have to warn you and there's not much time. You're in danger. You're not safe in that house, not alone."

The cookbook slid to the floor and landed on her foot. "What? Who is this?"

"Just listen. You're alone because it was arranged. Someone's going to try to break in tonight."

"Someone?" She shifted the phone and listened hard. It wasn't malice she detected, but nervousness. Whoever was on the other end was as shaky as she was. She was certain—almost certain—it was a man's voice. "If you're trying to frighten me—"

"I'm trying to warn you. When I found out..." Already low and indistinct, the voice became hesitant. "You shouldn't have sent the champagne. I don't like what's going on, but it won't stop. No one was going to be hurt, do you understand? But I'm afraid of what might happen next."

Pandora felt fear curl in her stomach. Outside the kitchen windows it was dark, pitch-dark. She was alone in the house with two old, sick servants. "If you're afraid, tell me who you are. Help me stop what's going on."

"I'm already risking everything by warning you. You don't understand. Get out, just get out of the house."

It was a ploy, she told herself. A ploy to make her leave. Pandora straightened her shoulders, but her gaze shifted from blank window to blank window. "I'm not going anywhere. If you want to help, tell me who I should be afraid of."

"Just get out," the voice repeated before the line went dead.

Pandora stood holding the silent receiver. The oil in the fryer had begun to sizzle, competing with the radio. Watching the windows, listening, she hung up the phone. It was a trick, she told herself. It was only a trick to get her out of the house in hopes she'd be

frightened enough to stay out. She wouldn't be shooed away by a quivering voice on the telephone.

Besides, Michael had already called the police. They knew she was alone in the house. At the first sign of trouble, she only had to pick up the phone.

Her hands weren't completely steady, but she went back to cooking with a vengeance. She slipped coated chicken into the fryer, tested the potatoes she had cooking, then decided a little glass of wine while she worked was an excellent idea. She was pouring it when Bruno raced into the room to run around her feet.

"Bruno." Pandora crouched and gathered the dog close. He felt warm, solid. "I'm glad you're here," she murmured. But for a moment, she allowed herself to wish desperately for Michael.

Bruno licked her face, made a couple of clumsy leaps toward the counter, then dashed to the door. Jumping up against it, he began to bark.

"Now?" Pandora demanded. "I don't suppose you could wait until morning."

Bruno raced back to Pandora, circled her then raced back to the door. When he'd gone through the routine three times, she relented. The phone call had been no more than a trick, a clumsy one at that. Besides, she told herself as she turned the lock, it wouldn't hurt to open the door and take a good look outside.

The moment she opened it, Bruno jumped out and tumbled into the snow. He began to sniff busily while Pandora stood shivering in the opening and straining her eyes against the dark. Music and the smells of cooking poured out behind her.

There was nothing. She hugged herself against the cold and decided she hadn't expected to see anything.

The snow was settled, the stars bright and the woods quiet. It was as it should have been; a very ordinary evening in the country. She took a deep breath of winter air and started to call the dog back. They saw the movement at the edge of the woods at the same time.

Just a shadow, it seemed to separate slowly from a tree and take on its own shape. A human shape. Before Pandora could react, Bruno began to bark and plow through the snow.

"No, Bruno! Come back." Without giving herself a chance to think, Pandora grabbed the old pea coat that hung beside the door and threw it on. As an afterthought, she reached for a cast-iron skillet before bolting through the door after her dog. "Bruno!"

He was already at the edge of the woods and hot on the trail. Picking up confidence as she went, Pandora raced in pursuit. Whoever had been watching the house had run at the sight of the clumsy, overgrown puppy. She'd found she was susceptible to fear, but she refused to be frightened by a coward. With as much enthusiasm as Bruno, Pandora sprinted into the woods. Out of breath and feeling indestructible, she paused long enough to look around and listen. For a moment there was nothing, then off to the right, she heard barking and thrashing.

"Get 'em, Bruno!" she shouted, and headed toward the chaos. Excited by the chase, she called encouragement to the dog, changing direction when she heard his answering bark. As she ran, snow dropped from the branches to slide cold and wet down the back of her neck. The barking grew wilder, and in her rush, Pandora fell headlong over a downed tree. Spitting out snow and swearing, she struggled to her knees. Bruno

bounded out of the woods and sent her sprawling again.

"Not me." Flat on her back, Pandora shoved at the dog. "Dammit, Bruno, if you don't—" She broke off when the dog stiffened and began to growl. Sprawled on the snow, Pandora looked up and saw the shadow move through the trees. She forgot she was too proud to fear a coward.

Though her hands were numb from cold, she gripped the handle of the skillet and, standing, inched her way along toward the nearest tree. Struggling to keep her breathing quiet, she braced herself for attack and defense. Relative or stranger, she'd hold her own. But her knees were shaking. Bruno tensed and hurled himself forward. The moment he did, Pandora lifted the skillet high and prepared to swing.

"What the hell's going on?"

"Michael!" The skillet landed in the snow with a plop as she followed Bruno's lead and hurled herself forward. Giddy with relief, she plastered kisses over Michael's face. "Oh, Michael, I'm so glad it's you."

"Yeah. You sure looked pleased when you were hefting that skillet. Run out of hair spray?"

"It was handy." Abruptly she drew back and glared at him. "Dammit, Michael, you scared me to death. You're supposed to be halfway to New York, not skulking around the woods."

"And you're supposed to be locked in the house."

"I would've been if you hadn't been skulking in the woods. Why?"

In an offhanded gesture, he brushed snow from her face. "I got ten miles away, and I couldn't get rid of

this bad feeling. It was too pat. I decided to stop at a gas station and phone my neighbor.''

''But your apartment.''

''I talked to the police, gave them a list of my valuables. We'll both run into New York in a day or two.'' Snow was scattered through her hair and matted to her coat. He thought of what might have happened and resisted the urge to shake her. ''I couldn't leave you alone.''

''I'm going to start believing you're chivalrous after all.'' She kissed him. ''That explains why you're not in New York, but what were you doing in the woods?''

''Just a hunch.'' He bent to retrieve the frying pan. A good whack with that, he discovered, and he'd have been down for the count.

''The next time you have a hunch, don't stand at the edge of the woods and stare at the house.''

''I wasn't.'' Michael took her arm and headed back toward the house. He wanted her inside again, behind locked doors.

''I saw you.''

''I don't know who you saw.'' Disgusted, Michael looked back at the dog. ''But if you hadn't let the dog out we'd both know. I decided to check around outside before coming in, and I saw footprints. I followed them around, then cut into the woods.'' He glanced over his shoulder, still tight with tension. ''I was just coming up behind whoever made them when Bruno tried his attack. I started chasing.'' He swore and slapped a palm against the skillet. ''I was gaining when this hound ran between my legs and sent me face first into the snow. About that time, you started yelling at the

dog. Whoever I was chasing had enough time to disappear.''

Pandora swore and kicked at the snow. ''If you'd let me know what was going on, we could've worked together.''

''I didn't know what was going on until it was already happening. In any case, the deal was you'd stay inside with the doors locked.''

''The dog had to go out,'' Pandora muttered. ''And I had this phone call.'' She looked back over her shoulder and sighed. ''Someone called to warn me.''

''Who?''

''I don't know. I thought it was a man's voice, but— I'm just not sure.''

Michael's hand tightened on her arm. ''Did he threaten you?''

''No, no it wasn't like a threat. Whoever it was certainly seemed to know what's been going on and isn't happy about it. That much was clear. He—she said someone was going to try to break into the Folley, and I should get out.''

''And, of course, you handled that by running into the woods with a skillet. Pandora.'' This time he did shake her. ''Why didn't you call the police?''

''Because I thought it was another trick and it made me mad.'' She sent Michael a stubborn look. ''Yes, it frightened me at first, then it just plain made me mad. I don't like intimidation. When I looked out and saw someone near the woods, I only wanted to fight back.''

''Admirable,'' he said but took her shoulders. ''Stupid.''

''You were doing the same thing.''

''It's not the same thing. You've got brains, you've

got style. I'll even give you guts. But, cousin, you're not a heavyweight. What if you'd caught up with whoever was out there and they wanted to play rough?''

"I can play rough, too," Pandora muttered.

"Fine." With a quick move, he hooked a foot behind hers and sent her bottom first into the snow. She didn't have the opportunity to complain before he was standing over her, gesturing with the skillet. Bruno decided it was a game and leaped on top of her. "I might've come back tomorrow and found you half-buried in the snow." Before she could speak, he hauled her to her feet again. "I'm not risking that."

"You caught me off balance," she began.

"Shut up." He had her by the shoulders again, and this time his grip wasn't gentle. "You're too important, Pandora, I'm through taking chances. We're going inside and calling the cops. We're going to tell them everything."

"What can they do?"

"We'll find out."

She let out a long breath, then leaned against him. The chase might have been exciting, but her knees had yet to stop shaking. "Okay, maybe you're right. We're no farther along now than when we started."

"Calling the police isn't giving up, it's just changing the odds. I might not have come back here tonight, Pandora. The dog may not have frightened anyone off. You'd have been alone." He took both her hands, pressing them to his lips and warming them. "I'm not going to let anything happen to you."

Confused by the sense of pleasure his words gave her, she tried to draw her hands away. "I can take care of myself, Michael."

He smiled but didn't let go. "Maybe. But you're not going to have the chance to find out. Let's go home. I'm hungry."

"Typical," she began, needing to lighten the mood. "You'd think of your stomach—oh my God, the chicken!" Breaking away, Pandora loped toward the house.

"I'm not that hungry." Michael sprinted after her. The relief came again when he scooped her up into his arms. When he'd heard her shout in the woods, had realized she was outside and vulnerable, his blood had simply stopped flowing. "In fact," he said as he scooped her up, "I can think of more pressing matters than eating."

"Michael." She struggled, but laughed. "If you don't put me down, there won't be a kitchen to eat in."

"We'll eat somewhere else."

"I left the pan on. There's probably nothing left of the chicken but charred bones."

"There's always soup." With that, he pushed open the kitchen door.

Rather than a smoky, splattered mess, they found a platter piled high with crisp, brown chicken. Sweeney had wiped up the spills, and had the pans soaking in the sink.

"Sweeney." From her perch in Michael's arms, Pandora surveyed the room. "What are you doing out of bed?"

"My job," she said briskly, but gave them a quick sidelong look. As far as she was concerned, her plans were working perfectly. She imagined Pandora and Michael had decided to take a little air while dinner

was cooking, and, as young people would, had forgotten the time.

"You're supposed to be in bed," Pandora reminded her.

"Posh. I've been in bed long enough." And the days of little or no activity had nearly bored her to tears. It was worth it, however, to see Pandora snug in Michael's arms. "Feeling fit as a fiddle now, I promise you. Wash up for dinner."

Michael and Pandora each took separate and careful studies. Sweeney's cheeks were pink and round, her eyes bright. She bustled from counter to counter in her old businesslike fashion. "We still want you to take it easy," Michael decided. "No heavy work."

"That's right. Michael and I'll take care of the washing up." She saw him scowl, just a little, and patted his shoulder. "We like to do it."

At Michael and Pandora's insistence, all four ate in the kitchen. Charles, sitting next to Sweeney, was left uncertain how much he should cough and settled on a middle road, clearing his throat every so often. In an unspoken agreement, Pandora and Michael decided to keep the matter of trespassers to themselves. Both of them felt the announcement that someone was watching the house would be too upsetting for the two old people while they were recuperating.

On the surface, dinner was an easy meal, but Pandora kept wondering how soon they could nudge the servants along to bed and contact the police. More than once, Pandora caught Sweeney looking from her to Michael with a smug smile. Sweet old lady, Pandora mused, innocently believing the cook to be pleased to have her kitchen back. It made Pandora only more de-

termined to protect her and Charles from any unpleasantness. She concentrated on cleaning up and packing them off to bed, and it was nearly nine before she was able to meet Michael in the parlor.

"Settled?"

She heard the familiar restlessness in his voice and merely nodded, pouring a brandy. "It's a bit like cajoling children, but I managed to find a Cary Grant movie that interested them." She sipped the brandy, waiting for her muscles to relax with it. "I'd rather be watching it myself."

"Another time." Michael took a sip from her snifter. "I've called the police. They'll be here shortly."

She took the glass back. "It still bothers me to take the business to outsiders. After all, anything beyond simple trespass is speculation."

"We'll let the police speculate."

She managed to smile. "Your Logan always handles things on his own."

"Someone told me once that that was just fiction." He poured himself a brandy and toasted her. "I discovered I don't like having you in the middle of a story line."

The brandy and firelight gave the evening an illusion of normalcy. Pandora took his statement with a shrug. "You seem to have developed a protect-the-woman syndrome, Michael. It's not like you."

"Maybe not." He tossed back a gulp. "It's different when it's my woman."

She turned, brow lifted. It was ridiculous to feel pleasure at such a foolish and possessive term. "Yours?"

"Mine." He cupped the back of her neck with his hand. "Got a problem with that?"

Her heart beat steadily in her throat until she managed to swallow. Maybe he meant it—now. In a few months when he was back moving in his own world, with his own people, she'd be no more than his somewhat annoying cousin. But for now, just for now, maybe he meant it. "I'm not sure."

"Give it some thought," he advised before he lowered his mouth to hers. "We'll come back to it."

He left her flustered and went to answer the door.

When he returned, Pandora was sitting calmly enough in a high-backed chair near the fire. "Lieutenant Randall, Pandora McVie."

"How d'you do?" The lieutenant pulled off a wool muffler and stuck it in his coat pocket. He looked, Pandora thought, like someone's grandfather. Comfy, round and balding. "Miserable night," he announced, and situated himself near the fire.

"Would you like some coffee, Lieutenant?"

Randall gave Pandora a grateful look. "Love it."

"Please, have a seat. I'll be back in a minute."

She took her time heating coffee and arranging cups and saucers on a tray. Not putting off, Pandora insisted, just preparing. She'd never had occasion to talk to a policeman on any subject more complex than a parking ticket. She'd come out on the short end on that one. Now, she was about to discuss her family and her relationship with Michael.

Her relationship with Michael, she thought again as she fussed with the sugar bowl. That's what really had her hiding in the kitchen. She hadn't yet been able to dull the feeling that had raced through her when he'd

called her his woman. Adolescent, Pandora told herself. It was absolutely absurd to feel giddy and self-satisfied and unnerved because a man had looked at her with passion in his eyes.

But they'd been Michael's eyes.

She found linen napkins and folded them into triangles. She didn't want to be anyone's woman but her own. It had been the strain and excitement of the evening that had made her react like a sixteen-year-old being offered a school ring. She was an adult; she was self-sustaining. She was in love. Talk yourself out of that one, Pandora challenged herself. Taking a long breath, she hefted the tray and went back to the parlor.

"Gentlemen." Pandora set the tray on a low table and stuck on a smile. "Cream and sugar, Lieutenant?"

"Thanks. A healthy dose of both." He set a dog-eared notepad on his knee when Pandora handed him a cup. "Mr. Donahue's been filling me in. Seems you've had a few annoyances."

She smiled at the term. Like his looks, his voice was comfortable. "A few."

"I'm not going to lecture." But he gave them both a stern look. "Still, you should've notified the police after the first incident. Vandalism's a crime."

"We'd hoped by ignoring it, it would discourage repetition." Pandora lifted her cup. "We were wrong."

"I'll need to take the champagne with me." Again, he sent them a look of disapproval. "Even though you've had it analyzed, we'll want to run it through our own lab."

"I'll get it for you." Michael rose and left them alone.

"Miss McVie, from what your cousin tells me, the terms of Mr. McVie's will were a bit unconventional."

"A bit."

"He also tells me he talked you into agreeing to them."

"That's Michael's fantasy, Lieutenant." She sipped her coffee. "I'm doing exactly what I chose to do."

Randall nodded and noted. "You agree with Mr. Donahue's idea that these incidents are connected and one of your relatives is responsible."

"I can't think of any reason to disagree."

"Do you have any reason to suspect one more than another?"

Pandora thought it through as she'd thought it through before. "No. You see, we're not at all a close family. The truth is I don't know any of them very well."

"Except Mr. Donahue."

"That's right. Michael and I often visited our uncle, and we ran into each other here at the Folley." Whether we wanted to or not, she added to herself in her own private joke. "None of the others came by very often."

"The champagne, Lieutenant." Michael brought in the box. "And the report from Sanfield Laboratories."

Randall skimmed the printout, then tucked the sheet into the box. "Your uncle's attorney..." He referred quickly to his notes. "Fitzhugh reported trespassing several weeks ago. We've had a squad car cruise the area, but at this point you might agree to having a man patrol the grounds once a day."

"I'd prefer it," Michael told him.

"I'll contact Fitzhugh." Seeing his cup was empty,

Pandora took it and filled it again. "I'll also need a list of the relatives named in the will."

Pandora frowned over her rim. Between her and Michael, they tried to fill in the lieutenant, as best as they could. When they had finished, Pandora sent Randall an apologetic look. "I told you we aren't close."

"I'll get the lawyer to fill in the details." Randall rose and tried not to think about the cold drive back to town. "We'll keep the inquiries as quiet as possible. If anything else happens, call me. One of my men will be around to look things over."

"Thank you, Lieutenant." Michael helped the pudgy man on with his coat.

Randall took another look around the room. "Ever think of installing a security system?"

"No."

"Think again," he advised, and made his way out.

"We've just been scolded," Pandora murmured.

Michael wondered if *Logan's Run* had room for a cranky, well-padded cop. "Seems that way."

"You know, Michael, I have two schools of thought on bringing in the police."

"Which are?"

"It's either going to calm things down or stir things up."

"You pay your money and take your choice."

She gave him a knowing look. "You're counting on the second."

"I came close tonight." He bypassed the coffee and poured another brandy. "I nearly had my hands on something. Someone." When he looked at her, the faint amusement in his eyes had faded. The reckless-

ness was back. "I like my fights in the open, face-to-face."

"It's better if we look at it as a chess game rather than a boxing match." She came close to wrap her arms around him and press her cheek to his shoulder. It was the kind of gesture he didn't think he'd ever get used to from her. As he rested his head on her hair, he realized that the fact that he wouldn't only added to the sweetness of the feeling. When had he stopped remembering that she didn't fit into his long-established picture of the ideal woman? Her hair was too red, her body too thin, her tongue too sharp. Michael nuzzled against her and found they fit very well.

"I've never had the patience for chess."

"Then we'll just leave it to the police." She held him tighter. The need to protect rose as sharply as the desire to be protected. "I've been thinking about what might have happened out there tonight. I don't want you hurt, Michael."

With two fingers under her chin, he lifted it. "Why not?"

"Because..." She looked into his eyes and felt her heart melt. But she wouldn't be a fool; she wouldn't risk her pride. "Because then I'd have to do the dishes by myself."

He smiled. No, he didn't have a great deal of patience, but he could call on it when circumstances warranted. He brushed a kiss on either side of her mouth. Sooner or later, he'd have more out of her. Then he'd just have to decide what to do with it. "Any other reason?"

Absorbing the sensations, Pandora searched her

mind for another easy answer. "If you were hurt, you couldn't work. I'd have to live with your foul temper."

"I thought you were already living with it."

"I've seen it fouler."

He kissed her eyes closed in his slow, sensuous way. "Try one more time."

"I care." She opened her eyes, and her look was tense and defiant. "Got a problem with that?"

"No." His kiss wasn't gentle this time, it wasn't patient. He had her caught close and reeling within moments. If there was tension in her still, he couldn't feel it. "The only problem's been dragging it out of you."

"You're family after all—"

With a laugh, he nipped the lobe of her ear. "Don't try to back out."

Indignant, she stiffened. "I never back out."

"Unless you can rationalize it. Just remember this." He had her molded against him again. "The family connection's distant." Their lips met, urgently, then parted. "This connection isn't."

"I don't know what you want from me," she whispered.

"You're usually so quick."

"Don't joke, Michael."

"It's no joke." He drew her away, holding her by the shoulders. Briefly, firmly, he ran his hands down to her elbows, then back. "No, I'm not going to spell it out for you, Pandora. I'm not going to make it easy on you. You have to be willing to admit we both want the same thing. And you will."

"Arrogant," she warned.

"Confident," he corrected. He had to be, or he'd be on his knees begging. There'd come a time, he'd

promised himself, when she'd drop the last of her restrictions. ''I want you.''

A tremor skipped up her spine. ''I know.''

''Yeah.'' He linked his fingers with hers. ''I think you do.''

Chapter 11

Winter raged its way through February. There came a point when Pandora had to shovel her way from the house to her workshop. She found herself grateful for the physical labor. Winter was a long quiet time that provided too many hours to think.

In using this time, Pandora came to several uncomfortable realizations. Her life, as she'd known it, as she'd guided it, would never be the same. As far as her art was concerned, she felt the months of concentrated effort with dashes of excitement had only improved her crafting. In truth, she often used her jewelry to take her mind off what was happening to and around her. When that didn't work, she used what was happening to and around her in her work.

The sudden blunt understanding that her health, even her life, had been endangered made her take a step away from her usual practical outlook. It caused

her to appreciate little things she'd always taken for granted. Waking up in a warm bed, watching snow fall while a fire crackled beside her. She'd learned that every second in life was vital.

Already she was considering taking a day to drive back to New York and pack what was important to her. More than packing, it would be a time of decision making. What she kept, what she didn't, would in some ways reflect the changes she'd accepted in herself.

Both the lease on her apartment and the lease on the shop over the boutique were coming up for renewal. She'd let them lapse. Rather than living alone, she'd have the company and the responsibility of her uncle's old servants. Though she'd once been determined to be responsible only to herself and her art, Pandora made the choice without a qualm. Though she had lived in the city, in the rush, in the crowds, she'd isolated herself. No more.

Through it all wove Michael.

In a few short weeks, what they had now would be over. The long winter they'd shared would be something to think of during other winters. As she prepared for a new and different life, Pandora promised herself she'd have no regrets. But she couldn't stop herself from having wishes. Things were already changing.

The police had come, and with their arrival had been more questions. Everything in her shop had to be locked up tightly after dark, and there were no more solitary walks in the woods after a snowfall. It had become a nightly ritual to go through the Folley and check doors and windows that had once been casually ignored. Often when she walked back to the house

from her shop, she'd see Michael watching from the
window of his room. It should have given her a warm,
comfortable feeling, but she knew he was waiting for
something else to happen. She knew, as she knew him,
that he wanted it. Inactivity was sitting uneasily on
him.

Since they'd driven into New York to deal with the
break-in at his apartment, he'd been distant, with a
restlessness roiling underneath. Though they both understood the wisdom of having the grounds patrolled,
she thought they felt intruded upon.

They had no sense of satisfaction from the police
investigation. Each one of their relatives had alibis for
one or more of the incidents. So far the investigation
seemed to have twin results. Since the police had been
called in, nothing else had happened. There'd been no
anonymous phone calls, no shadows in the woods, no
bogus telegrams. It had, as Pandora had also predicted,
stirred things up. She'd dealt with an irate phone call
from Carlson who insisted they were using the investigation in an attempt to undermine his case against
the will.

On the heels of that had come a disjointed letter
from Ginger who'd had the idea that the Folley was
haunted. Michael had had a two-minute phone conversation with Morgan who'd muttered about private
family business, overreacting and hogwash. Biff, in his
usual style, had wired a short message:

Cops and robbers? Looks like you two are playing games with each other.

From Hank they heard nothing.
The police lab had confirmed the private analysis of

the champagne; Randall was plodding through the investigation in his precise, quiet way. Michael and Pandora were exactly where they'd been weeks before: waiting.

He didn't know how she could stand it. As Michael made his way down the narrow path Pandora had shoveled, he wondered how she could remain so calm when he was ready to chew glass. It had only taken him a few days of hanging in limbo to realize it was worse when nothing happened. Waiting for someone else to make the next move was the most racking kind of torture. Until he was sure Pandora was safe, he couldn't relax. Until he had his hands around someone's throat, he wouldn't be satisfied. He was caught in a trap of inactivity that was slowly driving him mad. Pausing just outside her shop, he glanced around.

The house looked big and foolish with icicles hanging and dripping from eaves, gutters and shutters. It belonged in a book, he thought, some moody, misty gothic. A fairy tale—the grim sort. Perhaps one day he'd weave a story around it himself, but for now, it was just home.

With his hands in his pockets he watched smoke puff out of chimneys. Foolish it might be, but he'd always loved it. The longer he lived in it, the surer he was that he was meant to. He was far from certain how Pandora would take his decision to remain after the term was over.

His last script for the season was done. It was the only episode to be filmed before the show wrapped until fall. He could, as he often did, take a few weeks in the early spring and find a hot, noisy beach. He

could fish, relax and enjoy watching women in under-size bikinis. Michael knew he wasn't going anywhere.

For the past few days, he'd been toying with a screenplay for a feature film. He'd given it some thought before, but somehow something had always interfered. He could write it here, he knew. He could perfect it here with Pandora wielding her art nearby, criticizing his work so that he was only more determined to make it better. But he was waiting. Waiting for something else to happen, waiting to find who it was who'd used fear and intimidation to try to drive them out. And most of all, he was waiting for Pandora. Until she gave him her complete trust, willingly, until she gave him her heart unrestrictedly, he had to go on waiting.

His hands curled into fists and released. He wanted action.

He tried the door and satisfied himself that she'd kept her word and locked it from the inside. "Pandora?" He knocked with the side of his fist. She opened the door with a drill in her hand. After giving her flushed face and tousled hair a quick look, Michael lifted his hands, palms out. "I'm unarmed."

"And I'm busy." But her lips curved. There was a light of pleasure in her eyes. He found it easy to notice such small things.

"I know, I've invaded scheduled working hours, but I have a valid excuse."

"You're letting in the cold," she complained. Once, she might have shut the door in his face without a second thought. This time she shut it behind him.

"Not a hell of a lot warmer in here."

"It's fine when I'm working. Which I am."

"Blame Sweeney. She's sending me in for supplies, and she insisted I take you." He sent Pandora a bland look. "'That girl holes herself up in that shed too much. Needs some sun.'"

"I get plenty of sun," Pandora countered. Still, the idea of a drive into town appealed. It wouldn't hurt to talk to the jeweler in the little shopping center. She was beginning to think her work should spread out a bit, beyond the big cities. "I suppose we should humor her, but I want to finish up here first."

"I'm in no hurry."

"Good. Half an hour then." She went to exchange the drill for a jeweler's torch. Because she didn't hear the door open or shut, she turned and saw Michael examining her rolling mill. "Michael," she said with more than a trace of exasperation.

"Go ahead, take your time."

"Don't you have anything to do?"

"Not a thing," he said cheerfully.

"Not one car chase to write?"

"No. Besides, I've never seen you work."

"Audiences make me cranky."

"Broaden your horizons, love. Pretend I'm an apprentice."

"I'm not sure they can get that broad."

Undaunted, he pointed to her worktable. "What is that thing?"

"This thing," she began tightly, "is a pendant. A waterfall effect made with brass wire and some scraps of silver I had left over from a bracelet."

"No waste," he murmured. "Practical as ever. So what's the next step?"

With a long breath, she decided it would be simpler

to play along than to throw him out. "I've just finished adjusting the curves of the wires. I've used different thicknesses and lengths to give it a free-flowing effect. The silver scraps I've cut and filed into elongated tear-drops. Now I solder them onto the ends of the wires."

She applied the flux, shifting a bit so that he could watch. After she'd put a square of solder beside each wire, she used the torch to apply heat until the solder melted. Patient, competent, she repeated the procedure until all twelve teardrops were attached.

"Looks easy enough," he mused.

"A child of five could do it."

He heard the sarcasm and laughed as he took her hands. "You want flattery? A few minutes ago I saw a pile of metal. Now I see an intriguing ornament. Ornate and exotic."

"It's supposed to be exotic," Pandora replied. "Jessica Wainwright will wear it in the film. It's to have been a gift from an old lover. The countess claims he was a Turkish prince."

Michael studied the necklace again. "Very appropriate."

"It'll droop down from brass and silver wires twisted together. The lowest teardrop should hang nearly to her waist." Pleased, but knowing better than to touch the metal before the solder cooled, Pandora held up her sketch. "Ms. Wainwright was very specific. She wants nothing ordinary, nothing even classic. Everything she wears should add to the character's mystique."

She set the sketch down and tidied her tools. She'd solder on the hoop and fashion the neck wire when they returned from town. Then if there was time, she'd

begin the next project. The gold-plated peacock pin with its three-inch filigree tail would take her the better part of two weeks.

"This thing has potential as a murder weapon," Michael mused, picking up a burnisher to examine the curved, steel tip.

"I beg your pardon?"

He liked the way she said it, so that even with her back turned she was looking down her nose. "For a story line."

"Leave my tools out of your stories." Pandora took the burnisher from him and packed it away. "Going to buy me lunch in town?" She stripped off her apron then grabbed her coat.

"I was going to ask you the same thing."

"I asked first." She locked the shop and welcomed the cold. "The snow's beginning to melt."

"In a few weeks, the five dozen bulbs Jolley planted during his gardening stage will be starting to bloom."

"Daffodils," she murmured. It didn't seem possible when you felt the air, saw the mounds of snow, but spring was closing in. "The winter hasn't seemed so long."

"No, it hasn't." He slipped an arm around her shoulders. "I never expected six months to go so quickly. I figured one of us would've attempted murder by this time."

With a laugh, Pandora matched her step to his. "We've still got a month to go."

"Now we have to behave ourselves," he reminded her. "Lieutenant Randall has his eye on us."

"I guess we blew our chance." She turned to wind

her arms around his neck. "There have been times I've wanted to hit you with a blunt instrument."

"Feeling's mutual," he told her as he lowered his mouth. Her lips were cool and curved.

At the side window, Sweeney drew back the drape. "Look at this!" Cackling, she gestured to Charles. "I told you it would work. In a few more weeks, I'll be putting bells on a wedding cake."

As Charles joined Sweeney at the window, Pandora scooped a hand into the snow and tossed it in Michael's face. "Don't count your chickens," he muttered.

In a desperate move to avoid retaliation, Pandora raced to the garage. She ducked seconds before snow splattered against the door. "Your aim's still off, cousin." Hefting the door, she sprinted inside and jumped into his car. Smug, she settled into the seat. He wouldn't, she was sure, mar his spotless interior with a snowball. Michael opened the door, slid in beside her and dumped snow over her head. She was still squealing when he turned the key.

"I'm better at close range."

Pandora sputtered as she wiped at the snow. Because she'd appreciated the move, it was difficult to sound indignant. "One would have thought that a man who drives an ostentatious car would be more particular with it."

"It's only ostentatious if you buy it for status purposes."

"And, of course, you didn't."

"I bought it because it gets terrific gas mileage." When she snorted, he turned to grin at her. "And because it looks great wrapped around redheads."

"And blondes and brunettes."

"Redheads," he corrected, twining her hair around his finger. "I've developed a preference."

It shouldn't have made her smile, but it did. She was still smiling when they started down the long, curvy road. "We can't complain about the road crews," she said idly. "Except for those two weeks last month, the roads've been fairly clear." She glanced toward the mounds of snow the plows had pushed to the side of the road.

"Too bad they won't do the driveway."

"You know you loved riding that little tractor. Uncle Jolley always said it made him feel tough and macho."

"So much so he'd race it like a madman over the yard."

As they came to a curve, Michael eased on the brake and downshifted. Pandora leaned forward and fiddled with the stereo. "Most people have equipment like this in their den."

"I don't have a den."

"You don't have a stereo to put in one, either," she remembered. "Or a television."

He shrugged, but mentally listed what he'd lost from his apartment. "Insurance'll cover it."

"The police are handling that as though it were a normal break-in." She switched channels. "It might've been."

"Or it might've been a smoke screen. I wish we—" He broke off as they approached another curve. He'd pressed the brake again, but this time, the pedal had gone uselessly to the floor.

"Michael, if you're trying to impress me with your

skill as a driver, it's not working.'' Instinctively Pandora grabbed the door handle as the car careered down the curve.

Whipping the steering wheel with one hand, Michael yanked on the emergency brake. The car continued to barrel down. He gripped the wheel in both hands and fought the next curve. ''No brakes.'' As he told her, Michael glanced down to see the speedometer hover at seventy.

Pandora's knuckles turned white on the handle. ''We won't make it to the bottom without them.''

He never considered lying. ''No.'' Tires squealed as he rounded the next curve. Gravel spit under the wheels as the car went wide. There was the scrape and scream of metal as the fender kissed the guardrail.

She looked at the winding road spinning in front of her. Her vision blurred then cleared. The sign before the S-turn cautioned for a safe speed of thirty. Michael took it at seventy-five. Pandora shut her eyes. When she opened them and saw the snowbank dead ahead, she screamed. With seconds to spare, Michael yanked the car around. Snow flew skyward as the car skidded along the bank.

Eyes intense, Michael stared at the road ahead and struggled to anticipate each curve. Sweat beaded on his forehead. He knew the road, that's what terrified him. In less than three miles, the already sharp incline steepened. At high speed, the car would ram straight through the guardrail and crash on the cliffs below. The game Jolley had begun would end violently.

Michael tasted his own fear, then swallowed it. ''There's only one chance; we've got to turn off on the lane leading into the old inn. It's coming up after

that curve.'' He couldn't take his eyes from the road to look at her. His fingers dug into the wheel. ''Hang on.''

She was going to die. Her mind was numb from the thought of it. She heard the tires scream as Michael dragged at the wheel. The car tilted, nearly going over. She saw trees rush by as the car slid on the slippery edge of the lane. Almost, for an instant, the rubber seemed to grip the gravel beneath. But the turn was too sharp, the speed too fast. Out of control, the car spiraled toward the trees.

''I love you,'' she whispered, and grabbed for him before the world went black.

He came to slowly. He hurt, and for a time didn't understand why. There was noise. Eventually he turned his head toward it. When he opened his eyes, Michael saw a boy with wide eyes and black hair gawking through the window.

''Mister, hey, mister. You okay?''

Dazed, Michael pushed open the door. ''Get help,'' he managed, fighting against blacking out again. He took deep gulps of air to clear his head as the boy dashed off through the woods. ''Pandora.'' Fear broke through the fog. In seconds, he was leaning over her.

His fingers shook as he reached for the pulse of her neck, but he found it. Blood from a cut on her forehead ran down her face and onto his hands. With his fingers pressed against the wound, he fumbled in the glove compartment for the first-aid kit. He'd stopped the bleeding and was checking her for broken bones when she moaned. He had to stop himself from dragging her against him and holding on.

''Take it easy,'' he murmured when she began to

stir. "Don't move around." When she opened her
eyes, he saw they were glazed and unfocused. "You're
all right." Gently he cupped her face in his hands and
continued to reassure her. Her eyes focused gradually.
As they did, she reached for his hand.

"The brakes...."

"Yeah." He rested his cheek against hers a moment. "It was a hell of a trip, but it looks like we
made it."

Confused, she looked around. The car was stopped,
leaning drunkenly against a tree. It had been the deep,
slushy snow that had slowed them down enough to
prevent the crash from being fatal. "We—you're all
right?" The tears started when she reached out and
took his face in her hands as he had with hers. "You're
all right."

"Terrific." His wrist throbbed like a jackhammer
and his head ached unbelievably, but he was alive.
When she started to move, he held her still. "No, don't
move around. I don't know how badly you're hurt.
There was a kid. He's gone for help."

"It's just my head." She started to take his hand,
and saw the blood. "Oh God, you're bleeding.
Where?" Before she could begin her frantic search, he
gripped her hands together.

"It's not me. It's you. Your head's cut. You probably have a concussion."

Shaky, she lifted her hand and touched the bandage.
The wound beneath it hurt, but she drew on that. If
she hurt, she was alive. "I thought I was dead." She
closed her eyes but tears slipped through the lashes.
"I thought we were both dead."

"We're both fine." They heard the siren wail up the

mountain road. He was silent until she opened her eyes again. "You know what happened?"

Her head ached badly, but it was clear. "Attempted murder."

He nodded, not turning when the ambulance pulled into the slushy lane. "I'm through waiting, Pandora. I'm through waiting all around."

Lieutenant Randall found Michael in the emergency-room lounge. He unwrapped his muffler, unbuttoned his coat and sat down on the hard wooden bench. "Looks like you've had some trouble."

"Big time."

Randall nodded toward the Ace bandage on Michael's wrist. "Bad?"

"Just a sprain. Few cuts and bruises and a hell of a headache. Last time I saw it, my car looked something like an accordion."

"We're taking it in. Anything we should look for?"

"Brake lines. It seemed I didn't have any when I started the trip down the mountain."

"When's the last time you used your car?" Randall had his notepad in hand.

"Ten days, two weeks." Wearily, Michael rubbed a temple. "I drove into New York to talk to police about the robbery in my apartment."

"Where do you keep your car?"

"In the garage."

"Locked?"

"The garage?" Michael kept his eye on the hallway where Pandora had been wheeled away. "No. My uncle had installed one of those remote control devices a few years back. Never worked unless you turned on

the television. Anyway, he took it out again and never replaced the lock. Pandora's car's in there,'' he remembered suddenly. "If—"

"We'll check it out," Randall said easily. "Miss McVie was with you?"

"Yeah, she's with a doctor." For the first time in weeks, Michael found himself craving a cigarette. "Her head was cut." He looked down at his hands and remembered her blood on them. "I'm going to find out who did this, Lieutenant, and then I'm going to—"

"Don't say anything to me I might have to use later," Randall warned. There were some people who threatened as a means to let off steam or relieve tension. Randall didn't think Michael Donahue was one of them. "Let me do my job, Mr. Donahue."

Michael gave him a long, steady look. "Someone's been playing games, deadly ones, with someone very important to me. If you were in my place, would you twiddle your thumbs and wait?"

Randall smiled, just a little. "You know, Donahue, I never miss your show. Great entertainment. Some of this business sounds just like one of your shows."

"Like one of my shows," Michael repeated slowly.

"Problem is, things don't work the same way out here in the world as they do on television. But it sure is a pleasure to watch. Here comes your lady."

Michael sprang up and headed for her.

"I'm fine," she told him before he could ask.

"Not entirely." Behind her a young, white coated doctor stood impatiently. "Miss McVie has a concussion."

"He put a few stitches in my head and wants to

hold me prisoner.'' She gave the doctor a sweet smile and linked arms with Michael. "Let's go home."

"Just a minute." Keeping her beside him, Michael turned to the doctor. "You want her in the hospital?"

"Michael—"

"Shut up."

"Anyone suffering from a concussion should be routinely checked. Miss McVie would be wise to remain overnight with professional care."

"I'm not staying in the hospital because I have a bump on the head. Good afternoon, Lieutenant."

"Miss McVie."

Lifting her chin, she looked back at the doctor. "Now, Doctor…"

"Barnhouse."

"Dr. Barnhouse," she began. "I will take your advice to a point. I'll rest, avoid stress. At the first sign of nausea or dizziness, I'll be on your doorstep. I can assure you, now that you've convinced Michael I'm an invalid, I'll be properly smothered and hovered over. You'll have to be satisfied with that."

Far from satisfied, the doctor directed himself to Michael. "I can't force her to stay, of course."

Michael lifted a brow. "If you think I can, you've got a lot to learn about women."

Resigned, Barnhouse turned back to Pandora. "I want to see you in a week, sooner if any of the symptoms we discussed show up. You're to rest for twenty-four hours. That means horizontally."

"Yes, Doctor." She offered a hand, which he took grudgingly. "You were very gentle. Thank you."

His lips twitched. "A week," he repeated and strode back down the hall.

"If I didn't know better," Michael mused, "I'd say he wanted to keep you here just to look at you."

"Of course. I look stunning with blood running down my face and a hole in my head."

"I thought so." He kissed her cheek, but used the gesture to get a closer look at her wound. The stitches were small and neat, disappearing into her hairline. After counting six of them, his determination iced. "Come on, we'll go home so I can start pampering you."

"I'll take you myself." Randall gestured toward the door. "I might as well look around a bit while I'm there."

Sweeney clucked like a mother hen and had Pandora bundled into bed five minutes after she'd walked in the door. If she'd had the strength, Pandora would have argued for form's sake. Instead she let herself be tucked under a comforter, fed soup and sweet tea, and fussed over. Though the doctor had assured her it was perfectly safe to sleep, she thought of the old wives' tale and struggled to stay awake. Armed with a sketch pad and pencil, she whiled away the time designing. But when she began to tire of that, she began to think.

Murder. It would have been nothing less than murder. Murder for gain, she mused, an impossible thing for her to understand. She'd told herself before that her life was threatened, but somehow it had seemed remote. She had only to touch her own forehead now to prove just how direct it had become.

An uncle, a cousin, an aunt? Which one wanted Jolley's fortune so badly to murder for it? Not for the first time, Pandora wished she knew them better, under-

stood them better. She realized she'd simply followed Jolley's lead and dismissed them as boring.

And that was true enough, Pandora assured herself. She'd been to a party or two with all of them. Monroe would huff, Biff would preen, Ginger would prattle, and so on. But boring or not, one of them had slipped over the line of civilized behavior. And they were willing to step over her to do it. Slowly, from memory, she began to sketch each of her relatives. Perhaps that way, she'd see something that was buried in her subconscious.

When Michael came in, she had sketches lined in rows over her spread. "Quite a rogues' gallery."

He'd come straight from the garage, where he and Randall had found the still-wet brake fluid on the concrete. Not all of it, Michael mused. Whoever had tampered with the brakes had left enough fluid in so that the car would react normally for the first few miles. And then, nothing. Michael had already concluded that the police would find a hole in the lines. Just as they'd find one in the lines of Pandora's, to match the dark puddle beneath her car. It had been every bit as lethal as his.

He wasn't ready to tell Pandora that whoever had tried to kill them had been as close as the garage a day, perhaps two, before. Instead he looked at her sketches.

"What do you see?" she demanded.

"That you have tremendous talent and should give serious thought to painting."

"I mean in their faces." Impatient with herself, she drew her legs up Indian style. "There's just nothing

there. No spark, no streak of anything that tells me this one's capable of killing.''

"Anyone's capable of killing. Oh yes,'' Michael added when she opened her mouth to disagree. ''Anyone. It's simply that the motive has to fit the personality, the circumstances, the need. When a person's threatened, he kills. For some it's only when their lives or the lives of someone they love are threatened.''

"That's entirely different.''

"No.'' He sat on the bed. ''It's a matter of different degrees. Some people kill because their home is threatened, their possessions. Some kill because a desire is threatened. Wealth, power, those are very strong desires.

"So a very ordinary, even conventional person might kill to achieve that desire.''

He gestured to her sketches. ''One of them tried. Aunt Patience with her round little face and myopic eyes.''

"You can't seriously believe—''

"She's devoted to Morgan, obsessively so. She's never married. Why? Because she's always taken care of him.''

He picked up the next sketch. ''Or there's Morgan himself, stout, blunt, hard-nosed. He thought Jolley was mad and a nuisance.''

"They all did.''

"Exactly. Carlson, straitlaced, humorless, and Jolley's only surviving son.''

"He tried contesting the will.''

"Going the conventional route. Still, he knew his father was shrewd, perhaps better than anyone. Who's to say he wouldn't cover his bases in a more direct

way? Biff..." He had a laugh as he looked at the sketch. Pandora had drawn him precisely as he was. Self-absorbed.

"I can't see him getting his hands dirty."

"For a slice of a hundred fifty million? I can. Pretty little Ginger. One wonders if she can possibly be as sweet and spacey as she appears. And Hank." Pandora had drawn him with his arm muscle flexed. "Would he settle for a couple of thousand when he could have millions?"

"I don't know—that's just the point." Pandora shuffled the sketches. "Even when I have them all lined up in front of me, I don't know."

"Lined up," Michael murmured. "Maybe that is the answer. I think it's time we had a nice, family party."

"Party? You don't mean actually invite them all here."

"It's perfect."

"They won't come."

"Oh yes, they will." He was already thinking ahead. "You can bank on it. A little hint that things aren't going well around here, and they'll jump at the chance to give us an extra push. You see the doctor in a week. If he gives you a clean bill of health, we're going to start a little game of our own."

"What game?"

"In a week," he repeated, and took her face in his hands. It was narrow, dominated by the mop of hair and sharp eyes. Not beautiful, but special. It had taken him a long time to admit it. "A bit pale."

"I'm always pale with a concussion. Are you going to pamper me?"

"At least." But his smile faded as he gathered her close. "Oh God, I thought I'd lost you."

The trace of desperation in his voice urged her to soothe. "We'd both have been lost if you hadn't handled the car so well." She snuggled into his shoulder. It was real and solid, like the one she'd sometimes imagined leaning on. It wouldn't hurt, just this once, to pretend it would always be there. "I never thought we'd walk away from that one."

"But we did." He drew back to look at her. She looked tired and drawn, but he knew her will was as strong as ever. "And now we're going to talk about what you said to me right before we crashed."

"Wasn't I screaming?"

"No."

"If I criticized your driving, I apologize."

He tightened his grip on her chin. "You told me you loved me." He watched her mouth fall open in genuine surprise. Some men might have been insulted. Michael could bless his sense of humor. "It could technically be called a deathbed confession."

Had she? She could only remember reaching for him in those last seconds, knowing they were about to die together. "I was hysterical," she began, and tried to draw back.

"It didn't sound like raving to me."

"Michael, you heard Dr. Barnhouse. I'm not supposed to have any stress. If you want to be helpful, see about some more tea."

"I've something better for relaxing the muscles and soothing the nerves." He laid her back against the pillows, sliding down with her. Sweetly, tenderly, he ran

his lips down the lines of her cheekbones. "I want to hear you tell me again, here."

"Michael—"

"No, lie back." And his hands, gentle and calm, stilled her. "I need to touch you, just touch you. There's plenty of time for the rest."

He was so kind, so patient. More than once she'd wondered how such a restive, volatile man could have such comforting hands. Taking off only his shoes, he slipped into bed with her. He held her in the crook of his arm and stroked until he felt her sigh of relief. "I'm going to take care of you," he murmured. "When you're well, we'll take care of each other."

"I'll be fine tomorrow." But her voice was thick and sleepy.

"Sure you will." He'd keep her in bed another twenty-four hours if he had to chain her. "You haven't told me again. Are you in love with me, Pandora?"

She was so tired, so drained. It seemed she'd reached a point where she could fight nothing. "What if I am?" She managed to tilt her head back to stare at him. His fingers rubbed gently at her temple, easing even the dull echo of pain. "People fall in and out of love all the time."

"People." He lowered his head so that he could just skim her lips with his. "Not Pandora. It infuriates you, doesn't it?"

She wanted to glare but closed her eyes instead. "Yes. I'm doing my best to reverse the situation."

He snuggled down beside her, content for now. She loved him. He still had time to make her like the idea. "Let me know how it works out," he said, and lulled her to sleep.

Chapter 12

Michael studied the dark stains on the garage floor with a kind of grim fascination. Draining the brake fluid from an intended victim's car was a hackneyed device, one expected from time to time on any self-respecting action-adventure show. Viewers and readers alike developed a certain fondness for old, reliable angles in the same way they appreciated the new and different. Though it took on a different picture when it became personal, the car careering out of control down a steep mountain road was as old as the Model T.

He'd used it himself, just as he'd used the anonymous gift of champagne. And the bogus-telegram routine, he mused as an idea began to stir. Just last season one of *Logan's* heroines of the week had been locked in a cellar—left in the dark after going to investigate a window slamming in the wind. It too was a classic. Each and every one of the ploys used against himself

and Pandora could have been lifted from one of his own plots. Randall had pointed it out, though he'd been joking. It didn't seem very funny.

Michael cursed himself, knowing he should have seen the pattern before. Perhaps he hadn't simply because it had been a pattern, a trite one by Hollywood standards. Whether it was accidental or planned, Michael decided he wasn't about to be outplotted. He'd make his next move taking a page from the classic mystery novels. Going into the house, Michael went to the phone and began to structure his scene.

He was just completing his last call when Pandora came down the hall toward him. "Michael, you've got to do something about Sweeney."

Michael leaned back against the newel post and studied her. She looked wonderful—rested, healthy and annoyed. "Isn't it time for your afternoon nap?"

"That's just what I'm talking about." The annoyance deepened between her brows and pleased him. "I don't need an afternoon nap. It's been over a week since the accident." She pulled a leather thong out of her hair and began to run it through her fingers. "I've seen the doctor, and he said I was fine."

"I thought it was more something along the lines of you having a head like a rock."

She narrowed her eyes. "He was annoyed because I healed perfectly without him. The point is, I am healed, but if Sweeney keeps nagging and hovering, I'll have a relapse." It came out as a declaration as she stood straight in front of him, chin lifted, looking as though she'd never been ill a day in her life.

"What would you like me to do?"

"She'll listen to you. For some reason she has the idea that you're infallible. Mr. Donahue this, Mr. Donahue that." She slapped the leather against her palm. "For the past week all I've heard is how charming, handsome and strong you are. It's a wonder I recovered at all."

His lips twitched, but he understood Sweeney's flattery could undo any progress he'd made. "The woman's perceptive. However..." He stopped Pandora's retort by holding up a hand. "Because I'd never refuse you anything—" when she snorted he ignored it "—and because she's been driving me crazy fussing over my wrist, I'm going to take care of it."

Pandora tilted her head. "How?"

"Sweeney's going to be too busy over the next few days to fuss over us. She'll have the dinner party to fuss over."

"What dinner party?"

"The dinner party we're going to give next week for all our relatives."

She glanced at the phone, remembering he'd been using it when she'd come down the hall. "What have you been up to?"

"Just setting the scene, cousin." He rocked back on his heels, already imagining. "I think we'll have Sweeney dig out the best china, though I doubt we'll have time to use it."

"Michael." She didn't want to seem a coward, but the accident had taught her something about caution and self-preservation. "We won't just be inviting relatives. One of them tried to kill us."

"And failed." He took her chin in his hand. "Don't you think he'll try again, Pandora, and again? The po-

lice can't patrol the grounds indefinitely. And,'' he added with his fingers tightening, ''I'm not willing to let bygones be bygones.'' His gaze skimmed up to where her hair just covered the scar on her forehead. The doctor had said it would fade, but Michael's memory of it never would. ''We're going to settle this, my way.''

''I don't like it.''

''Pandora.'' He gave her a charming smile and pinched her cheek. ''Trust me.''

The fact that she did only made her more nervous. With a sigh, she took his hand. ''Let's tell Sweeney to kill the fatted calf.''

Right down to the moment the first car arrived, Pandora was certain no one would come. She'd sat through a discussion of Michael's plan, argued, disagreed, admired and ultimately she'd given up. Theatrics, she'd decided. But there was enough Jolley in her to look forward to the show, especially when she was one of the leads. And she had, as they said in the business, her part cold.

She'd dressed for the role in a slim, strapless black dress. For flair, she'd added a sterling silver necklace she'd fashioned in an exaggerated star burst. Matching earrings dripped nearly to her chin. If Michael wanted drama, who was she to argue? As the night of the dinner party had grown closer, her nerves had steeled into determination.

When he saw her at the top of the stairs, he was speechless. Had he really convinced himself all these years she had no real beauty? At the moment, poised, defiant and enjoying herself, she made every other

woman he'd known look like a shadow. And if he told her so, she wouldn't believe it for a moment. Instead he merely nodded and rocked back on his heels.

"Perfect," he told her as she walked down the main stairs. Standing at the base in a dark suit, Michael looked invincible, and ruthless. "The sophisticated heroine." He took her hand. "Cool and sexy. Hitchcock would've made you a star."

"Don't forget what happened to Janet Leigh."

He laughed and sent one of her earrings spinning. "Nervous?"

"Not as much as I'd thought I'd be. If this doesn't work—"

"Then we're no worse off than we are now. You know what to do."

"We've rehearsed it a half-dozen times. I still have the bruises."

He leaned closer to kiss both bare shoulders. "I always thought you'd be a natural. When this is over, we have a scene of our own to finish. No, don't pull back," he warned as she attempted to. "It's too late to pull back." They stood close, nearly mouth to mouth. "It's been too late all along."

Nerves she'd managed to quell came racing back, but they had nothing to do with plots or plans. "You're being dramatic."

With a nod, he tangled his fingers in her hair. "My sense of drama, your streak of practicality. An interesting combination."

"An uneasy one."

"If life's too easy you sleep through it," Michael decided. "It sounds like the first of our guests are ar-

riving,'' he murmured as they heard the sound of a car. He kissed her briefly. ''Break a leg.''

She wrinkled her nose at his back. ''That's what I'm afraid of.''

Within a half hour, everyone who had been at the reading of the will, except Fitzhugh, was again in the library. No one seemed any more relaxed than they'd been almost six months before. Jolley beamed down on them from the oil painting. From time to time Pandora glanced up at it almost expecting him to wink. To give everyone what they'd come for, Pandora and Michael kept arguing about whatever came to mind. Time for the game to begin, she decided.

Carlson stood with his wife near a bookshelf. He looked cross and impatient and glowered when Pandora approached.

''Uncle Carlson, I'm so glad you could make it. We don't see nearly enough of each other.''

''Don't soft-soap me.'' He swirled his scotch but didn't drink. ''If you've got the idea you can talk me out of contesting this absurd will, you're mistaken.''

''I wouldn't dream of it. Fitzhugh tells me you don't have a chance.'' She smiled beautifully. ''But I have to agree the will's absurd, especially after being forced to live in the same house with Michael all these months.'' She ran a finger down one of the long, flattened prongs of her necklace. ''I'll tell you, Uncle Carlson, there have been times I've seriously considered throwing in the towel. He's done everything possible to make the six months unbearable. Once he pretended his mother was ill, and he had to go to California. Next thing I knew I was locked in the basement. Childish games,'' she muttered sending Michael

a look of utter dislike. Out of the corner of her eye, she saw Carlson take a quick, nervous drink. "Well, the sentence is nearly up." She turned back with a fresh smile. "I'm so glad we could have this little celebration. Michael's finally going to open a bottle of champagne he's been hoarding since Christmas."

Pandora watched Carlson's wife drop her glass on the Turkish carpet. "Dear me," Pandora said softly. "We'll have to get something to mop that up. Freshen your drink?"

"No, she's fine." Carlson took his wife by the elbow. "Excuse me."

As they moved away, Pandora felt a quick thrill of excitement. So, it had been Carlson.

"I quit smoking about six months ago," Michael told Hank and his wife, earning healthy approval.

"You'll never regret it," Hank stated in his slow, deliberate way. "You're responsible for your own body."

"I've been giving that a lot of thought lately," Michael said dryly. "But living with Pandora the past few months hasn't made it easy. She's made this past winter miserable. She had someone send me a fake telegram so I'd go flying off to California thinking my mother was ill." He glanced over his shoulder and scowled at Pandora's back.

"If you've gotten through six months without smoking…" Meg began, guiding the conversation back to Michael's health.

"It's a miracle I have living with that woman. But it's almost over." He grinned at Hank. "We're having champagne instead of carrot juice for dinner. I've been

saving this bottle since Christmas for just the right occasion.''

He saw Hank's fingers whiten around his glass of Perrier and Meg's color drain. "We don't—" Hank looked helplessly at Meg. "We don't drink."

"Champagne isn't drinking," Michael said jovially. "It's celebrating. Excuse me." He moved to the bar as if to freshen his drink and waited for Pandora to join him. "It's Hank."

"No." She added a splash of vermouth to her glass. "It's Carlson." Following the script, she glared at him. "You're an insufferable bore, Michael. Putting up with you isn't worth any amount of money."

"Intellectual snob." He toasted her. "I'm counting the days."

With a sweep of her skirts, Pandora walked over to Ginger. "I don't know how I manage to hold my temper with that man."

Ginger checked her face in a pretty silver compact. "I've always thought he was kind of cute."

"You haven't had to live with him. We were hardly together a week when he broke into my workshop and vandalized it. Then he tried to pass the whole thing off as the work of a vagrant."

Ginger frowned and touched a bit of powder to her nose. "It didn't seem like something he'd do to me. I told—" She caught herself and looked back at Pandora with a vague smile. "Those are pretty earrings."

Michael steeled himself to listen to Morgan's terse opinion on the stock market. The moment he found an opening, he broke in. "Once everything's settled, I'll have to come to you for advice. I've been thinking about getting more actively involved with one of Jol-

ley's chemical firms. There's a lot of money in fertil-
izer—and pesticides.'' He watched Patience flutter her
hands and subside at a glare from Morgan.

"Software,'' Morgan said briefly.

Michael only smiled. "I'll look into it.''

Pandora tried unsuccessfully to pump Ginger. The
five-minute conversation left her suspicious, confused
and with the beginnings of a headache. She decided to
try her luck on Biff.

"You're looking well.'' She smiled at him and nodded at his wife.

"You're looking a bit pale, cousin.''

"The past six months haven't been a picnic.'' She
cast a look at Michael. "Of course, you've always detested him.''

"Of course,'' Biff said amiably.

"I've yet to discover why Uncle Jolley was fond of
him. Besides being a bore, Michael has an affection
for odd practical jokes. He got a tremendous kick out
of locking me in the cellar.''

Biff smiled into his glass. "He's never quite been
in our class.''

Pandora bit her tongue, then agreed. "Do you know,
he even called me one night, disguising his voice. He
tried to frighten me by saying someone was trying to
kill me.''

Biff's brows drew together as he stared into Pandora's eyes. "Odd.''

"Well, things are almost settled. By the way, did
you enjoy the champagne I sent you?''

Biff's fingers froze on his glass. "Champagne?''

"Right after Christmas.''

"Oh yes." He lifted his glass again, studying her as he drank. "So it was you."

"I got the idea when someone sent Michael a bottle at Christmastime. He promises to finally open it tonight. Excuse me, I want to check on dinner."

Her eyes met Michael's briefly as she slipped from the room. They'd set his scene, she thought. Now she had to move the action along. In the kitchen she found Sweeney finishing up the final preparation for the meal.

"If they're hungry," Sweeney began, "they'll just have to wait ten minutes."

"Sweeney, it's time to turn off the main power switch."

"I know, I know. I was just finishing this ham."

Sweeney had been instructed to, at Pandora's signal, go down to the cellar, turn off the power, then wait exactly one minute and turn it on again. She had been skeptical about the whole of Michael and Pandora's plan but had finally agreed to participate in it. Wiping her hands on her apron, the cook went to the cellar door. Pandora took a deep breath and walked back to the library.

Michael had positioned himself near the desk. He gave Pandora the slightest of nods when she entered. "Dinner in ten minutes," she announced brightly as she swept across the room.

"That gives us just enough time." Michael took the stage and couldn't resist starting with a tried and true line. He didn't have to see Pandora to know she was taking her position. "You all must be wondering why we brought you here tonight." He lifted his glass and

looked from one face to the next. "One of you is a murderer."

On cue, the lights went out and pandemonium struck. Glasses shattered, women screamed, a table was overturned. When the lights blinked on, everyone froze. Lying half under the desk, facedown, was Pandora. Beside her was a letter opener with a curved, ornate hilt and blood on the blade. In an instant Michael was beside her, lifting her into his arms before anyone had a chance to react. Silently, he carried her from the room. Several minutes passed before he returned, alone. He gazed, hot and hard, at every face in the room.

"A murderer," he repeated. "She's dead."

"What do you mean she's dead?" Carlson pushed his way forward. "What kind of game is this? Let's have a look at her."

"No one's touching her." Michael effectively blocked his way. "No one's touching anything or leaving this room until the police get here."

"Police?" Pale and shaken, Carlson glanced around. "We don't want that. We'll have to handle this ourselves. She's just fainted."

"Her blood's all over this," Michael commented gesturing to the bloodstained letter opener.

"No!" Meg pushed forward until she'd broken through the crowd around the desk. "No one was supposed to be hurt. Only frightened. It wasn't supposed to be like this. Hank." She reached out, then buried her face against his chest.

"We were only going to play some tricks," he murmured.

"First degree murder isn't a trick."

"We never—" He looked at Michael in shock. "Not murder," he managed, holding Meg as tightly as she was holding him.

"You didn't want to drink the champagne, either, did you, Hank?"

"That's when I wanted to stop." Still sobbing, Meg turned in her husband's arms. "I even called and tried to warn her. I thought it was wrong all along, just a mean trick, but we needed money. The gym's drained everything we have. We thought if we could make the two of you angry enough with each other, you'd break the terms of the will. But that's all. Hank and I stayed in the cabin and waited. Then he went into Pandora's shop and turned things upside down. If she thought you did it—"

"I never thought she would," Ginger piped up. Two tears rolled down her cheeks. "Really, it all seemed silly and—exciting."

Michael looked at his pretty, weeping cousin. "So you were part of it."

"Well, I didn't really do anything. But when Aunt Patience explained it to me…"

"Patience?" There were patterns and patterns. A new one emerged.

"Morgan deserved his share." The old woman wrung her hands and looked everywhere but at the bloodstained letter opener. She'd thought she'd done the right thing. It all sounded so simple. "We thought we could make one of you leave, then it would all be the way it should be."

"Telegram," Morgan said, puffing wide-eyed on his cigar. "Not murder." He turned to Carlson. "Your idea."

"It's preposterous." Carlson mopped his brow with a white silk handkerchief. "The lawyers were incompetent. They haven't been able to do a thing. I was merely protecting my rights."

"With murder."

"Don't be ridiculous." He nearly sounded staid and stuffy again. "The plan was to get you out of the house. I did nothing more than lock—her—in the cellar. When I heard about the champagne, I had a doubt or two, but after all, it wasn't fatal."

"Heard about the champagne." It was what Michael had waited for. "From whom?"

"It was Biff," Meg told him. "Biff set it all up, promised nothing would go wrong."

"Just an organizer." Biff gauged the odds, then shrugged. "All's fair, cousin. Everyone in this room had their hand in." He held his up, examining it. "There's no blood on mine. I'd vote for you." He gave Michael a cool smile. "After all, it's no secret you couldn't abide each other."

"You set it up." Michael took a step closer. "There's also a matter of tampering with my car."

Biff moved his shoulders again, but Michael saw the sweat bead above his lips. "Everyone in this room had a part in it. Any of you willing to turn yourselves in?" His breath came faster as he backed away. "One of them panicked and did this. You won't find my fingerprints on that letter opener."

"When someone's attempted murder once," Michael said calmly, "it's easier to prove he tried again."

"You won't prove anything. Any of us might have drained the brake lines in your car. You can't prove I did."

"I don't need to." In a quick move, Michael caught him cleanly on the jaw and sent him reeling. Before he could fall, Michael had him by the collar. "I never said anything about draining the lines."

Feeling the trap close, Biff struck out blindly. Fists swinging, they tumbled to the floor. A Tiffany lamp shattered in a pile of color. They rolled, locked together, into a Belker table that shook from the impact. Shocked and ineffective, the rest stepped back and gave them room.

"Michael, that's quite enough." Pandora entered the room, her hair mussed and her clothes disheveled. "We have company."

Panting, he dragged Biff to his feet. His wrist sang a bit, but he considered it a pleasure. Charles, looking dignified in his best suit, opened the library doors. "Dinner is served."

Two hours later, Pandora and Michael shared a small feast in the library. "I never thought it would work," Pandora said over a mouthful of ham. "It shouldn't have."

"The more predictable the moves, the more predictable the end."

"Lieutenant Randall didn't seem too pleased."

"He wanted to do it his way." Michael moved his shoulders. "Since he'd already discovered Biff had been visiting other members of the family and making calls to them, he was bound to find out something eventually."

"The easy way." She rubbed the back of her neck. "Do you know how uncomfortable it is to play dead?"

"You were great." He leaned over to kiss her. "A star."

"The letter opener with the stage blood was a nice touch. Still, if they'd all stuck together..."

"We already knew someone was weakening because of the warning call. Turned out that Meg had had enough."

"I've been thinking about investing in their gym."

"It wouldn't hurt."

"What do you think's going to happen?"

"Oh, Carlson'll get off more or less along with the rest of them, excluding Biff. I don't think we have to worry about going to court over the will. As for our dear cousin—" Michael lifted a glass of champagne "—he's going to be facing tougher charges than malicious mischief or burglary. I may never get my television back, but he isn't going to be wearing any Brooks Brothers suits for a while. Only prison blues."

"You gave him another black eye," Pandora mused.

"Yeah." With a grin, Michael drank the wine. "Now you and I only have to cruise through the next two weeks."

"Then it's over."

"No." He took her hand before she could rise. "Then it begins." He slipped the glass from her other hand and pressed her back against the cushions. "How long?"

Pandora struggled to keep the tension from showing. "How long what?"

"Have you been in love with me?"

She jerked, then was frustrated when he held her back. "I'm not sitting here feeding your ego."

"All right, we'll start with me." He leaned back companionably and boxed her in. "I think I fell in love with you when you came back from the Canary Islands and walked into the parlor. You had legs all the way to your waist and you looked down your nose at me. I've never been the same."

"I've had enough games, Michael," she said stiffly.

"So've I." He traced a finger down her cheek. "You said you loved me, Pandora."

"Under duress."

"Then I'll just have to keep you under duress because I'm not giving you up now. Why don't we get married right here?"

She'd started to give him a hefty shove and stopped with her hands pressed against his chest. "What?"

"Right here in the library." He glanced around, ignoring the overturned tables and broken china. "It'd be a nice touch."

"I don't know what you're talking about."

"It's very simple. Here's the plot. You love me, I love you."

"That's not simple," she managed. "I've just been accessible. Once you get back to your blond dancers and busty starlets, you'll—"

"What blond dancers? I can't stand blond dancers."

"Michael, this isn't anything I can joke about."

"Just wait. You buy a nice white dress, maybe a veil. A veil would suit you. We get a minister, lots of flowers and have a very traditional marriage ceremony. After that, we settle into the Folley, each pursuing our respective careers. In a year, two at the most, we give Charles and Sweeney a baby to fuss over. See?" He kissed her ear.

"People's lives aren't screenplays," she began.

"I'm crazy about you, Pandora. Look at me." He took her chin and held it so that their faces were close. "As an artist, you're supposed to be able to see below the surface. That should be easy since you've always told me I'm shallow."

"I was wrong." She wanted to believe. Her heart already did. "Michael, if you're playing games with me, I'll kill you myself."

"Games are over. I love you, it's that simple."

"Simple," she murmured, surprised she could speak at all. "You want to get married?"

"Living together's too easy."

She was more surprised that she could laugh. "Easy?"

"That's right." He shifted her until she was lying flat on the sofa, his body pressed into hers. When his mouth came down, it wasn't patient, wasn't gentle, and everything he thought, everything he felt, communicated itself through that one contact. As she did rarely, as he asked rarely, she went limp and pliant. Her arms went around him. Perhaps it was easy after all.

"I love you, Michael."

"We're getting married."

"It looks that way."

His eyes were intense when he lifted his head. "I'm going to make life tough on you, Pandora. That's just to pay you back for the fact that you'll be the most exasperating wife on record. Do we understand each other?"

Her smile bloomed slowly. "I suppose we always have."

Michael pressed a kiss to her forehead, to the tip of her nose, then to her lips. "He understood both of us."

She followed his gaze to Jolley's portrait. "Crazy old goat has us right where he wants us. I imagine he's having a good laugh." She rubbed her cheek against Michael's. "I just wish he could be here to see us married."

Michael lifted a brow. "Who says he won't be?" He pulled her up and picked up both glasses. "To Maximillian Jolley McVie."

"To Uncle Jolley." Pandora clinked her glass to Michael's. "To us."

* * * * *

Boundary Lines

Chapter 1

The wind whipped against her cheeks. It flowed through her hair, smelling faintly of spring and growing things. Jillian lifted her face to it, as much in challenge as in appreciation. Beneath her, the sleek mare strained for more speed. They'd ride, two free spirits, as long as the sun stayed high.

Short, tough grass was crushed under hooves, along with stray wildflowers. Jillian gave no thought to the buttercups as she crossed to the path. Here the soil was hard, chestnut in color and bordered by the silver-gray sage.

There were no trees along this rough, open plain, but Jillian wasn't looking for shade. She galloped by a field of wheat bleaching in the sun with hardly a stray breeze to rustle it. Farther on there was hay, acres of it, nearly ready for the first harvesting. She heard and recognized the call of a meadowlark. But she

wasn't a farmer. If someone had termed her one, Jillian would have laughed or bristled, depending on her mood.

The crops were grown because they were needed, in the same way the vegetable patch was sown and tended. Growing your own feed made you self-reliant. There was nothing more important than that in Jillian's estimation. In a good year there were enough crops left over to bring in a few extra dollars. The few extra dollars would buy more cattle. It was always the cattle.

She was a rancher—like her grandfather had been, and his father before him.

The land stretched as far as she could see. Her land. It was rolling and rich. Acre after acre of grain sprouted up, and beyond it were the plains and pastures where the cattle and horses grazed. But she wasn't riding fence today, counting head, or poring over the books in her grandfather's leather-and-oak office. To-day she wanted freedom, and was taking it.

Jillian hadn't been raised on the rugged, spacious plains of Montana. She hadn't been born in the saddle. She'd grown up in Chicago because her father had chosen medicine over ranching, and east over west. Jillian hadn't blamed him as her grandfather had—it was a matter of choice. Everyone was entitled to the life they chose. That was why she'd come here, back to her heritage, five years before when she'd turned twenty.

At the top of the hill Jillian stopped the mare. From here she could see over the planted fields to the pastures, fenced in with wire that could hardly be seen from that distance. It gave the illusion of open range where the cattle could roam at will. Once, it would've

been like that, she mused as she tossed her hair back over her shoulder. If she narrowed her eyes, she could almost see it—open, free—the way it had been when her ancestors had first come to settle. The gold rush had brought them, but the land had kept them. It kept her.

Gold, she thought with a shake of her head. Who needed gold when there was priceless wealth in space alone? She preferred the spread of land with its isolated mountains and valleys. If her people had gone farther west, into the higher mountains, her great-great-grandparents might have toiled in the streams and the mines. They might have staked their claim there, plucking out nuggets and digging out gold dust, but they would never have found anything richer than this. Jillian had understood the land's worth and its allure the first moment she'd seen it.

She'd been ten. At her grandfather's invitation—command, Jillian corrected with a smirk—both she and her brother, Marc, had made the trip west, to Utopia. Marc had been there before, of course. He'd been sixteen and quietly capable in the way of their father. And no more interested in ranching than his father had been.

Her first glimpse of the ranch hadn't surprised her, though it wasn't what many children might've expected after years of exposure to western cinema. It was vast, and somehow tidy. Paddocks, stables, barns, and the sturdy charm of the ranch house itself. Even at ten, even after one look, Jillian had known she hadn't been meant for the streets and sidewalks of Chicago, but for this open sky and endless land. At ten, she'd had her first experience with love at first sight.

But it wasn't love at first sight with her grandfather. He'd been a tough, weathered, opinionated old man. The ranch and his herd had been his life. He hadn't the least idea what to do with a spindly girl who happened to be his son's daughter. They'd circled each other warily for days, until he'd made the mistake of letting out some caustic remark about her father and his choice of pills and needles. Quick tempered, Jillian had flown to her father's defense. They'd ended up shouting at each other, Jillian red-faced and dry-eyed even after being threatened with a razor strap.

They'd parted at the end of that visit with a combination of mutual respect and dislike. Then he'd sent her a custom-made, buff-colored Stetson for her birthday. And it began...

Perhaps they'd grown to love one another so deeply because they'd taken their time about it. Those sporadic weeks during her adolescence he'd taught her everything, hardly seeming to teach at all: how to gauge the weather by the smell of the air, the look of the sky; how to deliver a breech calf; how to ride fence and herd a steer. She'd called him Clay because they'd been friends. And when she'd tried her first and only plug of tobacco, he'd held her head when she'd been sick. He hadn't lectured.

When his eyes had grown weak, Jillian had taken over the books. They'd never discussed it—just as they'd never discussed that her move there in the summer of her twentieth year would be permanent. When his illness had begun to take over, she'd gradually assumed the responsibilities of the ranch, though no words had passed between them to make it official.

When he died, the ranch was hers. Jillian hadn't

needed to hear the will read to know it. Clay had known she would stay. She'd left the east behind— and if there were memories from there that still twisted inside her, she buried them. More easily than she'd buried her grandfather.

It was herself she grieved for, and knowing it made her impatient. Clay had lived long and hard, doing as he chose the way he chose. His illness had wasted him, and would have brought him pain and humiliation had it continued. He would have hated that, would have railed at her if he could have seen how she'd wept over him.

God Almightly, girl! What're you wasting time here for? Don't you know there's a ranch to run? Get some hands out to check the fence in the west forty before we've got cattle roaming all over Montana.

Yes, she thought with a half smile. He'd have said something like that—cursed her a bit, then would've turned away with a grunt. Of course, she'd have cursed right back at him.

"You mangy old bear," she muttered. "I'm going to turn Utopia into the best ranch in Montana just to spite you." Laughing, she threw her face up to the sky. "See if I don't!"

Sensing her change of mood, the mare began to dance impatiently, tossing her head. "All right, Delilah." Jillian leaned over to pat her creamy neck. "We've got all afternoon." In a deft move she turned the mare around and started off at an easy lope.

There weren't many free hours like this, so they were prized. As it was, Jillian knew she'd stolen them. That made it all the sweeter. If she had to work eighteen hours tomorrow to make up for it, she'd do it

without complaint. Even the bookwork, she thought with a sigh. Though there was that sick heifer that needed watching, and the damn Jeep that'd broken down for the third time this month. And the fence along the boundary line. The Murdock boundary line, she thought with a grimace.

The feud between the Barons and the Murdocks stretched back to the early 1900's when Noah Baron, her great-grandfather, came to southeast Montana. He'd meant to go on, to the mountains and the gold, but had stayed to homestead. The Murdocks had already been there, with their vast, rich ranch. The Barons had been peasants to them, intruders doomed to fail—or to be driven out. Jillian gritted her teeth as she remembered the stories her grandfather had told her: cut fences, stolen cattle, ruined crops.

But the Barons had stayed, survived, and succeeded. No, they didn't have the amount of land the Murdocks did, or the money, but they knew how to make the best use of what they did have. If her grandfather had struck oil as the Murdocks had, Jillian thought with a smirk, they could have afforded to specialize in pure-bred beef as well. That had been a matter of chance, not skill.

She told herself she didn't care about the purebred part of it. Let the Murdock clan wave their blue ribbons and shout about improving the line. She'd raise her Herefords and shorthorns and get the best price for them at the Exchange. Baron beef was prime, and everyone knew it.

When was the last time one of the high-and-mighty Murdocks rode the miles of fence, sweating under the sun while checking for a break? When was the last

time one of them had eaten dust on a drive? Jillian knew for a fact that Paul J. Murdock, her grandfather's contemporary, hadn't bothered to ride fence or flank cattle in more than a year.

She let out a short, derisive laugh. All they knew about was the figures in the account books and politicking. By the time she was finished, Utopia would make the Double M look like a dude ranch.

The idea put her in a better mood, so that the line between her brows vanished. She wouldn't think of the Murdocks today, or of the back-breaking work that promised to begin before the sun came up tomorrow. She would think only of the sweetness of these stolen hours, of the rich smell of spring…and the endless hard blue of the sky.

Jillian knew this path well. It ran along the westernmost tip of her land. Too tough for the plow, too stubborn for grazing, it was left alone. It was here she always came when she wanted both a sense of solitude and excitement. No one else came here, from her own ranch or from the Murdock spread that ran parallel to it. Even the fence that had once formed the boundary had fallen years before, and had been forgotten. No one cared about this little slice of useless land but her, which made her care all the more.

Now there were a few trees, the cottonwood and aspen just beginning to green. Over the sound of the mare's hooves she heard a warbler begin to sing. There might be coyotes too, and certainly rattlesnakes. Jillian wasn't so enchanted she didn't remember that. There was a rifle, oiled and loaded, strapped to the back of her saddle.

The mare scented the water from the pond, and Jil-

lian let her have her head. The thought of stripping off her sweaty clothes and diving in appealed immensely. Five minutes in that clear, icy water would be exhilarating, and Delilah could rest and drink before they began the long trip back. Spotting the glistening water, Jillian let the reins drop, relaxing. Her grandfather would have cursed her for her lack of attention, but she was already thinking about the luxury of sliding naked into the cold water, then drying in the sun.

But the mare scented something else. Abruptly she reared, plunging so that Jillian's first thought was rattler. While she struggled to control Delilah with one hand, she reached behind for the rifle. Before she could draw a breath, she was hurtling through space. Jillian only had time for one muttered oath before she landed bottom first in the pond. But she'd seen that the rattlesnake had legs.

Sputtering and furious, she struggled to her feet, wiping her wet hair out of her eyes so that she could glare at the man astride a buckskin stallion. Delilah danced nervously while he held the glistening stallion still.

He didn't need to have his feet on the ground for her to see that he was tall. His hair was dark, waving thick and long beneath a black Stetson that shadowed a raw-boned, weathered face. His nose was straight and aristocratic, his mouth well shaped and solemn. Jillian didn't take the time to admire the way he sat the stallion—with a casual sort of control that exuded confidence and power. What she did see was that his eyes were nearly as black as his hair. And laughing.

Narrowing her own, she spat at him, ''What the hell are you doing on my land?''

He looked at her in silence, the only movement a very slow lifting of his left brow. Unlike Jillian, he was taking the time to admire. Her fiery hair was darkened almost to copper with the water and clung wetly to accent the elegance of bone and skin—fine boned, honey-toned skin. He could see the flash of green that was her eyes, dark as jade and dangerous as a cat's. Her mouth, clamped together in fury, had a luxuriously full, promising lower lip that contrasted with the firm stubborn chin.

Casually he let his gaze slide down. She was a long one, he thought, with hardly more curves than a boy. But just now, with the shirt wet and snug as a second skin... Slowly his gaze climbed back to hers. She didn't blush at the survey, though she recognized it. There wasn't apprehension or fear in her eyes. Instead, she shot him a hard look that might have withered another man.

"I said," Jillian began in a low, clipped voice, "what the hell are you doing on my land?"

Instead of answering he swung out of the saddle—the move smooth and economic enough to tell her he'd been in and out of one most of his life. He walked toward her with a loose, easy stride that still carried the air of command. Then he smiled. In one quick flash his face changed from dangerously sexy to dangerously charming. It was a smile that said, you can trust me...for the moment. He held out a hand.

"Ma'am."

Jillian drew in one deep breath and let it out again. Ignoring the offered hand, she climbed out of the water by herself. Dripping, cold, but far from cooled off,

Jillian stuck her hands on her hips. "You haven't answered my question."

Nerve, he thought, still studying her. She's got plenty of that. Temper and—he noticed the way her chin was thrown up in challenge—arrogance. He liked the combination. Hooking his thumbs in his pockets, he shifted his weight, thinking it was a shame she'd dry off quickly in the full sun.

"This isn't your land," he said smoothly, with only a hint of a western drawl. "Miss…"

"Baron," Jillian snapped. "And who the hell are you to tell me this isn't my land?"

He tipped his hat with more insolence than respect.

"Aaron Murdock." His lips twitched at her hiss of breath. "Boundary runs straight up through here." He looked down at the toes of his boots inches away from the toes of hers as if he could see the line drawn there. "Cuts about clean down the middle of the pond." He brought his gaze back to hers—mouth solemn, eyes laughing. "I think you landed on my side."

Aaron Murdock, son and heir. Wasn't he supposed to be out in Billings playing in their damn oil fields? Frowning, Jillian decided he didn't look like the smooth college boy her grandfather had described to her. That was something she'd think about later. Right now, it was imperative she make her stand, and make it stick.

"*If* I landed on your side," she said scathingly, "it was because you were lurking around with that." She jerked her thumb at his horse. Gorgeous animal, she thought with an admiration she had to fight to conceal.

"Your hands were slack on the reins," he pointed out mildly.

The truth of it only added fuel to the fire. "His scent spooked Delilah."

"Delilah." A flicker of amusement ran over his face as he pushed back his hat and studied the smooth clean lines of Jillian's mare. "Must've been fate," he murmured. "Samson." At the sound of his name the stallion walked over to nuzzle Aaron's shoulder.

Jillian choked back a chuckle, but not in time to conceal the play of a small dimple at the side of her mouth. "Just remember what Samson's fate was," she retorted. "And keep him away from my mare."

"A mighty pretty filly," Aaron said easily. While he stroked his horse's head his eyes remained on Jillian. "A bit high strung," he continued, "but well built. She'd breed well."

Jillian's eyes narrowed again. Aaron found he liked the way they glinted through the thick, luxurious lashes. "I'll worry about her breeding, Murdock." She planted her feet in the ground that soaked up the water still dripping from her. "What're you doing up here?" she demanded. "You won't find any oil."

Aaron tilted his head. "I wasn't looking for any. I wasn't looking for a woman either." Casually he reached over and lifted a strand of her heavy hair. "But I found one."

Jillian felt that quick, breathless pressure in her chest and recognized it. Oh, no, she'd let that happen to her once before. She let her gaze drop down to where his long brown fingers toyed with the ends of her hair, then lifted it to his face again. "You wouldn't want to lose that hand," she said softly.

For a moment, his fingers tightened, as if he considered picking up the challenge she'd thrown down.

Then, as casually as he'd captured her hair, he released it. "Testy, aren't you?" Aaron said mildly. "But then, you Barons've always been quick to draw."

"To defend," Jillian corrected, standing her ground.

They measured each other a moment, both surprised to find the opposition so attractive. Tread carefully. The command went through each of their minds, though it was an order both habitually had trouble carrying out.

"I'm sorry about the old man," Aaron said at length. "He'd have been your—grandfather?"

Jillian's chin stayed up, but Aaron saw the shadow that briefly clouded her eyes. "Yes."

She'd loved him, Aaron thought with some surprise. From his few run-ins with Clay Baron, he'd found a singularly unlovable man. He let his memory play back with the snatches of information he'd gleaned since his return to the Double M. "You'd be the little girl who spent some summers here years back," he commented, trying to remember if he'd ever caught sight of her before. "From back east." His hand came back to stroke his chin, a bit rough from the lack of razor that morning. "Jill, isn't it?"

"Jillian," she corrected coldly.

"Jillian." The swift smile transformed his face again. "It suits you better."

"Miss Baron suits me best," she told him, damning his smile.

Aaron didn't bother to acknowledge her deliberate unfriendliness, instead giving in to the urge to let his gaze slip briefly to her mouth again. No, he didn't believe he'd seen her before. That wasn't a mouth a

man forgot. "If Gil Haley's running things at Utopia, you should do well enough."

She bristled. He could almost see her spine snap straight. "I run things at Utopia," she said evenly.

His mouth tilted at one corner. "You?"

"That's right, Murdock, me. I haven't been pushing papers in Billings for the last five years." Something flashed in his eyes, but she ignored it and plunged ahead. "Utopia's mine, every inch of ground, every blade of grass. The difference is I work it instead of strutting around the State Fair waving my blue ribbons."

Intrigued, he took her hands, ignoring her protest as he turned them over to study the palms. They were slender, but hard and capable. Running his thumb over a line of callus, Aaron felt a ripple of admiration—and desire. He'd grown very weary of pampered helpless hands in Billings. "Well, well," he murmured, keeping her hands in his as he looked back into her eyes.

She was furious—that his hands were so strong, that they held hers so effortlessly. That her heartbeat was roaring in her ears. The warbler had begun to sing again and she could hear the gentle swish of the horses' tails as they stood.

He smelled pleasantly of leather and sweat. Too pleasantly. There was a rim of amber around the outside of his irises that only accented the depth of brown. A scar, very thin and white, rode along the edge of his jaw. You wouldn't notice it unless you looked very closely. Just as you might not notice how strong and lean his hands were unless yours were caught in them.

Jillian snapped back quickly. It didn't pay to notice things like that. It didn't pay to listen to that roaring

in your head. She'd done that once before and where
had it gotten her? Dewy-eyed, submissive, and soft-
headed. She was a lot smarter than she'd been five
years before. The most important thing was to remember who he was—a Murdock. And who she was—a
Baron.

"I warned you about your hands before," she said
quietly.

"So you did," Aaron agreed, watching her face.
"Why?"

"I don't like to be touched."

"No?" His brow lifted again, but he didn't yet release her hands. "Most living things do—if they're
touched properly." His eyes locked on hers abruptly,
very direct, very intuitive. "Someone touch you wrong
once, Jillian?"

Her gaze didn't falter. "You're trespassing, Murdock."

Again, that faint inclination of the head. "Maybe.
We could always string the fence again."

She knew he hadn't misunderstood her. This time,
when she tugged on her hands, he released them. "Just
stay on your side," she suggested.

He adjusted his hat so that the shadow fell over his
face again. "And if I don't?"

Her chin came up. "Then I'll have to deal with
you." Turning her back, she walked to Delilah and
gathered the reins. It took an effort not to pass her
hand over the buckskin stallion, but she resisted. Without looking at Aaron, Jillian swung easily into the saddle, then fit her own damp, flat-brimmed hat back on
her head. Now she had the satisfaction of being able
to look down at him.

In a better humor, Jillian leaned on the saddle horn. Leather creaked easily beneath her as Delilah shifted her weight. Her shirt was drying warm on her back. "You have a nice vacation, Murdock," she told him with a faint smile. "Don't wear yourself out while you're here."

He reached up to stroke Delilah's neck. "Now, I'm going to try real hard to take your advice on that, Jillian."

She leaned down a bit closer. "Miss Baron."

Aaron surprised her by tugging the brim of her hat down to her nose. "I like Jillian." He grabbed the string tie of the hat before she could straighten, then gave her a long, odd look. "I swear," he murmured, "you smell like something a man could just close his eyes and wallow in."

She was amused. Jillian told herself she was amused while she pretended not to feel the quick trip of her pulse. She removed his hand from the string of her hat, straightened, and smiled. "You disappoint me. I'd've thought a man who'd spent so much time in college and the big city would have a snappier line and a smoother delivery."

He slipped his hands into his back pockets as he looked up at her. It was fascinating to watch the way the sun shot into her eyes without drawing out the smallest fleck of gold or gray in that cool, deep green. The eyes were too stubborn to allow for any interference; they suited the woman. "I'll practice," Aaron told her with the hint of a smile. "I'll do better next time."

She gave a snort of laughter and started to turn her horse. "There won't be a next time."

His hand was firm on the bridle before she could trot off. The look he gave her was calm, and only slightly amused. "You look smarter than that Jillian. We'll have a number of next times before we're through."

She didn't know how she'd lost the advantage so quickly, only that she had. Her chin angled. "You seem determined to lose that hand, Murdock."

He gave her an easy smile, patted Delilah's neck, then turned toward his own horse. "I'll see you soon, Jillian."

She waited, seething, until he'd swung into the saddle. Delilah sidestepped skittishly until the horses were nearly nose to nose. "Stay on your own side," Jillian ordered, then pressed in her heels. The straining mare lunged forward.

Samson tossed his head and pranced as they both watched Jillian race off on Delilah. "Not this time," Aaron murmured to himself, soothing his horse. "But soon." He gave a quick laugh, then pointed his horse in the opposite direction. "Damn soon."

Jillian could get rid of a lot of anger and frustration with the speed and the wind. She rode as the mare wanted—fast. Perhaps Delilah needed to outrace her blood as well, Jillian thought wryly. Both male animals had been compelling. If the stallion had belonged to anyone but a Murdock, she would've found a way to have Delilah bred with him—no matter what the stud fee. If she had any hope of increasing and improving Utopia's line of horses, the bulk of the burden rested with her own mare. And there wasn't a stallion on her ranch that could compare with Murdock's Samson.

It was a pity Aaron Murdock hadn't been the

smooth, fastidious, boring businessman she'd envisioned him. That type would never have made her blood heat. A woman in her position couldn't afford to acknowledge that kind of attraction, especially with a rival. It would put her at an immediate disadvantage when she needed every edge she could get.

So much depended on the next six months if she was going to have the chance to expand. Oh, the ranch could go on, making its cozy little profit, but she wanted more. The fire of her grandfather's ambition hadn't dimmed so much with age as it had been transferred to her. With her youth and energy, and with that fickle lady called luck, she could turn Utopia into the empire her ancestors had dreamed about.

She had the land and the knowledge. She had the skill and the determination. Already, Jillian had poured the cash portion of her inheritance back into the ranch. She'd put a down payment on the small plane her grandfather had been too stubborn to buy. With a plane, the ranch could be patrolled in hours, stray cattle spotted, broken fences reported. Though she still believed in the necessity of a skilled puncher and cow pony, Jillian understood the beauty of mixing new techniques with the old.

Pickups and Jeeps roamed the range as well as horses. C.B.'s could be used to communicate over long distances, while the lariat was still carried by every hand—in the saddle or behind the wheel. The cattle would be driven to feed lots when necessary and the calves herded into the corral for branding, though the iron would be heated by a butane torch rather than an open fire. Times had changed, but the spirit and the code remained.

Above all, the rancher, like any other country person, depended on two things: the sky and the earth. Because the first was always fickle and the second often unyielding, the rancher had no choice but to rely, ultimately, on himself. That was Jillian's philosophy.

With that in mind, she changed directions without changing her pace. She'd ride along the Murdock boundary and check the fences after all.

She trotted along an open pasture while broad-rumped, white-faced Herefords barely glanced up from their grazing. The spring grass was growing thick and full. Hearing the rumble of an engine, she stopped. In almost the same manner as her mount, Jillian scented the air. Gasoline. It was a shame to spoil the scent of grass and cattle with it. Philosophically she turned Delilah in the direction of the sound and rode.

It was easy to spot the battered pickup in the rolling terrain. Jillian lifted her hand in half salute and rode toward it. Her mood had lifted again, though her jeans were still damp and her boots soggy. She considered Gil Haley one of the few dyed-in-the-wool cowboys left on her ranch or any other. A hundred years before, he'd have been happy riding the range with his saddle, bedroll, and plug of tobacco. If he had the chance, she mused, he'd be just as happy that way today.

"Gil." Jillian stopped Delilah by the driver's window and grinned at him.

"You disappeared this morning." His greeting was brusque in a voice that sounded perpetually peppery. He didn't expect an explanation, nor would she have given one.

Jillian nodded to the two men with him, another breed of cowhand, distinguished by their heavy work

shoes. Gil might give in to the pickup because he could patrol fifty thousand acres quicker and more thoroughly than on horseback, but he'd never give up his boots. "Any problem?"

"Dumb cow tangled in the wire a ways back." He shifted his tobacco plug while looking up at her with his perpetual squint. "Got her out before she did any damage. Looks like we've got to clear out some of that damn tumbleweed again. Knocked down some line."

Jillian accepted this with a nod. "Anyone check the fence along the west section today?"

There was no change in the squint as he eyed her. "Nope."

"I'll see to it now, then." Jillian hesitated. If there was anyone who knew the gossip, it would be Gil. "I happened to run into Aaron Murdock about an hour ago," she put in casually. "I thought he was in Billings."

"Nope."

Jillian gave him a mild look. "I realize that, Gil. What's he doing around here?"

"Got himself a ranch."

Gamely Jillian hung on to her temper. "I realize that too. He's also got himself an oil field—or his father does."

"Kid sister married herself an oil man," Gil told her. "The old man did some shifting around and got the boy back where he wants him."

"You mean…" Jillian narrowed her eyes. "Aaron Murdock's staying on the Double M?"

"Managing it," Gil stated, then spit expertly. "Guess things've simmered down after the blowup a

few years back. Murdock's getting on, you know, close on to seventy or more. Maybe he wants to sit back and relax now.''

"Managing it," Jillian muttered. So she was going to be plagued with a Murdock after all. At least she and the old man had managed to stay out of each other's way. Aaron had already invaded what she considered her private haven—even if he did own half of it. "How long's he been back?"

Gil took his time answering, tugging absently at the grizzled gray mustache that hung over his lip—a habit Jillian usually found amusing. "Couple weeks."

And she'd already plowed into him. Well, she'd had five years of peace, Jillian reminded herself. In country with this much space, she should be able to avoid one man without too much trouble. There were other questions she wanted to ask, but they'd wait until she and Gil were alone.

"I'll check the fence," she said briefly, then turned the mare and rode west.

Gil watched her with a twinkle. He might squint, but his eyesight was sharp enough to have noticed her damp clothes. And the fire in her eyes. Ran into Aaron Murdock, did she? With a wheeze and a chuckle, he started the pickup. It gave a man something to speculate on.

"Keep your eyes front, son," he grumbled to the young hand who was craning his neck to get a last look of Jillian as she galloped over the pasture.

Chapter 2

The day began before sunrise. There was stock to be fed, eggs to be gathered, cows to be milked. Even with machines, capable hands were needed. Jillian had grown so accustomed to helping with the early morning chores, it never occurred to her to stop now that she was the owner. Ranch life was a routine that varied only in the number of animals to be tended and the weather in which you tended them.

It was pleasantly cool when Jillian made the trip from the ranch house to the stables, but she'd crossed the same ground when the air had been so hot and thick it seemed to stick to her skin, or when the snow had been past her boot tops. There was only a faint lessening in the dark, a hint of color in the eastern sky, but the ranch yard already held signs of life. She caught the scent of grilled meat and coffee as the ranch cook started breakfast.

Men and women went about their chores quietly, with an occasional oath, or a quick laugh. Because all of them had just been through a Montana winter, this sweet spring morning was prized. Spring gave way to summer heat, and summer drought too quickly.

Jillian crossed the concrete passageway and opened Delilah's stall. As always, she would tend her first before going on to the other horses, then the dairy cows. A few of the men were there before her, measuring out grain, filling troughs. There was the click of boot heels on concrete, the jingle of spurs.

Some of them owned their own horses, but the bulk of them used Utopia's line. All of them owned their own saddles. Her grandfather's hard-and-fast rule.

The stables smelled comfortably of horses and hay and sweet grain. By the time the stock had been fed and led out to the corrals, it was nearly light. Automatically, Jillian headed for the vast white barn where cows waited to be milked.

"Jillian."

She stopped, waiting for Joe Carlson, her herdsman, to cross the ranch yard. He didn't walk like a cowboy, or dress like one, simply because he wasn't one. He had a smooth, even gait that suited his rather cocky good looks. The early sun teased out the gold in his curling hair. He rode a Jeep rather than a horse and preferred a dry wine to beer, but he knew cattle. Jillian needed him if she was to make a real success out of what was now just dabbling in the purebred industry. She'd hired him six months before over her grandfather's grumbles, and didn't regret it.

"Morning, Joe."

"Jillian." He shook his head when he reached her,

then pushed back the powder-gray hat he kept meticulously clean. "When are you going to stop working a fifteen-hour day?"

She laughed and started toward the dairy barn again, matching her longer, looser stride with his. "In August, when I have to start working an eighteen-hour day."

"Jillian." He put a hand on her shoulder, stopping her at the entrance of the barn. His hand was neat and well shaped, tanned but not callused. For some reason it reminded her of a stronger hand, a harder one. She frowned at the horizon. "You know it's not necessary for you to tie yourself down to every aspect of this ranch. You've got enough hands working for you. If you'd hire a manager..."

It was an old routine and Jillian answered it in the usual way. "I am the manager," she said simply. "I don't consider the ranch a toy or a tax break, Joe. Before I hire someone to take over for me, I'll sell out."

"You work too damn hard."

"You worry too much," she countered, but smiled. "I appreciate it. How's the bull?"

Joe's teeth flashed, straight, even, and white. "Mean as ever, but he's bred with every cow we've let within ten feet of him. He's a beauty."

"I hope so," Jillian murmured, remembering just what the purebred Hereford bull had cost her. Still, if he was everything Joe had claimed, he was her start in improving the quality of Utopia's beef.

"Just wait till the calves start dropping," Joe advised, giving her shoulder a quick squeeze. "You want to come take a look at him?"

"Mmmm, maybe later." She took a step inside the barn, then shot a look over her shoulder. "I'd like to see that bull take the blue ribbon over the Murdock entry in July." She grinned, quick and insolent. "Damned if I wouldn't."

By the time the stock had been fed and Jillian had bolted down her own breakfast, it was full light. The long hours and demands should have kept her mind occupied. They always had. Between her concerns over feed and wages and fence, there shouldn't have been room for thoughts of Aaron Murdock. But there was. Jillian decided that once she had the answers to her questions she'd be able to put him out of her mind. So she'd better see about getting them. She hailed Gil before he could climb into his pickup.

"I'm going with you today," she told him as she hopped into the passenger's seat.

He shrugged and spit tobacco out the window. "Suit yourself."

Jillian grinned at the greeting and pushed her hat back on her head. A few heavy red curls dipped over her brow. "Why is it you've never gotten married, Gil? You're such a charmer."

Beneath his grizzled mustache his lips quivered. "Always was a smart aleck." He started the engine and aimed his squint at her. "What about you? You might be skinny, but you ain't ugly."

She propped a booted foot on his dash. "I'd rather run my own life," she said easily. "Men want to tell you what to do and how to do it."

"Woman ain't got no business out here on her own," Gil said stubbornly as he drove out of the ranch yard.

"And men do?" Jillian countered, lazily examining the toe of her boot.

"Men's different."

"Better?"

He shifted, knowing he was already getting out of his depth. "Different," he said again and clamped his lips.

Jillian laughed and settled back. "You old coot," she said fondly. "Tell me about this blowup at the Murdocks'."

"Had a few of them. They're a hardheaded bunch."

"So I've heard. The one that happened before Aaron Murdock went to Billings."

"Kid had lots of ideas when he come back from college." He snorted at education in the way of a man who considered the best learning came from doing. "Maybe some of them were right enough," he conceded. "Always was smart, and knew how to sit a horse."

"Isn't that why he went to college?" Jillian probed. "To get ideas?"

Gil grunted. "Seems the old man felt the boy was taking over too quick. Rumor is the boy agreed to work for his father for three years, then he was supposed to take over. Manage the place like."

Gil stopped at a gate and Jillian climbed out to open it, waiting until he'd driven through before closing and locking it behind her. Another dry day, she thought with a glance at the sky. They'd need some rain soon. A pheasant shot out of the field to her right and wheeled with a flash of color into the sky. She could smell sweet clover.

"So?" she said when she hopped into the truck again.

"So when the three years was up, the old man balked. Wouldn't give the boy the authority they'd agreed on. Well, they got tempers, those Murdocks." He grinned, showing off his dentures. "The boy up and quit, said he'd start his own spread."

"That's what I'd've done," Jillian muttered. "Murdock had no right to go back on his word."

"Maybe not. But he talked the boy into going to Billings 'cause there was some trouble there with the books and such. Nobody could much figure why he did it, unless the old man made it worth his while."

Jillian sneered. Money, she thought derisively. If Aaron had had any guts, he'd've thumbed his nose at his father and started his own place. Probably couldn't handle the idea of starting from the ground up. But she remembered his face, the hard, strong feel of his hand. Something, she thought, puzzled, just didn't fit.

"What do you think of him, Gil—personally?"

"Who?"

"Aaron Murdock," she snapped.

"Can't say much," Gil began slowly, rubbing a hand over his face to conceal another grin. "Was a bright kid and full of sass, like one or two others I've known." He gave a hoot when Jillian narrowed her eyes at him. "Wasn't afraid of work neither. By the time he'd grown whiskers, he had the ladies sighing over him too." Gil put a hand to his heart and gave an exaggerated sigh of his own. Jillian punched him enthusiastically in the arm.

"I'm not interested in his love life, Gil," she began

and then immediately changed gears. "He's never married?"

"Guess he figured a woman might want to tell him what to do and how to do it," Gil returned blandly.

Jillian started to swear at him, then laughed instead. "You're a clever old devil, Gil Haley. Look here!" She put a hand on his arm. "We've got calves."

They got out to walk the pasture together, taking a head count and enjoying one of the first true pleasures of spring: new life.

"These'd be from the new bull." Jillian watched a calf nurse frantically while its mother half dozed in the sun.

"Yep." Gil's squint narrowed further while he skimmed over the grazing herd and the new offspring. "I reckon Joe knows what he's about," he murmured and rubbed his chin. "How many younguns you count?"

"Ten and looks like twenty more cows nearly ready to drop." She frowned over the numbers a moment. "Wasn't there—" Jillian broke off as a new sound came over the bored mooing and rustling. "Over there," she said even as Gil started forward.

They found him collapsed and frightened beside his dying mother. A day old, no more than two, Jillian estimated as she gathered up the calf, crooning to him. The cow lay bleeding, barely breathing. The birth had gone wrong. Jillian didn't need Gil to tell her that. The cow had survived the breech, then had crawled off to die.

If the plane had been up…Jillian thought grimly as Gil walked silently back to the pickup. If the plane had been up, someone would've spotted her from the air,

and… She shook her head and nuzzled the calf. This was the price of it, she reminded herself. You couldn't mourn over every cow or horse you lost in the course of a year. But when she saw Gil returning with his rifle, she gave him a look of helpless grief. Then she turned and walked away.

One shudder rippled through her at the sound of the shot, then she forced herself to push the weakness away. Still carrying the calf, she went back to Gil.

"Going to have to call for some men on the C.B.," he told her. "It's going to take more than you and me to load her up." He cupped the calf's head in his hand and studied him. "Hope this one's got some fight in him or he ain't going to make it."

"He'll make it," Jillian said simply. "I'm going to see to it." She went back to the truck, murmuring to soothe the newborn in her arms.

By nine o'clock that evening she was exhausted. Antelope had raced through a hay field and damaged half an acre's crop. One of her men fractured his arm when his horse was spooked by a snake. They'd found three breaks in the wire along the Murdock boundary and some of her cows had strayed. It had taken the better part of the day to round them up again and repair the fence.

Every spare minute Jillian had been able to scrape together had been dedicated to the orphaned calf. She'd given him a warm, dry stall in the cattle barn and had taken charge of his feeding herself. She ended her day there, with one low light burning and the scent and sound of animals around her.

"Here, now." She sat cross-legged on the fresh hay and stroked the calf's small white face. "You're feel-

ing better." He let out a high, shaky sound that made her laugh. "Yes, Baby, I'm your momma now."

To her relief he took the nipple easily. Twice before, she'd had to force feed him. This time, she had to take a firm hold on the bottle to prevent him from tugging it right out of her hand. He's catching on, she thought, stroking him as he sucked. It's a tough life, but the only one we've got.

"Pretty Baby," she murmured, then laughed when he wobbled and sat down hard, back legs spread, without releasing the nipple. "Go ahead and be greedy." Jillian tilted the bottle higher. "You're entitled." His eyes clung to hers as he pulled in his feed. "In a few months you'll be out in the pasture with the rest of them, eating grass and raising hell. I've got a feeling about you, Baby," she said thoughtfully as she scratched his ears. "You might just be a real success with the ladies."

When he started to suck air, Jillian pulled the nipple away. The calf immediately began to nibble at her jeans. "Idiot, you're not a goat." Jillian gave him a gentle shove so that he rolled over and lay, content to have her stroke him.

"Making a pet out of him?"

She whipped her head around quickly and stared up at Aaron Murdock. While he watched, the laughter died out of her eyes. "What are you doing here?"

"One of your favorite questions," he commented as he stepped inside the stall. "Nice-looking calf." He crouched beside her.

Sandalwood and leather. Jillian caught just a whiff of it on him and automatically shifted away. She wanted no scent to creep up and remind her of him

when he was gone. "Did you take a wrong turn, Murdock?" she asked dryly. "This is my ranch."

Slowly, he turned his head until their eyes met. Aaron wasn't certain just how long he'd stood watching her—he hadn't intended to watch at all. Maybe it had been the way she'd laughed, that low, smoky sound that had a way of rippling along a man's skin. Maybe it had been the way her hair had glistened—firelike in the low light. Or maybe it had just been that softness he'd seen in her eyes when she'd murmured to the calf. There'd been something about that look that had had tiny aches rushing to the surface. A man needed a woman to look at him like that—first thing in the morning, last thing at night.

There was no softness in her eyes now, but a challenge, a defiance. That stirred something in him as well, something he recognized with more ease. Desire was so simple to label. He smiled.

"I didn't take a wrong turn, Jillian. I wanted to talk to you."

She wouldn't allow herself the luxury of shifting away from him again, or him the pleasure of knowing how badly she wanted to. She sat where she was and tilted her chin. "About what?"

His gaze skimmed over her face. He was beginning to wish he hadn't stayed in Billings quite so long. "Horse breeding—for a start."

Excitement flickered into her eyes and gave her away even though she schooled her voice to casual disinterest. "Horse breeding?"

"Your Delilah." Casually he wound her hair around his finger. What kind of secret female trick did she use

to make it so soft? he wondered. "My Samson. I'm too romantic to let a coincidence like that pass."

"Romantic, my foot." Jillian brushed his hand aside only to find her fingers caught in his.

"You'd be surprised," Aaron said softly. So softly only a well-tuned ear would have heard the steel in it. "I also know a—" his gaze skimmed insolently over her face again—"prime filly when I see one." He laughed when her eyes flashed at him. "Are you always so ready to wrestle, Jillian?"

"I'm always ready to talk business, Murdock," she countered. *Don't be too anxious.* Jillian remembered her grandfather's schooling well. *Always play your cards close to your chest.* "I might be interested in breeding Delilah with your stallion, but I'll need another look at him first."

"Fair enough. Come by tomorrow—nine."

She wanted to jump at it. Five years in Montana and she'd never seen the Murdock spread. And that stallion... Still, she'd been taught too well. "If I can manage it. Middle of the morning's a busy time." Then she was laughing because the calf, weary of being ignored, was butting against her knee. "Spoiled already." Obligingly she tickled his belly.

"Acts more like a puppy than a cow," Aaron stated, but reached over to scratch the calf's ears. It surprised her how gentle his fingers could be. "How'd he lose his mother?"

"Birthing went wrong." She grinned when the calf licked the back of Aaron's hand. "He likes you. Too young to know better."

Amused, Aaron lifted a brow. "Like I said, it's a matter of touching the right way." He slid one lean

hand over the calf's head and massaged its neck.
"There's one technique for soothing babies, another
for breaking horses, and another for gentling a
woman."

"Gentling a woman?" Jillian sent him an arch look
that held humor rather than annoyance. "That's a remarkable phrase."

"An apt one, in certain cases."

She watched as the calf, satisfied, his belly full,
curled up on the hay to sleep. "A typical male animal," Jillian remarked, still smiling, "Apparently,
you're another."

There wasn't any heat in the comment, but an acceptance. "Could be," he agreed, "though I wouldn't
say you were typical."

Unconsciously relaxed, Jillian studied him. "I don't
think you meant that as a compliment."

"No, it was an observation. You'd spit a compliment back in my face."

Delighted, Jillian threw back her head and laughed.
"Whatever else you are, Murdock, you're not stupid."
Still chuckling, she leaned back against the wall of the
stall, bringing up one knee and circling it with her
hands. At the moment she didn't want to question why
she was pleased to have his company.

"I have a first name." A trick of the angle had the
light slanting over her eyes, highlighting them and
casting her face in shadow. He felt the stir again.
"Ever thought of using it?"

"Not really." But that was a lie, she realized. She
already thought of him as Aaron. The real trouble was
that she thought of him at all. Yet she smiled again,

too comfortable to make an issue of it. "Baby's asleep," she murmured.

Aaron glanced over, grinning. Would she still call him Baby when he was a bull weighing several hundred pounds? Probably. "It's been a long day."

"Mmmm." She stretched her arms to the ceiling, feeling her muscles loosen. The exhaustion she dragged into the barn with her had become a rather pleasant fatigue. "They're never long enough. If I had just ten hours more in a week, I'd catch up."

With what? he wondered. Herself? "Ever heard of overachievement, Jillian?"

"Ambition," she corrected. Her eyes met his again and held. "I'm not the one who's willing to settle for what's handed to her."

Temper surged into him so quickly he clenched at the hay under him. It was clear she was referring to his father's ranch and his own position there. His expression remained completely passive as he battled back the need to strike out where he was struck. "Each of us does what he has to do," Aaron said mildly and let the hay sift through his hands.

It annoyed her that he didn't defend himself. She wanted him to give her his excuses, his reasons. It shouldn't matter, Jillian reminded herself. He shouldn't matter. He didn't, she assured herself with something perilously close to panic. Of course he didn't. Rising, she dusted off her jeans.

"I've got paperwork to see to before I turn in."

He rose too, more slowly, so that it was too late when she realized she was backed into the corner of the stall. "Not even going to offer me a cup of coffee, Jillian?"

There was a band of tension at the back of her neck, a thudding at her ribs. She recognized the temper in his eyes, and though she wondered that she hadn't noticed it before, it wasn't his temper that worried her. It was her own shaky pulse. "No," she said evenly. "I'm not."

He hooked his thumbs through his belt loops and studied her lazily. "You've got a problem with manners."

Her chin came up. "Manners don't concern me."

"No?" He smiled then, in a way that made her brace herself. "Then we'll drop them."

In a move too quick for her to evade, he gathered her shirtfront in one hand and yanked her against him. The first shock came from the feel of that long, hard body against hers. "Damn you, Murdock—" The second shock came when his mouth closed over hers.

Oh, no... It was that sweet, weak thought that drifted through her mind even as she fought back like a tiger. Oh, no. He shouldn't feel so good, taste so wonderful. She shouldn't want it to go on and on and on.

Jillian shoved against him and found herself caught closer so that she couldn't shove again. She squirmed and only succeeded in driving herself mad at the feel of her body rubbing against his. Stop it! her mind shouted as the fire began to flicker inside her. She couldn't—wouldn't—let it happen. She knew how to outwit desire. For five years she'd done so with hardly an effort. But now...now something was sprinting inside her too fast, twisting and turning so that she couldn't grab on and stop it from getting further and further out of her reach.

Her blood began to swim, her hands began to clutch. And her mouth began to answer.

He'd expected her temper. Because his own had peaked, he'd wanted it. He'd known she'd be furious, that she'd fight against him for outmaneuvering her and taking something without her permission. His anger demanded that she fight, just as his desire demanded that he take.

He'd expected her mouth to be soft. Why else would he have wanted to taste it so badly that he'd spent two days thinking of little else? He'd known her body would be firm with only hints of the subtle dips and curves of woman. It fit unerringly to his as though it had been fashioned to do so. She strained away from him, shifting, making his skin tingle at the friction her movements caused.

Then, abruptly, her arms were clasped around him. Her lips parted, not in surrender but with an urgency that rocked him. If her passion had been simmering, she'd concealed it well. It seemed to explode in one blinding white flash of heat that came from nowhere. Shaken, Aaron drew back, trying to judge his own reaction, fighting to keep his own needs in perspective.

Jillian stared up at him, her breath coming in jerks. Her hair streamed behind her back, catching the light while her eyes glinted in the dark. Her mind was reeling and she shook her head as if to clear it. Just as she began to draw her first coherent thought, he swore and crushed his mouth to hers again.

There was no hint of struggle this time, nor any hint of surrender. Passion for passion she met him, matching his need with hers, degree by degree. Sandalwood and leather. Now she drew it in, absorbed the aroma

as she absorbed the hard, relentless texture of his lips. She let her tongue toy with his while she drank up all those hot, heady male tastes. There was something un-apologetically primitive in the way he held her, kissed her. Jillian reveled in it. If she was to take a man, she neither needed nor wanted any polish or gloss that clouded or chipped away so easily.

She let her body take control. How long had she yearned for this? To have someone hold her, spin her away so that she couldn't think, couldn't worry? There were no responsibilities here, and the only demands were of the flesh. Here, with a warm, moist mouth on hers, with a hard body against her, she was finally and ultimately only a woman. Selfishly a woman. She'd forgotten just how glorious it could feel, or perhaps she'd never fully known the sensation before.

What was she doing to him? Aaron tried to pull himself back and found his hands were trapped in the thick softness of her hair. He tried to think and found his senses swimming with the scent of her. And the taste... A low sound started in his throat as he ravaged her mouth. How could he have known she'd taste like this? Seductive, pungent, alluring. Her flavor held all the lushness her body lacked, and the combination was devastating. He wondered how he'd ever lived without it. With that thought came the knowledge that he was getting in much too deep much too fast.

Aaron drew away carefully because the hands on her shoulders weren't as steady as he'd have liked.

Jillian started to sway and caught herself. Good God, what was she doing? What had she done? As the breath rushed swiftly and unevenly through her lips, she stared up at him. Those dark, wicked looks and

clever mouth... She'd forgotten. She'd forgotten who she was, and who he was. Forgotten everything but that heady feeling of freedom and heat. He'd use that against her, she thought grimly. If she let him. But something had happened when—

Don't think now! she ordered herself. Just get him out of here before you make a complete fool of yourself. Very carefully, Jillian brushed Aaron's hands from her shoulders. Tilting her chin, she prayed her voice would be steady.

"Well, Murdock, you've had your fun. Now clear out."

Fun? he thought, staring at her. Whatever had happened it didn't have anything to do with fun. The room was tilting a bit, like it had when he'd downed his first six-pack of beer a hundred years before. That hadn't been much fun either, but it'd been a hell of an experience. And he'd paid for it the next day. He supposed he'd pay for this one as well.

He wouldn't apologize, he told himself as he forced himself to relax. Damned if he would, but he would back off while he still could. Casually he bent down to pick up the hat that had fallen off when her fingers had combed through his hair. He took his time putting it on.

"You're right, Jillian," he said mildly—when he could. "A man would have a hard time resisting a woman like you." He grinned at her and tipped his hat. "But I'll do my best."

"See that you do, Murdock!" she called out after him, then hugged herself because she'd begun to tremble.

Even after his footsteps died away, she waited five

full minutes before leaving the barn. When Jillian stepped outside, the ranch yard was dark and quiet. She thought she could just hear the murmur of a television or radio from the bunkhouse. There were a few lights farther down the road where her grandfather had built quarters for the married hands. She stopped and listened, but couldn't hear the engine of whatever vehicle Aaron had used to drive from his ranch to hers.

Long gone, she thought, and turned on her heel to stride to the house. It was a two-story stone-and-wood structure. All native Montana material. The rambling building had been constructed on the site of the original homestead. Her grandfather had been fond of bragging that he'd been born in a house that would have fit into the kitchen of this one. Jillian entered by the front door, which was still never locked.

She'd always loved the space, and the clever use of wood and tile and stone that made up the living area. You could roast one of Utopia's steers in the fireplace. Her grandmother's ivory lace curtains still hung at the windows. Jillian often wished she'd known her. All she knew was that she'd been an Irishwoman with dainty looks and a strong back. Jillian had inherited her coloring and, from her grandfather's accounting, her temper. And perhaps, Jillian thought wryly as she climbed the stairs, her back.

God, she wished she had a woman to talk to. Halfway up the stairs she paused and pressed her fingers to her temple. Where did that come from? she wondered. As far back as she could remember, she'd never sought out the company of women. So few of them were interested in the same things she was. And, when

there was no niggling sexual problem to overcome, she found men easier to deal with.

But now, with the house so empty around her, with her blood still churning, she wished for a woman who might understand the war going on inside her. Her mother? With a quiet laugh, Jillian pushed open the door to her bedroom. If she called her mother and said she was burning up with desire and had no place to put it, the gentle doctor's wife would blush crimson and stammer out a recommendation for a good book on the subject.

No, as fond as she was of her mother, she wasn't a woman who would understand—well, cravings, Jillian admitted, stripping out of her work shirt. If she was going to be honest, that's what she'd felt in Aaron's arms. Perhaps it was all she was capable of feeling. Frowning, she dropped her jeans into a heap on top of her work shirt and walked naked to the bath.

She should probably be grateful she'd felt that. With a jerk of the wrist, she turned the hot water on full, then added a trickle of cold. She'd felt nothing at all for any man in years. Five years, Jillian admitted and dumped in bath salts with a lavish hand. With an expert twist and a couple of pins, she secured her hair to the top of her head.

It was a good thing she remembered Kevin and that very brief, very unhappy affair. Did one night in bed equal an affair? she wondered ruefully, then lowered herself into the steaming water. Whatever you called it, it had been a fiasco. That's what she had to remember. She'd been so young. Jillian could almost—almost—think of it with amusement now.

The young, dewy-eyed virgin, the smooth, charming

intern with eyes as clear as a lake. He hadn't talked
her into bed, hadn't pressured her. No, Jillian had to
admit that she'd wanted to go with him. And he'd been
gentle and sweet with her. It had simply been that the
words *I love you* had meant two different things to
each of them. To Jillian, they'd been a pledge. To him,
they'd been a phrase.

She'd learned the hard way that making love didn't
equal love or commitment or marriage. He'd laughed
at her, perhaps not unkindly, when she'd naively talked
of their future together. He hadn't wanted a wife, or
even a partner, but a companion willing to share his
bed from time to time. His casualness had devastated
her.

She'd been willing to mold herself into whatever
he'd wanted—a tidy, socially wise doctor's wife like
her mother; a clever, dedicated housewife; an organized marriage partner who could juggle career and
family. It had taken her months before she'd realized
that she'd made a fool of herself over him, taking
every compliment or sweet word literally, because
that's what she'd wanted to hear. It had taken more
time and several thousand miles of distance before
she'd been able to admit that he'd done her a favor.

Not only had he saved her from trying to force her
personality into a mold that would never have fit, but
he'd given her a solid view of the male species. They
weren't to be trusted on a personal level. Once you
gave them your love, the power to hurt you, you were
lost, ready to do anything to please them even at the
loss of self.

When she was young, she'd tried to please her father
that way and had failed because she was too like her

grandfather. The only man she'd ever loved who'd accepted her for what she was had been Clay Baron. And he was gone.

Jillian lay back, closed her eyes, and let the hot water steam away her fatigue. Aaron Murdock wasn't looking for a partner and neither was she. What had happened between them in the barn was a mistake that wouldn't be repeated. He might be looking for a lover, but she wasn't.

Jillian Baron was on her own, and that's the way she liked it.

Chapter 3

He wondered if she would come. Aaron drove back from a line camp on a road that had once been fit only for horses or mules. It wasn't in much better shape now. The Jeep bucked along much like a bad-tempered bronc might, dipping into ruts, bounding over rocks. He rather liked it. Just as he'd enjoyed the early morning visit with five of his men at the line camp. If he could spare the time, he would appreciate a few days at one of the camps in unabashedly male company. Hard, sweaty work during the day, a few beers and a poker game at night. Riding herd far enough from the ranch so that you could forget there was civilization anywhere. Yes, he'd enjoy that, but...

He appreciated the conservative, traditional ways of his father—particularly when they were mixed with his own experimental ideas. The men would still rope and flank cattle in the open pasture, but two tractors drag-

ging a cable would clear off more brush in a day than axmen could in a month. And a plane...

With a wry smile Aaron remembered how he'd fought six years before for the plane his father had considered a foolish luxury. He'd ended up paying for it himself and flying it himself. His father had never admitted that the plane had become indispensable. That didn't matter to Aaron, as long as it was used. He had no desire to push the cowboy out of existence, just to make him sweat a little less.

Downshifting for the decline, he let the Jeep bump its way down the hill. The differences with his father that had come to a head five years before had eased, but not vanished. Aaron knew he'd have to fight for every change, every improvement, every deviation. And he'd win. Paul Murdock might be stubborn, but he wasn't stupid. And he was sick. In six months...

Aaron rammed the Jeep back into fourth. He didn't like to dwell on the battle his father was losing. A battle Aaron could do nothing about. Helplessness was something Aaron wasn't accustomed to. He was too much like his father. Perhaps that's why they spent most of their time arguing.

He pushed his father and mortality out of his mind and thought of Jillian. There was life, and youth, and vitality.

Would she come? Grinning, Aaron sped past a pasture covered with mesquite grass. Damn right she would. She'd come if for no other reason than to prove to him that she couldn't be intimidated. She'd throw her chin up and give him one of those cool go-to-hell looks. No wonder he wanted her so badly it caused an

ache in the pit of his belly. The ache had burned like fire when he'd kissed her.

There hadn't been a female who'd made him come so close to stammering since Emma Lou Swanson had initiated him into life's pleasures in the hayloft. It was one thing for a teenager to lose the power of speech and reason with soft arms around him, and quite another for it to happen to a grown man who'd made a study of the delights and frustrations of women. Aaron couldn't quite account for it, but he knew he was going to have to have more. Soon.

She was a typical Baron, he decided. Hotheaded, stubborn, opinionated. Aaron grinned again. He figured the main reason the Barons and Murdocks had never gotten on was that they'd been too much alike. She wasn't going to have an easy time taking over the ranch, but he didn't doubt she'd do it. He didn't doubt he was going to enjoy watching her. Almost as much as he was going to enjoy bedding her.

Whistling between his teeth, Aaron braked in front of the ranch house. Over near the cattle barn a dog was barking halfheartedly. Someone was playing a radio by the feed lot—a slow, twangy country lament. There were asters popping up in the flower bed and not a weed in sight. As he climbed out of the Jeep he heard the porch door open and glanced over. His mother walked out, lips curved, eyes weary.

She was so beautiful—he'd never gotten used to it. Very small, very slender, Karen Murdock walked with the gliding step of a runway model. She was twenty-two years younger than her husband, and neither the cold winters nor the bright sun of Montana had dimmed the luster of her skin. His sister had those

looks, Aaron mused, the classic blond beauty that went on and on with the years. Karen wore slimming slacks, a rose-colored blouse, with her hair loosely coiled at the neck. She could've walked into the Beverly Wilshire without changing a stitch. If the need had arisen, she could've saddled up a horse and ridden out to string wire.

"Everything all right?" she asked him, holding out a hand.

"Fine. They've rounded up the strays we were losing through the south fence." Studying her face, Aaron took her hand. "You look tired."

"No." She squeezed his fingers as much for support as reassurance. "Your father didn't sleep well last night. You didn't come by to see him."

"That wouldn't've made him sleep any better."

"Arguing with you is about all the entertainment he has these days."

Aaron grinned because she wanted him to. "I'll come in later and tell him about the five hundred acres of mesquite I want to clear."

Karen laughed and put her hands on her son's shoulders. With her standing on the porch and him on the ground, their eyes were level. "You're good for him, Aaron. No, don't raise your brow at me," she told him mildly.

"When I saw him yesterday morning, he told me to go to the devil."

"Exactly." Her fingers kneaded absently at his shoulders. "I tend to pamper him, even though I shouldn't. He needs you around to make him angry enough to live a bit longer. He knows you're right— that you've been right all along. He's proud of you."

"You don't have to explain him to me." The steel had crept into his voice before he could prevent it. "I know him well enough."

"Almost well enough," Karen murmured, laying her cheek against Aaron's.

When Jillian drove into the ranch yard, she saw Aaron with his arms around a slim, elegant blonde. The surge of jealousy stunned, then infuriated her. He was a man after all, she reminded herself, gripping the steering wheel tightly for a moment. It was so easy for a man to enjoy quick passion in a horse stall one evening, then a sweet embrace in the sunshine the next day. True emotion never entered into it. Why should it? she thought, setting her teeth. She braked sharply beside Aaron's Jeep.

He turned, and while she had the disadvantage of the sun in her eyes, she met his amused look with ice. Not for a moment would she give him the satisfaction of knowing she'd spent a restless, dream-disturbed night. Jillian stepped out of her aging compact and managed not to slam the door.

"Murdock," she said curtly.

"Good morning, Jillian." He gave her a bland smile with something sharper hovering in his eyes.

She walked to him, since he didn't seem inclined to drop the blonde's hand and come to her. "I've come to see your stud."

"We talked about manners last night, didn't we?" His grin only widened when she glared at him. "I don't think you two have met."

"No, indeed." Karen came down the porch steps, amused by the gleam in her son's eye, and the fire in

the woman's. "You must be Jillian Baron. I'm Karen Murdock, Aaron's mother."

As her mouth fell open Jillian turned to look at Mrs. Murdock. Soft, elegant, beautiful. "Mother?" she repeated before she could stop herself.

Karen laughed, and rested a hand on Aaron's shoulder. "I think I've just been given a wonderful compliment."

He grinned down at her. "Or I have."

Laughing again, she turned back to Jillian. Karen filed away her quick assessment. "I'll leave you two to go about your business. Please, stop in for coffee before you go if you've time, Jillian. I have so little opportunity these days to talk with another woman."

"Yes, ah—thank you." With her brows drawn together, Jillian watched her go back through the porch door.

"I don't think you're often at a loss for words," Aaron commented.

"No." With a little shake of her head she looked up at him. "Your mother's beautiful."

"Surprised?"

"No. That is, I'd heard she was lovely, but..." Jillian shrugged and wished he'd stop looking down at her with that infernal smile on his face. "You don't look a thing like her."

Aaron swung his arm around her shoulder as they turned away from the house. "You're trying to charm me again, Jillian."

She had to bite down on her lip to keep the chuckle back. "I've better uses for my time." Though the weight felt good, she plucked his arm away.

''You smell of jasmine,'' he said lazily. ''Did you wear it for me?''

Rather than dignify the question with an answer, Jillian stopped, tilted her chin, and gave him one long icy look that only wavered when he began to laugh. With a careless flick he knocked the hat from her head, pulled her against him, and gave her a hard, thorough kiss. She felt her legs dissolve from the knees down.

Though he released her before she'd even thought to demand it, Jillian gathered her wits quickly enough. ''What the hell do you think—''

''Sorry.'' His eyes were laughing, but he held his hands up, palms out in a gesture of peace. ''Lost my head. Something comes over me when you look at me as though you'd like to cut me into small pieces. *Very* small pieces,'' he added as he took the hat from where it hung at her back and placed it back on her head.

''Next time I won't just look,'' she said precisely, wheeling away toward the corral.

Aaron fell into step beside her. ''How's the calf?''

''He's doing well. Vet's coming by to check him over this afternoon, but he took the bottle again this morning.''

''Was he sired by that new bull of yours?'' When Jillian sent him a sharp look, Aaron smiled blandly. ''Word gets around. As it happens, you snatched him up from under my nose. I was making arrangements to go to England to check him out for myself when I heard you'd bought him.''

''Really?'' It was news—and news she couldn't help but be pleased to hear.

''Thought that might make your day,'' Aaron said mildly.

"Nasty of me," Jillian admitted as they came to the corral fence. Resting a foot on the lower rail, she smiled at him. "I'm not a nice person, Murdock."

He gave her an odd look and nodded. "Then we'll deal well enough together. What's the nickname your hands have dubbed that bull?"

Her smile warmed so that the dimple flickered. He was going to have to find out what it felt like to put his lips just there. "The Terror's the cleanest in polite company."

He chuckled. "I don't think that was the one I heard. How many calves so far?"

"Fifty. It's early yet."

"Mmm. Are you using artificial insemination?"

Her eyes narrowed. "Why?"

"Just curious. We are in the same business, Jillian."

"That's not something I'll forget," she said evenly.

Annoyance tightened his mouth. "Which doesn't mean we have to be opponents."

"Doesn't it?" Jillian shifted her hat lower on her forehead. "I came to look at your stud, Murdock."

He stood watching her a moment, long enough, directly enough, to make Jillian want to squirm. "So you did," Aaron said quietly. Plucking a halter from the fence post, he swung lithely over the corral fence.

Rude, Jillian condemned herself. It was one thing to be cautious, even unfriendly, but another to be pointedly rude. It wasn't like her. Frowning, Jillian leaned on the fence and rested her chin in her open hand. Yet she'd been rude to Aaron almost continually since their first encounter. Her frown cleared as she watched him approach the stallion.

Both males were strong and well built, and each was

inclined to want his own way. At the moment the stallion wasn't in the mood for the halter. He pranced away from Aaron to lap disinterestedly at his water trough. Aaron murmured something that had Samson shaking his head and trotting off again.

"You devil," she heard Aaron say, but there was a laugh in his voice. Aaron crossed to him again, and again the stallion danced off in the opposite direction.

Laughing, Jillian climbed the fence and sat on the top rung. "Round 'em up, cowboy," she drawled.

Aaron flashed her a grin, then shrugged as though he'd given up and turned his back on the stallion. By the time he'd crossed the center of the corral, Samson had come up behind him to nudge his head into Aaron's back.

"Now you wanna make up," he murmured, turning to ruffle the horse's mane before he slipped on the halter. "After you've made me look like a greenhorn in front of the lady."

Greenhorn, hell, Jillian thought, watching the way he handled the skittish stallion. If he cared about impressing anyone, he'd have made the difficult look difficult instead of making it look easy. With a sigh, she felt her respect for him go up another notch.

Automatically she reached out to stroke the stallion's neck as Aaron led him to her. He had a coat like silk, and eyes that were wary but not mean. "Aaron..." She glanced down in time to see his brow lift at her voluntary use of his name. "I'm sorry," she said simply.

Something flickered in his eyes, but they were so dark it was difficult to read it. "All right," he said just

as simply and held out a hand. She took it and hopped down.

"He's beautiful." Jillian ran her hands along Samson's wide chest and sleek flank. "Have you bred him before?"

"Twice in Billings," he said, watching her.

"How long have you had him?" She went to Samson's head, then passed under him to the other side.

"Since he was a foal. It took me five days to catch his father." Jillian looked up and caught the light in his eyes. "There must've been a hundred and fifty mustangs in his herd. He was a cagey devil, damn near killed me the first time I got a rope around him. Then he busted down the stall and nearly got away again. You should've seen him, blood spurting out of his leg, fire in his eyes. It took six of us to control him when we bred him to the mare."

"What did you do with him?" Jillian swallowed, thinking how easy it would be to breed the wild stallion again and again, then geld him. Break his spirit.

Aaron's eyes met hers over Samson's withers. "I let him go. Some things you don't fence."

She smiled. Before she realized it, she reached over Samson for Aaron's hand. "I'm glad."

With his eyes on hers, Aaron stroked a thumb over her knuckles. The palm of his hand was rough, the back of hers smooth. "You're an interesting woman, Jillian, with a few rather appealing soft spots."

Disturbed, she tried to slip her hand from his. "Very few."

"Which is why they're appealing. You were beautiful last night, sitting in the hay, crooning to the calf, with the light in your hair."

She knew about clever words. Why were these making her pulse jerky? "I'm not beautiful," she said flatly. "I don't want to be."

He tilted his head when he realized she was perfectly serious. "Well, we can't have everything we want, can we?"

"Don't start again, Murdock," she ordered, sharply enough that the stallion moved restlessly under their joined hands.

"Start what?"

"You know, I wondered why I always end up being rude to you," she began. "I realize it's simply because you don't understand anything else. Let go of my hand."

His eyes narrowed at her tone. "No." Tightening his hold, he gave the stallion a quick pat that sent him trotting off, leaving nothing between himself and Jillian. "I wondered why I always end up wanting to toss you over my knee—or my shoulder," he added thoughtfully. "Must be for the same reason."

"Your reasons don't interest me, Murdock."

His lips curved slowly, but his eyes held something entirely different from humor. "Now, I might've believed that, Jillian, if it hadn't been for last night." He took a step closer. "Maybe I kissed you first, but, lady, you kissed me right back. I had a whole long night to think about that. And about just what I was going to do about it."

Maybe it was because he'd spoken the truth when she didn't care to hear it. Maybe it had something to do with the wicked gleam in his eyes or the insolence of his smile. It might have been a combination of all three that loosened Jillian's temper. Before she had a

chance to think about it, or Aaron a chance to react, she'd drawn back her fist and plunged it hard into his stomach.

"That's what *I* intend to do about it!" she declared as he grunted. She had only a fleeting glimpse of the astonishment on his face before she spun on her heel and strode away. She didn't get far.

Jillian's breath was knocked out of her as he brought her down in a tackle. She found herself flat on her back, pinned under him with a face filled with fury rather than astonishment looming over hers. It only took her a second to fight back, and little more to realize she was outmatched.

"You hellion," Aaron grunted as he held her down. "You've been asking for a thrashing since the first time I laid eyes on you."

"It'll take a better man than you, Murdock." She nearly succeeded in bringing her knee up and scoring a very important point. Instead he shifted until her position was only more vulnerable. Heat that had nothing to do with temper surged into her stomach.

"By God, you tempt me to prove you wrong." She squirmed again and stirred something dangerous in him. "Woman, if you want to fight dirty, you've come to the right place." He closed his mouth over hers before she could swear at him. At the instant of contact he felt the pulse in her wrist bound under his hands. Then he felt nothing but the hot give of her mouth.

If she was still struggling beneath him, he wasn't aware of it. Aaron felt himself sinking, and sinking much deeper than he'd expected. The sun was warm on his back, she was soft under him, yet he felt only that moist, silky texture that was her lips. He thought

he could make do with that sensation alone for the rest
of his life. It scared him to death.

Pulling himself back, he stared down at her. She'd
stolen the breath from him much more successfully
this time than she had with the quick jab to the gut.
''I ought to beat you,'' he said softly.

Somehow in her prone position she managed to
thrust her chin out. ''I'd prefer it.'' It wasn't the first
lie she'd told, but it might have been the biggest.

She told herself a woman didn't want to be kissed
by a man who tossed her on the ground. Yet her conscience played back that she'd deserved that at the
least. She wasn't a fragile doll and didn't want to be
treated like one. But she shouldn't want him to kiss
her again…want it so badly she could already taste it.
''Will you get off me?'' she said between her teeth.
''You're not as skinny as you look.''

''It's safer talking to you this way.''

''I don't want to talk to you.''

The gleam shot back in his eyes. ''Then we won't
talk.''

Before Jillian could protest, or Aaron could do what
he'd intended, Samson lowered his head between their
faces.

''Get your own filly,'' Aaron muttered, shoving him
aside.

''He's got a smoother technique than you,'' Jillian
began, then choked on a laugh as the horse bent down
again. ''Oh, for God's sake, Aaron, let me up. This is
ridiculous.''

Instead of obliging he looked back down at her. Her
eyes were bright with laughter now, her dimple flash-

ing. Her hair spread like fire in the dust. "I'm beginning to like it. You don't do that enough."

She blew the hair out of her eyes. "What?"

"Smile at me."

She laughed again and he felt the arms under his hands relax. "Why should I?"

"Because I like it."

She tried to give a long-winded sigh, but it ended on a chuckle. "If I apologize for hitting you, will you let me up?"

"Don't spoil it—besides, you won't catch me off guard again."

No, she didn't imagine she would. "Well, in any case you deserved it—and you paid me back. Now, get up, Murdock. This ground's hard."

"Is it? You're not." He lifted a brow as he shifted into a more comfortable position. He wondered if her legs would look as nice as they felt. "Anyway, we still have to discuss that remark about my technique."

"The best I can say about it," Jillian began as Aaron pushed absently at Samson's head again, "is that it needs some polishing. If you'll excuse me, I really have to get back. Some of us work for a living."

"Polishing," he murmured, ignoring the rest. "You'd like something a little—smoother." His voice dropped intimately as he brushed his lips over her cheek, light as a whisper. He heard the quick, involuntary sound she made as he moved lazily toward her mouth.

"Don't." Her voice trembled on the word so that he looked down at her again. Vulnerability. It was in her eyes. That, and a touch of panic. He hadn't expected to see either.

"An Achilles' heel," he murmured, moved, aroused. "You've given me an advantage, Jillian." Lifting a hand, he traced her mouth with a fingertip and felt it tremble. "It's only fair to warn you that I'll use it."

"Your only advantage at the moment is your weight."

He grinned, but before he could speak a shadow fell over them.

"Boy, what're you doing with that little lady on the ground?"

Jillian turned her head and saw an old man with sharp, well-defined features and dark eyes. Though he was pale and had an air of fragility, she saw the resemblance. Astonished, she stared at him. Could this bent old man who leaned heavily on a cane, who was so painfully thin, be the much feared and respected Paul Murdock? His eyes, dark and intense as Aaron's, skimmed over her. The hand on the cane had the faintest of tremors.

Aaron looked up at his father and grinned. "I'm not sure yet," he said easily. "It's a choice between beating her or making love."

Murdock gave a wheezing laugh and curled one hand around the rail of the fence. "It's a stupid man who wouldn't know which choice to make, but you'll do neither here. Let the filly up so I can have a look at her."

Aaron obliged, taking Jillian by the arm and hauling her unceremoniously to her feet. She slanted him a killing glare before she looked back at his father. What nasty twist of fate had decided that she would meet Paul J. Murdock for the first time with corral dust

clinging to her and her body still warm from his son's? she wondered as she silently cursed Aaron. Then she tossed back her hair and lifted her chin.

Murdock's face remained calm and unexpressive. "So, you're Clay Baron's granddaughter."

She met his steady hawklike gaze levelly. "Yes, I am."

"You look like your grandmother."

Her chin lifted a fraction higher. "So I've been told."

"She was a fire-eater." A ghost of a smile touched his eyes. "Hasn't been a Baron on my land since she marched over here to pay her respects to Karen after the wedding. If some young buck had tried to wrestle with her, she'd have blackened his eye."

Aaron leaned on the fence, running a hand over his stomach. "She hit me first," he drawled, grinning at Jillian. "Hard."

Jillian slipped her hat from her back and meticulously began to dust it off and straighten it. "Better tighten up those muscles, Murdock," she suggested as she set the hat back on her head. "I can hit a lot harder." She glanced over as Paul Murdock began to laugh.

"I always thought I should've thrashed him a sight more. What's your name, girl?"

She eyed him uncertainly. "Jillian."

"You're a pretty thing," he said with a nod. "And it doesn't appear you lack for sense. My wife would be glad for some company."

For a minute she could only stare at him. This was the fierce Murdock—her grandfather's arch rival—inviting her into his home? "Thank you, Mr. Murdock."

"Come in for coffee, then," he said briskly, then shot a look at Aaron. "You and I have some business to clear up."

Jillian felt something pass between the two men that wasn't entirely pleasant before Murdock turned to walk back toward the house. "You'll come in," Aaron said as he unlatched the gate. It wasn't an invitation but a statement. Curious, Jillian let it pass.

"For a little while. I've got to get back."

They walked through the gate together and relatched it. Though they moved slowly, they caught up with Murdock as he reached the porch steps. Seeing his struggle to negotiate them with the cane, Jillian automatically started to reach out for his arm. Aaron grabbed her wrist. He shook his head, then waited until his father had painstakingly gained the porch.

"Karen!" It might have been a bellow if it hadn't been so breathless. "You've got company." Murdock swung open the front door and gestured Jillian in.

It was more palatial than Utopia's main building, but had the same western feel that had first charmed a little girl from Chicago. All the wood was highly polished—the floor, the beams in the ceilings, the woodwork—all satiny oak. But here was something Utopia lacked. That subtle woman's touch.

There were fresh flowers arranged in a pottery bowl, and softer colors. Though Jillian's grandfather had kept the ivory lace curtains at the windows, his ranch house had reverted to a man's dwelling over the years. Until she walked into the Murdock home and felt Karen's presence, Jillian hadn't realized it.

There was a huge Indian rug spread over the floor in the living area and glossy brass urns beside the fire-

place that held tall dried flowers. A seat was fashioned into a bow window and piled with hand-worked pillows. The room had a sense of order and welcome.

"Aren't either of you men going to offer Jillian a chair?" Karen asked mildly as she wheeled in a coffee cart.

"She seems to be Aaron's filly," Murdock commented as he lowered himself into a wing-backed chair and hooked his cane over the arm.

Jillian's automatic retort was stifled as Aaron nudged her onto the sofa. Gritting her teeth, she turned to Karen. "You have a lovely home, Mrs. Murdock."

Karen didn't attempt to disguise her amusement. "Thank you. I believe I saw you at the rodeo last year," she continued as she began to pour coffee. "I remember thinking you looked like Maggie—your grandmother. Do you plan to compete again this year?"

"Yes." Jillian accepted the cup, declining cream or sugar. "Even though my foreman squawked quite a bit when I beat his time in the calf roping."

Aaron reached over to toy with her hair. "That tempts me to enter myself."

"It'd be a pretty sorry day when a son of mine couldn't rope a calf quicker than a female," Murdock muttered.

Aaron sent him a bland look. "That would depend on the female."

"You might be out of practice," Jillian said coolly as she sipped her coffee. "After five years behind a desk." As soon as she'd said it, Jillian felt the tension between father and son, a bit more strained, a bit more unpleasant than she'd felt once before.

"I suppose things like that are in the blood," Karen said smoothly. "You've taken to ranch life, but you were raised back east, weren't you?"

"Chicago," Jillian admitted, wondering what she'd stirred up. "I never fit in." It was out before she realized it. A frown flickered briefly in her eyes before she controlled it. "I suppose ranching just skipped a generation in my family," she said easily.

"You have a brother, don't you?" Karen stirred the slightest bit of cream into her own coffee.

"Yes, he's a doctor. He and my father share a practice now."

"I remember the boy—your father," Murdock told her, then chugged down half a cup of coffee. "Quiet, serious fellow who never said three words if two would do."

Jillian had to smile. "You remember him well."

"Easy to understand why Baron left the ranch to you instead." Murdock held out his cup for more coffee, but Jillian noticed that Karen only filled it halfway. "Guess you can't do much better than Gil Haley for running things."

Her dimple flickered. It was, she supposed, a compliment of sorts. "Gil's the best foreman I could ask for," Jillian said mildly. "But I run Utopia."

Murdock's brows drew together. "Women don't run ranches, girl."

Her chin angled. "This one does."

"Nothing but trouble when you start having cowboys in skirts," he said with a snort.

"I don't wear them when I'm hazing cattle."

He set down his cup and leaned forward. "Whatever I felt about your grandfather, it wouldn't sit well with

me to see what he worked for blown away because of some female.''

''Paul,'' Karen began, but Jillian was already rolling.

''Clay wasn't so narrow-minded,'' Jillian shot back. ''If a person was capable, it didn't matter what sex they were. I run Utopia, and before I'm done you'll be watching your back door.'' She rose, unconsciously regal. ''I've got work to do. Thank you for the coffee, Mrs. Murdock.'' She shot a look at Aaron, who was still lounging back on the sofa. ''We still have to discuss your stud.''

''What's this?'' Murdock demanded, banging his cane.

''I'm breeding Samson to one of Jillian's mares,'' Aaron said easily.

Color surged into Murdock's pale face. ''A Murdock doesn't do business with a Baron.''

Aaron unfolded himself slowly and stood. ''I do business as I please,'' Jillian heard him say as she started for the door. She was already at her car when Aaron caught up with her.

''What's your fee?'' she said between her teeth.

He leaned against the car. If he was angry, she couldn't see it. ''You spark easily, Jillian. I'm usually the only one who can put my father in a rage these days.''

''Your father,'' she said precisely, ''is a bigot.''

With his thumbs hooked idly in his pockets, Aaron studied the house. ''Yeah. But he knows his cows.''

She let out a long breath because she wanted to chuckle. ''About the stud fee, Murdock.''

''Come to dinner tonight, we'll talk about it.''

"I haven't time for socializing," she said flatly.

"You've been around long enough to know the advantages of a business dinner."

She frowned at the house. An evening with the Murdocks? No, she didn't think she could get through one without throwing something. "Look, Aaron, I'd like to breed Delilah with Samson—if the terms are right. I'm not interested in anything more to do with you or your family."

"Why?"

"There's been bad blood between the Barons and Murdocks for almost a century."

He gave her a lazy look under lowered lids. "Now who's a bigot?"

Bull's-eye, she thought and sighed. Putting her hands on her hips, she tried to bring her temper to order. Murdock was an old man, and from the looks of him, a sick one. He was also, though she'd choke rather than admit it, a great deal like her grandfather. She'd be a pretty poor individual if she couldn't drum up some understanding. "All right, I'll come to dinner." She turned back to him. "But I won't be responsible if it ends up with a lot of shouting."

"I think we might avoid that. I'll pick you up at seven."

"I know the way," she countered and started to push him aside to open her door. His hand curled over her forearm.

"I'll pick you up, Jillian." The steel was back, in his eyes, his voice.

She shrugged. "Suit yourself."

He cupped the back of her head and kissed her before she could prevent it. "I intend to," he told her easily, then left her to walk back into the house.

Chapter 4

Jillian was still smarting when she returned to Utopia. Murdock's comments, and Aaron's arrogance, had set her back up. She wasn't the sort of woman who made a habit of calming down gracefully. She told herself the only reason she was going back to the Double M to deal with the Murdocks again was because she was interested in a breeding contract. She wanted to believe it.

Dust flew out from her wheels as she drove up the hard-packed road to the ranch yard. It was nearly deserted now at mid-morning, with most of the men out on the range, others busy in the outbuildings. But even an audience wouldn't have prevented her from springing out of her car and slamming the door with a vicious swing. She'd never been a woman who believed in letting her temper simmer if it could boil.

The sound of the door slam echoed like a pistol shot.

Fleetingly she thought of the paperwork waiting for her in the office, then brushed it aside. She couldn't deal with ledgers and numbers at the moment. She needed something physical to drain off the anger before she tackled the dry practicality of checks and balances. Spinning on her heel, she headed for the stables. There'd be stalls to muck out and tack to clean.

"Anybody in particular you'd like to mow down?"

With her eyes still sparkling with anger, Jillian whipped her head around. Joe Carlson walked toward her, his neat hat shading his eyes, a faint, friendly smile on his lips.

"*Murdocks.*"

He nodded after the short explosion of the word. "Figured it was something along those lines. Couldn't come to an agreement on the stud fee?"

"We haven't started negotiating yet." Her jaw clenched. "I'm going back this evening."

Joe scanned her face, wondering that a woman who played poker so craftily should be so utterly readable when riled. "Oh?" he said simply and earned a glare.

"That's right." She bit off each word. "If Murdock didn't have such a damn beautiful horse, I'd tell him to go to the devil and to take his father with him."

This time Joe grinned. "You met Paul Murdock, then."

"He gave me his opinion on cowboys in skirts." Her teeth shut with an audible click.

"Really?"

The dry tone was irresistible. Jillian grinned back at him. "Yes, really." Then she sighed, remembering how difficult it had been for Paul Murdock to climb the four steps to his own porch. "Oh, hell," she mur-

mured, cooling off as quickly as she'd flared. "I shouldn't have let him get under my skin. He's an old man and—"

She broke off, stopping herself before she added *ill*. For some indefinable reason she found it necessary to allow Murdock whatever illusions he had left. Instead she shrugged and glanced toward the corral. "I suppose I'm just used to the way Clay was. If you could ride and drive cattle, he didn't care if you were male or female."

Joe gave her one sharp glance. It wasn't what she'd started to say, but he'd get nothing out of her by probing. One thing he'd learned in the past six months was that Jillian Baron was a woman who did things her way. If a man got too close, one freezing look reminded him how much distance was expected.

"Maybe you'd like to take another look at the bull now, if you've got a few minutes."

"Hmm?" Abstracted, she looked back at him.

"The bull," Joe repeated.

"Oh, yeah." Hooking her thumbs in her pockets, she began to walk with him. "Gil told you about the calves we counted yesterday?"

"Took a look in the south section today. You've got some more."

"How many?"

"Oh, thirty or so. In another week all the calves should be dropped."

"You know, when we were checking the pasture yesterday, I thought the numbers were a little light." Frowning, she went over the numbers in her head again. "I'm going to need someone to go out there and see that some of the bred cows haven't strayed."

"I'll take care of it. How's the orphan?"

With a grin Jillian glanced back toward the cattle barn. "He's going to be fine." Attachments were a mistake, she knew. But it was already too late between her and Baby. "I'd swear he's grown since yesterday."

"And here's Poppa," Joe announced as they came to the bull's paddock.

After angling the hat farther over her eyes, Jillian leaned on the fence. Beautiful, she thought. Absolutely beautiful.

The bull eyed them balefully and snorted air. He didn't have the bulk or girth of an Angus but was built, Jillian thought, like a sleek tank. His red hide glistened as he stood in the full sun. She didn't see boredom in his expression as she'd seen in so many of the steers or cows, but arrogance. His horns curved around the wide white face and gave him a sense of dangerous royalty. It occurred to her that the little orphan she had sheltered in the cattle barn would look essentially the same in a year's time. The bull snorted again and pawed the ground as if daring them to come inside and try their luck.

"His personality's grim at best," Joe commented.

"I don't need him to be polite," Jillian murmured. "I just need him to produce."

"Well, you don't have any problem there." His gaze skimmed over the bull. "From the looks of the calves in this first batch, he's already done a good job for us. Since we're using artificial insemination now, he should be able to service every Hereford cow on the ranch this spring. Your shorthorn bull's a fine piece of beef, Jillian, but he doesn't come up to this one."

"No." Smiling, she rested her elbows on the rail. "As a matter of fact, I found out today that Aaron Murdock was interested in our, ah, Casanova. I can't help but pat myself on the back when I remember how I sent off to England for him on a hunch. Damned expensive hunch," she added, thinking of the hefty dent in the books. "Aaron told me today that he was planning on going over to England to take a look at the bull himself when he learned we'd bought him."

"That was a year ago," Joe commented with a frown. "He was still in Billings."

Jillian shrugged. "I guess he was keeping his finger in the pie. In any case, we've got him." She pushed away from the rail. "I meant what I said about the fair in July, Joe. I can't say I cared much about competition and ribbons before. This year I want to win."

Joe brought his attention from the bull and studied her. "Personal?"

"Yeah." She gave him a grim smile. "You could say it's personal. In the meantime, I'm counting on this guy to give me the best line of beef cattle in Montana. I need a good price in Miles City if I'm going to keep the books in the black. And next year when some of his calves are ready..." She trailed off with a last look at the bull. "Well, we'll just take it a bit at a time. Get back to me on those numbers, Joe. I want to take a look at Baby before I go into the office."

"I'll take care of it," he said again and watched her walk away.

By five Jillian had brought the books up to date and was, if not elated with the figures, at least satisfied. True, the expenses had taken a sharp increase over the

last year, but by roundup time, she anticipated a tidy profit from the Livestock Auction Saleyard in Miles City. The expenses had been a gamble, but a necessary one. The plane would be in use within the week and the bull had already proved himself.

Tipping back in her grandfather's worn leather chair, she studied the ceiling. If she could find the time, she'd like to learn how to fly the plane herself. As owner she felt it imperative that she have at least a working knowledge of every aspect of the ranch. In a pinch she could shoe a horse or stitch up a rent hide. She'd learned to operate a hay baler and a bulldozer during a summer visit when she'd still been a teenager—the same year she'd wielded her first and last knife to turn a calf into a steer.

When and if she could afford the luxury, she thought, she'd hire someone to take over the books. Grimacing, she closed the ledger. She had more energy left after ten hours on horseback than she did after four behind a desk.

For now it couldn't be helped. She could justify adding another puncher to the payroll, but not a paper pusher. Next year... She laughed at herself and rested her feet on the desk.

Trouble was, she was counting too heavily on next year and too many things could happen. A drought could mean the loss of crops, a blizzard the loss of cattle. And that was just nature. If feed prices continued to rise, she was going to have to seriously consider selling off a larger portion of the calves as baby beef. Then there was the repair bill for the Jeep, the vet bill, the food bill for the hands. The bill for fuel that would rise once the plane was in use. Yes, she was going to

need top dollar in Miles City and a blue ribbon or two wouldn't hurt.

In the meantime she was going to keep an eye on her spring calves. And Aaron Murdock. With a half smile, Jillian thought of him. He was an arrogant son of a bitch, she mused with something very close to admiration, and sharp as they came. It was a pity she didn't trust him enough to discuss ranch business with him and kick around ideas. She'd missed that luxury since her grandfather died. The men were friendly enough, but you didn't talk about your business with a hand who might be working for someone else next year. And Gil was...Gil was Gil, she thought with a grin. He was fond of her, even respected her abilities, though he wouldn't come out and say so. But he was too steeped in his own ways to talk about ideas and changes. So that left—no one, Jillian admitted.

There had been times in Chicago when she could have screamed for privacy, for solitude. Now there were times she ached just to have someone to share an hour's conversation with. With a shake of her head she rose. She was getting foolish. She had dozens of people to talk to. All she had to do was go down to the barn or the stables. Wherever this sudden discontent had come from it would fade again quickly enough. She didn't have time for it.

Her boots clicked lightly on the floor as she walked through the house and up the stairs. From outside she could hear the ring of the triangle, those quick three notes that ran faster and faster until it was one high sound. Her hands would be sitting down to their meal. She'd better get ready for her own.

Jillian toyed with the idea of just slipping into clean

jeans and a shirt. The deliberate casualness of such an outfit would be pointedly rude. She was still annoyed enough at both Aaron and his father to do it, but she thought of Karen Murdock. With a sigh, Jillian rejected the idea and hunted through her closet.

It was a matter of her own choice that she had few dresses. They were relegated to one side of her closet, and she rooted them out on the occasions when she entertained other ranchers or businessmen. She stuck with simple styles, having found it to her advantage not to call her femininity to attention. Standing in a brief teddy, she skimmed over her options.

The oversized white cotton shirt wasn't precisely masculine in cut, but it was still casual. Matched with a full white wrap skirt with yards of sash, it made an outfit she thought not only suitable but understated. She made a small concession with a touch of makeup, hesitated over jewelry, then, shrugging, clipped small swirls of gold at her ears. Her mother, Jillian thought, would have badgered her to do something more sophisticated with her hair. Instead she ran a brush through it and left it down. She didn't need elegant styles to discuss breeding contracts.

When she heard the sound of a car drive up outside, she stopped herself from going to the window to peer out. Deliberately she took her time going back downstairs.

Aaron wasn't wearing a hat. Without it Jillian realized he still looked like what he was—a rugged outdoorsman with touches of the aristocracy. He didn't need the uniform to show it.

Looking at him, she wondered how he had found the patience to sit in Billings behind a desk. Trim black

slacks and a thin black sweater fit him as truly as his work clothes, yet they seemed to accent the wickedness of his dark looks. She felt an involuntary stir and met his eyes coolly.

"You're prompt," she commented and let the door swing shut behind her. It might not be wise to be alone with him any longer than necessary.

"So are you." He let his gaze move over her slowly, appreciating the simplicity of her outfit—the way the sash accented her small waist and narrow hips, the way the unrelieved white made her skin glow and her hair spark like fire. "And beautiful," he added, taking her hand. "Whether you like it or not."

Because her pulse reacted immediately, Jillian knew she had to tread carefully. "You keep risking that hand of yours, Murdock." When she tried to slip hers from it, he merely tightened his fingers.

"One thing I've learned is that nothing's worth having if you don't have trouble getting it." Very deliberately he brought her hand to his lips, watching her steadily.

It wasn't a gesture she expected from him. Perhaps that was why she did nothing but stare at him as the sun dipped lower in the sky. She should've jerked her hand away—she wanted to spread her fingers so that she could touch that high curve of cheekbone, that lean line of jaw. She did nothing—until he smiled.

"Maybe I should warn you," Jillian said evenly, "that the next time I hit you, I'm going to aim a bit lower."

He grinned, then kissed her hand again before he released it. "I believe it."

Because she couldn't stop her own smile, she gave

up. "Are you going to feed me, Murdock, or not?" Without waiting for an answer, she walked down the steps in front of him.

His car was more in tune with the oil man she'd first envisioned. A low, sleek Maserati. She admired anything well built and fast and settled into her seat with a little sigh. "Nice toy," she commented with a hint of the smile still playing around her mouth.

"I like it," Aaron said easily when he started the engine. It roared into life, then settled down to a purr. "A man doesn't always like to take a woman out in a Jeep or pickup."

"This isn't a date," she reminded him but skimmed her fingers over the smooth leather of the upholstery.

"I admire your practical streak—most of the time."

Jillian turned in her seat to watch the way he handled the car. As well as he handles a horse, she decided. As well as she was certain he handled a woman. The smile curved her lips again. He was going to discover that she wasn't a woman who took to being handled. She settled back to enjoy the ride.

"How does your father feel about me coming to dinner?" she asked idly. Those last slanting rays of the sun were tipping the grass with gold. She heard a cow moo lazily.

"How should he feel about it?" Aaron countered.

"He was amiable enough when I was simply Clay Baron's granddaughter," Jillian pointed out. "But once he found out I was *the* Baron, so to speak, he changed his tune. You're fraternizing with the enemy, aren't you?"

Aaron took his eyes off the road long enough to

meet her amused look with one of his own. "So to speak. Aren't you?"

"I suppose I prefer to look at it as making a mutually advantageous bargain. Aaron..." She hesitated, picking her way carefully over what she knew was none of her business. "Your father's very ill, isn't he?"

She could see his expression draw inward, though it barely changed at all. "Yes."

"I'm sorry." Jillian turned to look out the side window. "It's hard," she murmured, thinking of her grandfather. "It's so hard for them."

"He's dying," Aaron said flatly.

"Oh, but—"

"He's dying," he repeated. "Five years ago they told him he had a year, two at most. He outfoxed them. But now..." His fingers contracted briefly on the wheel, then relaxed again. "He might make it to the first snow, but he won't make it to the last."

He sounded so matter-of-fact. Perhaps she'd imagined that quick tension in his fingers. "There hasn't even been a rumor of his illness."

"No, we intend to keep it that way."

She frowned at his profile. "Then why did you tell me?"

"Because you understand about pride and you don't play games."

Jillian studied him another moment, then turned away. No soft words or whispered compliments could have moved her more than that brisk, emotionless statement. "It must be difficult for your mother."

"She's tougher than she looks."

''Yes.'' Jillian smiled again. ''She'd have to be to put up with him.''

They drove under the high-arched *Double M* at the entrance to the ranch. The day was hovering at dusk when the light grew lazy and the air soft. Cattle stood slack-hipped in the pasture to the right. She saw a mother licking patiently to clean her baby's hide while other calves were busy at their evening feeding. In another few months they'd be heifers and steers, the maternal bond forgotten, but for now they were just babies with awkward legs and demanding stomachs.

''I like this time of day,'' she murmured, half to herself. ''When work's over and it isn't time to think about tomorrow yet.''

He glanced down at her hand that lay relaxed against the seat. Competent, unpampered, with narrow bones and slender fingers. ''Did you ever consider that you work too hard?''

Jillian turned and met his gaze calmly. ''No.''

''I didn't think you did.''

''Cowboys in skirts again, Murdock?''

''No.'' But he'd made a few discreet inquiries. Jillian Baron had a reputation for working a twelve-hour day—on a horse, in a pickup, on her feet. If she wasn't riding fence or hazing cattle, she was feeding her stock, overseeing repairs, or poring over the books. ''What do you do to relax?'' he asked abruptly. Her blank look gave him the answer before she did.

''I don't have a lot of time for that right now. When I do there are books or the toy Clay bought a couple years ago.''

''Toy?''

"Videotape machine," she said with a grin. "He loved the movies."

"Solitary entertainments," Aaron mused.

"It's a solitary way of life," Jillian countered, then glanced over curiously when he stopped in front of a simple white frame house. "What's this?"

"It's where I live," Aaron told her easily before he stepped from the car.

She sat where she was, frowning at the house. She'd taken it for granted that he lived in the sprawling main house another quarter mile or so up the road. Just as she'd taken it for granted that they were having dinner there, with his parents. Jillian turned her head as he opened her door and sent him an uncompromising look. "What are you up to, Murdock?"

"Dinner." Taking her hand, he pulled her from the car. "Isn't that what we'd agreed on?"

"I was under the impression we were having it up there." She gestured in the general direction of the ranch house.

Aaron followed the movement of her hand. When he turned back to her, his mouth was solemn, his eyes amused. "Wrong impression."

"You didn't do anything to correct it."

"Or to promote it," he countered. "My parents don't have anything to do with what's between us, Jillian."

"Nothing is."

Now his lips smiled as well. "There's a matter of the horses—yours and mine." When she continued to frown, he stepped closer, his body just brushing hers. "Afraid to be alone with me, Jillian?"

Her chin came up. "You overestimate yourself, Murdock."

He saw from the look in her eyes that she wouldn't back down no matter what he did. The temptation was too great. Lowering his head, he nipped at her bottom lip. "Maybe," he said softly. "Maybe not. We can always ride on up to the main house if you're—nervous."

Her heart had already risen to the base of her throat to pound. But she knew what it was to deal with a stray wildcat. "You don't worry me," she said mildly, then turned to walk to the house.

Oh, yes, I do, Aaron thought, and admired her all the more because she was determined to face him down. He decided, as he moved to open the front door, that it promised to be an interesting evening.

She couldn't fault his taste. Jillian glanced around his living quarters, wondering just how much she could learn about him from his choice of furnishings. Apparently, he had his mother's flair for style and color, though there were no subtle feminine touches here. Buffs and creams were offset by a stunning wall hanging slashed with vivid blues and greens. He favored antiques and clean lines. Though the room was small, there was no sense of clutter. Curious, she wandered to a curved mahogany shelf and studied his collection of pewter.

The mustang at full gallop caught her attention, though all the animals in the miniature menagerie were finely crafted. For a moment she wished he wasn't a man who appreciated what appealed to her quite so much. Then, remembering the stand she had to take,

she turned around. "This is very nice. Though it is a bit simple for a man who grew up the way you did."

His brow lifted. "I'll take the compliment. How do you like your steak?"

Jillian dipped her hands in the wide pockets of her skirt. "Medium rare."

"Keep me company while I fix them." He curled a hand around her arm and moved through the house with her.

"So, I get Murdock beef prepared by a Murdock." She shot him a look. "I suppose I should be complimented."

"We might consider it a peace offering."

"We might," Jillian said cautiously, then smiled. "Providing you know how to cook. I haven't eaten since breakfast."

"Why not?"

He gave her such a disapproving look that she laughed. "I got bogged down in paperwork. I can't work up much of an appetite sitting at a desk. Well, well," she added, glancing around his kitchen. Its simplicity suited the house, with its hardwood floor and plain counters. There wasn't a crumb out of place. "You're a tidy one, aren't you?"

"I lived in the bunkhouse for a while." Aaron uncorked a bottle of wine that stood on the counter next to two glasses. "It either corrupts or reforms you."

"Why the bunkhouse when—" She cut herself off, annoyed that she'd begun to pry again.

"My father and I deal together better when there's some distance." He poured wine into both glasses. "You'd have heard by now that we don't always agree."

"I heard you'd had a falling-out a few years ago, before you went to Billings."

"And you wondered why I—buckled under instead of telling him to go to hell and starting my own place."

Jillian accepted the wine he handed her. "All right, yes, I wondered. It's none of my business."

He looked into his glass a moment, as if studying the dark red color of the wine. "No." Aaron glanced back up and sipped. "It's not."

Without another word he turned to take two hefty steaks out of the refrigerator. Jillian sipped her wine and remained quiet, watching him as he began preparation of the meal with the deft, economical moves that were characteristic of him. Five years ago they'd given his father a year, perhaps two, to live. Aaron had told her that without even a hint of emotion in his voice. And he'd gone to Billings five years before.

To wait his father out? she wondered and winced at the thought. No, she couldn't believe that of him—a man cool and calculating enough to wait for his father to die? Even if his feelings for his father didn't run deep, it was too cold, too heartless. With a shudder, Jillian took a deep swallow of her wine, then set it down. She wouldn't believe it of him.

"Anything I can do?"

Aaron glanced over his shoulder to see her calmly watching him. He knew what direction her thoughts had taken—the logical direction. Now he saw she'd decided in his favor. He told himself he didn't give a damn one way or the other. It wasn't just astonishing to find out he did, it was enervating. He could feel the emotion stir, and drain him. To give himself a moment

to settle, he slipped the steaks under the broiler and turned it on.

"Yeah, there's something you can do." Crossing to her, Aaron framed her face in his hands, seeing her eyes widen in surprise just before his mouth closed over hers. He meant to keep it hard and brief. A gesture—a gesture only to rid him of whatever emotion had suddenly sprung up in him. But as his lips moved over hers the emotion swelled, threatening to take over as the kiss lingered.

She stiffened, and lifted her hands to his chest in automatic defense. Aaron found he didn't want the struggle that usually appealed to him, but the softness he knew she'd give to very few. "Jillian, don't." His fingers tangled in her hair. His voice had roughened with feelings—mysterious, unnamed—he didn't pause to question. "Don't fight me—just this once."

Something in his voice, that quiet hint of need, had her hands relaxing against him before the thought to do so had registered. So she yielded, and in yielding brought herself a moment of sweet, mindless pleasure.

His mouth gentled on hers even as he took her deeper. Her hands crept up to his shoulders, her head tilted back so that he might take what he needed and bring her more of that soft, soft delight she hadn't been aware existed. With a sigh that came from discovery, she gave.

He hadn't known he was capable of tenderness. There'd never been a woman who'd drawn it from him before. He hadn't been aware that desire could ever be calm and easy. Yet while the need built inside of him, he felt a quiet wave of contentment. Aaron basked in it until it made him light-headed. Shaken, he eased her

away, studying her face like a man who had seen something he didn't quite understand. And wasn't sure he wanted to.

Jillian took a step back, regaining her balance by placing her palm down on the scrubbed wooden table. She found sweetness in the last place she expected to. There was nothing she was more determined to fight. "I came here for dinner," she began, eyeing him just as warily as he was eyeing her. "And to talk business. Don't do that again."

"You've got a point," he murmured before he turned back to the stove to tend the steaks. "Drink your wine, Jillian. We'll both be safer."

She did as he suggested only because she wanted something to calm her nerves. "I'll set the table," she offered.

"Dishes're up there." Aaron pointed to a cabinet without looking up. The steaks sizzled when he flipped them. "There's salad in the refrigerator."

They finished up the cooking and preparation in silence, with only the sound of sizzling meat and frying potatoes. Jillian finished off her first glass of wine and looked at the food with real enthusiasm.

"Either you know what you're doing, or I'm starved."

"Both." Aaron passed her some ranch dressing. "Eat. When you're skinny you can't afford to miss meals."

Unoffended, she shrugged. "Metabolism," she told him as she speared into the salad. "It doesn't matter how much I eat, nothing sticks."

"Some people call it nervous energy."

She glanced up as he tilted more wine into her glass. "I call it metabolism. I'm never nervous."

"Not often, in any case," he acknowledged. "Why did you leave Chicago?" Aaron asked before she could formulate a response.

"I didn't belong there."

"You could have, if you'd chosen to."

Jillian gave him a long neutral look, then nodded. "I didn't choose to, then. I felt at home here the first summer I visited."

"What about your family?"

She laughed. "They didn't."

"I mean, how do they feel about you living here, running Utopia?"

"How should they feel?" Jillian countered. She frowned into her wine a moment, then shrugged again. "I suppose you could say my father feels about Chicago the way I feel about Montana. It's where he belongs. You'd think he'd been born and raised there. And of course, my mother was, so... We just never worked out as a family."

"How?"

Jillian dashed some salt on her steak and cut into it. "I hated my piano lessons," she said simply.

"As easy as that?"

"As basic as that. Marc—my brother—he just melded right in. I suppose it helped that he developed an interest in medicine early, and he loves opera. My mother's quite a fan," she said with a smile. "Anyway, I still cringe a bit when I have to use a needle on a cow, and I've never been able to appreciate *La Traviata*."

"Is that what it takes to suit as a family?" Aaron wondered.

"It was important in mine. When I came here the first time, things started to change. Clay understood me. He yelled and swore instead of lecturing."

Aaron grinned, offering her more steak fries. "You like being yelled at?"

"Patient lecturing is the worst form of punishment."

"I guess I've never had to deal with it. We had a wood shed." He liked the way she laughed, low, appreciative. "Why didn't you come out to stay sooner?"

She moved her shoulders restlessly as she continued to eat. "I was in college. Both my parents thought a degree was vital, and I felt it was important to try to please them in that if nothing else. Then I got involved with—" She stopped herself, stunned that she'd almost told him of her relationship with that long-ago intern. Meticulously she cut a piece of steak. "It just didn't work out," she concluded, "so I came out here."

The someone who touched her wrong, Aaron decided. The astonishment in her eyes had been brief, her cover-up swift and smooth, but not smooth enough. He wouldn't probe there, not on a spot that was obviously tender. But he wondered who it had been who had touched her, and hurt her while she'd still been too young to build defenses.

"I think my mother was right," he commented. "Some things are just in the blood. You belong here."

There was something in the tone that made her look up carefully. She wasn't certain at that moment

whether he referred to the ranch or to himself. His eyes reminded her just how ruthless he could be when he wanted something. "I belong at Utopia," she said precisely. "And I intend to stay. Your father said something today too," she reminded him. "That a Murdock doesn't do business with a Baron."

"My father doesn't run my life, personally or professionally."

"Are you going to breed your stallion with Delilah to spite him?"

"I don't waste time with spite." It was said very simply, with that undercurrent of steel that made her think if he wanted revenge, he'd choose a very direct route. "I want the mare"—his dark eyes met hers and held—"for reasons of my own."

"Which are?"

Lifting his wine, he drank. "My own."

Jillian opened her mouth to speak, then shut it again. His reasons didn't matter. Business was business. "All right, what fee are you asking?"

Aaron took his time, calmly watching her face. "You seem to be finished."

Distracted, Jillian looked down to see that she'd eaten every bite on her plate. "Apparently," she said with a half laugh. "Well, I almost hate to admit it, Murdock, but it was good—almost as good as Utopia beef."

He answered her grin as he rose to clear off the table. "Why don't we take the wine in the other room, unless you'd like some coffee."

"No." She got up to help him stack the dishes. "I drank a full pot when I was fooling with the damn books."

"Don't care for paperwork?" Aaron picked up the half-full bottle of wine as they walked out of the kitchen.

"Putting it mildly," she murmured. "But someone has to do it."

"You could get a bookkeeper."

"The thought's crossed my mind. Maybe next year," she said with a move of her shoulders. "I've gotten used to keeping my finger on the pulse, let's say."

"Rumor is you rope a steer with the best of them."

Jillian sat on the couch, the full white skirt billowing around her. "Rumor's fact, Murdock," she said with a cocky smile. "Anytime you want to put some money on it, we'll go head to head."

He sat down beside her and toyed with the end of her sash. "I'll keep that in mind. But I have to admit, it isn't a hardship to look at you in a skirt."

Over the rim of her glass she watched him. "We were talking stud fees. What'd you have in mind for Samson?"

Idly he twisted a lock of her hair around his finger. "The first foal."

Chapter 5

For a moment there was complete silence in the room as they measured each other. She'd thought she had him pegged. It infuriated her to realize he was still a step ahead of her. "The first—" Jillian set down her glass of wine with a snap. "You're out of your mind."

"I'm not interested in cash. Two guaranteed breedings. I take the first foal, colt or filly. You take the second. I like the looks of your mare."

"You expect me to breed Delilah, cover all the expenses while she's carrying a foal, lose the use of her for three to four months, deal with the vet fees, then turn the result over to you?"

Relaxed, Aaron leaned back. He'd almost forgotten how good it was to haggle. "You'd have the second for nothing. I'd be willing to negotiate on the expenses."

"A flat fee," Jillian said, rising. "We're not talking about dogs, where you can take the pick of the litter."

"I don't need cash," Aaron repeated, lounging back on the couch. "I want a foal, take it or leave it."

Oh, she'd like to leave it. She'd like to have tossed it back in his face. Simmering, she stalked over to the window and stared out. It surprised her that she didn't. Until that moment Jillian hadn't realized just how much she wanted to breed those two horses. Another hunch, she thought, remembering the bull. She could feel that something special would come out of it. Clay had often told her she had a feel. More than once she'd singled out an animal for no other reason than a feeling. Now she had to weigh that with the absurdity of Aaron's suggestion.

She stared hard out of the window into the full night, full dark. Behind her, Aaron remained silent, waiting, watching her with a faint smile. He wondered if she knew just how lovely she was when she was annoyed. It was tempting to keep her that way.

"I get the first foal," she said suddenly. "You get the second. It's my mare who's taking the risk in pregnancy, who won't be any use for working when she's at term and nursing. I'm the one bearing the brunt of the expense."

Aaron considered a moment. She was playing it precisely as he'd have done himself if the situation was reversed. He found it pleased him. "We breed her back as soon as she's weaned the foal."

"Agreed. You pay half the vet bills—on both foalings."

His brows raised. Whatever she knew about cattle, she wasn't a fool when it came to horse trading. "Half," he agreed. "We breed them as soon as she comes in season."

With a nod, Jillian offered her hand on it. "Do you want to draw up the papers or shall I?"

Standing, Aaron took her hand. "I'm not particular. A handshake's binding enough for me."

"Agreed," she said again. "But it never hurts to have words written down."

He grinned, skimming his thumb over her knuckles. "Don't you trust me, Jillian?"

"Not an inch," she said easily, then laughed because he seemed more pleased than offended. "No, not an inch. And you'd be disappointed if I did."

"You have a way of cutting through to the heart of things. It's a pity I've been away for five years." He inclined his head. "But I have a feeling we'll be making up for lost time."

"I haven't lost any time," Jillian countered. "Now that we've concluded our business successfully, Murdock, I have a long day tomorrow."

He tightened his fingers on hers before she could turn away. "Not all our business."

"All I came for." Her voice was cool, even when he stepped closer. "I don't want to make a habit out of hitting you."

"You won't connect this time." He took her other hand and held both lightly, though not so lightly she could draw away. "I'm going to have you, Jillian."

She didn't try to pull her hands away. She didn't back up. Her eyes stayed level with his and her voice just as matter-of-fact. "The hell you are."

"And when I do," he went on as if she hadn't spoken, "it's not going to be something either one of us is going to forget. You stirred something in me—" he yanked her closer so that the unrelieved white of her

skirt flowed against the stark black of his slacks
"—from the first minute I saw you. It hasn't settled
yet."

"Your problem." She angled her chin, but her voice
was breathless. "You don't interest me, Murdock."

"Tell me that again," he challenged, "in just a minute."

He brought his mouth down on hers, harder, rougher
than he'd intended. His emotions seemed to have no
middle ground with her. It was either all soft tenderness or raw passion. Her arms strained against his hold,
her body jerked as if to reject him. Then he felt it—
the instant she became as consumed as he. In seconds
his arms were around her, and hers around him.

It felt just as she'd wanted it to. Heady, overpow-
ering. She could forget everything but that delicious
churning within her own body. The rich flavor of wine
that lingered on his tongue would make her drunk, but
it didn't matter. Her head could whirl and spin, but she
could only be grateful for the giddiness. With unapol-
ogetic passion, she met his demand with demand.

When his mouth left hers, she would have protested,
but the sound became a moan as his lips raced down
her throat. Instinctively she tilted her head back to give
him more freedom, and the sharp scent of soap drifted
over her, laced with a hint of sandalwood. Then his
mouth was at her ear, his teeth tugging and nipping
before he whispered something she didn't understand.
The words didn't matter, the sound alone made her
tremble. With a murmur of desperation, she dragged
his lips back to hers.

Jillian was demanding he take more. Aaron could
feel the strain of her body against his and knew she
was aching to be touched. But his hands were still

tangled in her hair as they tumbled onto the couch. Then his hands were everywhere, and he couldn't touch enough fast enough. Her body was so slender under all those yards of thin white cotton. So responsive. Her breast was almost lost under the span of his hand, yet it was so firm. And her heartbeat pounded like thunder beneath it.

His legs tangled with hers before he slipped between them. When she sank into the cushions, he nearly lost himself in the simple give of her body. His mouth ravaged hers—he couldn't prevent it, she didn't protest. She only answered and demanded until he was half mad again. Her scent, part subtle, part sultry, enveloped him so that he knew he'd be able to smell her when she was miles from him. He could hear her breath rush from between her lips into his mouth, where it whispered warm and sweet and promising.

Her body was responding of its own accord while her mind raced off in a dozen directions. His weight, that hard, firm press of his body, felt so good, so natural against hers. Those rough, ruthless kisses gave her everything she needed long before she knew she needed. He threatened her with words of passion that were only whispered madness in a world of color without form.

His cheek grazed hers as his lips raced over her face. No one had ever wanted her like this. But more, she'd never wanted this wildly. Her only taste of lovemaking had been so mild, so quiet. Nothing had prepared her for a violence of need that came from within herself. She wanted to fly with it. Too much.

His hand skimmed up her leg, seeking, and everything that was inside her built to a fever pitch. If it

exploded, she'd be lost. Pieces of herself might scatter so that she'd never be strong enough to stand on her own again.

In a panic, she began to struggle while part of her fought to yield. And to take.

"No." Moaning, she pushed against him.

"Jillian, for God's sake." Her name came out in a gasp as he felt himself drowning.

"No!" With the strength of fear, she managed to shove him aside and scramble up. Before either of them could think, she was dashing outside, running away from something that followed much too closely. Aaron was cursing steadily when he caught her.

"What the hell's wrong with you?" he demanded as he whipped her back around.

"Let me go! I won't be pawed that way."

"Pawed?" He didn't even hear her gasp as his fingers tightened. "Damn you," he said under his breath. "You were doing some pawing of your own, if that's what you want to call it."

"Just let me go," she said unsteadily. "I told you I don't like to be touched."

"Oh, you like to be touched," he grated, then caught the glint of fear in her eyes. There was pride there as well, a kind of terrorized pride laced with passion. It reminded him sharply of the eyes of a stallion he'd once tied in a stall. Then he realized his fingers were digging into the flesh of very slender arms.

No, he wasn't a gentle man, but she was the first and only woman who'd caused him to lose control to the point where he'd mark her skin. Carefully he loosened his hold without releasing her. Even as his fingers

relaxed, he knew he could drag her back inside and have her willing to give herself to him within moments. But some things you didn't fence.

"Jillian." His voice was still rough, only slightly calmer. "You can postpone what's going to happen between us, but you can't stop it." She opened her mouth, but he shook his head in warning. "No, you'd be much better off not to say anything just now. I want you, and at the moment it's a damned uncomfortable feeling. I'm going to take you home while I've got myself convinced I play by the rules. It wouldn't take me long to remember I've never followed any."

He pulled open the passenger door, then strode around to the driver's seat without another word. They drove away in a silence that remained thick for miles. Because her body was still throbbing, Jillian sat very straight. She cursed Aaron, then when she began to calm, she cursed herself. She'd wanted him, and every time he touched her, her initial restraint vanished within moments.

The hands in her lap balled into fists. There was a name for a woman who was willing and eager one moment and hurling accusations the next. It wasn't pleasant. She'd never played that kind of game and had nothing but disdain for anyone who did.

He had a right to be furious, Jillian admitted, but then, so did she. He was the one who'd come barging into her life, stirring things up she wanted left alone. She didn't want to feel all those hungers, all those aches that raged through her when he held her.

She couldn't give in to them. Once she did, she'd start depending. If that happened, she'd start chipping away at her own self-reliance until he had more of who

and what she was than she did. It had happened before
and the need had been nothing like this. She'd gotten
a hint, during that strangely gentle kiss in his kitchen,
just how easily she could lose herself to him. And
yet... Yet when it was all said and done, Jillian was
forced to admit, she'd acted like an idiot. The one
thing she detested more than anything else was finding
herself in the wrong.

A deer bounded over the fence to the left, pausing
in the road, as it was trapped in the headlights. Even
as Aaron braked, it was sprinting off, slender legs lifting as it took the next fence and disappeared into the
darkness. The sight warmed Jillian as it always did.
With a soft laugh, she turned back to see the smile in
Aaron's eyes. The flood of emotion swamped her.

"I'm sorry." The words came quickly, before she
realized she would say them. "I overreacted."

He gave her a long look. He'd wanted to stay angry.
Somehow it was easier—now it was impossible.
"Maybe we both did. We have a tendency to spark
something off each other."

She couldn't deny that, but neither did she want to
think about it too carefully just then. "Since we're
going to have to deal with each other from time to
time, maybe we should come to some kind of understanding."

A smile began to tug at his mouth. "That sounds
reasonable. What kind of understanding did you have
in mind?"

"We're business associates," she said very dryly
because of the amusement in his question.

"Uh-huh." Aaron rested his arm on the back of the
seat as he began to enjoy himself.

"Do you practice being an idiot, Murdock, or does it come naturally?"

"Oh, no, no insults, Jillian. We're coming to an understanding."

Jillian fought against a grin and lost. "You have a strange sense of humor."

"A keen sense of the ridiculous," he countered. "So we're business associates. You forgot neighbors."

"And neighbors," she agreed with a nod. "Colleagues, if you want to belabor a point."

"Belabor it," Aaron suggested. "But can I ask you a question?"

"Yes." She drew out the word cautiously.

"What *is* the point?"

"Damn it, Aaron," she said with a laugh. "I'm trying to put things in order so I don't end up apologizing again. I hate apologizing."

"I like the way you do it, very simple and sincere right before you lose your temper again."

"I'm not going to lose my temper again."

"I'll give you five to one."

"Damn it, Aaron." Her laugh rippled, low and smooth. "If I took that bet, you'd go out of your way to make me mad."

"You see, we understand each other already. But you were telling me your point." He pulled into the darkened ranch yard. The light from Jillian's front porch spilled into the car and cast his face in shadows.

"We could have a successful business association *if* we both put a lot of effort into it."

"Agreed." He turned and in the small confines of the car was already touching her. Just the skim of his fingers over her shoulder, the brush of leg against leg.

"We'll continue to be neighbors because neither of us is moving. As long as we remember those things, we should be able to deal with each other without too much fighting."

"You forgot something."

"Did I?"

"You've said what we are to each other, not what we're going to be." He watched her eyes narrow.

"Which is?"

"Lovers." He ran his finger casually down the side of her neck. "I still mean to have you."

Jillian let out a long breath and worked on keeping her temper in check. "It's obvious you can't carry on a reasonable conversation."

"A lot of things are obvious." He put his hand over hers as she reached for the handle. With their faces close, he let his gaze linger on her mouth just long enough for the ache to spread. "I'm not a patient man," Aaron murmured. "But there are some things I can wait for."

"You'll have a long wait."

"Maybe longer than I'd like," he agreed. "But shorter than you think." His hand was still over hers as he pressed down the handle to release the door. "Sleep well, Jillian."

She swung out of the car, then gave him a smoldering look. "Don't cross the line until you're invited, Murdock." Slamming the door, she sprinted up the steps, cursing the low, easy laughter that followed her.

In the days that followed, Jillian tried not to think about Aaron. When she couldn't stop him from creeping into her mind, she did her best to think of him with

scorn. Occasionally she was successful enough to dismiss him as a spoiled, willful man who was used to getting what he wanted by demanding it. If she were successful, she could forget that he made her laugh, made her want.

Her days were long and full and demanding enough that she had little time to dwell on him or her feelings. But though the nights were growing shorter, she swore against the hours she spent alone and unoccupied. It was then she remembered exactly how it felt to be held against him. It was then she remembered how his eyes could laugh while the rest of his face remained serious and solemn. And how firm and strong his mouth could be against hers.

She began to rise earlier, to work later. She exhausted herself on the range or in the outbuildings until she could tumble boneless into bed. But still there were dreams.

Jillian was out in the pasture as soon as it was light. The sky was still tipped with the colors of sunrise so that gold and rose tinted the hazy blue. Like most of her men, she wore a light work jacket and chaps as they began the job of rounding up the first hundred calves and cows for corral branding. This part of the job would be slow and easy. It was too common to run twenty-five pounds off a cow with a lot of racing and roping. A good deal of the work could be done on foot, the rest with experienced horses or four wheels. If they hazed the mothers along gently, the babies would follow.

Jillian turned Delilah, keeping her at a walk as she urged a cow and calf away from a group of heifers. She looked forward to a long hard morning and the

satisfaction of a job well done. When she saw Joe slowly prodding cows along on foot, she tipped her hat to him.

"I always thought branding was a kind of stag party," he commented as he came alongside of her.

Looking down, she laughed. "Not on Utopia." She looked around as punchers nudged cows along with soft calls and footwork. "When we brand again in a couple of days, the plane should be in. God knows it'll be easier to spot the strays."

"You've been working too hard. No, don't give me that look," he insisted. "You know you have. What's up?"

Aaron sneaked past her defenses, but now she just shook her head. "Nothing. It's a busy time of year. We'll be haying soon, first crop should come in right after the spring branding. Then there's the rodeo." She glanced down again as Delilah shifted under her. "I'm counting on those blue ribbons, Joe."

"You've been working from first light to last for a week," he pointed out. "You're entitled to a couple days off."

"The boss is the last one entitled to a couple days off." Satisfied that her cows had joined the slowly moving group headed for the pasture, she wheeled Delilah around. She spotted a calf racing west, spooked by the number of men, horses, and trucks. Sending Delilah into an easy lope, Jillian went after him.

Her first amusement at the frantic pace the dogie was setting faded as she saw he was heading directly for the wire. With a soft oath, she nudged more speed out of her mare and reached for her rope. With an expert movement of arm and wrist, she swung it over

her head, then shot it out to loop over the maverick's neck. Jillian pulled him up a foot from the wire where he cried and struggled until his mother caught up.

"Dumb cow," she muttered as she dismounted to release him. "Fat lot of good you'd've done yourself if you'd tangled in that." She cast a glance at the sharp points of wire before she slipped the rope from around his head. The mother eyed her with annoyance as she began to recoil the rope. "Yeah, you're welcome," Jillian told her with a grin. Glancing over, she saw Gil crossing to her on foot. "Still think you can beat my time in July?" she demanded.

"You put too much fancy work on the spin."

Though his words were said in his usual rough-and-ready style, something in his eyes alerted her. "What is it?"

"Something you oughta see down here a ways."

Without a word, she gathered Delilah's reins in her hand and began to walk beside him. There was no use asking, so she didn't bother. Part of her mind still registered the sights and sounds around her—the irritated mooing, the high sound of puzzled calves, the ponderous majestic movements of their mothers, the swish of men and animals through grass. They'd start branding by mid-morning.

"Look here."

Jillian saw the small section of broken fence and swore. "Damn it, we just took care of this line a week ago. I rode this section myself." Jillian scowled into the opposite pasture wondering how many of her cattle had strayed. That would account for the fact that though the numbers reported to her were right, her eye

had told her differently that morning. "I'll need a few hands to round up the strays."

"Yeah." Reaching over, he caught a strand of wire in his fingers. "Take a look."

Distracted, she glanced down. Almost immediately, Jillian stiffened and took the wire in her own fingers. The break was much too sharp, much too clean. "It's been cut," she said quietly, then looked up and over into the next pasture. Murdock land.

She expected to feel rage and was stunned when she felt hurt instead. Was he capable? Jillian thought he could be ruthless, even lawless if it suited him. But to deliberately cut wire... Could he have found his own way to pay her back for their personal differences and professional enmity? She let the wire fall.

"Send three of the men over to check for strays," she said flatly. "I'd like you to see to this wire yourself." She met Gil's eyes coolly and on level. "And keep it to yourself."

He squinted at her, then spit. "You're the boss."

"If I'm not back by the time the cattle are ready in the corral, get started. We don't have any time to waste getting brands on the calves."

"Maybe we waited a few days too long already."

Jillian swung into the saddle. "We'll see about that." She led Delilah carefully through the break in the wire, then dug in her heels.

It didn't take her long to come across her first group of men. Delilah pulled up at the Jeep and Jillian stared down her nose. "Where's Murdock?" she demanded. "Aaron Murdock."

The man tipped his hat, recognizing an outraged fe-

male when he saw one. "In the north section, ma'am, rounding up calves."

"There's a break in the fence," she said briefly. "Some of my men are coming over to look for strays. You might want to do the same."

"Yes, ma'am." But he said it to her back as she galloped away.

The Murdock crew worked essentially the same way her own did. She saw them fanned out, moving slowly, steadily, with the cows plodding along in front of them. A few were farther afield, outflanking the mavericks and driving them back to the herd.

Jillian saw him well out to the right, twisting and turning Samson around a reluctant calf. Ignoring the curious glances of his men, Jillian picked her way through them. She heard them laugh, then shout something short and rude at the calf before he saw her.

The brim of his hat shaded his face from the early morning sun. She couldn't see his expression, only that he watched her come toward him. Delilah pricked up her ears as she scented the stallion and sidestepped skittishly.

Aaron waited until they were side by side. "Jillian." Because he could already see that something was wrong, he didn't bother with any more words.

"I want to talk to you, Murdock."

"So talk." He nudged the calf, but Jillian reached over to grip his saddle horn. His eyes flicked down to rest on her restraining hand.

"Alone."

His expression remained placid—but she still couldn't see his eyes. Signaling to one of his men to take charge of the maverick, Aaron turned his horse

and walked farther north. "You'll have to keep it short, I haven't got time to socialize right now."

"This isn't a social call," she bit off, controlling Delilah as the mare eyed the stallion cautiously.

"So I gathered. What's the problem?"

When she was certain they were out of earshot, Jillian pulled up her mount. "There's a break in the west boundary line."

He looked over her head to watch his men. "You want one of my hands to fix it?"

"I want to know who cut it."

His eyes came back to hers quickly. She could see only that they were dark. The single sign of his mood was the sudden nervous shift of his stallion. Aaron controlled him without taking his eyes off Jillian. "Cut it?"

"That's right." Her voice was even now, with rage bubbling just beneath. "Gil found it, and I saw it myself."

Very slowly he tipped back his hat. For the first time she saw his face unshadowed. She'd seen that expression once before—when it had loomed over her as he pinned her to the ground in Samson's corral. "What are you accusing me of?"

"I'm telling you what I know." Her eyes caught the slant of the morning sun and glittered with it. "You can take it from there."

In what seemed to be a very calm, very deliberate motion, he reached over and gathered the front of her jacket in his hand. "I don't cut fence."

She didn't jerk away from him and her gaze remained steady. A single stray breeze stirred the flame-colored curls that flowed from her hat. "Maybe you

don't, but you've got a lot of men working your place. Three of my men are in your pasture now, rounding up my strays. I'm missing some cows.''

"I'll send some men to check your herd for any of mine.''

"I already suggested that to one of your hands in the border pasture.''

He nodded, but his eyes remained very intense and very angry. "A wire can be cut from either side, Jillian.''

Dumbfounded, she stared at him. Rage boiled out as she knocked his hand away from her jacket. "That's ridiculous. I wouldn't be telling you about the damn wire if I'd cut it.''

Aaron watched her settle her moody mare before he gave her a grim smile. "You have a lot of men working your place,'' he repeated.

As she continued to stare her angry color drained. Hurt and anger hadn't allowed her to think through the logic of it. Some of her men she'd known and trusted for years. Others—they came and they went, earning a stake, then drifting to another ranch, another county. You rarely knew their names, only their faces. But it was her count that was short, she reminded herself.

"You missing any cattle?'' she demanded.

"I'll let you know.''

"I'll be doing a thorough count in the west section.'' She turned away to stare at the rising sun. It could've been one of her men just as easily as it could've been one of his. And she was responsible for everyone who was on Utopia's payroll. She had to face that. "I've no use for your beef, Aaron,'' she said quietly.

"Any more than I do for yours."

"It wouldn't be the first time." When she looked back at him, her chin stayed up. "The Murdocks made a habit out of cutting Baron wire."

"You want to go back eighty years?" he demanded. "There's two sides to a story, Jillian, just like there's two sides to a line. You and I weren't even alive then, what the hell difference does it make to us?"

"I don't know, but it happened—it could happen again. Clay may be gone, but your father still has some bad feelings."

Temper sprang back into his eyes. "Maybe he dragged himself out here and cut the wire so he could cause you trouble."

"I'm not a fool," she retorted.

"No?" Furious, he wheeled his horse so that they were face-to-face. "You do a damn good imitation. I'll check the west line myself and get back to you."

Before she could throw any of her fury back at him, he galloped away. Teeth gritted, Jillian headed south, back to Utopia.

Chapter 6

By the time Jillian galloped into the ranch yard the cattle were already penned. A glance at the sun told her it was only shortly after eight. Cows and calves were milling and mooing in the largest board pen and the workmen had already begun to separate them. No easy task. Listening to the sounds of men and cattle, Jillian dismounted and unsaddled her mare. There wasn't time to brood over the cut wire when branding was under way.

Some of the men remained on horseback, keeping the cows moving as they worked to chase the frantic mothers into a wire pen while the calves were herded into another board corral. The air was already peppered with curses that were more imaginative than profane.

With blows and shouts, a cow and her calf were driven out of the big corral. Men on foot were strung

out in a line too tight to allow the cow to follow as
the calf slipped through. Relying mostly on arm waving, shrieks, and whistles, the men propelled the cow
into the wire pen. Then the process repeated itself. She
watched Gil spinning his wiry little body and cheering
with an energy that promised to see him through the
day despite his years. With a half laugh, Jillian settled
her hat firmly on her head and went to join them, lariat
in hand.

Calves streaked like terriers back into the cow pen.
Dust flew. Cows bullied their way through the line for
a reunion with their offspring. Men ran them back with
shouts, brute force, or ropes. Men might be outnum-
bered and outweighed, but the cattle were no match
for western ingenuity.

Gil singled a calf out in the cow pen, roped it, and
dragged it to him, cursing all the way. With a swat on
the flank, he sent it into the calf corral, then squinted
at Jillian.

"Fence repaired?" she asked briefly.

"Yep."

"I'll see to the rest myself." She paused, then
swung her lariat. "I'm going to want to talk to you
later, Gil."

He removed his hat, swiped the sweat off his brow
with the arm of his dusty shirt, then perched it on his
head again. "When you're ready." He glanced around
as Jillian pulled in a calf. "Just about done—time to
gang up on 'em."

So saying, he joined the line of men who closed in
on the unruly cows to drive the last of them into their
proper place. Inside the smaller corral calves bawled
and crowded together.

"It isn't pleasant," Jillian muttered to them. "But it'll be quick."

The gate creaked as it was swung across to hold them in. The rest wasn't a business she cared for, though she never would've admitted it to anyone but herself. Knife and needle and iron were used with precision, with a rhythm that started off uneven, then gained fluidity and speed. Calves came through the chute one at a time, dreaming of liberation, only to be hoisted onto the calf table.

She watched the next calf roll his big eyes in astonishment as the table tilted, leaving him helpless on his side, as high as a man's waist. Then he was dealt with as any calf is at a roundup.

It was hot, dirty work. There was a smell of sweat, blood, smoking hide, and medicine. Throughout the steady action reminiscences could be heard—stories no one would believe and everyone tried to top. Cows surged in the wire pen; their babies squealed at the bite of needle or knife. The language grew as steamy as the air in the pen.

It wasn't Jillian's first branding, and yet each one—for all the sweat and blood—made her remember why she was here instead of on one of the wide busy streets back east. It was hard work, but honest. It took a special brand of person to do it. The cattle milling and calling in the corral were hers. Just as the land was. She relieved a man at the table and began her turn at the vaccinations.

The sun rose higher, heading toward afternoon before the last calf was released. When it was done, the men were hungry, the calves exhausted and bawling pitifully for their mothers.

Hot and hungry herself, Jillian sat on a handy crate
and wiped the grime from her face. Her shirt stuck to
her with patches of wet cutting through the dirt. That
was only the first hundred, she thought as she arched
her back. They wouldn't finish with the spring brand-
ings until the end of that week or into the next. She
waited until nearly all the men had made their way
toward the cookhouse before she signaled to Gil. He
plucked two beers out of a cooler and went to join her.

"Thanks." Jillian twisted off the cap, then let the
cold, yeasty taste wash away some of the dust. "Murdock's going to check the rest of the line himself,"
she began without preamble. "Tell me straight"—she
held the bottle to her brow a moment, enjoying the
chill—"is he the kind of man who'd play this sort of
game?"

"What do you think?" he countered.

What could she think? Jillian asked herself. No matter how hard she tried, her feelings kept getting in the
way. Feelings she'd yet to understand because she
didn't dare. "I'm asking you."

"Kid's got class," Gil said briefly. "Now, the old
man…" He grinned a bit, then squinted into the sun.
"Well, he might've done something of the sort years
back, just for devilment. Give your grandpaw something to swear about. But the kid—don't strike me like
his devilment runs that way. Another thing…" He spit
tobacco and shifted his weight. "I did a head count in
the pasture this morning. Might be a few off, seeing
as they were spread out and scattered during
roundup."

Jillian took another swig from the bottle, then set it
aside. "But?"

"Looked to me like we were light an easy hundred."

"A hundred?" she repeated in a whisper of shock. "That many cattle aren't going to stray through a break in the fence, not on their own."

"Boys got back midway through the branding. Only rounded up a dozen on Murdock land."

"I see." She let out a long breath. "Then it doesn't look like the wire was cut for mischief, does it?"

"Nope."

"I want an accurate head count in the morning, down to the last calf. Start with the west pasture." She looked down at her hands. They were filthy. Her fingers ached. It was as innate in her to work for what was hers as it was to fight for it. "Gil, the chances are pretty good that someone on the Murdock payroll's rustling our cattle, maybe for the Double M, but more likely for themselves."

He tugged on his ear. "Maybe."

"Or, it's one of our own."

He met her eyes calmly. He'd wondered if that would occur to her. "Just as likely," he said simply. "Murdock might find his numbers light too."

"I want that head count by sundown tomorrow." She rose to face him. "Pick men you're sure of, no one that's been here less than a season. Men who know how to keep their thoughts to themselves."

He nodded, understanding the need for discretion. Rustling wasn't any less deadly a foe than it had been a century before. "You gonna work with Murdock on this?"

"If I have to." She remembered the fury on his face—something she recognized as angry pride. She

had plenty of that herself. The sigh came before she could prevent it and spoke of weariness. "Go get something to eat."

"You coming?"

"No." She walked back to Delilah and hefted the saddle. Mechanically she began to hook cinches and tighten them. In the corral the cattle were beginning to calm.

When she'd finished, Gil tapped her on the shoulder. Turning her head, she saw him hold out a thick biscuit crammed with meat.

"You eat this, dammit," he said gruffly. "You're going to blow away in a high wind if you keep it up."

Accepting the biscuit, she took a huge bite. "You mangy old dog," she muttered with her mouth full. Then, because no one was around to see and razz him, she kissed both his cheeks. Though it pleased him, he cursed her for it and made her laugh as she vaulted into the saddle.

Jillian trotted the mare out of the ranch yard, then, turning toward solitude, rode her hard.

To satisfy her own curiosity, she headed for the west pasture first. Riding slowly now, she checked the repaired fence, then began to count the cattle still grazing. It didn't take long for her to conclude that Gil's estimate had been very close to the mark. A hundred head. Closing her eyes, she tried to think calmly.

The winter had only cost her twenty—that was something every rancher had to deal with. But it hadn't been nature who'd taken these cows from her. She had to find out who, and quickly, before the losses continued. Jillian glanced over the boundary line. On both sides cattle grazed placidly, at peace now that man had

left them to their own pursuits. As far as she could see there was nothing but rolling grass and the cattle growing sleek on it. A hundred head, she thought again. Enough to put a small but appreciable dent in her herd—and her profit. She wasn't going to sit still for it.

Grimly she sent Delilah into a gallop. She couldn't afford the luxury of panicking. She'd have to take it step by step, ascertaining a firm and accurate account of her losses before she went to the authorities. But for now she was tired, dirty, and discouraged. The best thing to do was to take care of that before she went back to the ranch.

It had been only a week since she'd last ridden out to the pond, but even in that short time the aspen and cottonwood were greener. She could see hints of bitterroot and of the wild roses that were lovely and so destructive when they sprang up in the pastures. The sun was beginning its gradual decline westward. Jillian judged it to be somewhere between one and two. She'd give herself an hour here to recharge before she went back to begin the painstaking job of checking and rechecking the number of cattle in her books, and their locations. Dismounting, she tethered her mare to a branch of an aspen and let her graze.

Carelessly Jillian tossed her hat aside, then sat on a rock to pull off her boots. As her jeans and shirt followed she listened to the sound of a warbler singing importantly of spring and sunshine. Black-eyed Susans were springing up at the edge of the grass.

The water was deliciously cool. When she lowered herself into it, she could forget about the aches in her muscles, the faint, dull pain in her lower back, and the

sense of despair that had followed her out of the west pasture. As owner and boss of Utopia, she'd deal with what needed to be dealt with. For now, she needed to be only Jillian. It was spring, the sun was warm. If the breeze was right, she could smell the young roses. Dipping her head back, she let the water flow over her face and hair.

Aaron didn't ask himself how he'd known she'd be there. He didn't ask himself why knowing it, he'd come. Both he and the stallion remained still as he watched her. She didn't splash around but simply drifted quietly so that the water made soft lapping sounds that didn't disturb the birdsong. He thought he could see the fatigue drain from her. It was the first time he'd seen her completely relaxed without the light of adventure or temper or even laughter in her eyes. This was something she did for herself, and though he knew he intruded, he stayed where he was.

Her skin was milky pale where the sun hadn't touched it. Beneath the rippling water, he could see the slender curves of her body. Her hair clung to her head and shoulders and burned like fire. So did the need that started low in his stomach and spread through his blood.

Did she know how exquisite she was with that long, limber body and creamy skin? Did she know how seductive she looked with that mass of chestnut hair sleek around a face that held both delicacy and strength? No, he thought as she sank beneath the surface, she wouldn't know—wouldn't allow herself to know. Perhaps it was time he showed her. With the slightest of signals, he walked Samson to a tree on his side of the boundary.

Jillian surfaced and found herself looking directly up into Aaron's eyes. Her first shock gave way to annoyance and annoyance to outrage when she remembered her disadvantage. Aaron saw all three emotions. His lips twitched.

"What're you doing here?" she demanded. She knew she could do nothing about modesty and didn't attempt to. Instead she relied on bravado.

"How's the water?" Aaron asked easily. Another woman, he mused, would've made some frantic and useless attempt to conceal herself. Not Jillian. She just tossed up her chin.

"It's cold. Now, why don't you go back to wherever you came from so I can finish what I'm doing."

"It was a long, dusty morning." He sat on a rock near the edge of the pool and smiled companionably. Like Jillian's, his clothes and skin were streaked with grime and sweat. The signs of hard work and effort suited him. Aaron tilted back his hat. "Looks inviting."

"I was here first," she said between her teeth. "If you had any sense of decency, you'd go away."

"Yep." He bent over and pulled off his boots.

Jillian watched first one then the other hit the grass. "What the hell do you think you're doing?"

"Thought I'd take a dip." He gave her an engaging grin as he tossed his hat aside.

"Think again."

He rose, and his brow lifted slowly as he unbuttoned his shirt. "I'm on my own land," he pointed out. He tossed the shirt aside so that Jillian had an unwanted and fascinating view of a hard, lean torso with brown skin stretched tight over the rib cage and a dark vee

of hair that trailed down to the low-slung waist of his jeans.

"Damn you, Murdock," she muttered, and judged the distance to her own clothes. Too far to be any use.

"Relax," he suggested, enjoying himself. "We can pretend there's wire strung clean down the middle." With this he unhooked his belt.

His eyes stayed on hers. Jillian's first instinct to look away was overruled by the amusement she saw there. Coolly she watched him strip. If she had to swallow, she did it quietly.

Damn, did he have to be so beautiful? she asked herself and kept well to her own side as he slid into the water. The ripples his body made spread out to tease her own skin. Shivering, she sank a little deeper.

"You're really getting a kick out of this, aren't you?"

Aaron gave a long sigh as the water rinsed away dust and cooled his blood. "Have to admit I am. View from in here's no different from the one I had out there," he reminded her easily. "And I'd already given some thought to what you'd look like without your clothes. Most redheads have freckles."

"I'm just lucky, I guess." Her dimple flickered briefly. At least they were on equal ground again. "You're built like most cowboys," she told him in a drawl. "Lots of leg, no hips." She let her arms float lazily. "I've seen better," she lied. Laughing, she tilted her head and let her legs come up, unable to resist the urge to tease him.

He had only to reach out to grab her ankle and drag her to him. Aaron rubbed his itchy palm on his thigh

and relaxed. "You make a habit of skinny-dipping up here?"

"No one comes here." Tossing the hair out of her eyes, she shot him a look. "Or no one did. If you're going to start using the pond regularly, we'll have to work out some kind of schedule."

"I don't mind the company." He drifted closer so that his body brushed the imaginary line.

"Keep to your own side, Murdock," she warned softly, but smiled. "Trespassers still get shot these days." To show her lack of concern, she closed her eyes and floated. "I like to come here on Sunday afternoons, when the men are in the ranch yard, pitching horseshoes and swapping lies."

Aaron studied her face. No, he'd never seen her this relaxed. He wondered if she realized just how little space she gave herself. "Don't you like to swap lies?"

"Men tend to remember I'm a woman on Sunday afternoons. Having me around puts a censor on the— ah, kind of lies."

"They only remember on Sunday afternoons?"

"It's easy to forget the way a person's built when you're out on the range or shoveling out stalls."

He let his eyes skim down the length of her, covered by only a few inches of water. "You say so," he murmured.

"And they need time to complain." With another laugh, she let her legs sink. "About the food, the pay, the work. Hard to do all that when the boss is there." She spun her hand just under the surface and sent the water waving all the way to the edge. He thought it was the first purely frivolous gesture he'd ever seen her make. "Your men complain, Murdock?"

''You should've heard them when my sister decided to fix up the bunkhouse six or seven years back.'' The memory made him grin. ''Seems she thought the place needed some pretty paint and curtains—gingham curtains, baby-blue paint.''

''Oh, my God.'' Jillian tried to imagine what her crew's reaction would be if they were faced with gingham. Throwing back her head, she laughed until her sides ached. ''What did they do?''

''They refused to wash anything, sweep anything, or throw anything away. In two weeks' time the place looked like the county dump—smelled like it too.''

''Why'd your father let her do it?'' Jillian asked, wiping her eyes.

''She looks like my mother,'' Aaron said simply.

Nodding, she sighed from the effort of laughing. ''But they got rid of the curtains.''

''I—let's say they disappeared one night,'' he amended.

Jillian gave him a swift appraising look. ''You took them down and burned them.''

''If I haven't admitted that in seven years, I'm not going to admit it now. It took damned near a week to get that place cleared out,'' he remembered. She was smiling at him in such an easy, friendly way it took all his willpower not to reach over and pull her to his side. ''Did you do the orphan today?''

''Earmarked, vaccinated, and branded,'' Jillian returned, trailing her hands through the water again.

''Is that all?''

She grinned, knowing his meaning. ''In a couple of years Baby's going to be giving his poppa some competition.'' She shrugged, so that her body shifted and

the water lapped close at the curve of her breast. The less she seemed concerned about her body, the more he became fascinated by it. "I have a feeling about him," she continued. "No use making a steer out of a potential breeder." A cloud of worry came into her eyes. "I rode the west fence before I came up here. I didn't see any more breaks."

"There weren't any more." He'd known they had to discuss it, but it annoyed him to have the few moments of simple camaraderie interrupted. He couldn't remember sharing that sort of simplicity with a woman before. "My men rounded up six cows that had strayed to your side. Seemed like you had about twice that many on mine."

She hesitated a moment, worrying her bottom lip. "Then your count balances?"

He heard the tension in her voice and narrowed his eyes. "Seems to. Why?"

She kept her eyes level and expressionless. "I'm a good hundred head short."

"Hundred?" He'd grabbed her arm before he realized it. "A hundred head? Are you sure?"

"As sure as I can be until we count again and go over the books. But we're short, I'm sure of that."

He stared at her as his thoughts ran along the same path hers had. That many cows didn't stray on their own. "I'll do a count of my own herd in the morning, but I can tell you, I'd know if I had that much extra cattle in my pasture."

"I'm sure you would. I don't think that's where they are."

Aaron reached up to touch her cheek. "I'd like to help you—if you need some extra hands. We can take

the plane up. Maybe they wandered in the other direction.''

She felt something soften inside her that shouldn't have. A simple offer of help when she needed it—and his hand was gentle on her face. ''I appreciate it,'' Jillian began unsteadily. ''But I don't think the cattle wandered any more than you do.''

''No.'' He combed the hair away from her face. ''I'll go with you to the sheriff.''

Unused to unselfish support, she stared at him. Neither was aware that they were both drifting to the line, and each other. ''No—I...it isn't necessary, I can deal with it.''

''You don't have to deal with it alone.'' How was it he'd never noticed how fragile she was? he wondered. Her eyes were so young, so vulnerable. The curve of her cheek was so delicate. He ran his thumb over it and felt her tremble. Somehow his hand was at her lower back, bringing her closer. ''Jillian...'' But he didn't have the words, only the needs. His mouth came to hers gently.

Her hands ran up his back, skimming up wet, cool skin. Her lips parted softly under his. The tip of his tongue ran lazily around the inside of her mouth, stopping to tease hers. Jillian relaxed against him, content for the long, moist kiss to go on and on. She couldn't remember ever feeling so pliant, so much in tune with another's movements and wishes. His lips grew warmer and heated hers. Against her own, she could feel his heartbeat—quick and steady. His mouth left hers only long enough to change the angle before he began to slowly deepen the kiss.

It happened so gradually she had no defense. It was

an emptiness that started in her stomach like a hunger, then spread until it was an ache to be loved. Her body yearned for it. Her heart began to tell her he was the one she could share herself with, not without risk, not without pain, but with something she'd almost forgotten to ask for: hope.

But when her mind started to cloud, she struggled to clear it. It wasn't sharing, she told herself even as his lips slanted over hers to persuade her. It was giving, and if she gave she could lose. Only a fool would forget the boundary line that stood between them.

She pulled out of his hold and stared at him. Was she mad? Making love to a Murdock when her fence had been cut and a hundred of her cows were missing? Was she so weak that a gentle touch, a tender kiss, made her forget her responsibilities and obligations?

"I told you to stay on your own side," she said unsteadily. "I meant it." Turning away, she cut through the water and scrambled up the bank.

Breathing fast, Aaron watched her. She'd been so soft, so giving in his arms. He'd never wanted a woman more—never felt just that way. It came like a blow that she was the first who'd really mattered, and the first to throw his own emotion back in his face. Grimly he swam back to his own side.

"You're one tough lady, aren't you?"

Jillian heard the water lap as he pulled himself from it. Without bothering to shake it out, she dragged on her dusty shirt. "That's right. God knows why I was fool enough to think I could trust you." Why did she want so badly to weep when she never wept? she wondered and buttoned her shirt with shaky fingers. "All that talk about helping me, just so you could get what

you wanted.'' Keeping her back to him, she pulled up her brief panties.

Aaron's hands paused on the snap of his jeans. Rage and frustration tumbled through him so quickly he didn't think he'd be able to control it. ''Be careful, Jillian.''

She whirled around, eyes brilliant, breasts heaving. ''Don't you tell me what to do. You've been clear right from the beginning about what you wanted.''

Muscles tense, he laid a hand on the saddle of his stallion. ''That's right.''

The calm answer only filled her with more fury. ''I might've respected your honesty if it wasn't for the fact that I've got a cut fence and missing cattle. Things like that didn't happen when you were in Billings waiting for your father to—'' She cut herself off, appalled at what she'd been about to say. Whatever apology she might have made was swallowed at the murderous look he sent her.

''Waiting for him to what?'' Aaron said softly—too softly.

The ripple of fear made her lift her chin. ''That's for you to answer.''

He knew he didn't dare go near her. If he did she might not come out whole. His fingers tightened on the rope that hung on his saddle. ''Then you'd better keep your thoughts to yourself.''

She'd have given half her spread to have been able to take those hateful, spiteful words back. But they'd been said. ''And you keep your hands to yourself,'' she said evenly. ''I want you to stay away from me and mine. I don't need soft words, Murdock. I don't want them from you or anyone. You're a damn sight

easier to take without the pretense.'' She stalked away to grab at her jeans.

He acted swiftly. He didn't think. His mind was still reeling from her words—words that had stung because he'd never felt or shown that kind of tenderness to another woman. What had flowed through him in the pond had been much more than a physical need and complex enough to allow him to be hurt for the first time by a woman.

Jillian gave out a gasp of astonishment as the circle of rope slipped around her, snapping snugly just about her waist and pinning her arms above the elbows. Whirling on her heel, she grabbed at the line. ''What the hell do you think you're doing?''

With a jerk, Aaron brought her stumbling forward. ''What I should've done a week ago.'' His eyes were nearly black with fury as she fell helplessly against him. ''You won't get any more soft words out of me.''

She struggled impotently against the rope, but her eyes were defiant and fearless. ''You're going to pay for this, Murdock.''

He didn't doubt it, but at that moment he didn't give a damn. Gathering her wet hair in one hand, he dragged her closer. ''By God,'' he muttered. ''I think it'll be worth it. You make a man ache, Jillian, in the middle of the night when he should have some peace. One minute you're so damn soft, and the next you're snarling. Since you can't make up your mind, I'll do it for you.''

His mouth came down on hers so that she could taste enraged desire. She fought against it even as it found some answering chord in her. His chest was still naked, still wet, so that her shirt soaked up the mois-

ture. The air rippled against her bare legs as he
scooped them out from under her. With her mouth still
imprisoned by his, she found herself lying on the sun-
warmed grass beneath him. Her fury didn't leave room
for panic.

She squirmed under him, kicking and straining
against the rope, cursing him when he released her
mouth to savage her neck. But an oath ended on a
moan when his mouth came back to hers. He nipped
into her full bottom lip as if to draw out passion. Her
movements beneath him altered in tone from protest
to demand, but neither of them noticed. Jillian only
knew her body was on fire, and that this time she'd
submit to it no matter what the cost.

He was drowning in her. He'd forgotten about the
rope, forgotten his anger and his hurt. All he knew
was that she was warm and slender beneath him and
that her mouth was enough to drive a man over the
line of reason. Nothing about her was calm. Her lips
were avid and seeking; her fingers dug into his waist.
He could feel the thunder of her heart race to match
his. When she caught his lip between her teeth and
drew it into her mouth, he groaned and let her have
her way.

Jillian flew with the sensations. The grass rubbed
against her legs as she shifted them to allow him more
intimacy. His hair smelled of the water that ran from
it onto her skin. She tasted it, and the light flavor of
salt and flesh when she pressed her lips to his throat.
Her name shivered in a desperate whisper against her
ear. No soft words. There was nothing soft, nothing
gentle about what they brought to each other now. This
was a raw, primitive passion that she understood even

as it was tapped for the first time. She felt his fingers skim down her shirt, releasing buttons so that he could find her. But it was his mouth not his hand that closed over the taut peak, hot and greedy. The need erupted and shattered her.

Lips, teeth, and tongue were busy on her flesh as she lay dazed from the first swift, unexpected crest. While she fought to catch her breath, Aaron tugged on her shirt to remove it, cursing when it remained tight at her waist. In an urgent move his hand swept down. His fingers touched rope. He froze, his breath heaving in his lungs.

Good God, what was he doing? Squeezing his eyes tight, he fought for reason. His face was nuzzled in the slender valley between her breasts so that he could feel as well as hear the frantic beat of her heart.

He was about to force himself on a helpless woman. No matter what the provocation, there could be no absolution for what he was on the edge of doing. Cursing himself, Aaron tugged on the rope, then yanked it over her head. After he'd tossed it aside, he looked down at her.

Her mouth was swollen from his. Her eyes were nearly closed and so clouded he couldn't read them. She lay so still he could feel each separate tremor from her body. He wanted her badly enough to beg. "You can make me pay now," he said softly and rolled from her onto his back.

She didn't move, but looked up into the calm blue sky while needs churned inside her. The warbler was still singing, the roses still blooming.

Yes, she could make him pay—she'd recognized the look of self-disgust in his eyes. She had only to get

up and walk away to do it. She'd never considered
herself a fool. Deliberately she rolled over on top of
him. Aaron automatically put his hands on her arms to
steady her. Their eyes met so that desire stared into
desire.

"You'll pay—if you don't finish what you've
started." Diving her hands into his hair, she brought
her mouth down on his.

Her shirt fluttered open so that her naked skin slid
over his. Jillian felt his groan of pleasure every bit as
clearly as she heard it. Then it was all speed and fire,
so fast, so hot, there wasn't time for thought. Tasting,
feeling was enough as they raced over each other in a
frenzy of demand. Her shirt fell away just before she
pulled at the snap of his jeans.

She tugged them down, then lost herself in the long
lean line of his hips. Her fingers found a narrow raised
scar that ran six inches down the bone. She felt a ripple
of pain as if her own skin had been rent. Then he was
struggling out of his jeans and the feel of him, hot and
ready against her, drove everything else out of her
mind. But when she reached for him, he shifted so she
was beneath him again.

"Aaron…" What she would have demanded ended
in a helpless moan as he slid a finger under the elastic
riding high on her thigh. With a clever, thorough touch
of fingertips he brought her to a racking climax.

She was pulsing all over, inside and out. No longer
was she aware that she clung to him, her hands bringing him as much torturous pleasure as his brought her.
She only knew that her need built and was met time
and time again while he held off that last, that ultimate
fulfillment. With eyes dazed with passion, she watched

his mouth come toward hers again. Their lips met—he plunged into her, swallowing her gasps.

For a long time she lay spent. The sky overhead was still calm. With her hands on Aaron's shoulders, she could feel each labored breath. There seemed to be no peace for them even in the aftermath of passion. Was this the way it was supposed to be? she wondered. She'd known nothing like this before. Needs that hurt and remained unsettled even after they'd been satisfied. She still wanted him—that moment when her body was hot and trembling from their merging.

After all the years she'd been so careful to distance herself from any chance of an involvement, she found herself needing a man she hardly knew. A man she'd been schooled to distrust. Yet she did trust him…that's what frightened her most of all. She had no reason to—no logical reason. He'd made her forget her ambitions, her work, her responsibilities, and reminded her that beneath it all, she was first a woman. More, he'd made her glory in it.

Aaron raised his head slowly, for the first time in his memory unsure of himself. She'd gotten to a place inside him no one had ever touched. He realized he didn't want her to walk away and leave it empty again—and that he'd never be able to hold her unless she was willing. "Jillian…" He brushed her damp, tangled hair from her cheek. "This was supposed to be easy. Why isn't it?"

"I don't know." She held onto the weakness another moment, bringing his cheek down to hers so that she could draw in his scent and remember. "I need to think."

"About what?"

She closed her eyes a moment and shook her head. "I don't know. Let me go now, Aaron."

His fingers tightened in her hair. "For how long?"

"I don't know that either. I need some time."

It would be easy to keep her—for the moment. He had only to lower his mouth to hers again. He remembered the wild mustang—the hell he'd gone through to catch it, the hell he'd gone through to set it free. Saying nothing, he released her.

They dressed in silence—both of them too battered by feelings they'd never tried to put into words. When Jillian reached for her hat, Aaron took her arm.

"If I told you this meant something to me, more than I'd expected, maybe more than I'd wanted, would you believe me?"

Jillian moistened her lips. "I do now. I have to be sure I do tomorrow."

Aaron picked up his own hat and shaded his face with it. "I'll wait—but I won't wait long." Lifting a hand, he cupped her chin. "If you don't come to me, I'll come after you."

She ignored the little thrill of excitement that rushed up her spine. "If I don't come to you, you won't be able to come after me." Turning away, she untied her mare and vaulted into the saddle. Aaron slipped his hand under the bridle and gave her one long look.

"Don't bet on it," he said quietly. He walked back over the boundary line to his own mount.

Chapter 7

If you don't come to me, I'll come after you.

They weren't words Jillian would forget. She hadn't yet decided what to do about them—any more than she'd decided what to do about what had happened between her and Aaron. There'd been more than passion in that fiery afternoon at the pond, more than pleasure, however intense. Perhaps she could have faced the passion and the pleasure, but it was the something more that kept her awake at nights.

If she went to him, what would she be going to? A man she'd yet to scratch the surface of—an affair that promised to have more hills and valleys than she knew how to negotiate. The risk—she was beginning to understand the risk too well. If she relaxed her hands on the reins this time, she'd tumble into love before she could regain control. That was difficult for her to admit, and impossible for her to understand.

She'd always believed that people fell in love because they wanted to, because they were looking for, or were ready for, romance. Certainly she'd been ready for it once before, open for all those soft feelings and heightened emotions. Yet now, when she believed she was on the border of love again, she was neither ready for it, nor was she experiencing any soft feelings. Aaron Murdock didn't ask for them—and in not asking, he demanded so much more.

If she went to him…could she balance her responsibilities, her ambitions, with the needs he drew out of her? When she was in his arms she didn't think of the ranch, or her position there that she had to struggle every day to maintain.

If she fell in love with him…could she deal with the imbalance of feelings between them and cope when the time came for him to go his own way? She never doubted he would. Other than Clay, there'd never been a man who'd remained constant to her.

Indecision tore at her, as it would in a woman accustomed to following her own route in her own way.

And while her personal life was in turmoil, her professional one fared no better. Five hundred of her cattle were missing. There was no longer any doubt that her herd had been systematically and successfully rustled.

Jillian hung up the phone, rubbing at the headache that drummed behind her temples.

"Well?" Hat in lap, Joe Carlson sat on the other side of her desk.

"They can't deliver the plane until the end of the week." Grimly she set her jaw as she looked over at him. "It hardly matters now. Unless they're fools,

they've got the cattle well away by this time. Probably transported them over the border into Wyoming.''

He studied the brim of his neat Stetson. "Maybe not, that would make it federal.''

"It's what I'd do,'' she murmured. "You can't hide five hundred head of prime beef." Rising, she dragged her hands through her hair. *Five hundred.* The words continued to flash in her mind—a sign of failure, impotence, vulnerability. "Well, the sheriff's doing what he can, but they've got the jump on us, Joe. There's nothing I can do." On a sound of frustration, she balled her fists. "I hate being helpless.''

"Jillian…" Joe ran the brim of his hat through his hands, frowning down at it another moment. During his silence she could hear the old clock on her grandfather's desk tick the time away. "I wouldn't feel right if I didn't bring it up," he said at length and looked back at her. "It wouldn't be too difficult to hide five hundred head if they were scattered through a few thousand.''

Her eyes chilled. "Why don't you speak plainly, Joe?''

He rose. After more than six months on Utopia, he still looked more businessman than outdoorsman. And she understood it was the businessman who spoke now. "Jillian, you can't just ignore the fact that the west boundary line was cut. That pasture leads directly onto Murdock land.''

"I know where it leads,'' she said coolly. "Just as I know I need more than a cut line to accuse anyone, particularly the Murdocks, of rustling.''

Joe opened his mouth to speak again, met her uncompromising look, then shut it. "Okay.''

The simplicity of his answer only fanned her temper. And her doubts. "Aaron told me he was going to take a thorough head count. He'd know if there were fifty extra head on his spread, much less five hundred."

It was her tone much more than her words that told him where the land lay now. "I know."

Jillian stared at him. His eyes were steady and compassionate. "Damn it, he doesn't need to steal cattle from me."

"Jillian, you lose five hundred head now and your profit dwindles down to nothing. Lose that much again, half that much again, and…you might have to start thinking about selling off some of your pasture. There're other reasons than the price per head for rustling."

She spun around, shutting her eyes tight. She'd thought of that—and hated herself for it. "He would've asked me if he wanted to buy my land."

"Maybe, but your answer would've been no. Rumor is he was going to start his own place a few years back. He didn't—but that doesn't mean he's content to make do with what his father has."

She couldn't contradict him, not on anything he'd said. But she couldn't live with it either. "Leave the investigating to the sheriff, Joe. That's his job."

He drew very straight and very stiff at the clipped tone of her voice. "All right. I guess I better get back to mine."

On a wave of frustration and guilt, she turned before he reached the door. "Joe—I'm sorry. I know you're only thinking about Utopia."

"I'm thinking about you, too."

"I appreciate it, I really do." She picked up her worn leather work glove from the desk and ran it through her hands. "I have to handle this my own way, and I need a little more time to decide just what that is."

"Okay." He put his hat on and lowered the brim with his finger. "Just so you know you've got support if you need it."

"I won't forget it."

When he'd gone, Jillian stopped in the center of the office. God, she wanted so badly to panic. Just to throw up her hands and tell whoever'd listen that she couldn't deal with it. There had to be someone else, somewhere, who could take over and see her through until everything was back in order. But she wasn't allowed to panic, or to turn over her responsibilities even for a minute. The land was hers, and all that went with it.

Jillian picked up her hat and her other glove. There was work to be done. If they cleaned her out down to the last hundred head, there would still be work to be done, and a way to build things back up again. She had the land, and her grandfather's legacy of determination.

Even as she opened the front door to go out, she saw Karen Murdock drive up in front of the house. Surprised, Jillian hesitated, then went out on the porch to meet her.

"Hello, I hope you don't mind that I just dropped by."

"No, of course not." Jillian smiled, marveling for the second time at the soft, elegant looks of Aaron's mother. "It's nice to see you again, Mrs. Murdock."

"I've caught you at a bad time," she said, glancing down at the work gloves in Jillian's hand.

"No." Jillian stuck the gloves in her back pocket. "Would you like some coffee?"

"I'd love it."

Karen followed Jillian into the house, glancing around idly as they walked toward the kitchen. "Lord, it's been years since I've been in here. I used to visit your grandmother," she said with a rueful smile. "Of course your grandfather and Paul both knew, but we were all very careful not to mention it. How do you feel about old feuds, Jillian?"

There was a laugh in her voice that might have set Jillian's back up at one time. Now it simply nudged a smile from her. "Not precisely the same way I felt a few weeks ago."

"I'm glad to hear it." Karen took a seat at the kitchen table while Jillian began to brew a fresh pot of coffee. "I realize Paul said some things the other day that were bound to rub you the wrong way. I have to confess he does some of it on purpose. Your reaction was the high point of his day."

Jillian smiled a little as she looked over her shoulder. "Maybe he's more like Clay than I'd imagined."

"They were out of the same mold. There aren't many of them," she murmured. "Jillian—we've heard about your missing cattle. I can't tell you how badly I feel. I realize the words *if there's anything I can do* sound empty, but I mean them."

Turning back to the coffeepot, Jillian managed to shrug. She wasn't sure she could deal easily with sympathy right then. "It's a risk we all take. The sheriff's doing what he can."

"A risk we all take," Karen agreed. "When it happens to one of us, all of us feel it." She hesitated a moment, knowing the ground was delicate. "Jillian, Aaron mentioned the cut line to me, though he's kept it from his father."

"I'm not worried about the cut line," Jillian told her quietly. "I know Aaron didn't have any part in it—I'm not a fool."

No, Karen thought, studying the clean-lined profile. A fool you're not. "He's very concerned about you."

"He needn't be." She swung open a cupboard door for cups. "It's my problem, I have to deal with it."

Karen watched calmly as Jillian poured. "No support accepted?"

With a sigh, Jillian turned around. "I don't mean to be rude, Mrs. Murdock. Running a ranch is a difficult, chancy business. When you're a woman you double those stakes." Bringing the coffee to the table, she sat across from her. "I have to be twice as good as a man would be in my place because this is still a man's world. I can't afford to cave in."

"I understand that." Karen sipped and glanced around the room. "There's no one here you have to prove anything to."

Jillian looked up from her own cup and saw the compassion, and the unique bond one woman can have with another. As she did, the tight band of control loosened. "I'm so scared," she whispered. "Most of the time I don't dare admit it to myself because there's so much riding on this year. I've taken a lot of gambles—if they pay off... Five hundred head." She let out a long breath as the numbers pounded in her mind.

"It won't put me under, I can't let it put me under, but it's going to take a long time to recover."

Reaching out, Karen covered her hand with her own. "They could be found."

"You know the chances of that now." For a moment she sat still, accepting the comfort of the touch before she put her hand back on her cup. "Whichever way it goes, I'm still boss at Utopia. I have a responsibility to make what was passed on to me work. Clay trusted me with what was his. I'm going to make it work."

Karen gave her a long, thorough look very much like one of her son's. "For Clay or for yourself?"

"For both of us," Jillian told her. "I owe him for the land, and for what he taught me."

"You can put too much of yourself into this land," Karen said abruptly. "Paul would swear I'd taken leave of my senses if he heard me say so, but it's true. Aaron—" She smiled, indulgent, proud. "He's a great deal like his father, but he doesn't have Paul's rigidity. Perhaps he hasn't needed it. You can't let the land swallow you, Jillian."

"It's all I have."

"You don't mean that. Oh, you think you do," she murmured when Jillian said nothing. "But if you lost every acre of this land tomorrow, you'd make something else. You've the guts for it. I recognize it in you just as I've always seen it in Aaron."

"He had other options." Agitated, Jillian rose to pour coffee she no longer wanted.

"You're thinking of the oil." For a moment Karen said nothing as she weighed the pros and cons of what she was going to say. "He did that for me—and for

his father," she said at length. "I hope I don't ever have to ask anything like that of him again."

Jillian came back to the table but didn't sit. "I don't understand."

"Paul was wrong. He's a good man and his mistakes have always been made with the same force and vigor as he does everything." A smile flickered on her lips, but her eyes were serious. "He'd promised something to Aaron, something that had been understood since Aaron was a boy. The Double M would be his, if he'd earned it. By God, he did," she whispered. "I think you understand what I mean."

"Yes." Jillian looked down at her cup, then set it down. "Yes, I do."

"When Aaron came back from college, Paul wasn't ready to let go. That's when Aaron agreed to work it his father's way for three years. He was to take over as manager after that—with full authority."

"I've heard," Jillian began, then changed her tack. "It can't be easy for a man to give up what he's worked for, even to his own son."

"It was time for Paul to give," Karen told her, but she held her head high. "Perhaps he would have if..." She gestured with her hands as though she were slowing herself down. "When he refused to stick to the bargain, Aaron was furious. They had a terrible argument—the kind that's inevitable between two strong, self-willed men. Aaron was determined to go down to Wyoming, buy some land for himself, and start from scratch. As much as he loved the ranch, I think it was something he'd been itching to do in any case."

"But he didn't."

"No." Karen's eyes were very clear. "Because I

asked him not to. The doctors had just diagnosed Paul as terminal. They'd given him two years at the outside. He was infuriated that age had caught up with him, that his body was betraying him. He's a very proud man, Jillian. He'd beaten everything he'd ever gone up against.''

She remembered the hawklike gaze and trembling hands. ''I'm sorry.''

''He didn't want anyone to know, not even Aaron. I can count the times I've gone against Paul on one hand.'' She glanced down at her own palms. Something in her expression told Jillian very clearly that if the woman had acquiesced over the years, it had been because of strength and not weakness. ''I knew if Aaron went away like that, Paul would stop fighting for whatever time he had left. And then Aaron, once he knew, would never be able to live with it. So I told him.'' She let out a long sigh and turned her hands over. ''I asked him to give up what he wanted. He went to Billings, and though I'm sure he's always thought he did it for me, I know he did it for his father. I don't imagine the doctors would agree, but Aaron gave his father five years.''

Jillian turned away as her throat began to ache. ''I've said some horrible things to him.''

''You wouldn't be the first, I'm sure. Aaron knew what it would look like. He's never given a damn what people think of him. What most people think,'' she corrected softly.

''I can't apologize,'' Jillian said as she fought to control herself. ''He'd be furious if I told him I knew.''

''You know him well.''

''I don't,'' Jillian returned with sudden passion. ''I

don't know him, I don't understand him, and—'' She cut herself off, amazed that she was about to bare her soul to Aaron's mother.

"I'm his mother," Karen said, interpreting the look. "But I'm still a woman. And one who understands very well what it is to have feelings for a man that promise to lead to difficulties.'' This time she didn't weigh her words but spoke freely. "I was barely twenty when I met Paul, he was past forty. His friends thought he was mad and that I wanted his money.'' She laughed, then sat back with a little sigh. "I can promise you, I didn't see the humor in it thirty years ago. I'm not here to offer advice on whatever's between you and Aaron, but to offer support if you'll take it.''

Jillian looked at her—the enduring beauty, the strength that showed in her eyes, the kindness. "I'm not sure I know how.''

Rising, Karen placed her hands on Jillian's shoulders. So young, she thought wistfully. So dead set. "Do you know how to accept friendship?''

Jillian smiled and touched Karen's hands, still resting on her shoulders. "Yes.''

"That'll do. You're busy,'' she said briskly, giving Jillian a quick squeeze before she released her. "But if you need a woman, as we sometimes do, call me.''

"I will. Thank you.''

Karen shook her head. "No, it's not all unselfish. I've lived over thirty years in this man's world.'' Briefly she touched Jillian's cheek. "I miss my daughter.''

Aaron stood on the porch and watched the moon rise. The night was so still he heard the whisk of a

hawk's wings over his head before it dove after its night prey. In one hand he held a can of iced beer that he sipped occasionally, though he wasn't registering the taste. It was one of those warm spring nights when you could taste the scent of the flowers and smell the hint of summer, which was creeping closer.

He'd be damned if he'd wait much longer.

It had been a week since he'd touched her. Every night after the long, dusty day was over, he found himself aching to have her with him, to fill that emptiness inside him he'd become so suddenly aware of. It was difficult enough to have discovered he didn't want Jillian in the same way he'd wanted any other woman, but to have discovered his own vulnerabilities...

She could hurt him—had hurt him. That was a first, Aaron thought grimly and lifted his beer. He hadn't yet worked out how to prevent it from happening again. But that didn't stop him from wanting her.

She didn't trust him. Though he'd once agreed that he didn't want her to, Aaron had learned that was a lie. He wanted her to give him her trust—to believe in him enough to share her problems with him. She must be going through hell now, he thought as his fingers tightened on the can. But she wouldn't come to him, wouldn't let him help. Maybe it was about time he did something about that—whether she liked it or not.

Abruptly impatient, angry, he started toward the steps. The sound of an approaching car reached him before the headlights did. Glancing toward the sound, he watched the twin beams cut through the darkness. His initial disinterest became a tension he felt in his shoulder and stomach muscles.

Aaron set the half-empty beer on the porch rail as Jillian pulled up in front of his house. Whatever his needs were, he still had enough sense of self-preservation to prevent himself from just rushing down the stairs and grabbing her. He waited.

She'd been so sure her nerves would calm during the drive over. It was difficult for her, as a woman who simply didn't permit herself to be nervous, to deal with a jumpy stomach and dry throat. Not once since his mother had left her that morning had Aaron been out of her thoughts. Yet Jillian had gone through an agony of doubt before she'd made the final decision to come. In coming, she was giving him something she'd never intended to—a portion of her private self.

With the moon at her back she stood by her car a moment, looking up at him. Perhaps because her legs weren't as strong as they should've been, she kept her chin high as she walked up the porch steps.

"This is a mistake," she told him.

Aaron remained where he was, one shoulder leaning against the rail post. "Is it?"

"It's going to complicate things at a time when my life's complicated enough."

His stomach had twisted into a mass of knots that were only tugging tighter as he looked at her. She was pale, but there wasn't a hint of a tremor in her voice. "You took your sweet time coming here," he said mildly, but he folded his fingers into his palm to keep from touching her.

"I wouldn't have come at all if I could've stopped myself."

"That so?" It was more of an admission than he'd

expected. The first muscles began to relax. "Well, since you're here, why don't you come a little closer?"

He wasn't going to make it easy for her, Jillian realized. And she'd have detested herself if she'd let him. With her eyes on his, she stepped forward until their bodies brushed. "Is this close enough?"

His eyes skimmed her face, then he smiled. "No."

Jillian hooked her hands behind his head and pressed her lips to his. "Now?"

"Closer." He allowed himself to touch her—one hand at the small of her back rode slowly up to grip her hair. His eyes glittered in the moonlight, touched with triumph, amusement, and passion. "A damn sight closer, Jillian."

Her eyes stayed open as she fit her body more intimately to his. She felt the answering response of his muscles against her own, the echoing thud of his heart. "If we get much closer out here on the porch," she murmured with her mouth a whisper from his, "we're going to be illegal."

"Yeah." He traced her bottom lip, moistening it, and felt her little jerk of breath on his tongue. "I'll post bond if you're worried."

Her lips throbbed from the expert flick of his tongue. "Shut up, Murdock," she muttered and crushed her mouth to his. Jillian let all the passions, all the emotions that had been chasing her around for days, have their way. Even as they sprang out of her, they consumed her. Mindlessly she pressed against him so that he was caught between her body and the post.

The thrill of pleasure was so intense it almost sliced through his skin. Aaron's arm came around her so that he could cup the back of her head and keep that wildly

aggressive mouth on his own. Then, swiftly, his arm scooped under her knees and lifted her off her feet.

"Aaron—" Her protest was smothered by another ruthless kiss before he walked across the porch to the door. Though she admired the way he could swing the screen open, and slam the heavy door with his arms full, she laughed. "Aaron, put me down. I can walk."

"Don't see how when I'm carrying you," he pointed out as he started up the narrow steps to the second floor.

"Is this the sort of thing you do to express male dominance?"

She was rewarded with a narrow-eyed glare and smiled sweetly.

"No," Aaron said in mild tones. "This is the sort of thing I do to express romance. Now, when I want to express male dominance..." As he drew near the top of the steps he shifted her quickly so that she hung over his shoulder.

After the initial shock Jillian had to acknowledge a hit. "Had that one coming," she admitted, blowing the hair out of her face. "I think my point was that I wasn't looking for romance or dominance."

Aaron's brow lifted as he walked into the bedroom. The words had been light enough, but he'd caught the sincerity of tone. Slowly he drew her down so that before her feet had touched the floor every angle of her body had rubbed against his. Weakened by the maneuver, she stared up at him with eyes already stormy with desire. "Don't you like romance, Jillian?"

"That's not what I'm asking for," she managed, reaching for him.

He grabbed her wrists, holding her off. "That's too

bad, then.'' Very lightly he nipped at her ear. ''You'll just have to put up with it. Do you reckon straight passion's safer?''

''As anything could be with you.'' She caught her breath as his tongue traced down the side of her throat.

Aaron laughed, then began lazily, determinedly, to seduce her with his mouth alone. ''This right here,'' he murmured, nibbling at a point just above her collar. ''So soft, so delicate. A man could almost forget there're places like this on you until he finds them for himself. You throw up that damn-the-devil chin and it's tempting to give it one good clip, but then''—he tilted his head to a new angle and his lips skimmed along her skin—''right under it's just like silk.''

He tugged with his teeth at the cord of her neck and felt her arms go boneless. That's what he wanted, he thought with rising excitement. To have her melting and pliant and out of control, if only for a few minutes. Hot blood and fire were rewards in themselves, but this time, perhaps only this time, he wanted the satisfaction of knowing he could make her as weak as she could make him.

He slanted his mouth over hers, teasing her tongue with the tip of his until her breath was short and shallow. Her pulse pounded into his palms. He was going to take his time undressing her, he thought. A long, leisurely time that would drive them both crazy.

Without hurry Aaron backed her toward the bed, then eased her down until she sat on the edge. In the moonlight he could see that her eyes had already misted with need, her skin softly flushed with it. Watching her, he ran a long finger down her throat to the first button on her shirt. His eyes remained steady

as he undid it, then the second—then the third. He stopped there to move his hands down her, lightly over her breasts, the nipped waist, and narrow hips to the long, slender thighs. She was very still but for the quiver of her flesh.

Turning, he tucked her leg between his and began pulling off her boot. The first hit the floor, but when he took the other and tugged, Jillian gave him some assistance with a well-placed foot.

Surprised, he glanced back to see her shoot him a cocky smile. She recovered quickly, he thought. It would be all the more exciting to turn her to putty again. "You might do the same for me," Aaron suggested, then dropped on the bed, leaned back on his elbows, and held out a booted foot.

Jillian rose to oblige him and straddled his leg. This—the wicked grin, the reckless eyes—she knew how to deal with. It might light a fire in her, but it didn't bring on that uncontrollable softness. When she'd finally made her decision to come, she'd made it to come on equal terms, with no quiet promises or tender phrases that meant no more than the breath it took to make them. She'd told herself she wouldn't fall in love with him as long as she listened to her body and blocked off her heart.

The minute his second boot hit the floor, Aaron grabbed her around the waist and swung her back so that she fell onto the bed, laughing. "You're a tough guy, Murdock." Jillian hooked her arms around his neck and grinned up at him. "Always tossing women around."

"Bad habit of mine." Lowering his head, he nibbled idly at her lips, resisting her attempt to deepen the kiss.

"I like your mouth," he murmured. "It's another of those soft, surprising places." Gently he sucked on her lower lip until he felt the hands at his neck grow lax.

The mists were closing in again and she forgot the ways and means to hold them off. This wasn't what she wanted...was it? Yet it seemed to be everything she wanted. Her mind was floating, out of her body, so that she could almost see herself lying languorous and pliant under Aaron. She could see the tension and anxieties of the past days drain out of her own face until it was soft and relaxed under the lazy touch of his mouth and tongue. She could feel her heartbeat drop to a light pace that wasn't quite steady but not yet frantic. Perhaps this was what it felt like to be pampered, to be prized. She wasn't sure, but knew she couldn't bear to lose the sensation. Her sigh came slowly with the release of doubts.

When he bent to whisper something foolish in her ear, she could smell his evening shower on him. His face was rough with the stubble of a long day, but she rubbed her cheek against it, enjoying the scrape. Then his lips grazed across the skin that was alive and tingling until they found their way back to hers.

She felt the brush of strong, clever fingers as they trailed down to release the last buttons of her shirt. Then they skimmed over her rib cage, lightly, effortlessly drawing her deeper into the realm of sensation. He barely touched her. The kisses remained soft, his hands gentle. All coherent thought spun away.

"My shirt's in the way," he murmured against her ear. "I want to feel you against me."

She lifted her hands, and though her fingers didn't fumble, she couldn't make them move quickly. It

seemed like hours before she felt the press of his flesh against hers. With a sigh, she slid her hands up to his shoulders and back until she'd drawn the shirt away. The ridge of muscle was so hard. As she rubbed her palms over him, Jillian realized she'd only had flashes of impressions the first time they'd made love. Everything had been so fast and wild she hadn't been able to appreciate just how well he was formed.

Tight sinew, taut flesh. Aaron was a man used to using his back and his hands to do a day's work. She didn't stop to reason why that in itself was a pleasure to her. Then she could reason nothing because his mouth had begun to roam.

He hadn't known he could gain such complete satisfaction in thinking of another's pleasure. He wanted her—wanted her quick and fast and furious, and yet it was a heady feeling to know he had the power to make her weak with a touch.

The underside of her breast was so soft...and he lingered. The skin above the waistband of her jeans was white and smooth...and his hand was content to move just there. He felt her first trembles; they rippled under his lips and hands until his senses swam. Denim strained against denim until he pulled the jeans down over her hips to find her.

Jillian wasn't certain when the languor had become hunger. She arched against him, demanding, but he continued to move without haste. She couldn't understand his fascination with her body when she'd always considered it too straight, too slim and practical. Yet now he seemed anxious to touch, to taste every inch. And the murmurs that reached her whispered approval. His hand cupped her knee so that his fingers trailed

over the sensitive back. Years of riding, walking, working, had made her legs strong, and very susceptible.

When his teeth scraped down her thigh, she cried out, stunned to be catapulted to the taut edge of the first peak. But he didn't allow her to go over. Not yet. His warm breath teased her, then the light play of his tongue. She felt the threat of explosion building, growing in power and depth. Yet somehow he knew the instant before it shattered her, and retreated. Again and again he took her to the verge and brought her back until she was weak and desperate.

Jillian shifted beneath Aaron, willing him to take anything, all that he wanted—not even aware that he'd removed the last barrier of clothing until he was once more lying full length on her. She felt each warm, unsteady breath on her face just before his lips raced over it.

"This time..." Aaron pulled air into his lungs so that he could speak. "This time you tell me—you tell me that you want me."

"Yes." She locked herself around him, shuddering with need. "Yes, I want you. Now."

Something flashed in his eyes. "Not just now," he said roughly and drove into her.

Jillian slid over the first edge and was blinded. But there was more, so much more.

Chapter 8

It was the scent of her hair that slowly brought him back to reason. His face was buried in it. The fragrance reminded him of the wildflowers his mother would sometimes gather and place in a little porcelain vase on a window ledge. It was tangled in his hands, and so soft against his skin he knew he'd be content to stay just as he was through the night.

She lay still beneath him, her breathing so quiet and even she might have been asleep. But when he turned his head to press his lips to her neck, her arms tightened around him. Lifting his head, he looked down at her.

Her eyes were nearly closed, heavy. He'd seen the shadows beneath them when she'd first walked toward him on the porch. With a small frown, Aaron traced his thumb over them. "You haven't been sleeping well."

Surprised by the statement, and his tone, she lifted her brows. After where they'd just gone together, she might've expected him to say something foolish or arousing. Instead his brows had drawn together and his tone was disapproving. She wasn't sure why it made her want to laugh, but it did.

"I'm fine," she said with a smile.

"No." He cut her off and cupped her chin in his hand. "You're not."

She stared up, realizing how easy it would be to just pour out her thoughts and feelings. The worries, the fears, the problems, that seemed to build up faster than she could cope with them—how reassuring it would be to say it all out loud, to him.

She'd done too much of that with his mother, but somehow Jillian could justify that. It was one thing to confess fears and doubts to another woman, and another to give a man an insight on your weaknesses. At dawn they'd both be ranchers again, with a boundary line between them that had stood for nearly a century.

"Aaron, I didn't come here to—"

"I know why you came," he interrupted. His voice was much milder than his eyes. "Because you couldn't stay away. I understand that. Now you're just going to have to accept what comes with it."

It was difficult to drum up a great deal of dignity when she was naked and warm beneath him, but she came close to succeeding. "Which is?"

The annoyance in his eyes lightened to amusement. "I like the way you say that—just like my third grade teacher."

Her lips quivered. "It's one of the few things I man-

aged to pick up from my mother. But you haven't answered the question, Murdock.''

''I'm crazy about you,'' he said suddenly and the mouth that had curved into a smile fell open. She wasn't ready to hear that one, Aaron mused. He wasn't sure he was ready for the consequences of it himself, and decided to play it light. ''Of course, I've always been partial to nasty tempered females. I mean to help you, Jillian.'' His eyes were abruptly sober. ''If I have to climb over your back to do it.''

''There isn't anything you can do even if I wanted you to.''

He didn't comment immediately but shifted, pulling the pillows up against the headboard, then leaning back before he drew her against him. Jillian didn't stiffen as much as go still. There was something quietly possessive about the move, and irresistibly sweet. Before she could stop it, she'd relaxed against him.

Aaron felt the hesitation but didn't comment. When you went after trust, you did it slowly. ''Tell me what's been done.''

''Aaron, I don't want to bring you into this.''

''I am in it, if for no other reason than that cut line.''

She could accept that, and let her eyes close. ''We did a full head count and came up five hundred short. As a precaution, we branded what calves were left right away. I estimate we lost fifty or sixty of them. The sheriff's been out.''

''What'd he find?''

She moved her shoulders. ''Can't tell where they took them out. If they'd cut any more wire, they'd fixed it. Very neat and tidy,'' she murmured, knowing something died inside her each time she thought of it.

"It seems as though they didn't take them all at once, but skimmed a few head here and there."

"Seems odd they left the one line down."

"Maybe they didn't have time to fix it."

"Or maybe they wanted to throw your attention my way until they'd finished."

"Maybe." She turned her face into his shoulder— only slightly, only for an instant—but for Jillian it was a large step toward sharing. "Aaron, I didn't mean the things I said about you and your father."

"Forget it."

She tilted her head back and looked at him. "I can't."

He kissed her roughly. "Try harder," he suggested. "I heard you were getting a plane."

"Yes." She dropped her head on his shoulder and tried to order her thoughts. "It doesn't look like it's going to be ready until next week."

"Then we'll go up in mine tomorrow."

"But why—"

"Nothing against the sheriff," he said easily. "But you know your land better."

Jillian pressed her lips together. "Aaron, I don't want to be obligated to you. I don't know how to explain it, but—"

"Then don't." Taking hold of her hair, he jerked it until her face came up to his. "You're going to find I'm not the kind who'll always give a damn about what you want. You can fight me, sometimes you might even win. But you won't stop me."

Her eyes kindled. "Why do you gear me up for a fight when I'm trying to be grateful?"

In one swift move he shifted so that they lay cross-

wise across the bed. "Maybe I like you better that way. You're a hell of a lot more dangerous when you soften up."

She threw up her chin. "That's not something that's going to happen very often around you."

"Good," he said and crushed his mouth onto hers. "You'll stay with me tonight."

"I'm not—" Then he silenced her with a savage kiss that left no room for thought, much less words.

"Tonight," he said with a laugh that held more challenge than humor, "you stay with me."

And he took her in a fury that whispered of desperation.

The birds woke her. There was a short stretch of time during the summer when the sun rose early enough that the birds were up before her. With a sigh, Jillian snuggled into the pillow. She could always fool her system into thinking she'd been lazy when she woke to daylight and birdsong.

Groggily she went over the day's workload. She'd have to check Baby before she went in to the horses. He liked to have his bottle right off. With one luxurious stretch, she rolled over, then stared blankly around the room. Aaron's room. He'd won that battle.

Lying back for a moment, she thought about the night with a mixture of pleasure and discomfort. He'd said once before that it wasn't as easy as it should've been. But could he have any idea what it had done to her to lie beside him through the night? She'd never known the simple pleasure of sleeping with someone else, sharing warmth and quiet and darkness. What had

made her believe that she could have an affair and remain practical about it?

But she wasn't in love with him. Jillian reached over to touch the side of the bed where he'd slept. She still had too much sense to let that happen. Her fingers dug into the sheet as she closed her eyes. Oh, God, she hoped she did.

The birdcalls distracted her so that she looked over at the window. The sun poured through. But it wasn't summer, Jillian remembered abruptly. What was she still doing in bed when the sun was up? Furious with herself, she sat up just as the door opened. Aaron walked in, carrying a mug of coffee.

"Too bad," he commented as he crossed to her. "I was looking forward to waking you up."

"I've got to get back," she said, tossing her hair from her eyes. "I should've been up hours ago."

Aaron held her in place effortlessly with a hand on her shoulder. "What you should do is sleep till noon," he corrected as he studied her face. "But you look better."

"I've got a ranch to run."

"And there isn't a ranch in the country that can't do without one person for one day." He sat down beside her and pushed the cup into her hand. "Drink your coffee."

She might've been annoyed by his peremptory order, but the scent of coffee was more persuasive. "What time is it?" she asked between sips.

"A bit after nine."

"Nine!" Her eyes grew comically wide. "Good God, I've got to get back."

Again Aaron held her in bed without effort.

"You've got to drink your coffee," he corrected. "Then you've got to have some breakfast."

After a quick, abortive struggle, Jillian shot him an exasperated look. "Will you stop treating me as though I were eight years old?"

He glanced down to where she held the sheet absently at her breasts. "It's tempting," he agreed.

"Eyes front, Murdock," she ordered when her mouth twitched. "Look, I appreciate the service," Jillian continued, gesturing with her cup, "but I can't sit around until midday."

"When's the last time you had eight hours' sleep?" He watched the annoyance flicker into her eyes as she lifted the coffee again, sipping rather than answering. "You'd have had more than that last night if you hadn't—distracted me."

She lifted her brows. "Is that what I did?"

"Several times, as I recall." Something in her expression, a question, a hint of doubt, made him study her a bit more carefully. Was it possible a woman like her would need reassurance after the night they'd spent together? What a strange mixture of tough and vulnerable she was. Aaron bent over and brushed his lips over her brow, knowing what would happen if he allowed himself just one taste of her mouth. "Apparently, you don't have to try very hard," he murmured. His lips trailed down to her temple before he could prevent them. "If you'd like to take advantage of me…"

Jillian let out an unsteady breath. "I think—I'd better have pity on you this morning, Murdock."

"Well…" He hooked a finger under the sheet and

began to draw it down. "Can't say I've ever cared much for pity."

"Aaron." Jillian tightened her hold on the sheet. "It's nine o'clock in the morning."

"Probably a bit past that by now."

When he started to lean closer, she lifted the mug and held it against his chest. "I've got stock to check and fences to ride," she reminded him. "And so do you."

He had a woman to protect, he thought, surprising himself. But he had enough sense not to mention it to the woman. "Sometimes," he began, then gave her a friendly kiss, "you're just no fun, Jillian."

Laughing, she drained the coffee. "Why don't you get out of here so I can have a shower and get dressed?"

"See what I mean." But he rose. "I'll fix your breakfast," he told her, then continued before she could say it wasn't necessary. "And neither of us is riding fence today. We're going up in the plane."

"Aaron, you don't have to take the time away from your own ranch to do this."

He hooked his hands in his pockets and studied her for so long her brows drew together. "For a sharp woman, you can be amazingly slow. If it's easier for you, just remember that rustling is every rancher's business."

She could see he was annoyed; she could hear it in the sudden coolness of tone. "I don't understand you."

"No." He inclined his head in a gesture that might've been resignation or acceptance. "I can see

that.'' He started for the door, and Jillian watched him, baffled.

''I...'' What the devil did she want to say? ''I have to drive over and let Gil know what I'm doing.''

''I sent a man over earlier.'' Aaron paused at the door and turned back to her. ''He knows you're with me.''

''He knows—you sent—'' She broke off, her fingers tightening on the handle of the mug. ''You sent a man over to tell him I was here, this morning?''

''That's right.''

She dragged a hand through her hair and sunlight shimmered gold at the ends. ''Do you realize what that looks like?''

His eyes became very cool and remote. ''It looks like what it is. Sorry, I didn't realize you wanted an assignation.''

''Aaron—'' But he was already closing the door behind him. Jillian brought the mug back in a full swing and barely prevented herself from following through. With a sound of disgust, she set it down and pulled herself from bed. That had been clumsy of her, she berated herself. How was he to understand that it wasn't shame, but insecurity? Perhaps it was better if he didn't understand.

Aaron could cheerfully have strangled her. In the kitchen, he slapped a slice of ham into the skillet. His own fault, he thought as it began to sizzle. Damn it, it was his own fault. He'd had no business letting things get beyond what they were meant to. If he stretched things, he could say that she had a wary sort of affection for him. It was unlikely it would ever go beyond

that. If his feelings had, he had only himself to blame, and himself to deal with.

Since when did he want fences around him? Aaron thought savagely as he plunged a kitchen fork into the grilling meat. Since when did he want more from a woman, any woman, than companionship, intelligence, and a warm bed? Maybe his feelings had slipped a bit past that, but he wasn't out of control yet.

Pouring coffee, he drank it hot and black. He'd been around too long to lose his head over a firebrand who didn't want anything more than a practical, uncomplicated affair. After all, he hadn't been looking for any more than that himself. He'd just let himself get caught up because of the problems she was facing, and the unwavering manner with which she faced them.

The coffee calmed him. Reassured, he pulled a carton of eggs out of the refrigerator. He'd help her as much as he could over the rustling, take her to bed as often as possible, and that would be that.

When she came into the room, he glanced over casually. Her hair was still wet, her face naked and glowing with health and a good night's sleep.

Oh, God, he was in love with her. And what the hell was he going to do?

The easy comment she'd been about to make about the smell of food vanished. Why was he staring at her as if he'd never seen her before? Uncharacteristically self-conscious, she shifted her weight. He looked as though someone had just knocked the wind from him. "Is something wrong?"

"What?"

His answer was so dazed she smiled. What in the world had he been thinking about when she'd inter-

rupted him? she wondered. "I said, is something wrong? You look like you've just taken a quick fall from a tall horse."

He cursed himself and turned away. "Nothing. How do you want your eggs?"

"Over easy, thanks." She took a step toward him, then hesitated. It wasn't a simple matter for her to make an outward show of affection. She'd met with too many lukewarm receptions in her life. Drawing up her courage, she crossed the room and touched his shoulder. He stiffened. She withdrew. "Aaron..." How calm her voice was, she mused. But then, she'd grown very adept very early at concealing hurt. "I'm not very good at accepting support."

"I've noticed." He cracked an egg and let it slide into the pan.

She blinked because her eyes had filled. Stupid! she railed at herself. Never put your weaknesses on display. Swallowing pride came hard to her, but there were times it was necessary. "What I'd like to say is that I appreciate what you're doing. I appreciate it very much."

Emotions were clawing him. He smacked another egg on the side of the pan. "Don't mention it."

She backed away. What else did you expect? she asked herself. You've never been the kind of person who inspires tender feelings. You don't want to be. "Fine," she said carelessly. "I won't." Moving to the coffeepot, she filled her mug again. "Aren't you eating?"

"I ate before." Aaron flipped the eggs, then reached for a plate.

She eyed his back with dislike. "I realize I'm keep-

ing you from a lot of pressing matters. Why don't you just send me up with one of your men?''

"I said I'd take you.'' He piled her plate with food, then dropped it unceremoniously on the table.

Chin lifted, Jillian took her seat. ''Suit yourself, Murdock.''

He turned to see her hack a slice from the ham. ''I always do.'' On impulse he grabbed the back of her head and covered her mouth in a long, ruthlessly thorough kiss that left them both simmering with anger and need.

When it was done, Jillian put all her concentration into keeping her hands steady. ''A man should be more cautious,'' she said mildly as she cut another slice, ''when a woman's holding a knife.''

With a short laugh, he dropped into the chair across from her. ''Caution doesn't seem to be something I hold on to well around you.'' Sipping his coffee, Aaron watched her as she worked her way systematically through the meal. Maybe it was too late to realize that intimacy between them had been a mistake, but if he could keep their relationship on its old footing otherwise, he might get his feelings back in line.

''You know, you should've bought a plane for Utopia years ago,'' he commented, perfectly aware that it would annoy her.

Her gaze lifted from her plate, slow and deliberate. ''Is that so?''

''Only an idiot argues with progress.''

Jillian tapped her fork against her empty plate. ''What a fascinating statement,'' she said sweetly. ''Do you have any other suggestions on how I might improve the running of Utopia?''

"As a matter of fact"—Aaron drained his coffee—"I could come up with several."

"Really." She set down the fork before she stabbed him with it. "Would you like me to tell you what you can do with each and every one of them?"

"Maybe later." He rose. "Let's get going. The day's half gone already."

Grinding her teeth, Jillian followed him out the back door. She thought it was a pity she'd wasted even a moment on gratitude.

The small two-seater plane gave her a bad moment. She eyed the propellers while Aaron checked the gauges before takeoff. She trusted things with four legs or four wheels. There, she felt, you had some control—a control she'd be relinquishing the moment Aaron took the plane off the ground. With a show of indifference, she hooked her seat belt while he started the engine.

"Ever been up in one of these?" he asked idly. He slipped on sunglasses before he started down the narrow paved runway.

"Of course I went up in the one I bought." She didn't mention the jitters that one ride had given her. As much as she hated to agree with him, a plane was a necessary part of ranch life in the late twentieth century.

The engine roared and the ground tilted away. She'd just have to get used to it, she reminded herself, since she was going to learn to fly herself. She let her hands lie loosely on her knees and ignored the rolling pitch of her stomach.

"Are you the only one who flies this?" This tuna can with propellers, she thought dismally.

"No, two of our men are licensed pilots. It isn't smart to have only one person who can handle a specific job."

She nodded. "Yes. I've had a man on the payroll for over a month who can fly, but I'm going to have to get a license myself."

He glanced over. "I could teach you." Aaron noticed that her fingers were moving back and forth rhythmically over her knees. Nerves, he realized with some surprise. She hid them very well. "These little jobs're small," he said idly. "But the beauty is maneuverability. You can set them down in a pasture if you have to and hardly disturb the cattle."

"They're very small," Jillian muttered.

"Look down," he suggested. "It's very big."

She did so because she wouldn't, for a moment, have let him know how badly she wanted to be safe on the ground. Oddly her stomach stopped jumping when she did. Her fingers relaxed.

The landscape rolled under them, green and fresh, with strips of brown and amber so neat and tidy they seemed laid out with a ruler. She saw the stream that ran through her property and his, winding blue. Cattle were clumps of black and brown and red. Two young foals frolicked in a pasture while adult horses sunned themselves and grazed. She saw men riding below. Now and again one would take off his hat and wave it in a salute. Aaron dipped his wings in answer. Laughing, Jillian looked farther, to the plains and isolated mountains.

"It's fabulous. God, sometimes I look at it and I can't believe it belongs to me."

"I know." He skimmed the border line and banked

the plane over her land. "You can't get tired of looking at it, smelling it."

She rested her head against the window. He loves it as much as I do, she thought. Those five years in Billings must have eaten at him. Every time she thought of it, of the five years he'd given up, her admiration for him grew.

"Don't laugh," she told him and watched him glance over curiously. No, he wouldn't laugh, she realized. "When I was little—the first time I came out—I got a box and dug up a couple handfuls of pasture to take home with me. It didn't stay sweet for long, but it didn't matter."

Good God, sometimes she was so totally disarming it took his breath away. "How long did you keep it?"

"Until my mother found it and threw it away."

He had to bite back an angry remark on insensitivity and ignorance. "She didn't understand you," Aaron said instead.

"No, of course not." She gave a quick laugh at the idea. Who could've expected her to? "Look, that's Gil's truck." The idea of waving down to him distracted her so that she missed Aaron's smoldering look. He'd had some rocky times with his own father, some painful times, but he'd always been understood.

"Tell me about your family."

Jillian turned her head to look at him, not quite trusting the fact that she couldn't see his eyes through his tinted sunglasses. "No, not now." She looked back out the window. "I wish I knew what I was looking for," she murmured.

So do I, he thought grimly and banked down his frustration. It wasn't going to work, he decided. He

wasn't going to be able to talk himself out of needing her, all of her, any time soon. "Maybe you'll know when you see it. Could you figure if they took more cattle from any specific section?"

"It seems the north section was the hardest hit. I can't figure out how it got by me. Five hundred head, right under my nose."

"You wouldn't be the first," he reminded her. "Or the last. If you were going to drive cattle out of your north section, where would you go with them?"

"If they weren't mine," she said dryly, "I suppose I'd load them up and get them over the border."

"Maybe." He wondered if his own idea would be any harder for her to take. "Packaged beef's a lot easier to transport than it is on the hoof."

Slowly she turned back to him. She'd thought of it herself—more than once. But every time she'd pushed it aside. The last fragile hope of recovering what was hers would be lost. "I know that." Her voice was calm, her eyes steady. "If that's what was done, there's still the matter of catching who did it. They're not going to get away with it."

Aaron grinned in pure admiration. "Okay. Then let's think about it from this angle a minute. You've got the cattle—the cows are worth a lot more than the calves at this point, so maybe you're going to ship them off to greener pastures for a while. Unless we're dealing with a bunch of idiots, they're not going to slaughter a registered cow for the few hundred the calf would bring."

"A bunch of idiots couldn't have rustled my cattle," she said precisely.

"No." He nodded in simple agreement. "The

steers, now…it might be a smart choice to pick out a quiet spot and butcher them. The meat would bring in some quick cash while you worked out the deal for the rest." He made a slight adjustment in course and headed north.

"If you were smarter still, you'd have already set up a deal for the cows and the yearlings," Jillian pointed out. "That accounts for nearly half of what I lost. If I were using a trailer, and slipping them out a few head at a time, I'd make use of one of the canyons in the mountains."

"Yeah. Thought we'd take a look."

Her euphoria was gone, though the landscape below was a rambling map of color and texture. The ground grew more uneven, with the asphalt two-lane road cutting through the twists and angles. The barren clump of mountain wasn't majestic like its brothers farther west, but sat alone, inhabited by coyotes and wildcats who preferred to keep man at a distance.

Aaron took the plane higher and circled. Jillian looked down at jagged peaks and flat-bottomed canyons. Yes, if she had butchering in mind, no place made better sense. Then she saw the vultures, and her heart sank down to her stomach.

"I'm going to set her down," Aaron said simply.

Jillian said nothing but began to check off her options if they found what she thought they would. There were a few economies she could and would have to make before winter, even after the livestock auction at the end of the summer. The old Jeep would simply have to be repaired again instead of being replaced. There were two foals she could sell and keep her books

in the black. Checks and balances, she thought as the plane bumped on the ground. Nothing personal.

Aaron shut off the engine. "Why don't you wait here while I take a look?"

"My cattle," she said simply and climbed out of the plane.

The ground was hard and dusty from the lack of rain. She could smell its faintly metallic odor, so unlike the scent of grass and animals that permeated her own land. With no trees for shade, the sun beat down hard and bright. She heard the flap of a vulture's wings as one circled in and settled on a ridge.

It wasn't difficult going over the low rocky ground through the break in the mountain. No problem at all for a four-wheel drive, she thought and angled the brim of her hat to compensate for the glare of sunlight.

The canyon wasn't large and was cupped between three walls of rock, worn gray with some stubborn sage clinging here and there. Their boots made echoing hollow sounds. From somewhere, surprisingly, she heard a faint tinkling of water. The spring must be small, she mused, or she'd smell it. All she smelled here was...

She stopped and let out a long breath. "Oh, God."

Aaron recognized the odor, sickeningly hot and sweet, even as she did. "Jillian—"

She shook her head. There was no longer room for comfort or hope. "Damn. I wonder how many."

They walked on and saw, behind a rock, the bones a coyote had dug up and picked clean.

Aaron swore in a low soft stream that was all the more pungent in its control. "There's a shovel in the

plane," he began. "We can see what's here, or go back for the sheriff."

"It's my business." Jillian wiped her damp hands on her jeans. "I'd rather know now."

He knew better than to suggest she wait at the plane again. In her place, he'd have done precisely what she was ready to do. Without another word, he left her alone.

When she heard his footsteps die away, she squeezed her eyes tight, doubled her hands into fists. She wanted to scream out the useless, impotent rage. What was hers had been stolen, slaughtered, and sold. There could be no restitution now, no bringing back this part of what she'd worked for. Slowly, painfully, she brought herself under tight control. No restitution, but she'd have justice. Sometimes it was just a cleaner word for revenge.

When Aaron returned with the shovel, he saw the anger glittering in her eyes. He preferred it to that brief glimpse of despair he'd seen. "Let's just make sure. After we know, we go into town for the sheriff."

She agreed with a nod. If they found one hide, it would be one too many. The shovel bit into the ground with a thud.

Aaron didn't have to dig long. He glanced up at Jillian to see her face perfectly composed, then uncovered the first stack of hides. Though the stench was vile, she crouched down and made out the *U* of her brand.

"Well, this should be proof enough," she murmured and stayed where she was because she wanted to drop her head to her knees and weep. "How many—"

"Let the sheriff deal with it," Aaron bit off, as infuriated by their find as he would have been if the hide had borne his own brand. With an oath, he scraped the shovel across the loosened dirt and dislodged something.

Jillian reached down and picked it up. The glove was filthy, but the leather was quality—the kind any cowhand would need for working with the wire. A bubble of excitement rose in her. "One of them must've lost it when they were burying these." She sprang to her feet, holding the glove in both hands. "Oh, they're going to pay for it," she said savagely. "This is one mistake they're going to pay for. Most of my hands score their initials on the inside." Ignoring the grime, she turned the bottom of the glove over and found them.

Aaron watched her color drain as she stared at the inside flap of the glove. Her fingers whitened against the leather before she lifted her eyes to his. Without a word, she handed it to him. Watching her, he took the soiled leather in his hand, then glanced down. There were initials inside. His own.

His face was expressionless when he looked back at her. "Well," he said coolly, "it looks like we're back to square one, doesn't it?" He passed the glove back to her. "You'll need this for the sheriff."

She sent him a look of smoldering anger that cut straight through him. "Do you think I'm stupid enough to believe you had anything to do with this?" Spinning around, she stalked away before he had a chance to understand, much less react. Then he stood where he was for another instant as it struck him, forcibly.

He caught her before she had clambered over the last rocks leading out of the canyon. His hands weren't gentle as he whirled her around, his breath wasn't steady.

"Maybe I do." She jerked away only to have him grab her again. "Maybe I want you to tell me why you don't."

"I might believe a lot of things of you, I might not like everything I believe. But not this." Her voice broke and she fought to even it. "Integrity—integrity isn't something that has to be polite. You wouldn't cut my lines and you wouldn't butcher my cattle."

Her words alone would've shaken him, but he saw her eyes were swimming with tears. What he knew about comforting a woman could be said in one sentence: get out of the way. Aaron held on to her and lifted a hand to her cheek. "Jillian..."

"No! For God's sake don't be kind now." She tried to turn away, only to find herself held close, her face buried against his shoulder. His body was like a solid wall of support and understanding. If she leaned against it now, what would she do when he removed it? "Aaron, don't do this." But her hands clutched at him as he held on.

"I've got to do something," he murmured, stroking her hair. "Lean on me for a minute. It won't hurt you."

But it did. She'd always found tears a painful experience. There was no stopping them, so she wept with the passion they both understood while he held her near the barren mountain under the strong light of the sun.

Chapter 9

Jillian didn't have time to grieve over her losses. Over two hundred hides had been unearthed from the canyon floor, all bearing the Utopia brand. She'd had interviews with the sheriff, talked to the Cattlemen's Association, and dealt with the visits and calls from neighboring ranchers. After her single bout of weeping, her despair had iced over to a frigid rage she found much more useful. It carried her through each day, pushing her to work just that much harder, helping her not to break down when she was faced with sympathetic words.

For two weeks she knew there was little talk of anything else, on her ranch or for miles around. There hadn't been a rustling of this size in thirty years. It became easier for her when the talk began to die down, though it became equally more difficult to go on believing that the investigation would yield fruit. She had

accepted the loss of her cattle because she had no choice, but she couldn't accept the total victory of the thieves.

They were clever—she had to admit it. They'd pulled off a rustling as smooth as anything the old-timers in the area claimed to remember. The cut wire, Aaron's glove; deliberate and subtle "mistakes" that were designed to turn her attention toward Murdock land. Perhaps the first of them had worked well enough to give the rustlers just enough extra time to cover their tracks. Jillian's only comfort was that she hadn't fallen for the second.

Aaron had given her no choice but to accept his support. She'd balked, particularly after recovering from her lapse in the canyon, but he'd proven to be every bit as obstinate as she. He'd taken her to the sheriff himself, stood by her with the Cattlemen's Association, and one evening had come by to drag her forty miles to a movie. Through it all he wasn't gentle with her, didn't pamper. For that more than anything else, Jillian felt she owed him. Kindness left her no defense and edged her back toward despair.

As the days passed, Jillian forced herself to take each one of them separately. She could fill the hours with dozens of tasks and worries and responsibilities. Then there wouldn't be time to mourn. For now, her first concern was the breeding of her mare with Aaron's stallion.

He'd brought two of his own men with him. With Gil and another of Jillian's hands, they would hold the restraining ropes on the stallion. Once he caught the scent of Jillian's mare in heat, he'd be as wild as his father had been, and as dangerous.

When Jillian brought Delilah into the paddock, she cast a look at the stallion surrounded by men. A gorgeous creature, she thought, wholly male—not quite tamed. Her gaze flicked over to Aaron, who stood at the horse's head.

His dark hair sprang from under his hat to curl carelessly over his neck and ears. His body was erect and lean. One might look at him and think he was perfectly relaxed. But Jillian saw more—the coiled tension beneath, the power that was always there and came out unexpectedly. Eyes nearly as dark as his hair were half hidden by the brim of his hat as he both soothed and controlled his stallion.

No mount could've suited him more. Her lover, she realized with the peculiar little jolt that always accompanied the thought. Would her nerves ever stop skidding along whenever she remembered what it was like to be with him—or imagined what it would be like to be with him again? He'd opened up so many places inside of her. When she was alone, it came close to frightening her; when she saw him, her feelings had nothing to do with fear.

Maybe it was the thick, heavy air that threatened rain or the half-nervous, half-impatient quiverings of her mare, but Jillian's heart was already pounding. The horses caught each other's scent.

Samson plunged and began to fight against the ropes. With his head thrown back, his mane flowing, he called the mare. One of the men cursed in reflex. Jillian tightened her grip on Delilah's bridle as the mare began to struggle—against the restraint or against the inevitable, Jillian would never be sure. She soothed her with words that weren't even heard. Samson gave

a long, passionate whinny that was answered. Delilah reared, nearly ripping the bridle from Jillian's hand. Watching the struggle and flying hooves, Aaron felt his heart leap into his throat.

"Help her hold the mare," he ordered.

"No." Jillian fought for new purchase and got it. "She doesn't trust anyone but me. Let's get it done." A long line of sweat held her shirt to her back.

The stallion was wild, plunging and straining, his coat glossy with sweat, his eyes fierce. With five men surrounding him, he reared back, hanging poised and magnificent for a heartbeat before he mounted the mare.

The horses were beyond any thought, any fear, any respect for the humans now. Instinct drove them, primitive and consuming. Jillian forgot her aching arms and the rivulets of sweat that poured down her sides. Her feet were planted, her leg muscles taut as she pitted all her strength toward keeping the mare from bolting or rearing and injuring herself.

She was caught up in the fire and desperation of the horses, and the elemental beauty. The air was ripe with the scent of sweat and animal passion. She couldn't breathe but that she drew it in. Since she'd been a child she'd seen animals breed, helped with the matings whenever necessary, but now, for the first time, she understood the consuming force that drove them. The need of a woman for a man could be equally unrestrained, equally primitive.

Then it began to rain, slowly, heavily, coolly over her skin. With her face lifted to the mare's, Jillian let it flow over her cheeks. Another of the men swore as the ropes grew wet and slippery.

When her eyes met Aaron's, she found her heart was still in her throat, the beat as lurching and uneven as the mare's would be. She felt the flash of need that was both shocking and basic. He saw and recognized. As the rain poured over him, he smiled. Her thigh muscles went lax so quickly she had to fight to strengthen them again and maintain her control of the mare. But she didn't look away. Excitement was nearly painful, knowledge enervating. As if his hands were on her, she felt the need pulse from him.

Gradually a softer feeling drifted in. There was a strange sensation of being safe even though the safety was circled with dangers. This time she didn't question it or fight against it. They were helping to create new life. Now there was a bond between them.

The horses' sides were heaving when they drew them apart. The rain continued to sluice down. She heard Gil give a cackle of laughter over something one of the men said under his breath. Jillian forgot them, giving her full attention to the mare. Soothing and murmuring, she walked her back into the stables.

The light was dim, the air heavy with the scent of dry hay and oiled leather. After removing the bridle, Jillian began to groom the mare with long slow strokes until the quivering stopped.

"There now, love." Jillian nuzzled her face into Delilah's neck. "There's not much any of us can do about their bodies."

"Is that how you look at it?"

Jillian turned her head to see Aaron standing at the entrance to the stall. He was drenched and apparently unconcerned about it. She saw his eyes make a short but very thorough scan of her face—a habit he'd de-

veloped since their discovery in the canyon. She knew he looked for signs of strain and somewhere along the line had stopped resenting it.

"I'm not a horse," she returned easily and patted Delilah's neck.

Aaron came into the stall and ran his hands over the mare himself. She was dry and still. "She all right?"

"Mmmm. We were right not to field breed them," she added. "Both of them are spirited enough to have done damage." Laughing, she turned to him. "The foal's going to be a champion. I can feel it. There was something special out there just now, something important." On impulse, she threw her arms around Aaron's neck and kissed him ardently.

Surprise held him very still. His hands came to her waist more in instinct than response. It was the first time she'd given him any spontaneous show of affection or offered him any part of herself without reluctance. The ache of need wove through him, throbbing with what he now understood was connected to passion but not exclusive of it.

She was still smiling when she drew away, but he wasn't. Before the puzzlement over what was in his eyes had fully registered with her, Aaron drew her back against him and just held on. Jillian found the unexpected sweetness disconcerting and wonderful.

"Hadn't you better see to Samson?" she murmured.

"My men have already taken him back."

She rubbed her cheek against his wet shirt. They'd steal some time, she thought. An hour, a moment— just some time. "I'll fix you some coffee."

"Yeah." He slipped an arm around her shoulders

as they went back into the rain. "Heard anything from the sheriff?"

"Nothing new."

They crossed the ranch yard together, both too accustomed to the elements to heed the rain as anything but necessary.

"It's got the whole county in an uproar."

"I know." They paused at the kitchen door to rid themselves of muddy boots. Jillian ran a careless hand through her hair and scattered rain. "It might do more good than anything else. Every rancher I know or've heard of in this part of Montana's got his eyes open. And any number over the border, from what I'm told. I'm toying with offering a reward."

"Not a bad idea." Aaron sat down at the table and stretched out long legs as Jillian brewed coffee. The rain was a constant soothing sound against the roof and windows. He found an odd comfort there in the gloomy light, in the warm kitchen. It might be like this if it were their ranch they were in rather than hers, or his. It might be like this if he could ever make her a permanent part of his life.

It took only a second for the thoughts to go through his head, and another for him to be jolted by them. Marriage. He was thinking marriage. He sat for a moment while the idea settled over him, not uncomfortably but inevitably. I'll be damned, he thought and nearly laughed before he brought himself back to what she'd been saying.

"Let me do it," he said briskly. She turned, words of refusal on the tip of her tongue. "Wait," Aaron ordered. "Hear me out. My father got wind of the cut wire." He watched her subside before she turned away

for mugs. "Obviously it didn't set well with him. These old stories between the Murdocks and Barons don't need much fanning to come to life again. Some people are going to think, even if they don't say, that he's eating your beef."

Jillian poured the coffee, then turned with a mug in each hand. "I don't think it."

"I know." He gave her an odd look, holding out a hand. She placed a mug in it, but Aaron set it down on the table and lightly took her fingers. "That means a great deal to me." Because she didn't know how to respond to that tone, she didn't respond at all but only continued to look down at him. "Jillian, this has set him back some. A few years ago the idea of people thinking he'd done something unethical or illegal would probably have pleased him. He's not as strong as he was. Your grandfather was a rival, but he was also a contemporary, someone he understood, even respected. It would help if he could do something. I don't like to ask for favors any more than you like to accept them."

She looked down at their joined hands, both tanned, both lean and strong, yet hers was so easily swallowed up by his. "You love him very much."

"Yes." It was said very simply, in the same emotionless tone he'd used to tell her his father was dying. This time Jillian understood him better.

"I'd appreciate it if you'd stake the reward."

He laced his fingers with hers. "Good."

"Want some more coffee?"

"No." That wicked light of humor shot into his eyes. "But I was thinking I should help you out of those wet clothes."

With a laugh, Jillian sat down. "You know I'm still planning on beating out the Double M on July Fourth."

"I was hoping you were planning on it," Aaron returned easily. "But about doing it…"

"You a gambling man, Murdock?"

He lifted his brow. "It's been said."

"I've got fifty that says my Hereford bull will take the blue ribbon over anything you have to put against him."

Aaron contemplated the dregs of his coffee as if considering. If everything he'd heard about Jillian's bull was true, he was tolerably sure he was throwing money away. "Fifty," he agreed and smiled. "And another fifty that says I beat your time in the calf roping."

"My pleasure." Jillian held out a hand to seal it.

"Are you competing in anything else?"

"I don't think so." She stretched her back, thinking what a luxury it was to sit stone still in the middle of the afternoon. "The barrel racing doesn't much interest me and I know better than to try bronc riding."

"Know better?"

"Two reasons. First the men would do a lot of muttering and complaining if I did. And second"—she grinned and shrugged—"I'd probably break my neck."

It occurred to him that she wouldn't have admitted the second to him even a week before. Laughing, he leaned over and kissed her. But the friendly kiss stirred something, and cupping the back of her neck, he kissed her again, lingeringly. "It's your mouth," he mur-

mured while his fingertips toyed with her skin. "Once I get started on it, I can't find a single reason to stop."

Her breath fluttered unevenly through her lips, through his. "It's the middle of the day."

He smiled, then teased her tongue with the tip of his. "Yeah. Are you going to take me to bed?"

The eyes that were nearly closed opened again. In them he saw desire and confusion, a combination he found very much to his liking. "I have to check the—" His teeth nipped persuasively into her bottom lip.

"The what?" he whispered as her words ended on a little shiver.

"The, uh…" His lips were skimming over hers in something much more provocative than a kiss. The lazy caress of his tongue kept them moist. His fingers were very light on the back of her neck. Their knees were brushing. Somehow she could already feel the press of his body against hers and the issuing warmth the pressure always brought. "I can't think," she murmured.

It was what he wanted. Or he wanted her to think of him and only him. For himself, he needed to know that she put him first this time, or at least her need for him. Over her ranch, her men, her cattle, her ambitions. If he could draw her feelings out to match his once, he might be able to do so again and again until she was as rashly in love with him as he was with her. "Why do you have to?" he asked and, rising, drew her to her feet. "You can feel."

Yes, with her arms around him and her head cradled against his chest, she could feel. Emotions nudging at her, urging her to acknowledge them—needs, pressing

and searingly urgent, demanding that she fulfill them. They were all connected to him, the hungers, the tiny fears, the wishes. She couldn't deny them all. Perhaps, just this once, she didn't need to.

"I want to make love with you." She sighed with the words and nuzzled closer. "I can't seem to stop wanting to."

He tilted her head back so that he could see her face, then, half smiling, skimmed his thumb over her jaw. "In the middle of the day?"

She tossed the hair out of her eyes and settled her linked hands comfortably behind his neck. "I'm going to have you now, Murdock. Right now."

He glanced at the tidy kitchen table and his grin was wicked. "Right now?"

"Your mind takes some unusual turns," she commented. "I think I can give you time enough to get upstairs." Releasing him, she walked over and flicked off the coffeepot. "If you hurry." Even as he grinned, she crossed back to him. Putting her hands on his shoulders, she leaped up, locking her legs around his waist, her arms around his neck. "You know where the stairs are?"

"I can find them."

She pressed her lips to his throat. "Top of the stairs, second door on the right," she told him as she began to please herself with his taste.

As Aaron wound through the house Jillian wondered what he would think or say if he knew she'd never done anything quite like this before. She'd come to realize that the man from her youth hadn't been a lover, but an incident. It took more than one night to make a lover. She'd feel much too foolish telling

Aaron he was the first—much too inadequate. How could she tell him that the first rush of passion had loosened the locks she'd put on parts of herself? How could she trust her own feelings when they were so muddled and new?

She rested her head on his shoulder a moment and closed her eyes. For once in her life she was going to enjoy without worrying about the consequences. Shifting, she leaned back so that she could smile at him. "You're out of shape, Murdock. One flight of stairs and your heart's pounding."

"So's yours," he pointed out. "And you had a ride up."

"Must be the rain," she said loftily.

"Your clothes're still damp." He moved into the room she'd directed him to and glanced around briefly.

It was consistent with her style—understated femininity, practicality. It was a room without frills or pastels, but he'd have known it for a woman's. It had none of the feminine disorder of his sister's old room at the ranch, nor the subtle elegance of his mother's. Like the woman he still held, Aaron found the room unique.

Plain walls, plain floors, easy colors, no clutter. No, Jillian wasn't a woman to clutter her life. She wouldn't give herself the time. Perhaps it was the few indulgences she'd allowed herself that gave him the most insight.

A stoneware vase with fluted edges held pussy willow—soft brown nubs that wouldn't quite be considered a flower. There was a small carved box on her dresser he was certain would play some soft tune when the top was lifted. She might lift it sometimes when she was alone, or lonely. On the wall was a watercolor

with all the bleeding passion of sunset. How carefully, how painstakingly, he thought, she'd controlled whatever romanticism she was prone to. How surprised she'd be to know that because she did, it only shouted out louder.

Recognizing his survey, Jillian cocked her head. "There's not a lot to see in here."

"You'd be surprised," he murmured.

The enigmatic answer made her glance around herself. "I don't spend a lot of time in here," she began, realizing it was rather sparse even compared to his room in the white frame house.

"You misunderstood me." Aaron let his hands run up her sides as she slid down. "I'd've known this was your room. It even smells like you."

She laughed, pleased without knowing why. "Are you being poetic?"

"Maybe."

Lifting a hand, she toyed with the top button of his shirt. "Want me to help you out of those wet clothes?"

"Absolutely."

She began to oblige him, then shot him an amused look as she slid the shirt over his shoulders. "If you expect me to seduce you, you're going to be disappointed."

His stomach muscles were already knotted with need. "I am?"

"I don't know any tricks." Before he could comment, she launched herself at him, overbalancing him so that they tumbled back onto the bed. "No wiles," she continued. "No subtlety."

"You're a pushy lady, all right." He could feel the heat of her body through her damp shirt.

"I like the way you look, Murdock." She trailed her fingers through his thick dark hair as she studied his face. "It used to annoy the hell out of me, but now it's kind of nice."

"The way I look?"

"That I like the way you look. It's ruthless," she decided, skimming a finger down his jawline. "And when you smile it can be very charming—the kind of charm a smart woman recognizes as highly dangerous."

He grinned, cupping her hips in his hands. "Did you?"

"I'm a smart woman." With a little laugh, she rubbed her nose against his. "I know a rattlesnake when I see one."

"But not enough to keep your distance."

"Apparently not—then I don't always look for a long, safe ride."

But a short, rocky one, he thought as her lips came down to his. He'd be happy to give her the wisps of danger and trouble, he decided, drawing her closer. But she was going to find out he intended it to last.

He started to shift her, but then her lips were racing over his face. Soft, light, but with a heat that seeped right into him. Her long, limber body seemed almost weightless over his, yet he could feel every line and curve. Moisture still clung to her hair and reminded him of the first time, when he'd dragged her to the ground, consumed with need and fury. Now he was helpless against her rapid assault on his senses. No, she had no wiles, nor he the patience for them.

He could hear the rain patter rhythmically against the window. He could smell it on her. When his lips

brushed through her hair, he could taste it. It was almost as though they were alone in a quiet field, with the scent of wet grass and the rain slipping over their skin. The light was gray and indistinct; her mouth was vivid wherever it touched him.

She hadn't known it could be so exciting to weaken a man with herself. Feeling the strength drain from him made her almost light-headed with power. She'd met him on equal terms, and from time to time to her disadvantage, but never when she'd been so certain she could dominate. Her laugh was low and confident as it whispered along his skin, warm and sultry as it brushed over his lips.

He seemed content to lie still while she learned of him. She thought the air grew thicker. Perhaps that alone weighed him down and kept him from challenging her control. Her hands were eager, rushing here then there to linger over some small fascination: tight cords of muscle that ran down his upper arms to bunch and gather at her touch; smooth, taut skin that was surprisingly soft over his rib cage; the narrow, raised scar along his hipbone.

"Where'd you get this?" she murmured, outlining it with a fingertip.

"Brahma," he managed as she tugged his jeans down infinitesimally lower. "Jillian—" But her lips drifted over his again and silenced him.

"A bull?"

"Rodeo, when I had more guts than brains."

She heard the sound of pleasure in his throat as her mouth journeyed down. His body was a treasure of delight to her. In the soft rainy light she could see it, brown and hard against the plain, serviceable bed-

spread. Rangy and loose limbed, it was made for riding well and long, toughened by physical work, burnished by the elements. Tiny jumping thrills coursed through her as she thought that it was hers to touch and taste, to look at as long as she liked.

She took a wandering route down him, feeling his skin heat and pulse as she stripped him. The room was filled with the sound of rain and quickening breathing. It was all she heard. The sweet scent of passion enveloped her—a fragrance mixed of the essence of both of them. Intimate. She could taste desire on his skin, a heady flavor that made her greedy when she felt the thud of his heart under her tongue. Even when her excitement grew until her blood was racing, she could have luxuriated in him for hours. The sharp urgency she'd once felt had mellowed into a glowing contentment. She pleasured him. It was more than she'd believed she could do for anyone.

There were flames in his stomach, spreading. God, she was like a drug and he was lost, half dreaming while his flesh was burning up. Her fingers were so cool as they tortured him, her mouth so hot. He'd never explored his own vulnerabilities; it had always been more important to work around them or ignore them altogether. Now he had no choice and he found the sensation incredible.

She aroused, teased, and withdrew only to arouse again. Her enervating, openmouthed kisses ranged over him while her hands stroked and explored lazily, finding point after sensitive point until he trembled. No woman had ever made him tremble. Even as this thought ran through his ravaged mind, she caused him

to do so again. Then he knew she was driving him mad.

The wind kicked up, hurling rain against the window, then retreating with a distant howl. Something crazed sprang into him. Roughly he grabbed her, rolling over and pinning her, her arms above her head. His breathing was labored as he looked down.

Her chin was up, her hair spread out, her eyes glowing. There was no fear on her face, and nothing of submission. Though her own breathing came quickly, there was challenge in the look she gave him. A dare. He could take her, take her anyway he chose. And when he did so, he'd be taken as well.

So be it, he thought with a muffled oath. His mouth devoured hers.

She matched his urgency, aroused simply by knowing she had taken him to the edge. He wanted her. Her. In some ways he knew her better than anyone ever had, and still he wanted her. She'd waited so long for that, not even knowing that she'd waited at all. She couldn't think of this, or what the effects might be when his long desperate kisses were rousing her, when she could see small, silvery explosions going on behind her closed lids.

She felt him tug at the buttons of her shirt, heard him swear. When she felt the material rip away she knew only that at last she could feel his flesh against hers. As it was meant to be. His hands wouldn't be still and drove her as she had driven him. He pulled clothes from her in a frenzy as his mouth greedily searched. Somewhere in her hazy brain she felt wonder that she could bring him to this just by being.

Their bodies pressed, their limbs entwined. Their

mouths joined. He thought the mixing of their tastes the most intimate thing he'd even known. Under him she arched, more a demand than an offer. He raised himself over her, wanting to see her, wanting her to see him when he made her his.

Her eyes were dark, misted with need. Need for him. He knew he had what he'd wanted: she thought of nothing and no one else. ''I wanted you from the first minute,'' he murmured as he slipped inside her.

He saw the change in her face as he moved slowly, the flicker of pleasure, the softening that came just before delirium. Pushing back the rushing need in his blood, he drew out the sensations with a control so exquisite it burned in his muscles. Lowering his head, he nibbled at her lips.

She couldn't bear it. She couldn't stop it. When she thought she finally understood what passion was, he showed her there was more. Sensation after sensation slammed into her, leaving her weak and gasping. Even as the pressure built inside her, drumming under her skin and threatening to implode, she wanted it to go on. She could have wept from the joy of it, moaned from the ache. Unwittingly it was she who changed things simply by breathing his name as if she knew no other.

The instant his control snapped, she felt it. There was time only for a tingle of nervous excitement before he was catapulting her with him into a dark, frantic sky where it was all thunder and no air.

Chapter 10

The lengthy, dusty drive into town and the soaring temperatures couldn't dull the spirit. It was the Fourth of July, and the long, raucous holiday had barely begun.

By early morning the fairgrounds were crowded—ranchers, punchers, wives and sweethearts, and those looking for a sweetheart to share the celebration with. Prized animals were on display to be discussed, bragged about, and studied. Quilts and pies and preserves waited to be judged. As always, there was a pervasive air of expectancy.

Cowboys wore their best uniform—crisp shirts and pressed jeans, with the boots and hats that were saved and cherished for special occasions. Belt buckles gleamed. Children sported their finest, which promised to be dirt streaked and grass stained by the end of the long day.

For Jillian, it was the first carefree day in the season, and one she was all the more determined to enjoy because of her recent problems. For twenty-four hours she was going to forget her worries, the numbers in her account books, and the title of boss she worked day after day to earn. On this one sun-filled, heat-soaked day, she was going to simply enjoy the fact that she was part of a unique group of men and women who both lived and played off the land.

There was an excited babble of voices near the paddock and stable areas. The pungent aroma of animals permeated the air. From somewhere in the distance she could already hear fiddle music. There'd be more music after sundown, and dancing. Before then, there'd be games for young and old, the judgings, and enough food to feed the entire county twice over. She could smell the spicy aroma of an apple pie, still warm, as someone passed her with a laden basket. Her mouth watered.

First things first, she reminded herself as she wandered over to check out her bull's competition.

There were six entries altogether, all well muscled and fierce to look at. Horns gleamed, sharp and dangerous. Hides were sleek and well tended. Objectively Jillian studied each one, noting their high points and their weaknesses. There wasn't any doubt that her stiffest competitor would be the Double M's entry. He'd taken the blue ribbon three years running.

Not this year, she told him silently as her gaze skimmed over him. Pound for pound, he probably had her bull beat, but she thought hers had a bit more breadth in the shoulders. And there was no mistaking

that her Hereford's coloring and markings were perfect, the shape of his head superior.

Time for you to move over and make room for new blood, she told the reigning champion. Rather pleased with herself, she hooked her thumbs in her back pockets. First place and that little swatch of blue ribbon would go a long way to making up for everything that'd gone wrong in the past few weeks.

"Know a winner when you see one?"

Jillian turned at the thready voice that still held a hint of steel. Paul Murdock was dressed to perfection, but his hawklike face had little color under his Stetson. His cane was elegant and tipped with gold, but he leaned on it heavily. As they met hers, however, his eyes were very much alive and challenging.

"I know a winner when I see one," she agreed, then let her gaze skim over to her own bull.

He gave a snort of laughter and shifted his weight. "Been hearing a lot about your new boy." He studied the bull with a faint frown and couldn't prevent a twinge of envy. He, too, knew a winner when he saw one.

He felt the sun warm on his back and for a moment, for just a moment, wished desperately for his youth again. Years ate at strength. If he were fifty again and owned that bull... But he wasn't a man to sigh. "Got possibilities," he said shortly.

She recognized something of the envy and smiled. Nothing could've pleased her more. "Nothing wrong with second place," she said lightly.

Murdock glanced over sharply, pinned her eyes with his, then laughed when she didn't falter. "Damn,

you're quite a woman, aren't you, Jillian Baron? The old man taught you well enough.''

Her smile held more challenge than humor. ''Well enough to run Utopia.''

''Could be,'' he acknowledged. ''Times change.'' There wasn't any mistaking the resentment in the statement, but she understood it. Sympathized with it. ''This rustling...'' He glanced over to see her face, impassive and still. Murdock had a quick desire to sit across a poker table from her with a large, juicy pot in between. ''It's a damn abomination,'' he said with a savagery that made him momentarily breathless. ''There was a time a man'd have his neck stretched for stealing another man's beef.''

''Hanging them won't get my cattle back,'' Jillian said calmly.

''Aaron told me about what you found in the canyon.'' Murdock stared at the well-muscled bulls. These were the life's blood of their ranches—the profit and the status. ''A hard thing for you—for all of us,'' he added, shifting his eyes to hers again. ''I want you to understand that your grandfather and I had our problems. He was a stubborn, stiff-necked bastard.''

''Yes,'' Jillian agreed easily, so easily Murdock laughed. ''You'd understand a man like that,'' she added.

Murdock stopped laughing to fix her with a glittering look. She returned it. ''I understand a man like that,'' he acknowledged. ''And I want you to know that if this had happened to him, I'd've been behind him, just as I'd've expected him to be behind me. Personal feelings don't come into it. We're ranchers.''

It was said with a sting of pride that made her own chin lift. "I do know it."

"It'd be easy to say the cattle could've been driven over to my land."

"Easy to say," Jillian said with a nod. "If you knew me better, Mr. Murdock, you'd know I'm not a fool. If I believed you'd had my beef on your table, you'd already be paying for it."

His lips curved in a rock-hard, admiring smile. "Baron did well by you," he said after a moment. "Though I still think a woman needs a man beside her if she's going to run a ranch."

"Be careful, Mr. Murdock, I was just beginning to think I could tolerate you."

He laughed again, so obviously pleased that Jillian grinned. "Can't change an old dog, girl." His eyes narrowed fractionally as she'd seen his son's do. It occurred to her that in forty years Aaron would look like this—that honed-down strength that was just a little bit mean. It was the kind of strength you'd want behind you when there was trouble. "I've heard my boy's had his eye on you—can't say I fault his taste."

"Have you?" she returned mildly. "Do you believe everything you hear?"

"If he hasn't had his eye on you," Murdock countered, "he's not as smart as I give him credit for. Man needs a woman to settle him down."

"Really?" Jillian said very dryly.

"Don't get fired up, girl," Murdock ordered. "There'd've been a time when I'd have had his hide for looking twice at a Baron. Times change," he repeated with obvious reluctance. "Our land has run side

by side for most of this century, whether we like it or not.''

Jillian took a moment to brush off her sleeve. ''I'm not looking to settle anyone, Mr. Murdock. And I'm not looking for a merger.''

''Sometimes we wind up getting things we're not looking for.'' He smiled as she stared at him. ''You take my Karen—never figured to hitch myself with a beauty who always made me feel like I should wipe my feet whether I'd been in the pastures or not.''

Despite herself Jillian laughed, then surprised them both by hooking her arm through his as they began to walk. ''I get the feeling you're trying to bury the hatchet.'' When he stiffened, she muffled a chuckle and continued. ''Don't *you* get fired up,'' she said easily. ''I'm willing to try a truce. Aaron and I have…we understand each other,'' she decided. ''I like your wife, and I can just about tolerate you.''

''You're your grandmother all over again,'' Murdock muttered.

''Thanks.'' As they walked Jillian noted the few speculative glances tossed their way. Baron and Murdock arm in arm; times had indeed changed. She wondered how Clay would feel and decided, in his grudging way, he would've approved. Especially if it caused talk.

When Aaron saw them walking slowly toward the arena area, he broke off the conversation he'd been having with a puncher. Jillian tossed back her hair, tilted her head slightly toward his father's, and murmured something that made the old man hoot with laughter. If he hadn't already, Aaron would've fallen in love with her at that moment.

"Hey, isn't that Jillian Baron with your paw?"

"Hmmm? Yeah." Aaron didn't waste time glancing back at the puncher when he could look at Jillian.

"She sure is easy on the eyes," the puncher concluded a bit wistfully. "Heard you and her—" He broke off, chilled by the cool, neutral look Aaron aimed at him. The cowboy coughed into his hand. "Just meant people wonder about it, seeing as the Murdocks and Barons never had much dealings with each other."

"Do they?" Aaron relieved the cowboy by grinning before he walked off. Murdocks, the puncher thought with a shake of his head. You could never be too sure of them.

"Life's full of surprises," Aaron commented as he walked toward them. "No blood spilled?"

"Your father and I've reached a limited understanding." Jillian smiled at him, and though they touched in no way, Murdock was now certain the rumors he'd heard about Jillian and his son were true. Intimacy was something people often foolishly believed they could conceal, and rarely did.

"Your mother's got me judging the mincemeat," Murdock grumbled. This time he didn't feel that twinge of regret for what he'd lost, but an odd contentment at seeing his slice of immortality in his son. "We'll be in the stands later to watch you." He gave Jillian an arch look. "Both of you."

He walked off slowly. Jillian had to stuff her hands in her pockets to keep from helping him. That, she knew, would be met with cold annoyance. "He came over to the pens," Jillian told Aaron when Murdock

was out of earshot. "I think he did it on purpose so
that he could talk to me. He was very kind."

"Not many people see him as kind."

"Not many people had a grandfather like Clay
Baron." She turned to Aaron and smiled.

"How are you?" He couldn't have resisted the urge
to touch her if he'd wanted to. His fingertips skimmed
along her jaw.

"How do I look?"

"You don't like me to tell you you're beautiful."

She laughed, and the under-the-lashes look she sent
him was the first flirtatious move he'd ever seen from
her. "It's a holiday."

"Spend it with me?" He held out a hand, knowing
if she put hers in it, in public, where there were curious
eyes and tongues that appreciated a nice bit of gossip,
it would be a commitment of sorts.

Her fingers laced with his. "I thought you'd never
ask."

They spent the morning doing what couples had
done at county fairs for decades. There was lemonade
to be drunk, contests to be watched. It was easy to
laugh when the sky was clear and the sun promised a
dry, golden day.

Children raced by with balloons held by sticky fingers. Teenagers flirted with the nonchalance peculiar
to their age. Old-timers chewed tobacco and out-lied
each other. The air was touched with the scent of food
and animals, and the starch in bandbox shirts had not
yet wilted with sweat.

With Aaron's arm around her, Jillian crowded to the
fence to watch the greased pig contest. The ground had
been flooded and churned up so that the state of the

mud was perfection. The pig was slick with lard and quick, so that he eluded the five men who lunged after him. The crowd called out suggestions and hooted with laughter. The pig squealed and shot, like a bullet, out of capturing arms. Men fell on their faces and swore good-naturedly.

Jillian shot him a look, then inclined her head toward the pen where the activity was still wild and loud. "Don't you like games, Murdock?"

"I like to make up my own." He swung her around. "Now, there's this real quiet hayloft I know of."

With a laugh, she eluded him. He'd never known her to be deliberately provocative and found himself not quite certain how to deal with it. The glitter in her eyes made him decide. In one smooth move, Aaron gathered her close and kissed her soundly. There was an approving whoop from a group of cowboys behind them. When Jillian managed to untangle herself, she glanced over to see two of her own men grinning at her.

"It's a holiday," Aaron reminded her when she let out a huff of breath.

She brought her head back slowly and took his measure. Oh, he was damn proud of herself, she decided. And two could play. Her smile had him wondering just what she had up her sleeve.

"You want fireworks?" she asked, then threw her arms around him and silenced him before he could agree or deny.

While his kiss had been firm yet still friendly, hers whispered of secrets only the two of them knew. Aaron never heard the second cheer go up, but he wouldn't have been surprised to feel the ground move.

"I missed you last night, Murdock," she whispered, then went from her toes to her flat feet so that their lips parted. She took a step back before she offered her hand, and the smile on those fascinating lips was cocky.

Carefully Aaron drew air into his lungs and released it. "You're going to finish that one later, Jillian."

She only laughed again. "I certainly hope so. Let's go see if Gil can win the pie eating contest again this year."

He went wherever she wanted and felt foolishly, and appealingly, like a kid on his first date. It was the sudden carefree aura around her. Jillian had dropped everything, all worries and responsibilities, and had given herself a day for fun. Perhaps because she felt a slight twinge of guilt, like a kid playing hooky, the day was all the sweeter.

She would have sworn the sun had never been brighter, the sky so blue. In all of her life, she couldn't remember ever laughing so easily. A slice of cherry pie was ambrosia. If she could have concentrated the day down, section by section, she would have put it into a box where she could have taken out an hour at a time when she was alone and tired. Because she was too practical to believe that possible, Jillian chose to live each moment to the fullest.

By the time the rodeo officially opened, Jillian was nearly drunk on freedom. As the Fourth of July Queen and her court rode sedately around the arena, she still clutched her bull's blue ribbon in her hand. "That's fifty you owe me," she told Aaron with a grin.

He sat on the ground exchanging dress boots for

worn, patched riding favorites. "Why don't we wait and see how the second bet comes out?"

"Okay." She perched on a barrel and listened to the crowd cheer from the stands. She was riding high and knew it. Her luck had turned—there wasn't a problem she could be hit with that she couldn't handle.

A lot of cowboys and potential competitors had already collected behind the chutes. Though it all seemed very casual—the lounging, the rigging bags set carelessly against the chain link fence—there was an air of suppressed excitement. There was the scent of tobacco from the little cans invariably carried in the right rear pocket of jeans, and mink oil on leather. Already she heard the jingle of spurs and harnesses as equipment was checked. The bareback riding was first. When she heard the announcement, Jillian rose and wandered to the fence to watch.

"I'm surprised you didn't give this one a try," Aaron commented.

She tilted her head so that it brushed his arm—one of the rare signs of affection that made him weak. "Too much energy," she said with a laugh. "I'm dedicating the day to laziness. I noticed you were signed up for the bronc riding." Jillian nudged her hat back as she looked up at him. "Still more guts than brains?"

He grinned and shrugged. "Worried about me?"

Jillian gave a snort of laughter. "I've got some good liniment—it'll take the soreness out of the bruises you're going to get."

He ran a fingertip down her spine. "The idea tempts me to make sure I get a few. You know"—he turned her into his arms in a move both smooth and posses-

sive—"it wouldn't take much for me to forget all about this little competition." Lowering his head, he nibbled at her lips, oblivious of whoever might be milling around them. "It's not such a long drive back to the ranch. Not a soul there. Pretty day like this—I start thinking about taking a swim."

"Do you?" She drew her head back so their eyes met.

"Mmmm. Water'd be cool, and quiet."

Chuckling, she pressed her lips to his. "After the calf roping," she said and drew away.

Jillian preferred the chutes to the stands. There she could listen to the men talk of other rodeos, other rides, while she checked over her own equipment. She watched a young girl in a stunning buckskin suit rev up her nerves before the barrel racing. An old hand worked rosin into the palm of a glove with tireless patience. The little breeze carried the scent of grilled meat from the concessions.

No, she thought, her family could never understand the appeal of this. The earthy smells, the earthy talk. They'd be just as much out of their element here as she'd always been at her mother's box at the opera. It was times like these, when she was accepted for simply being what she was, that she stopped remembering the little twinges of panic that had plagued her while she grew up. No, there was nothing lacking in her as she'd often thought. She was simply different.

She watched the bull riding, thrilling to the danger and daring as men pitted themselves against a ton of beef. There were spills and close calls and clowns who made the terrifying seem amusing. Half dreaming, she leaned on the fence as a riderless bull charged and

snorted around the arena, poking bad temperedly at a clown in a barrel. The crowd was loud, but she could hear Aaron in an easy conversation with Gil from somewhere behind her. She caught snatches about the little sorrel mare Aaron had drawn in the bronc riding. A fire-eater. Out of the chute, then a lunge to the right. Liked to spin. Relaxed, Jillian thought she'd enjoy watching Aaron pit himself against the little fire-eater. After she'd won another fifty from him.

She thought the day had simply been set aside for her, warm and sunny and without demands. Perhaps she'd been this relaxed before, this happy, but it was difficult to remember when she'd shared the two sensations so clearly. She savored them.

Then everything happened so quickly she didn't have time to think, only to act.

She heard the childish laughter as she stretched her back muscles. She saw the quick flash of red zip through the fence and bounce on the dirt without fully registering it. But she saw the child skim through the rungs of the fence and into the arena. He was so close his jeans brushed hers as he scrambled through after his ball. Jillian was over the fence and running before his mother screamed. Part of her registered Aaron's voice, either furious or terrified, as he called her name.

Out of the corner of her eye Jillian saw the bull turn. His eyes, already wild from the ride, met hers, though she never paused. Her blood went cold.

She didn't hear the chaos as the crowd leaped to their feet or the mass confusion from behind the chutes as she sprinted after the boy. She did feel the ground tremble as the bull began its charge. There wasn't time to waste her breath on shouting. Running on instinct,

she lunged, letting the momentum carry her forward. She went down hard, full length on the boy, and knocked the breath out of both of them. As the bull skimmed by them, she felt the hot rush of air.

Don't move, she told herself, mercilessly pinning the boy beneath her when he started to squirm. Don't even breathe. She could hear shouting, very close by now, but didn't dare move her head to look. She wasn't gored. Jillian swallowed on the thought. No, she'd know it if he'd caught her with his horns. And he hadn't trampled her. Yet.

Someone was cursing furiously. Jillian closed her eyes and wondered if she'd ever be able to stand up again. The boy was beginning to cry lustily. She tried to smother the sound with her body.

When hands came under her arms, she jolted and started to struggle. "You *idiot*!" Recognizing the voice, Jillian relaxed and allowed herself to be hauled to her feet. She might have swayed if she hadn't been held so tightly. "What kind of a stunt was that?" She stared up at Aaron's deathly white face while he shook her. "Are you hurt?" he demanded. "Are you hurt anywhere?"

"What?"

He shook her again because his hands were trembling. "Damn it, Jillian!"

Her head was spinning a bit like it had when she'd had that first plug of tobacco. It took her a moment to realize someone was gripping her hand. Bemused, she listened to the tearful gratitude of the mother while the boy wept loudly with his face buried in his father's shirt. The Simmons boy, she thought dazedly. The little Simmons boy, who played in the yard while his

mother hung out the wash and his father worked on her own land.

"He's all right, Joleen," she managed, though her mouth didn't want to follow the order of her brain. "I might've put some bruises on him, though."

Aaron cut her off, barely suppressing the urge to suggest someone introduce the boy to a razor strap before he dragged Jillian away. She had a misty impression of a sea of faces and Aaron's simmering rage.

"...get you over to first aid."

"What?" she said again as his voice drifted in and out of her mind.

"I said I'm going to get you over to first aid." He bit off the words as he came to the fence.

"No, I'm fine." The light went gray for a moment and she shook her head.

"As soon as I'm sure of that, I'm going to strangle you."

She pulled her hand from his and straightened her shoulders. "I said I'm fine," she repeated. Then the ground tilted and rushed up at her.

The first thing she felt was the tickle of grass under her palm. Then there was a cool cloth, more wet than damp, on her face. Jillian moaned in annoyance as water trickled down to her collar. Opening her eyes, she saw a blur of light and shadow. She closed them again, then concentrated on focusing.

She saw Aaron first, grim and pale as he hitched her up to a half sitting position and held a glass to her lips. Then Gil, shifting his weight from foot to foot while he ran his hat through his hands. "She ain't hurt none," he told Aaron in a voice raised to convince

everyone, including himself. "Just had herself a spell, that's all. Women do."

"A lot you know," she muttered, then discovered what Aaron held to her lips wasn't a glass but a flask of neat brandy. It burned very effectively through the mists. "I didn't faint," Jillian said in disgust.

"You did a damn good imitation, then," Aaron snapped at her.

"Let the child breathe." Karen Murdock's calm, elegant voice had the magic effect of moving the crowd back. She slipped through and knelt at Jillian's side. Clucking her tongue, she took the dripping cloth from Jillian's brow and wrung it out. "Men'll always try to overcompensate. Well, Jillian, you caused quite a sensation."

Grimacing, Jillian sat up. "Did I?" She pressed her forehead to her knees a minute until she was certain the world wasn't going to do any more spinning. "I can't believe I fainted," she mumbled.

Aaron swore and took a healthy swig from the flask himself. "She almost gets herself killed and she's worried about what fainting's going to do to her image."

Jillian's head snapped up. "Look, Murdock—"

"I wouldn't push it if I were you," he warned and meticulously capped the flask. "If you can stand, I'll take you home."

"Of course I can stand," she retorted. "And I'm not going home."

"I'm sure you're fine," Karen began and shot her son a telling look. For a smart man, Karen mused, Aaron was showing a remarkable lack of sense. Then again, when love was around, sense customarily went out the window. "Trouble is, you're a seven-day won-

der,'' she told Jillian with a brief glance at the gathering crowd. ''You're going to be congratulated to death if you stay around here.'' She smiled as she saw her words sink in.

Grumbling, Jillian rose. ''All right.'' The bruises were beginning to be felt. Rather than admit it, she brushed at the dust on her jeans. ''There's no need for you to go,'' she told Aaron stiffly. ''I'm perfectly capable of—''

His fingers were wrapped tight around her arm as he dragged her away. ''I don't know what your problem is, Murdock,'' she said through her teeth. ''But I don't have to take this.''

''I'd keep a lid on it for a while if I were you.'' The crowd fell back as he strode through. If anyone considered speaking to Jillian, Aaron's challenging look changed their minds.

After wrenching open the door of his truck, Aaron gave her a none-too-gentle boost inside. Jillian pulled her hat from her back and, taking the brim in both hands, slammed it down on her head. Folding her arms, she prepared to endure the next hour's drive in absolute silence. As Aaron pulled out it occurred to her that she had missed not only the calf roping, but also her sacred right to gloat over her bull's victory at the evening barbecue. The injustice of it made her smolder.

And just what's he so worked up about? Jillian asked herself righteously. He hadn't scared himself blind, wrenched his knee, or humiliated himself by fainting in public. Gingerly she touched her elbow where she'd scraped most of the skin away. After all, if you wanted to be technical, she'd probably saved

that kid's life. Jillian's chin angled as her arm began to ache with real enthusiasm. So why was he acting as though she'd committed some crime?

"One of these days you're going to put your chin out like that and someone's going to take you up on it."

Slowly she turned her head to glare at him. "You want to give it a shot, Murdock?"

"Don't tempt me." He punched on the gas until the speedometer hovered at seventy.

"Look, I don't know what your problem is," she said tightly. "But since you've got one, why don't you just spill it? I'm not in the mood for your nasty little comments."

He swung the truck over to the side of the road so abruptly she crashed into the door. By the time she'd recovered, he was out of his side and striding across the tough wild grass of a narrow field. Rubbing her sore arm, Jillian pushed out of the truck and went after him.

"What the hell is all this about?" Anger made her breathless as she caught at his shirtsleeve. "If you want to drive like a maniac, I'll hitch a ride back to the ranch."

"Just shut up." He jerked away from her. Distance, he told himself. He just needed some distance until he pulled himself together. He was still seeing those lowered horns sweeping past Jillian's tumbling body. His rope might've missed the mark, and then— He couldn't afford to think of any *and thens*. As it was, it had taken three well-placed ropes and several strong arms before they'd been able to drag the bull away

from those two prone bodies. He'd nearly lost her. In one split second he'd nearly lost her.

"Don't you tell me to shut up." Spinning in front of him, Jillian gripped his shirtfront. Her hat tumbled down her back as she tossed her head and rage poured out of her. "I've had all I'm going to take from you. God knows why I've let you get away with this much, but no more. Now you can just hop back in your truck and head it in whatever direction you like. To hell would suit me just fine."

She whirled away, but before she could storm off she was spun back and crushed in his arms. Spitting mad, she struggled only to have his grip tighten. It wasn't until she stopped to marshal her forces that she realized he was trembling and that his breathing came fast and uneven. Emotion ruled him, yes, but it wasn't anger. Subsiding, she waited. Not certain what she was offering comfort for, she stroked his back. "Aaron?"

He shook his head and buried his face in her hair. It was the closest he could remember to just falling apart. It hadn't been distance he'd needed, he discovered, but this. To feel her warm and safe and solid in his arms.

"Oh, God, Jillian, do you know what you did to me?"

Baffled, she let her cheek rest against his drumming heart and continued to stroke his back. "I'm sorry," she offered, hoping it would be enough for whatever she'd done.

"It was so close. Inches—just inches more. I wasn't sure at first that he hadn't gotten you."

The bull, Jillian realized. It hadn't been anger, but fear. Something warm and sweet moved through her.

"Don't," she murmured. "I wasn't hurt. It wasn't nearly as bad as it must've looked."

"The hell it wasn't." His hands came to her face and jerked it back. "I was only a few yards back when I got the first rope around him. He was more'n half crazy by then. Another couple of seconds and he'd've scooped you right up off that ground."

Jillian stared up at him and finally managed to swallow. "I—I didn't know."

He watched as the color her temper had given her fled from her cheeks. And I just had to tell you, he thought furiously. Taking both her hands, he brought them to his lips, burying his mouth in one palm, then the other. The gesture alone was enough to distract her. "It's done," Aaron said with more control. "I guess I overreacted. It's not easy to watch something like that." Because she needed it, he smiled at her. "I wouldn't have cared for it if you'd picked up any holes."

Relaxing a bit, she answered the smile. "Neither would I. As it is, I picked up a few bruises I'm not too fond of."

Still holding her hands, he bent over and kissed her with such exquisite gentleness that she felt the ground tilt for the second time. There was something different here, she realized dimly. Something... But she couldn't hold on to it.

Aaron drew away, knowing the time was coming when he'd have to tell her what he felt, whether she was ready to hear it or not. As he led her back to the truck he decided that since he was only going to bare his heart to one woman in his life, he was going to do it right.

''You're going to take a hot bath,'' he told her as he lifted her into the truck. ''Then I'm going to fix you dinner.''

Jillian settled back against the seat. ''Maybe fainting isn't such a bad thing after all.''

Chapter 11

By the time they drove into the ranch yard, Jillian had decided she'd probably enjoy a few hours of pampering. As far as she could remember, no one had ever fussed over her before. As a child, she'd been strong and healthy. Whenever she'd been ill, she'd been treated with competent practicality by her doctor father. She'd learned early that the fewer complaints you made the less likelihood there was for a hypodermic to come out of that little black bag. Clay had always treated bumps and blood as a routine part of the life. Wash up and get back to work.

Now she thought it might be a rather interesting experience to have someone murmur over her scrapes and bruises. Especially if he kissed her like he had on the side of the road…in that soft, gentle way that made the top of her head threaten to spin off.

Perhaps they wouldn't have the noise and lights and

music of the fairgrounds, but they could make their own fireworks, alone, on Utopia.

All the buildings were quiet, bunkhouse, barns, stables. Instead of the noise and action that would accompany any late afternoon, there was simple, absolute peace over acres of land. Whatever animals hadn't been taken to the fair had been left to graze for the day. It would be hours before anyone returned to Utopia.

"I don't think I've ever been here alone before," Jillian murmured when Aaron stopped the truck. She sat for a moment and absorbed the quiet and the stillness. It occurred to her that she could cup her hands and shout if she liked—no one would even hear the echo.

"It's funny, it even feels different. You always know there're people around." She stepped out of the truck, then listened to the echo of the slam. "Somebody in the bunkhouse or the cookhouse or one of the outbuildings. Some of the wives or children hanging out clothes or working in the gardens. You hardly think about it, but it's like a little town."

"Self-sufficient, independent." He took her hand, thinking that the words described her just as accurately as they described the ranch. They were two of the reasons he'd been drawn to her.

"It has to be, doesn't it? It's so easy to get cut off— one bad storm. Besides, it's what makes it all so special." Though she didn't understand the smile he sent her, she answered it. "I'm glad I've got so many married hands who've settled," she added. "It's harder to depend on the drifters." Jillian scanned the ranch yard, not quite understanding her own reluctance to go in-

side. It was as if she were missing something. With a shrug, she put it down to the oddity of being alone, but she caught herself searching the area again.

Aaron glanced down and saw the lowered-brow look of concentration. "Something wrong?"

"I don't know... It seems like there is." With another shrug, she turned to him. "I must be getting jumpy." Reaching up, she tipped back the brim of his hat. She liked the way it shadowed his face, accenting the angle of bone, adding just one more shade of darkness to his eyes. "You didn't mention anything about scrubbing my back when I took that hot bath, did you?"

"No, but I could probably be persuaded."

Agreeably she went into his arms. She thought she could catch just a trace of rosin on him, perhaps a hint of saddle soap. "Did I mention how sore I am?"

"No, you didn't."

"I don't like to complain..." She snuggled against him.

"But?" he prompted with a grin.

"Well, now that you mention it—there are one or two places that sting, just a bit."

"Want me to kiss them and make them better?"

She sighed as he nuzzled her ear. "If it wouldn't be too much trouble."

"I'm a humanitarian," he told her, then began to nudge her slowly toward the porch steps. It was then Jillian remembered. With a gasp, she broke out of his arms and raced across the yard. "Jillian—" Swearing, Aaron followed her.

Oh, God, how could she've missed it! Jillian raced to the paddock fence and leaned breathlessly against

it. Empty. *Empty.* She balled her hands into fists as she looked at the bottle she'd left hanging at an angle in the shade. The trough of water glimmered in the sun. The few scoops of grain she'd left were barely touched.

"What's going on?"

"Baby," she muttered, tapping her hand rhythmically against the fence. "They've taken Baby." Her tone started out calm, then became more and more agitated. "They walked right into my backyard, right into my backyard, and stole from me."

"Maybe one of your hands put him back in the barn."

She only shook her head and continued to tap her hand on the fence. "The five hundred weren't enough," she murmured. "They had to come here and steal within a stone's throw of my house. I should've left Joe—he offered to stay. I should've stayed myself."

"Come on, we'll check the barn."

She looked at him, and her eyes were flat and dark. "He's not in the barn."

He'd rather have had her rage, weep, than look so—resigned. "Maybe not, but we'll be sure. Then we'll see if anything else was taken before we call the sheriff."

"The sheriff." Jillian laughed under her breath and stared blindly into the empty paddock. "The sheriff."

"Jillian—" Aaron slipped his arms around her, but she drew away immediately.

"No, I'm not going to fall apart this time." Her voice trembled slightly, but her eyes were clear. "They won't do that to me again."

It might be better if she did, Aaron thought. Her face was pale, but he knew that expression by now. There'd be no backing down. "You check the barn," he suggested. "I'll look in the stables."

Jillian followed the routine, though she knew it was hopeless. Baby's stall was empty. She watched the little motes of hay and dust as they floated in the slant of sunlight. Someone had taken her yearling. Someone. Her hands balled into fists. Somehow, some way, she was going to get a name. Spinning on her heel, she strode back out. Though she itched with impatience, she waited until Aaron crossed the yard to her. There wasn't any need for words. Together, they went into the house.

She's not going to take this one lying down, he decided, with as much admiration as concern. Yes, she was still pale, but her voice was strong and clear as she spoke to the sheriff's office. Resigned—yes, she was still resigned that it had been done. But she didn't consider it over.

He remembered the way she'd nuzzled the calf when it'd been newborn—the way her eyes had softened when she spoke of it. It was always a mistake to make a pet out of one of your stock, but there were times it happened. She was paying for it now.

Thoughtfully he began to brew coffee. Aaron considered it a foolish move for anyone to have stolen Utopia's prize yearling. For butchering? It hardly seemed worth the risk or effort. Yet what rancher in the area would buy a young Hereford so easily identified? Someone had gotten greedy, or stupid. Either way, it would make them easier to catch.

Jillian leaned against the kitchen wall and talked

steadily into the phone. Aaron found himself wanting to shield, to protect. She took the coffee from him with a brief nod and continued talking. Shaking his head, he reminded himself he should know better by now. Protection wasn't something Jillian would take gracefully. He drank his own coffee, looking out of the kitchen window and wondering how a man dealt with loving a woman who had more grit than most men.

"He'll do what he can," she said as she hung up the phone with a snap. "I'm going to offer a separate reward for Baby." Jillian drank down half the coffee, hot and black. "Tomorrow I'll go see the Cattlemen's Association again. I want to put the pressure on, and put it on hard. People are going to realize this isn't going to stop at Utopia." She looked into her coffee, then grimly finished it off. "I kept telling myself it wasn't personal. Even when I saw the hides and bones in the canyon. Not this time. They got cocky, Aaron. It's always easier to catch arrogance."

There was relish in the tone of her voice, the kind of relish that made him smile as he turned to face her. "You're right."

"What're you grinning at?"

"I was thinking if the rustlers could see you now, they'd be shaking the dust of this county off their boots in a hurry."

Her lips curved. She hadn't thought it possible. "Thank you." She gestured with the cup, then set it back on the stove. "I seem to be saying that to you quite a bit these days."

"You don't have to say it at all. Hungry?"

"Hmmm." She put her hand on her stomach and thought about it. "I don't know."

"Go get yourself a bath, I'll rustle up something."

Walking to him, Jillian slipped her arms around his waist and rested her head on his chest. How was it he knew her so well? How did he understand that she needed a few moments alone to sort through her thoughts and feelings?"

"Why are you so good to me?" she murmured.

With a half laugh, Aaron buried his face in her hair. "God knows. Go soak your bruises."

"Okay." But she gave in to the urge to hug him fiercely before she left the room.

She wished she knew a better way to express gratitude. As she climbed the stairs to the second floor, Jillian wished she were more clever with words. If she were, she'd be able to tell him how much it meant that he offered no more than she could comfortably take. His support today had been steady but unobtrusive. And he was giving her time alone without leaving her alone. Perhaps it had taken her quite some time to discover just how special a man he was, but she had discovered it. It wasn't something she'd forget.

As Jillian peeled off her clothes she found she was a bit more tender in places than she'd realized. Better, she decided, and turned the hot water on in the tub to let it steam. A few bruises were something solid to concentrate on. They were easier than the bruises she felt on the inside. It might have been foolish to feel as though she'd let her grandfather down, but she couldn't rid herself of the feeling. He'd given her something in trust and she hadn't protected it well enough. It would have soothed her if he'd been around to berate her for it.

Wincing a bit, she lowered herself into the water.

The raw skin on her elbow objected and she ignored
it. One of her own men? she thought with a grimace.
It was too possible. Back up a truck to the paddock,
load up the calf, and go.

She'd start making a few discreet inquiries herself.
Stealing the calf would've taken time. Maybe she
could discover just who was away from the fair. Perhaps they'd be confident enough to throw a little extra
money around if they thought they were safe and
then... Then they'd see, she thought as she relaxed in
the water.

Poor Baby. No one would spend the time scratching
his ears or talking to him now. Sinking further in the
water, she waited until her mind went blank.

It was nearly an hour before she came downstairs
again. She'd soaked the stiffness away and nearly all
the depression. Nothing practical could be done with
depression. She caught the aroma of something spicy
that had her stomach juices churning.

Aaron's name was on the tip of her tongue as she
walked into the kitchen, but the room was empty. A
pot simmered on the stove with little hisses and puffs
of steam. It drew her, irresistibly. Jillian lifted the lid,
closed her eyes, and breathed deep. Chili, thick, and
fragrant enough to make the mouth water. She
wouldn't have to give it any thought if he asked if she
was hungry now.

Picking up a spoon, she began to stir. Maybe just
one little taste...

"My mother used to smack my hand for that,"
Aaron commented. Jillian dropped the lid with a
clatter.

"Damn, Murdock! You scared me to—" Turning, she saw the clutch of wildflowers in his hand.

Some men might've looked foolish holding small colorful blooms in a hand roughened by work and weather. Other men might've seemed awkward. Aaron was neither. Something turned over in her chest when he smiled at her.

She looked stunned—not that he minded. It wasn't often you caught a woman like Jillian Baron off-balance. As he watched, she put her hands behind her back and gripped them together. He lifted a brow. If he'd known he could make her nervous with a bunch of wildflowers, he'd have dug up a field of them long before this.

"Feel better?" he asked and slowly crossed to her.

She'd backed into the counter before she'd realized she made the defensive move. "Yes, thanks."

He gave her one of his long, serious looks while his eyes laughed. "Something wrong?"

"No. The chili smells great."

"Something I picked up at one of the line camps a few years back." Bending his head, he kissed the corners of her mouth. "Don't you want the flowers, Jillian?"

"Yes, I—" She found she was gripping her fingers together until they hurt. Annoyed with herself, she loosened them and took the flowers from his hand. "They're very pretty."

"It's what your hair smells like," he murmured and saw the cautious look she threw up at him. Tilting his head, he studied her. "Hasn't anyone ever given you flowers before?"

Not in years, she realized. Not since—florist boxes,

ribbons, and soft words. Realizing she was making a fool of herself, she shrugged. "Roses," she said carelessly. "Red roses."

Something in her tone warned him. He kept his touch very light as he wound her hair around his finger. It was the color of flame, the texture of silk. "Too tame," he said simply. "Much too tame."

Something flickered inside her—acknowledgment, caution, need. With a sigh, she looked down at the small bold flowers in her hand. "Once—a long time ago—I thought I could be too."

He tugged on her hair until she looked up at him. "Is that what you wanted to be?"

"Then, I—" She broke off, but something in his eyes demanded an answer. "Yes, I would've tried."

"Were you in love with him?" He wasn't certain why he was hacking away at a wound—his and hers—but he couldn't stop.

"Aaron—"

"Were you?"

She let out a long breath. Mechanically she began to fill a water glass for the flowers. "I was very young. He was a great deal like my father—steady, quiet, dedicated. My father loved me because he had to, never because he wanted to. There's a tremendous difference." The sharp, clean scent of the wildflowers drifted up to her. "Maybe somewhere along the line I thought if I pleased him, I'd please my father. I don't know, I was foolish."

"That isn't an answer." He discovered jealousy tasted bitter even after it was swallowed.

"I guess I don't have one I'm sure of." She moved her shoulders and fluffed the flowers in the glass.

"Shouldn't we eat?" She went very still when his hands came to her shoulders, but she didn't resist when he turned her around.

She had a moment's fear that he would say something gentle, something sweet, and undermine her completely. She saw something of it in his eyes, just as he saw the apprehension in hers. Aaron tugged her against him and brought his mouth down hard on hers.

She could understand the turbulence and let go. She could meet the desire, the violence of needs, without fear of stumbling past her own rules. Her arms went around him to hold him close. Her lips sought his hungrily. If through the relief came a stir of feeling, she could almost convince herself it was nothing more complex than passion.

"Eat fast," Aaron told her. "I've been thinking about making love with you for hours."

"Didn't we eat already?"

With a chuckle he nuzzled her neck. "No, you don't. When I cook for a woman, she eats." He gave her a companionable smack on the bottom as he drew away. "Get the bowls."

Jillian handed him two and watched him scoop out generous portions. "Smells fabulous. Want a beer?"

"Yeah."

Unearthing two from the refrigerator, she poured them into glasses. "You know, if you ever get tired of ranching, you could have a job in the cookhouse here at Utopia."

"Always a comfort to have something to fall back on."

"We've got a woman now," Jillian went on as she took her seat. "The men call her Aunt Sally. She's got

a way with biscuits—'' She broke off as she took the first bite. Heat spread through her and woke up every cell in her body. Swallowing, she met Aaron's grin. ''You use a free hand with the peppers.''

''Separates the men from the boys.'' He took a generous forkful. ''Too hot for you?''

Disdainfully she took a second bite. ''There's nothing you can dish out I can't take, Murdock.''

Laughing, he continued to eat. Jillian decided the first encounter had numbed her mouth right down to the vocal cords. She ate with as much relish as he, cooling off occasionally with sips of cold beer.

''Those people in town don't know what they're missing,'' she commented as she scraped down to the bottom of the bowl. ''It isn't every day you get battery acid this tasty.''

He glanced over as she ate the last forkful. ''Want some more?''

''I want to live,'' she countered. ''God, Aaron, a steady diet of that and you wouldn't have a stomach lining. It's fabulous.''

''We had a Mexican foreman when I was a boy,'' Aaron told her. ''Best damn cattleman I've ever known. I spent the best part of a summer with him up at the line camp. You should taste my flour tortillas.''

The man was a constant surprise, Jillian decided as she rested her elbows on the table and cupped her chin in her hand. ''What happened to him?''

''Saved his stake, went back to Mexico, and started his own spread.''

''The impossible dream,'' Jillian murmured.

''Too easy to lose a month's pay in a poker game.''

She nodded, but her lips curved. ''Do you play?''

"I've sat in on a hand or two. You?"

"Clay taught me. We'll have to arrange a game one of these days."

"Any time."

"I'm counting on a few poker skills to bring me out of this rustling business."

Aaron watched her rise to clear the table. "How?"

"People get careless when they think you're ready to fold. They made a mistake with the yearling, Aaron. I'm going to be able to find him—especially if nobody knows how hard I'm looking. I'm thinking about hiring an investigator. Whatever it costs, I'd rather pay it than have the stealing go on."

He sat for a moment, listening to her run water in the sink—a homey, everyday sound. "How hard is all this hitting your books, Jillian?"

She cast a look over her shoulder, calm and cool. "I can still raise the bet."

He knew better than to offer her financial assistance. It irked him. Rising, he paced the kitchen until he'd come full circle behind her. "The Cattlemen's Association would back you."

"They'd have to know about it to do that. The less people who know, the more effective a private investigation would be."

"I want to help you."

Touched, she turned and took him into her arms. "You have helped me. I won't forget it."

"I have to hog-tie you before you'll let me do anything."

She laughed and lifted her face to his. "I'm not that bad."

"Worse," he countered. "If I offered you some men to help patrol your land…"

"Aaron—"

"See." He kissed her before she could finish the protest. "I could work for you myself until everything was straightened out."

"I couldn't let you—" Then his mouth was hard and bruising on hers again.

"I'm the one who has to watch you worry and struggle," he told her as his hands began to roam down. "Do you know what that does to me?"

She tried to concentrate on his words, but his mouth—his mouth was demanding all her attention. The hot, spicy kiss took her breath away, but she clung to him and fought for more. Each time he touched her it was only seconds until the needs took over completely. She'd never known anything so liberating, or so imprisoning. Jillian might have struggled against the latter if she'd known how. Instead she accepted the bars and locks even as she accepted the open sky and the wind. He was the only man who could tempt her to.

This was something he could do for her, Aaron knew. Make her forget, thrust her problems away from her, if only temporarily. Even so, he knew, if she had a choice, she would have kept some distance there as well. She'd been hurt, and her trust wasn't completely his yet. The frustration of it made his mouth more ruthless, his hands more urgent. There was still only one way that she was his without question. He swept her up, then silenced her murmured protest.

Jillian was aware she was being carried. Some inner part of her rebelled against it. And yet… He wasn't

taking her anywhere she wouldn't have gone willingly. Perhaps he needed this—romance he'd once called it. Romance frightened her, as the flowers had frightened her. It was so easy to lie in candlelight, so easy to deceive with fragrant blossoms and soft words. And she was no longer sure the defenses she'd once had were still there. Not with him.

"I want you." The words drifted from her to shimmer against his lips.

He would've taken her to bed. But it was too far. He would have given her the slow, easy loving a cherished woman deserves. But he was too hungry. With his mouth still fused to hers, he tumbled onto the couch with her and let the fire take them both.

She understood desperation. It was honest and real. There could be no doubting the frantic search of his mouth or the urgent pressure of his fingers against her skin. Desire had no shadows. She could feel it pulsing from him even as it pulsed from her. His curses as he tugged at her clothes made her laugh breathlessly. *She* made him clumsy. It was the greatest compliment she'd ever had.

He was relentless, spinning her beyond time and space the moment he could touch her flesh. She let herself go. Every touch, every frenzied caress, every deep, greedy kiss, took her further from the strict, practical world she'd formed for herself. Once she'd sought solitude and speed when she'd needed freedom. Now she needed only Aaron.

She felt his hair brush over her bare shoulder and savored even that simple contact. It brought a sweetness flowing into her while the burn of his mouth brought the fire. Only with him had she realized it was

possible to have both. Only with him had she realized the great, yawning need in herself to have both. Her moan came as much from the revelation as from the passion.

Did she know how giving she was? How incredibly arousing? Aaron had to fight the need to take her quickly, ruthlessly, while they were both still half dressed. No woman had ever sapped his control the way she could. One look, one touch, and he was hers so completely— How could she not know?

Her body flowed, fluid as water, heady as wine, under his hands. Her lips had the punch of an electric current and the texture of silk. Could any woman remain unaware of such a deadly combination?

As if to catch his breath, he took his lips to her throat and burrowed there. He drew in the fragrance from her bath, some subtle woman's scent that lingered there, waiting to entice a lover. It was then he remembered the bruises. Aaron shook his head, trying to clear it.

"I'm hurting you."

"No." She drew him back, close. "No, you're not. You never do. I'm not fragile, Aaron."

"No?" He lifted his head so that he could see her face. There was the delicate line of bone she couldn't deny, the honey-touched skin that remained soft after hours in the sun. The frailty that came and went in her eyes at the right word, the right touch. "Sometimes you are," he murmured. "Let me show you."

"No—"

But even as she protested, his lips skimmed hers, so gentle, so reassuring. It did nothing to smother the fire, only banked it while he showed her what magic there

could be with mouth to mouth. With his fingers he traced her face as though he might never see it with his eyes again—over the curve of cheekbone, down the slim line of jaw.

Patient, soft, murmuring, he seduced where no seduction was needed. Tender, thorough, easy, he let his lips show her what he hadn't yet spoken. The hand on his shoulder slid bonelessly down to his waist. He touched the tip of her tongue with his, then went deeper, slowly, in a soul-wrenching kiss that left them both limp. Then he began a careful worship of her body. She floated.

Was there any kind of pleasure he couldn't show her? Jillian wondered. Was this humming world just one more aspect to passion? She wanted desperately to give him something in return, yet her body was so heavy, weighed down with sensations. Sandalwood and leather—it would always bring him to her mind. The ridge of callus on his hand where the reins rubbed daily—nothing felt more perfect against her skin. He shifted so that she sank deeper into the cushions, and he with her.

She could taste him—and what she realized must be a wisp of herself on his lips. His cheek grazed hers, not quite smooth. She wanted to burrow against it. He whispered her name and generated a new layer of warmth.

Even when his hands began to roam, the excitement stayed hazy. She couldn't break through the mists, and no longer tried. Her skin was throbbing, but it went deeper, to the blood and bone. His mouth was light at her breast, his tongue clever enough to make her shudder, then settle, then shudder again.

He kept the pace easy, though she began to writhe under him. Time dripped away as he gave himself the pleasure of showing her each new delight. He knew afternoon was ending only by the way the light slanted over her face. The quiet was punctuated only with murmurs and sighs. He'd never felt more alone with her.

He took her slowly, savoring each moment, each movement, until there could be no more.

As she lay beneath him, Jillian watched the light shift toward dusk. It had been like a dream, she thought, like something you sigh over in the middle of the night when your wishes take control. Should it move her more than the fire and flash they usually brought each other? Somehow she knew what she'd just experienced had been more dangerous.

Aaron shifted, and though she made no objection to his weight, sat up, bringing her with him. "I like the way you stay soft and warm after I make love to you."

"It's never been just like that before," she murmured.

The words moved him; he couldn't stop it. "No." Tilting back her head, he kissed her again. "It will be again."

Perhaps because she wanted so badly to hold on, to stay, to depend, she drew away. "I'm never sure how to take you." Something warned her it was time to play it light. She was out of her depth—far, far out of her depth.

"In what way?"

She gave in to the urge to hold him again, just to feel the way his hand slid easily up and down her bare back. Reluctantly she slipped out of his arms and

pulled on her shirt. "You're a lot of different people, Aaron Murdock. Every time I think I might get to know who you are, you're someone else."

"No, I'm not." Before she could button it, Aaron took her shirtfront and pulled her back to him. "Different moods don't make different people."

"Maybe not." She disconcerted him by kissing the back of his hand. "But I still can't get a handle on you."

"Is that what you want?"

"I'm a simple person."

He stared at her a moment as she continued to dress. "Are you joking?"

Because there was a laugh in his voice, she looked over, half serious, half embarrassed. "No, I am. I have to know where I stand, what my options are, what's expected of me. As long as I know I can do my job and take care of what's mine, I'm content."

He watched her thoughtfully as he pulled on his jeans. "Your job's what's vital in your life?"

"It's what I know," she countered. "I understand the land."

"And people?"

"I'm not really very good with people—a lot of people. Unless I understand them."

Aaron pulled his shirt on but left it open as he crossed to her. "And I'm one you don't understand?"

"Only sometimes," she murmured. "I guess I understand you best when I'm annoyed with you. Other times…" She was sinking even deeper and started to turn away.

"Other times," Aaron prompted, holding on to her arms.

"Other times I don't know. I never expected to get involved with you—this way."

He ran his thumbs over the pulses at the inside of her elbow. They weren't steady any longer. "This way, Jillian?"

"I didn't expect that we'd be lovers. I never expected—" Why was her heart pounding like this again, so soon? "To want you," she finished.

"Didn't you?" There was something about the way she looked at him—not quite sure of herself when he knew she was fighting to be—that made him reckless. "I wanted you from the first minute I saw you, riding hell for leather on that mare. There were other things I didn't expect. Finding those soft places, on you, in you."

"Aaron—"

He shook his head when she tried to stop him. "Thinking of you in the middle of the day, the middle of the night. Remembering just the way you say my name."

"Don't."

He felt her start to tremble before she tried to pull away. "Damn it, it's time you heard what I've been carrying around inside of me. I love you, Jillian."

Panic came first, even when she began to build up the reserve. "No, you don't have to say that." Her voice was sharp and fast. "I don't expect to hear those kinds of things."

"What the hell are you talking about?" He shook her once in frustration, and a second time in anger. "I know what I have to say. I don't care if you expect to hear it or not, because you're going to."

She hung on to her temper because she knew it was

emotion that brought on betrayal. If she hadn't had her pride, she would have told him just how much those words, that easily said, empty phrase hurt her. "Aaron, I told you before I don't need the soft words. I don't even like them. Whatever's between us—"

"What is between us?" he demanded. He hadn't known he could be hurt, not like this. Not so he could all but feel the blood draining out of him where he stood. He'd just told a woman he loved her—the only woman, the first time. And she was answering him with ice. "You tell me what there is between us. Just this?" He swung a hand toward the couch, still rumpled from their bodies. "Is that it for you, Jillian?"

"I don't—" There was a tug-of-war going on inside of her, so fierce she was breathless from it. "It's all I thought you—" Frightened, she dragged both hands through her hair. Why was he doing this now, when she was just beginning to think she understood what he wanted from her, what she needed from him? "I don't know what you want. But I—I just can't give you any more than I already have. It's already more than I've ever given to anyone else."

His fingers loosened on her arms one by one, then dropped away. They were a match in many ways, and pride was one of them. Aaron watched her almost dispassionately as he buttoned his shirt. "You've let something freeze inside you, woman. If all you want's a warm body on a cold night, you shouldn't have much trouble. Personally, I like a little something more."

She watched him walk out of the door, heard the sound of his truck as it broke the silence. The sun was just slipping over the horizon.

Chapter 12

He worked until his muscles ached and he could think about little more than easing them. He probably drank too much. He rode the cattle, hours in the saddle, rounded strays, and ate more dust than food. He spent the long, sweaty days of summer at the line camp, driving himself from sunup to sundown. Sometimes, only sometimes, he managed to push her out of his mind.

For three weeks Aaron was hell to be around. Or so his men mumbled whenever he was out of earshot. It was a woman, they told each other. Only a woman could drive a man to the edge, and then give him that gentle tap over. The Baron woman's name came up. Well, Murdocks and Barons had never mixed, so it was no wonder. No one'd expected much to come of that but hot tempers and bad feelings.

If Aaron heard the murmurs, he ignored them. He'd

come up to the camp to work—and he was going to do just that until she was out of his system. No woman was going to make him crawl. He'd told her he loved her, and she'd shoved his words, his emotions, right back in his face. Not interested.

Aaron dropped a new fence post into the ground as the sweat rolled freely down his back and sides. Maybe she was the first woman he'd ever loved—that didn't mean she'd be the last. He came down hard on the post with a sledgehammer, hissing with the effort.

He hadn't meant to tell her—not then, not that way. Somehow, the words had started rolling and he hadn't been able to stop them. Had she wanted them all tied up with a ribbon, neat and fancy? Cursing, he came down with the hammer again so that the post vibrated and the noise sang out. Maybe he had more finesse than he'd shown her, and maybe he could've used it. With someone else. Someone who didn't make his feelings come up and grab him by the throat.

Where in God's name had he ever come up with the idea that she had those soft parts, that sweet vulnerability under all that starch and fire? Must've been crazy, he told himself as he began running fresh wire. Jillian Baron was a cold, single-minded woman who cared more about her head count than any real emotion.

And he was almost sick with loving her.

He gripped the wire hard enough so that it bit through the leather of his glove and into his hand. He cursed again. He'd just have to get over it. He had his own land to tend.

Pausing, he looked out. It rolled, oceans of grass, high with summer, green and rippling. The sky was a

merciless blue, and the sun beat down, strong and clean. It could be enough for a man—these thousands of acres. His cattle were fat and healthy, the yearlings growing strong. In a few weeks they'd round them up, drive them into Miles City. When those long days were over, the men would celebrate. It was their right to. And so would he, Aaron told himself grimly. So, by God, would he.

He'd have given half of what was his just to get her out of his mind for one day.

At dusk he washed off the day's sweat and dirt. He could smell the night's meal through the open windows of the cabin. Good red meat. Someone was playing a guitar and singing of lonely, lamented love. He found he wanted a beer more than he wanted his share of the steak. Because he knew a man couldn't work and not eat, he piled food on his plate and transferred it to his stomach. But he worked his way through one beer, then two, while the men made up their evening poker game. As they grew louder he took a six-pack and went out on the narrow wood porch.

The stars were just coming out. He heard a coyote call at the moon, then fall silent. The air was as still as it had been all day and barely cooler, but he could smell the sweet clover and wild roses. Resting his back against the porch rail, Aaron willed his mind to empty. But he thought of her…

Fully dressed and spitting mad, standing in the pond—crooning quietly to an orphaned calf—laughing up at him with her hair spread out over the earth of the corral—weeping in his arms over her butchered cattle. Soft one minute, prickly the next—no, she wasn't a temperate woman. But she was the only one

he wanted. She was the only one he'd ever felt enough for to hurt over.

Aaron took a long swig from the bottle. He didn't care much for emotional pain. The poets could have it. She didn't want him. Aaron swore and scowled into the dark. The hell she didn't—he wasn't a fool. Maybe her needs weren't the same as his, but she had them. For the first time in weeks he began to think calmly.

He hadn't played his hand well, he realized. It wasn't like him to fold so early—then again, he wasn't used to being soft-headed over a woman. Thoughtfully he tipped back his hat and looked at the stars. She was too set on having her own way, and it was time he gave her a run for her money.

No, he wasn't going back on his knees, Aaron thought with a grim smile. But he was going back. If he had to hobble and brand her, he was going to have Jillian Baron.

When the screen door opened he glanced around absently. His mood was more open to company.

"My luck's pretty poor."

Jennsen, Aaron thought, running through a quick mental outline of the man as he offered him a beer. A bit jittery, he mused. On his first season with the Double M, though he wasn't a greenhorn. He was a man who kept to himself and whose past was no more than could be seen in a worn saddle and patched boots.

Jennsen sat on the first step so that his lantern jaw was shadowed by the porch roof. Aaron thought he might be anywhere from thirty-five to fifty. There was age in his eyes—the kind that came from too many years of looking into the sun at another man's land.

"Cards aren't falling?" Aaron said conversationally

while he watched Jennsen roll a cigarette. He didn't miss the fact that the fingers weren't quite steady.

"Haven't been for weeks." Jennsen gave a brief laugh as he struck a match. "Trouble is, I've never been much good at staying away from a gamble." He shot Aaron a sidelong look as he drank again. He'd been working his way up to this talk for days and nearly had enough beer in him to go through with it. "Your luck's pretty steady at the table."

"Comes and goes," Aaron said, deciding Jennsen was feeling his way along for an advance or a loan.

"Luck's a funny thing." Jennsen wiped his mouth with the back of his hand. "Had some bad luck over at the Baron place lately. Losing that cattle," he continued when Aaron glanced over at him. "Somebody made a pretty profit off that beef."

He caught the trace of bitterness. Casually he twisted the top from another bottle and handed it over. "It's easy to make a profit when you don't pay for the beef. Whoever skimmed from the Baron place did a smooth job of it."

"Yeah." Jennsen drew in strong tobacco. He'd heard the rumors about something going on between Aaron Murdock and the Baron woman, but there didn't seem to be anything to it. Most of the talk was about the bad blood between the two families. It'd been going on for years, and it seemed as though it would go on for years more. At the moment he needed badly to believe it. "Guess it doesn't much matter on this side of the fence how much cattle slips away from the Baron spread."

Aaron stretched out his legs and crossed them at the ankles. The lowered brim of his hat shadowed his eyes.

"People have to look out for themselves," he said lazily.

Jennsen moistened his lips and prodded a bit further. "I've heard stories about your grandpaw helping himself to Baron beef."

Aaron's eyes narrowed to slits, but he checked his temper. "Stories," he agreed. "No proof."

Jennsen took another long swallow of beer. "I heard that somebody waltzed right onto Baron land and loaded up a prize yearling, sired by that fancy bull."

"Did a tidy job of it." Aaron kept his voice expressionless. Jennsen was testing the waters all right, but he wasn't looking for a loan. "It'd be a shame if they took it for baby beef," he added. "The yearling has the look of his sire—a real moneymaker. 'Course, in a few months he'd stand out like a sore thumb on a small spread. Hate to see a good bloodline wasted."

"Man hears things," Jennsen mumbled, accepting the fresh beer Aaron handed him. "You were interested in the Baron bull."

Aaron took a swig from his bottle, tipped back his hat, and grinned agreeably. "I'm always interested in good stock. Know where I can get my hands on some?"

Jennsen searched his face and swallowed. "Maybe."

Jillian slowed down as she passed the white frame house. Empty. Of course it was empty, she told herself. Even if he'd come back, he wouldn't be home in the middle of the morning. She shouldn't be here on Murdock land when she had her hands full of her own work. She couldn't stay away. If he didn't come back

soon, she was going to make a fool of herself and go up to the line camp and...

And what? she asked herself. Half the time she didn't know what she wanted to do, how she felt, what she thought. The one thing she was certain of was that she'd never spent three more miserable weeks in her life. It was perilously close to grief.

Something had died in her when he'd left—something she hadn't acknowledged had been alive. She'd convinced herself that she wouldn't fall in love with him. It would be impossible to count the times she'd told herself it wouldn't happen—even after it already had. Why hadn't she recognized it?

Jillian supposed it wasn't always easy to recognize something you'd never experienced before. Especially when it had no explanation. A woman so accustomed to getting and going her own way had no business falling for a man who was equally obstinate and independent.

Falling in love. Jillian thought it an apt phrase. When it happened you just lost your foothold and plunged.

Maybe he'd meant it, she thought. Maybe they had been more than words to him. If he loved her back, didn't it mean she had someone to hold on to while she was falling? She let out a long breath as she pulled up in front of the ranch house. If he'd meant it, why wasn't he here? Mistake, she told herself with forced calm. It was always a mistake to depend too much. People pulled back or just went away. But if she could only see him again...

"Going to just sit there in that Jeep all morning?"

With a jerk, Jillian turned to watch Paul Murdock

take a few slow, measured steps out onto the porch. She got out of the Jeep, wondering which of the excuses she'd made up before she'd set out would work the best.

"Sit," Murdock ordered before she could come to a decision. "Karen's fixing up a pitcher of tea."

"Thank you." Feeling awkward, she sat on the edge of the porch swing and searched for something to say.

"He hasn't come down from the camp yet," Murdock told her bluntly as he lowered himself into a rocker. "Don't frazzle your brain, girl," he ordered with an impatient brush of his hand. "I may be old, but I can see what's going on under my nose. What'd the two of you spat about?"

"Paul." Karen carried a tray laden with glasses and an iced pitcher. "Jillian's entitled to her privacy."

"Privacy!" he snorted while Karen arranged the tray on a table. "She's dangling after my son."

"Dangling!" Jillian was on her feet in a flash. "I don't dangle after anything or anyone. If I want something, I get it."

He laughed, rocking back and forth and wheezing with the effort as she glared down at him. "I like you, girl, damn if I don't. Got a fetching face, doesn't she, Karen?"

"Lovely." With a smile, Karen offered Jillian a glass of tea.

"Thank you." Stiffly she took her seat again. "I just stopped by to let Aaron know that the mare's doing well. The vet was by yesterday to check her out."

"That the best you could do?" Murdock demanded.

"Paul." Karen sat on the arm of the rocker and laid a hand on his arm.

"If I want manure, all I have to do is walk my own pasture," he grumbled, then pointed his cane at Jillian. "You going to tell me you don't want my boy?"

"Mr. Murdock," Jillian began with icy dignity, "Aaron and I have a business arrangement."

"When a man's dying he doesn't like to waste time," Murdock said with a scowl. "Now, you want to look me in the eye and tell me straight you've got no feelings for that son of mine, fine. We'll talk about the weather a bit."

Jillian opened her mouth, then closed it again with a helpless shake of her head. "When's he coming back?" she whispered. "It's been three weeks."

"He'll come back when he stops being as thick-headed as you are," Murdock told her curtly.

"I don't know what to do." After the words had tumbled out, she sat in amazement. She'd never in her life said that out loud to anyone.

"What do you want?" Karen asked her.

Jillian looked over and studied them—the old man and his beautiful wife. Karen's hand was over his on top of the cane. Their shoulders brushed. A few scattered times in her life she'd seen that kind of perfect intimacy that came from deep abiding love. It was easy to recognize, enviable. And a little scary. It came as a shock to discover she wanted that for herself. One man, one lifetime. But if that was ultimately what love equaled for her, she understood it had to be a shared dream.

"I'm still finding out," she murmured.

"That Jeep." Murdock nodded toward it. "You wouldn't have any trouble getting up to the line camp in a four-wheel drive."

Jillian smiled and set her glass aside. "I can't do it that way. It wouldn't work for me if I didn't meet him on equal terms."

"Stubborn young fool," Murdock grumbled.

"Yes." Jillian smiled again as she rose. "If he wants me, that's what he's going to get." The sound of an engine had her glancing over. When she recognized Gil's truck, she frowned and started down the steps.

"Ma'am." He tipped his hat to Karen but didn't even open the door of the truck. "Mr. Murdock. Got a problem," he said briefly, shifting his eyes to Jillian.

"What is it?"

"Sheriff called. Seems your yearling's been identified on a spread 'bout hundred and fifty miles south of here. Wants you to go down and take a look for yourself."

Jillian gripped the bottom of the open window. "Where?"

"Old Larraby spread. I'll take you now."

"Leave your Jeep here," Murdock told her, getting to his feet. "One of my men'll take it back to your place."

"Thanks." Quickly she dashed around to the other side of the truck. "Let's go," she ordered the moment the door shut beside her. "How, Gil?" she demanded as they drove out of the ranch yard. "Who identified him?"

Gil spit out the window and felt rather pleased with himself. "Aaron Murdock."

"Aaron—"

Gil was a bit more pleased when Jillian's mouth fell

open. "Yep." When he came to the fork in the road, he headed south at a steady, mile-eating clip.

"But how? Aaron's been up at his line camp for weeks, and—"

"Maybe you'd like to settle down so I can tell you, or maybe you wouldn't."

Seething with impatience, Jillian subsided. "Tell me."

"Seems one of the Murdock men had a hand in the rustling, fellow named Jennsen. Well, he wasn't too happy with his cut and gambled away most of it anyhow. Decided if they could slice off five hundred and get away with it, he'd take one more for himself."

"Baby," Jillian muttered and crossed her arms over her chest.

"Yep. Had himself a tiger by the tail there. Knew the makings of a prize bull when he saw it and took it over to Larraby. Used to work there before Larraby fell on hard times. Anyhow, he started to get nervous once the man who headed up the rustling got wind of who took the little bull, figured he better get it off his hands. Last night he tried to sell him to Aaron Murdock."

"I see." That was one more she owed him, Jillian thought with a scowl. It was hard to meet a man toe to toe when you were piling up debts. "If it is Baby, and this Jennsen was involved, we'll get the rest of them."

"We'll see if it's Baby," Gil said, then eased a cautious look at her. "The sheriff's already rounding up the rest of them. Picked up Joe Carlson a couple hours ago."

"Joe?" Stunned, she turned completely around in her seat to stare at Gil. "Joe Carlson?"

"Seems he bought himself a little place over in Wyoming. From the sound of it, he's already got a couple hundred head of your cattle grazing there."

"Joe." Shifting, Jillian stared straight ahead. So much for trust, she thought. So much for her expert reading of character. Clay hadn't wanted to hire him— she'd insisted. One of her first major independent decisions on Utopia had been her first major mistake.

"Guess he fooled me too," Gil muttered after a moment. "Knew his cattle front and back." He spit again and set his teeth. "Shoulda known better than to trust a man with soft hands and a clean hat."

"I hired him," Jillian muttered.

"I worked with him," Gil tossed back. "Side by side. And if you don't think that sticks in my craw, then you ain't too smart. Bamboozled me," he grumbled. *"Me!"*

It was his insulted pride that made her laugh. Jillian propped her feet up on the dash. What was done was over, she told herself. She was going to get a good chunk of her cattle back and see justice done. And at roundup time her books would shift back into the black. Maybe they'd have that new Jeep after all. "Did you get the full story from the sheriff?"

"Aaron Murdock," Gil told her. "He came by right before I set out after you."

"He came by the ranch?" she asked with a casualness that wouldn't have fooled anyone.

"Stopped by so I'd have the details."

"Did he—ah—say anything else?"

"Just that he had a lot of things to see to. Busy man."

"Oh." Jillian turned her head and stared out the window. Gil took a chance and grinned hugely.

She waited until it was nearly dark. It was impossible to bank down the hope that he'd come by or call, if only to see that everything had gone well. She worked out a dozen opening speeches and revised them. She paced. When she knew that she'd scream if she spent another minute within four walls, Jillian went out to the stables and saddled her mare.

"Men," she grumbled as she pulled the cinch. "If this is all part of the game, I'm not interested."

Ready for a run, Delilah sniffed the air the moment Jillian led her outside. When Jillian swung into the saddle, the mare danced and strained against the bit. Within moments they'd left the lights of the ranch yard behind.

The ride would clear her head, she told herself. Anyone would be a bit crazed after a day like this one. Getting Baby back had eased the sting of betrayal she'd felt after learning Joe Carlson had stolen from her. Methodically stolen, she thought, while offering advice and sympathy. He'd certainly been clever, she mused, subtly, systematically turning her attention toward the Murdocks while he was slipping her own cattle through her own fences. Until she found a new herdsman, she'd have to add his duties to her own.

It would do her good, she decided, keep her mind off things. Aaron. If he'd wanted to see her, he'd known where to find her. Apparently, she'd done them both a favor by pushing him away weeks before. If

she hadn't, they'd have found themselves in a very painful situation. As it was, they were each just going their own way—exactly as she'd known they would from the beginning. Perhaps she'd had a few moments of weakness, like the one that morning on the Double M, but they wouldn't last. In the next few weeks she'd be too busy to worry about Aaron Murdock and some foolish dreams.

Jillan told herself she hadn't deliberately ridden to the pond, but had simply let Delilah go her own way. In any case, it was still a spot she'd choose for solitude, no matter what memories lingered there.

The moon was full and white, the brush silvered with it. She told herself she wasn't unhappy, just tired after a long day of traveling, dealing with the sheriff, answering questions. She couldn't be unhappy when she finally had what was hers back. When the weariness passed, she'd celebrate. She could have wept, and hated herself.

When she saw the moon reflected on the water, she slowed Delilah to an easy lope. There wasn't a sound but the steady hoofbeats of her own mount. She heard the stallion even as her mare scented him. With her own heart pounding, Jillian controlled the now skittish Delilah and brought her to a halt. Aaron stepped out of the shadow of a cottonwood and said nothing at all.

He'd known she'd come—sooner or later. He could've gone to her, or waited for her to come to him. Somehow he'd known they had to meet here on land that belonged to them both.

It was better to face it all now and be done with it, Jillian told herself, then found her hands were wet with nerves as she dismounted. Nothing could've stiffened

her spine more effectively. In thrumming silence she tethered her mare. When she turned, she found Aaron had moved behind her, as silently as the wildcat she'd once compared him to. She stood very straight, kept her tone very impassive.

"So, you came back."

His eyes were lazy and amused as he scanned her face. "Did you think I wouldn't?"

Her chin came up as he'd known it would. "I didn't think about it at all."

"No?" He smiled then—it should have warned her. "Did you think about this?" He dragged her to him, one hand at her waist, one at the back of her head, and devoured the mouth he'd starved for. He expected her to struggle—perhaps he would've relished it just then—but she met the demands of his mouth with the strength and verve he remembered.

When he tore his mouth from hers, she clung, burying her face in his shoulder. He still wanted her—the thought pounded inside her head. She hadn't lost him, not yet. "Hold me," she murmured. "Please, just for a minute."

How could she do this to him? Aaron wondered. How could she shift his mood from crazed to tender in the space of seconds? Maybe he'd never figure out quite how to handle her, but he didn't intend to stop learning.

When she felt her nerves come back, she drew away. "I want to thank you for what you did. The sheriff told me that you got the evidence from Jennsen, and—"

"I don't want to talk about the cattle, Jillian."

"No." Linking her hands together, she turned away.

No, it was time they put that aside and dealt with what was really important. What was vital. "I've thought about what happened—about what you said the last time we saw each other." Where were all those speeches she'd planned? They'd all been so calm, so lucid. She twisted her fingers until they hurt, then separated them. "Aaron, I meant it when I said that I don't expect to be told those things. Some women do."

"I wasn't saying them to some women."

"It's so easy to say," she told him in a vibrating whisper. "So easy."

"Not for me."

She turned slowly, warily, as if she expected him to make a move she wasn't prepared for. He looked so calm, she thought. And yet the way the moonlight hit his eyes... "It's hard," she murmured.

"What is?"

"Loving you."

He could have gone to her then, right then, and pulled her to him until there was no more talk, no more thought. But her chin was up and her eyes were swimming. "Maybe it's supposed to be. I'm not offering you an easy road."

"No one's ever loved me back the way I wanted." Swallowing, she stepped away. "No one but Clay, and he never told me. He never had to."

"I'm not Clay, or your father. And there's no one who's ever going to love you the way I do." He took a step toward her, and though she didn't back up, he thought he could see every muscle brace. "What are you afraid of?"

"I'm not afraid!"

He came closer. "Like hell."

"That you'll stop." It wrenched out of her as she gripped her hands behind her back. Once started, the words rushed out quickly and ran together. "That you'll decide you never really loved me anyway. And I'll have let myself want and start depending and needing you. I've spent most of my life working on not depending on anyone, not for anything."

"I'm not anyone," he said quietly.

Her breath came shuddering out. "Since you've been gone I haven't cared about anything except you coming back."

He ran his hands up her arms. "Now that I am?"

"I couldn't bear it if you didn't stay. And though I think I could stand the hurt, I just can't stand being afraid." She put her hands to his chest when he started to draw her to him.

"Jillian, do you think you can tell me things I've been waiting to hear and have me keep my hands off you? Don't you know there's risk on both sides? Dependence on both sides?"

"Maybe." She made herself breathe evenly until she got it all out. "But people aren't always looking for the same things."

"Such as?"

This time she moistened her lips. "Are you going to marry me?" The surprise in his eyes made her muscles stiffen again.

"You asking?"

She dragged herself out of his hold, cursing herself for being a fool and him for laughing at her. "Go to hell," she told him as she started for her horse.

He caught her around the waist, lifting her off the

ground as she kicked out. "Damn, you've got a short fuse," he muttered and ended by pinning her to the ground. "I have a feeling I'm going to spend the best part of my life wrestling with you." Showing an amazing amount of patience, he waited until she'd run out of curses and had subsided, panting. "I'd planned to put the question to you a bit differently," he began. "As in, will you. But as I see it, that's a waste of time." As she stared up at him, he smiled. "God, you're beautiful. Don't argue," he warned as she opened her mouth. "I'm going to tell you that whenever I please so you might as well start swallowing it now."

"You were laughing at me," she began, but he cut her off.

"At both of us." Lowering his head, he kissed her, gently at first, then with building passion. "Now…" Cautiously he let her wrists go until he was certain she wasn't going to take a swing at him. "I'll give you a week to get things organized at your ranch."

"A week—"

"Shut up," he suggested. "A week, then we're both taking the next week off to get married."

Jillian lay very still and soaked it in. It was pure joy. "It doesn't take a week to get married."

"The way I do it does. When we get back—"

"Get back from where?"

"From any place where we can be alone," he told her. "We're going to start making some plans."

She reached for his cheek. "So far I like them. Aaron, say it again, while I'm looking at you."

"I love you, Jillian. A good bit of the time I like

you as well, though I can't say I mind fighting with you.''

''I guess you really mean it.'' She closed her eyes a moment. When she opened them again, they were laughing. ''It's hard to take a Murdock at his word, but I'm going to gamble.''

''What about a Baron?''

''A Baron's word's gold,'' she said, angling her chin. ''I love you, Aaron. I'm going to make you a frustrating wife and a hell of a partner.'' She grinned as his lips pressed against hers. ''What about those plans?''

''You've got a ranch, I've got a ranch,'' he pointed out as he kissed her palm. ''I don't much care whether we run them separately or together, but there's a matter of living. Your house, my house—that's not going to work for either of us. So we'll build our house, and that's where we're going to raise our children.''

Our. She decided it was the most exciting word in the English language. She was going to use it a dozen times every day for the rest of her life. ''Where?''

He glanced over her head, skimming the pool, the solitude. ''Right on the damn boundary line.''

With a laugh, Jillian circled his neck. ''What boundary line?''

*   *   *   *   *

From No. 1 *New York Times* bestselling author Nora Roberts

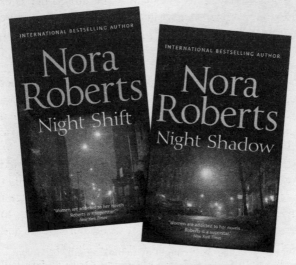

Night Shift available

When her stalker's threats start to escalate, late-night DJ Cilla O'Roarke and Detective Boyd Fletcher are led into a terrifying situation that they might not both walk away from…

Night Shadow available

Faced with a choice between her own life and the law, can prosecutor Deborah O'Roarke make the right decision – before someone else dies?

**Passion. Power. Suspense.
It's time to fall under the spell
of Nora Roberts.**

Nightshade

When a teenager gets caught up in making sadistic violent films, Colt Nightshade and Lieutenant Althea Grayson must find her before she winds up dead...

Night Smoke

When Natalie Fletcher's office is set ablaze, she must find out who wants her ruined – before someone is killed...

Night Shield

When a revengeful robber leaves blood-stained words on Detective Allison Fletcher's walls, she knows her cop's shield won't be enough to protect her...

Passion. Power. Suspense.
It's time to fall under the spell of Nora Roberts.

Nora Roberts' *The O'Hurleys*

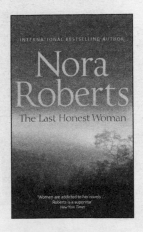

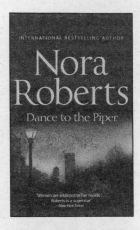

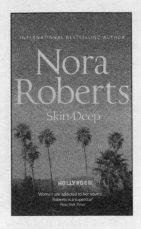

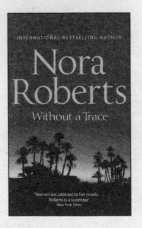

Meet Nora Robert's
The MacGregors family

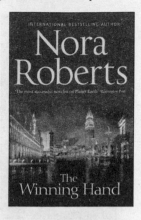

BL_265_TM

The Donovan Legacy

Four cousins. Four stories. One terrifying secret.

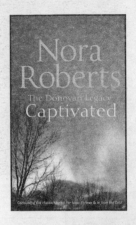

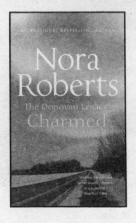

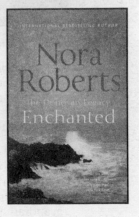

From international bestselling author Nora Roberts

Featuring two classic novels

Untamed
Jo Wilder couldn't deny the attraction between her and her charming new boss, Keane Prescott. Though his kisses left her breathless, it was his tenderness that threatened to tame her heart…

Less of a Stranger
Despite the passion David Katcherton aroused within Megan Miller, she wasn't about to fall for this irresistible stranger who was after her grandfather's business…